KIDNAPPING ANNA

THE KIDNAPPING ANNA TRILOGY: BOOK 1

A. B. ALVAREZ

BRUSHED STEEL BOOKS, INC

To Lindley

CONTENTS

PART IV
INCOMPLETE ANSWERS

FREE DOWNLOAD!

Get a free ebook copy of Part Two of the *Kidnapping Anna Trilogy,* *Kidnapping Anna: ADX Florence,* and a selection of short stories, after downloading the *A. B. Alvarez Reader* by going to https://www. abalvarez.com/free-book-en/!

KIDNAPPING

The crime of unlawfully seizing and carrying away a person by force or Fraud, or seizing and detaining a person against his or her will with an intent to carry that person away at a later time.

In most states, an asportation of a few feet may constitute the separate offense of kidnapping...

PROLOGUE

May 31, 2005

The man woke up for the last time.

A few seconds earlier, he thought he saw home. Trees along the sidewalk. The sun hot enough to make his scalp itch as it cooked the top of his head. He sauntered down the block to the muffled chirp of unidentified birds. Were his earplugs still in place? The bright orange foam was always the first thing he removed when he was done with target practice. He tried to move his arms to check, but they ignored his request.

His skin felt clammy. His fingers ached. What was that smell?

He walked down the block toward his home as he always did. He had parked his car, his old, deep green Toyota Camry, in the driveway and went for a walk.

He went for a walk. Why?

He saw himself walking, an observer of his life. His tie was loose, his gait sloppy. His thoughts seemed clear, but clear in the way someone felt after a shock, or a sudden deceleration due to a collision, with all their sensory input spilling out, unnoticed, like water being poured into a too-full glass. His eyes felt heavy, the lid muscles relaxed, that gentle smothered feeling.

Was he going to work, or returning? Did he pick up the groceries? If he didn't, he was going to hear it this time.

Sleep. He couldn't wait to get home and take a nap.

A fire suddenly burned in his brain, scorching from the back of his neck, over the top of his head, and down to his eyes. His nerves exploded in a silent scream that only the recently aware could feel, and he could do nothing to stop it.

WAKE UP! YOU'RE IN TROUBLE! WAKE UP!

The sweet smell of ether greeted him. He shook his head and realized that his arms were bound to the arms of the chair he was sitting in. He tried moving his legs. They too were bound. He shook his body with the energy that came from the realization that the darkness surrounding him was from a hood that enveloped his head.

The chair was bolted to the floor.

Adrenaline shot through him, clearing his head, but his vision did not get any clearer. It was a very dark hood. Dark, musty, and sweaty.

What was the last thing he remembered? His thoughts were cloudy. His breath was hot under the heavy cloth.

"Hello?" He swung his head left and right but couldn't discern anything. He heard rustling to his right. "I don't know who you are, but I sure hope you got the right guy."

He yanked his head to the left again when he felt the metal end of a tube push against his right temple.

"You hide very well," a voice that had smoked too many cigarettes responded. His interrogator. "But guys like you always make mistakes. Yes, we've got the right guy." The interrogator took a few steps toward his left. Deliberate. On concrete. "Tell me about Halon."

Oh, God. "Can you give me a hint?" The force of the interrogator's fist hitting his face was excruciating and snapped his head back in the unmoving chair. The dark transformed into stars. His nose felt broken and his brain crackled in response to the exploding pain.

"Halon," Smoky Voice said.

The voice was to his right. No, his left. Sweat slowly crawled down his face. Or was that blood?

"Everyone knows where I am. Agents are going to storm this place in a few minutes…" Another blow hammered his left temple. Stars. Electricity.

"I considered water boarding, but why waste water when duct tape and good old-fashioned persuasion are available?"

Sarcasm. *This guy knows he's got time on his side.* The rustling of Smoky's clothes told him that the man was walking back and forth.

He blinked over and over again in the dark hood. *This is bad. This is bad. This is bad.* He breathed through his mouth. There was too much pain through his nose. "What do you want to know?" Again on the left temple. It was the shoulder rest of a rifle. He smelled gun oil.

"Halon."

He heard someone move on the opposite side of his interrogator. Two people he would have to get past. His training didn't have much to say when you were in this much trouble.

"How many are you?"

"In here or around the world?" His interrogator turned and took a few steps away from him. He could hear the smile. "Five heavily armed men in the room. The rest don't matter."

"You sound American."

"I am."

"Why are you telling me?"

"You know why."

He spit in the hood. "Why should I tell you anything?" He turned his head toward Smoky Voice.

"Your family. We promise not to touch them. Even if you don't cooperate." The rifle butt slammed into the right side of his face and he felt bone cracking. "But you will." More movement. "Halon."

"You're a liar. You're all going to jail. You are an embarrassment…" The sound of a gun going off startled him for a split second before his knee exploded and he screamed. The interrogator grabbed the man's hair through the hood and lifted his head, along with his awareness.

"You have a lot of places I can shoot that won't kill you and only two that will." His head flopped back down when the interrogator let go. "This isn't meant to be a long conversation." The barrel of the gun pressed against his chest at his heart. "That's one."

"Doesn't matter anymore." He was shivering as he spoke through his teeth. The pain ran through him as if he were a giant exposed nerve ending.

Another shot. He screamed again. His other knee. Shaking. Screaming. He could barely think. The world. Very focused. This room. Pain. Liquid flowing down his legs. Something hit his face... once? Twice? *OH, OH, OH. STOP. OH, FUCK.* Words spilled out of his mouth. Fast. Slow. In no particular order. About Halon. *We don't know who you are, but we're getting close.* He didn't care. His world was only an inch outside the outline of his body. His shoulders sagged. His blinking slowed, along with his capacity to comprehend. *I guess this is when I die.*

The hood was yanked off his head. His eyes closed for a moment in the glare of the bright lights of the concrete-walled room. There were two men in dirty clothes standing to his left and right. He looked down at the shattered remnants of his knees and swung his eyes up to look at the man who must have been interrogating him. On the table behind him was the rifle used to strike his face. In the interrogator's hand was a Glock with a 12-round magazine protruding from the grip. He placed the barrel of the gun against his head.

"This is the second."

In that instant, he heard the gun go off and then nothing else.

PART I

CARPENTER POOLE

1

———

CONSPIRACY THEORY

May 31, 2005

Seventeen-year-old Anna Wodehouse, a junior in high school for just another few weeks, sat at her kitchen table in an immaculate kitchen, in an immaculate house, in a perfectly mediocre neighborhood in Brooklyn. She put her pencil down, sighed, and leaned back in her chair. The cushion sagged a little as she pushed against it, stretching her back and neck. The smell of disinfectant told her that her father must have had a bout of neat while she was out. Her math homework was done and now she was five chapters ahead of Mrs. Moran. She mentally congratulated herself, closed the book, and opened history. There was no way for her to get ahead in history. She was usually three to five chapters ahead of the class, but Mr. Dougherty had his own list of assignments and there was no way for her to do them ahead of time since she didn't know what they were. Pre-calc and physics were a snap; the exercises were right in the book.

History. Reading and waiting and taking notes. History was so boring! There were so many other interesting things to do and the sooner she got her schoolwork done, the sooner she could go do them.

Her neck felt hot, but the rest of her was fine. Her orange t-shirt did a good job of absorbing her sweat, and her jeans felt so comfortable she almost lived in them. Her Converse sneakers felt hot, but she would get rid of them later. She pushed a lock of curly black hair behind her ear and tugged at the neckline of her t-shirt with her left. The air-conditioner kept the house at a decent temperature, though she was pretty sure she could program the thermostat to be a little more understanding of her preference for cold weather.

Read, read, take notes. Read, read, take notes.

Where was Dad? Her aggravation level rose with her inability to cool down. She had a question about the mobile phone app she was working on and she needed to talk it out. Her dad was annoying, but at least he would listen to her. And she needed to ask him about the class trip. Anna hated class trips, but this one was to the Smithsonian and even though he already told her it was out of the question, she knew she might be able to get him to relent.

It was the Smithsonian! Glamorous Glynnis! Skylab! Maybe they would even see the Pentagon from the highway.

He never let her do anything. School trips, sleepovers, movies with some of the kids from school (well, she didn't like them anyway), but even school-sponsored trips to the movies were off-limits. At least he took her to the planetarium every few months. Ever since they moved to New York, he was a little more lenient. The other places they lived were black and white by comparison.

Maybe she could find a meetup.com group of high schoolers her age who were into computers and science the way she was. She found a blog for the Secret Science Club in Brooklyn, but you had to be at least twenty-one to attend. Four more years! She was counting down the days. Maybe, just maybe, she might give a talk there one day.

In the meantime, there had to be a way for her to sneak in.

The phone rang. The antique on the wall. She answered it just to stop the tinny sound from piercing her eardrum. "You are in so much trouble, Outhouse."

God! Not Jennifer again!

She hated being called Outhouse, but she hated fighting over it more. "What do you want, Banana?" She stopped a sigh before it escaped. Jennifer's Reign of Terror against Anna seemed neverending and getting worse.

"You are in so much trouble."

Heard that part.

"You forgot to feed the animals."

"Oh, go to…" A crash startled her out of her disdain. The front door smashed open and a blur of armed blue figures stormed into the house.

"Police! Don't move!"

Anna put her hands up and dropped the phone, her eyes wide, as two helmeted figures in full tactical gear ran over to her. Each roughly grabbed an arm and dragged her out of the house. *I'm going to kill Jennifer!* The words POLICE and SWAT were in large white letters on their chests and backs. A dark blue blur of other figures went through the hallway, backs against the walls, turning into the doorways. They called out someone's name, but she couldn't make it out. Where was Dad? She wanted to call out to him, but everything was happening so fast. *Daddy!*

The two officers pulled her through the narrow doorframe of her row house into the bright May afternoon sunlight. The air was still a little chilly. Her feet barely touched the ground as the two officers swung her around the various cars being used as barriers to the two police vans that were at ninety-degree angles to each other.

The neighborhood outside her drab, green vinyl-sided house was a cacophony of squad cars, SWAT vans, ambulances, and black SUVs. The lights and sounds overwhelmed her and she closed her eyes and put her hands on her face as the two officers stopped behind an ambulance. There were people everywhere. Spoke into radios. Took pictures. The neighborhood was out in full force. What did she do? How much trouble was she in?

"Are you alright?" One of the helmets bent down to meet her at eye level.

She leaned against the ambulance and slid down onto the cold polished chrome step. His words were just sounds, phonemes entering her ear, but not translated into anything she could comprehend.

A man in a suit came running over.

"What did I do?" she asked. Her hands trembled, her eyes scanned all around looking for something to latch onto, something to stabilize her. She looked down. The charcoal gray ground. Cars covered in grime. Exhaust fumes from the van's diesel engines.

"What?" the man in the suit asked.

"This is a mistake. One of the kids from school..." Her head was heavy. The sounds around her muffled. Her eyes darted back and forth. She was in trouble this time. What was she going to tell her father? She would never go on the trip now!

The man in the suit had a file in his hand and had to yell above all the noise. "Who else is in the house with you? Anyone? Do you know this man?" He held out a piece of paper.

Was that a helicopter overhead? *Omigod, those are news choppers.* "What's going on here?" Anna asked.

"What's your name?" The wind picked up. The man looked at her.

What did he want?

"What is your name?" he asked again.

"Anna!" She was yelling at the top of her lungs. Her throat was dry. "Anna Wodehouse."

"Do you live at 1836 76th Street in Brooklyn?"

"You just finished breaking into my house." *Is this guy kidding?*

"Please, answer the question."

"Yes, I do." Her hair fluttered onto her face.

"Do you know this man?" He clutched the folder at the bend to stop the papers from flying away.

She looked at the photo he held in front of her. Why wasn't he using a tablet? "That's my father." Anna wrapped her arms around her chest. Her eyes were starting to tear.

"What's his name?"

"Marshall..."

"What?"

"Marshall Wodehouse." Was she betraying him? Was this the moment he was so afraid of? That she used to tease him incessantly about? Conspiracies? Unknown men around every corner? Delusions of grandeur?

The man looked away and waved at someone. "His real name is Arnold Dashman."

Anna gaped at him. There had to be a way out of here. This couldn't be happening!

"Anna," the man put his hand out as if to hold her left arm, but he held it just out of reach, "your father, this man, is wanted for kidnapping."

She wiped a half-formed tear. The noise was making it hard to think. "I...I have to get back to my homework." A sob escaped her lips.

"I'm sorry they had to go in there and take you like that, but we were afraid of what he might do if he suspected anything."

An officer came through the doorway of her one-story violated home. "Clear!"

"You people are crazy! My dad is the most boring person on the planet. He didn't..." The words stuck in her throat. Her stomach was a mix of anger, fear, and anxiety. She jumped when she felt something on her shoulders. An EMT had just put a blanket on her. She pulled it off and threw it on the asphalt. "Who could he have possibly kidnapped?"

"You, Anna." He put his hand down. "He kidnapped you."

Are you kidding me?

She grabbed the folder from his hands and pushed him out of the way. She saw a squad car in front of her. She threw the folder off to the side and jumped onto the hood of the car, and then onto the roof and, as her voice echoed through the streets of her neighborhood, yelled, "Run! Run, Dad! Run!"

2

THE BASEMENT

June 1997

"But, Daddy," Anna said, "It's my tenth birthday. There has to be balloons and cake." She used her matter-of-fact voice.

She stood next to the worn wooden dining room table draped with one of the four bright tablecloths she liked so much. The tablecloths were mostly white, but had a bright colored margin with different patterns. This one had a double helix made of pink and white flowers on a green vine. Her father often talked about disposing of them, but Anna always put her foot down. She felt where they ate should be as bright as possible.

He agreed. He didn't often do that, but Anna always thought he was a reasonable man.

The curtains were drawn. It was dinnertime and he didn't like leaving the windows uncovered. Anna wanted them open, but she was a reasonable girl.

"I know," her father said, peering over the rims of his metal frame glasses. He sat at the head of the table staring at the screen of his notebook computer. Still wearing his work clothes (still-buttoned shirt, and dark slacks) he pulled at his chin. "But I just couldn't find any. I went to all the stores and they were all out."

"Daddy, that's impossible." Anna leaned against one of the dark wood dining room chairs. The overhead light cast noonday shadows. She looked at the centerpiece with its plastic leaves and fruits. The multiple shadows it cast intrigued her.

"What do you mean?" her father asked.

"There are 3 party stores in the area." She crossed her arms. "They have balloons. I called."

He took his glasses off and looked puzzled. "Three?" The glasses went on the table. "And you called them?" He stared at the ceiling, nodded in admiration, and returned his gaze to her. "They were out when I got there."

"And cake?"

"The bakery said they were all out."

"Of birthday cakes? You could have brought a cupcake." She motioned putting an invisible candle on an equally invisible cupcake. "I know we have to watch our budget, but, seriously? We have leftover candles."

"I know, but," he shrugged, "things are tight." He put the glasses on and looked at his screen over the top of the frame. "Did you tell you teacher about the rainbows?"

"That they're made of molecules the size of basketballs and colored in ROY G BIV?" Anna swiveled her hip and rested her right hand on it. "She didn't buy it."

Her father turned and focused his eyes past her. "Hmm." He shrugged. "I'll talk to her about it during the next parent-teacher night."

Not even a cupcake? Anna felt bad, but understood. Things were always tight. Maybe he bought her a new book. They could usually afford that. And he always surprised her with a gift even if it was something simple.

————

She went to the kitchen to get a glass of milk and wandered aimlessly from corner to corner stopping at the refrigerator. She leaned her head on brushed aluminum surface. She exhaled and a solitary tear fell. Maybe next year.

She heard something fall down the stairs to the basement. She ran to the door and called out, "Daddy? Are you alright?"

It was dark.

"I think I hurt my leg," his voice sounded in pain.

Anna ran down. *Oh, no! I hope he's not hurt!*

At the foot of the stairs, the lights turned on.

The basement was filled with balloons of every color imaginable. On the floor. In midair. Floating from the ceiling.

Like basketball-sized molecules in primary colors.

In the middle of the rainbow come to life was a table and on the table was a huge birthday cake that read:

Happy 10th Birthday, Squirrel!

Her face felt flush and her ears hurt from her smile. She blinked over and over as her eyes glazed from tears she didn't want to release, but couldn't help.

"You can take the leftovers to school tomorrow. You can share with your friends," he said.

Friends? Her smile didn't hurt her ears anymore. "Are you my friend?"

"No, Squirrel." He crouched down next to her and cupped her face in his right hand. His skin felt rough on her cheek. "That would be a step down from being your father." He smiled and she hugged him as tightly as she could.

3

___

TRANSCRIPT EXCERPT DATED MAY 31, 2005

U.S. Government vs. Arnold Dashman (a.k.a. Marshall Wodehouse)

Interview: Carpenter Poole (a.k.a. Anna Wodehouse)

Dr. Matheson: Tell me about your life prior to the kidnapping.

C. Poole: There was no kidnapping. I remember my life. My earliest memory is of my father holding me.

Dr. Matheson: Do you remember how old you were?

C. Poole: No, but I must have been younger than five. I was cold, and he held me, and I could feel the warmth of his arms and his chest through his coat.

Dr. Matheson: Tell me about your mother.

C. Poole: I don't remember her. Her name was Ingrid.

Dr. Matheson: Yes?

C. Poole: Do you hate me?

Dr. Matheson: I don't understand.

C. Poole: I don't know what to do. What am I supposed to do? Why did this happen?

Dr. Matheson: That man was not your father.

C. Poole: Stop saying that! He is my father. I am not the victim of a kidnapping.

Dr. Matheson: Okay, we'll call him your father if you prefer. Do you know where you are?

C. Poole: A police station.

Dr. Matheson: For now. We're going to be moving you to an FBI field office, but I wanted to see how you were doing.

C. Poole: I'm sorry, but there's been some kind of mistake. My dad was always worried about something, but I thought it was just work, or me...

Dr. Matheson: Did he ever punish you?

C. Poole: Of course he did.

Dr. Matheson: How?

C. Poole: He wouldn't let me do my homework. Or he made me do the dishes. The worst was...

Dr. Matheson: Yes?

C. Poole: He wouldn't let me watch TV because Billy Johnson tried coming over to visit.

Dr. Matheson: So he kept you isolated.

C. Poole: What do you mean?

Dr. Matheson: He kept you away from people.

C. Poole: No. [silence] I don't like the kids at school.

Dr. Matheson: Why?

C. Poole: Because they don't like me.

Dr. Matheson: Did your father every hit you?

C. Poole: What?

Dr. Matheson: Ever?

C. Poole: No.

Dr. Matheson: I find that hard to believe.

C. Poole: What? That a man who was afraid of ants and bumblebees and dragonflies wouldn't hurt his daughter?

Dr. Matheson: What was it like at the station house?

C. Poole: With the police?

Dr. Matheson: Yes.

C. Poole: Scary.

Dr. Matheson: What scared you?

C. Poole: All the guns.

Dr. Matheson: Did your father have a gun?

C. Poole: No! He was adamant that I know about guns, but we never had one. No.

Dr. Matheson: Would it surprise you to know that the police found a gun in your house?

C. Poole: We never had guns in the house!

Dr. Matheson: There was a semi-automatic hidden behind a false piece of dry wall.

C. Poole: That wasn't his.

Dr. Matheson: Do you want to know about your real mother and father?

C. Poole: I already have a real mother and father.

Dr. Matheson: A mother?

C. Poole: I told you. She died when I was younger.

Dr. Matheson: How old are you?

C. Poole: Seventeen.

Dr. Matheson: When was your birthday?

C. Poole: In June.

Dr. Matheson: Actually, it's in April.

C. Poole: It's in June.

Dr. Matheson: And your parents are dead.

C. Poole: They are not. Well, he's not. My mom died in a car accident.

Dr. Matheson: Tell me about the car accident.

C. Poole: When I was about two years old. The three of us were in a car accident. My mother died.

Dr. Matheson: Your mother did die in a car accident. Along with your father.

C. Poole: Stop.

Dr. Matheson: You were the only survivor of the crash. Do you know how I know that?

C. Poole: [no response]

Dr. Matheson: Do you want to know your real name?

C. Poole: [no response]

Dr. Matheson: You were abducted at the age of two by Arnold Dashman who raised you as his daughter for the last fifteen years. [flipping of paper]

C. Poole: Stop.

Dr. Matheson: Your aunt and uncle are on their way here. Did you know that you were born in Pennsylvania?

C. Poole: Stop! Stop! Stop! Stop it! My father's name is Marshall Wodehouse! My name is Anna Wodehouse! You kidnapped me! My life is boring and I have no friends, but my father loves me! He would never have done that to anyone!

Dr. Matheson: Your name is Carpenter Poole. You are the child of Harry and Lucy Poole of Littleton, PA. You were born seventeen years ago and had the unfortunate luck to be kidnapped by someone who raised you as his own.

C. Poole: Why would he do that?

Dr. Matheson: We don't know. We were hoping to ask him today, but he seems to have disappeared. Do you know where he is?

C. Poole: [no response]

Dr. Matheson: Carpenter?

C. Poole: [no response]

Dr. Matheson: Carpenter?

C. Poole: My name is Anna Wodehouse. And when my dad comes back, are you guys going to be sorry. He is going to sue you into kingdom come for false arrest, destroying property, wrongful detainment...

Dr. Matheson: You're free to go.

C. Poole: Liar.

Dr. Matheson: Carpenter...Anna, you've been manipulated and lied to for the last fifteen years by a man who was not your father. No matter what he may have done to you.

C. Poole: He never did anything to me except be my father.

Dr. Matheson: It's okay to tell me. I'm not here to judge you or Arnold.

C. Poole: Who's Arnold?

Dr. Matheson: Arnold Dashman, the man who said he was your father.

C. Poole: Marshall. My dad's name is Marshall. And what kind of name is that for a kidnapper? Arnold Dashman? Shouldn't he have sold me off for money or something? This is so stupid.

Dr. Matheson: Maybe. But if your dad really is Marshall Wodehouse then where is he? Why hasn't he come rushing here to tell us what a mistake we've made?

END OF TRANSCRIPT EXCERPT

4

IDENTITY

Anna wasn't quite sure where she was. Once the EMTs in the ambulance certified her unharmed outside her home, she was shunted into an unmarked police car. She peered through the crystal-clear tinted glass as the car made its way through closed off streets, and bridges over water, past abandoned buildings, and homes kept almost as good as new, but none of the visual details remained. Her journey was so much streaming data that her brain decided she didn't need and so disconnected the neural pathway between her eyes and her consciousness.

The car smelled stale like old chicken or dead rat.

Out of the car. Into an elevator.

The two men stood on either side of her speaking in firm tones but not raising their voices.

Walking. A lot of walking. Past offices with glass walls; people on telephones. No one looked up as she passed them in their aggregated fortresses of solitude behind their desks behind their monitors behind their keyboards.

They stopped before a closed, dark wood door and one of the men opened it. Anna entered the plain, nondescript room, but her escorts didn't cross inside with her. One of them mentioned something about something. The cream-colored walls in the room, about the size of her bedroom, were bare except for a cork bulletin board. *That's so much smaller than mine.* At the table was a woman she had met earlier.

Her next thought: *So this is what a real interrogation room looks like.*

A two-way mirror (she was sure of that), a wooden table with two side-by-side gray metal chairs with matching cushioned backs. Anna pursed her lips and sat down in the chair next to Dr. Matheson. Was that her name? They had met earlier, but Anna couldn't remember if it was at the ambulance or in one of the police vans.

Dr. Matheson wore heavy perfume and a dress that was definitely too tight over her pudgy frame. Anna did her best to breathe in while looking away, but she couldn't do it without being rude. Anna hated being rude. Why was everyone else always so rude to her?

"This is your paperwork." Dr. Matheson turned a few pages, took out four sheets, and placed them in front of Anna. The first read: *Child ID DNA Kit* with the name *Carpenter Poole* written in pen in very smooth cursive writing.

"Why isn't this in a computer?" Anna asked.

"It is, but I wanted you to see an almost-original of the paperwork pertaining to you. It was found by your aunt and uncle when they went to your real parents' home." Dr. Matheson moved the second page front and center of Anna. "To make the arrangements for your parents' funeral."

"I already told you, my mother died when I was young..."

"Yes, they both died when you were young. When you got here, we took a quick fingerprint of your index finger, remember?"

Anna nodded.

"We couldn't get a match. The fingerprints of a two year old are harder to match on a seventeen year old. A twenty year old to a ten year old, maybe. But fingerprints change substantially from when you are very young to even marginally older."

"But?"

"Around seventeen years ago, child DNA kits were very popular. Mr. and Mrs. Poole bought this one when you were about a year old. They took swabs of your cheek and a blood sample and a lock of your hair. The cheek swabs were all we needed." She slid the papers over to the side and extracted a printout from the folder.

Anna decided that she was going to hate file folders for the rest of her life. Their contents only brought bad news.

"This is the results of the DNA test of Carpenter Poole, who has been missing for fifteen years, and your cheek swab." Dr. Matheson pointed to the bottom of the page. "The samples are a match." She gave Anna a sympathetic smile. "I know you don't want to hear this, but you are Carpenter Poole."

Anna clenched her hands under the table. "I have to go. Please, I have to go." The air coming in and out of her nasal passages felt like they did when she got sick: cold and sharp.

"Anna, it's okay." Dr. Matheson put her hand on Anna's shoulder.

Anna shook it off. Her stomach felt tight and her shoulders hurt. Her palms tingled.

"I have to..." Anna started to stand, but not before she threw up on the table and on the paperwork. "I'm..." And then again. And again. She leapt from the chair and continued to vomit.

She stopped and a wave of exhaustion radiated from her chest into her arms and legs. She fell to the floor and landed hard on her butt. *Where's Dad? Where's Dad? Oh, why aren't you here?* She slid herself away from the table toward the wall and into the furthest corner. Dr. Matheson went over to her and Anna cringed. She pulled her legs in and leaned against the wall.

"Anna, please, let me help you..."

"Leave me alone! Leave ME ALONE!" Anna started to shake and tears escaped her clenched eyes. How could this be? Her entire life? Everything she'd ever known? No, that was not possible. Her dad was going to show up and straighten this all out. He did it before when things went wrong in school or when the neighbors blamed her for something she couldn't possibly have done.

He was there. He was always there.

Where was he? *Dad! I need you! Daddy! WHERE ARE YOU?*

She shivered with no sense of control. She huddled into a ball against the cold wall.

5

HOSPITAL VISIT

At the insistence of Dr. Gail Matheson, an ambulance transported Carpenter Poole from the FBI field office to New York Downtown Hospital in lower Manhattan. The hospital, one of the few near the financial district, founded in 1853 as the New York Infirmary for Indigent Women and Children, was one of the leaders in disaster management. During 9/11, while doctors were busy treating the first wave of injured people looking for help, the first tower of the World Trade Center went down with a roaring shock wave that engulfed the area, including the ER at the hospital, with a dust cloud so thick the medical staff couldn't see their hands in front of their faces. They still managed to treat fifteen hundred people and save the lives of thirty-three critical patients.

It was also the closest medical facility to the FBI facility at 26 Federal Plaza.

A New York City Police officer stood outside her room. Anna had never seen the outside of the hospital before and missed seeing it again as the ambulance took her straight to the Emergency Room door where they greeted her with a wheelchair, an escort, and an officer.

"I just threw up. I didn't need to be admitted." Anna was in bed and had an IV of saline solution going into her right arm. This was a day of firsts: she couldn't remember the last time she was in a hospital for any reason. The air was staler than the interrogation room. She confessed to herself that she was feeling a little better from her earlier episode, but she didn't need to tell them that. The walls were a different shade of beige and the light, which seemed to come from everywhere, made her squint. *Is this entire room designed to annoy patients?*

"It's late. They're not sending you home. You are still a minor and while New York doesn't have explicit emancipation laws, you don't quite fit the criteria for independence in any case." Dr. Matheson crossed her legs. She sat in a wooden chair to Anna's right. "Yet. First, you meet and go with your aunt and uncle and then you can decide what to do next. Maybe emancipation is in your future."

"You can't keep me here against my will without charging me with something," Anna said. *These sheets! Don't they use fabric softener?*

A voice came from the doorway and a middle-aged man came in through the door. "Actually we can. You're a minor and the victim of a crime and you have not yet been released into the custody of your nearest living relatives. If you didn't have any, we might be talking to a judge right now about making you a ward of the state because you are obviously overwrought and need medical attention." He walked up to the bed and looked around. "I would call this medical attention."

"I threw up."

"I know. I'm the Agent in Charge. Special Agent Gavin Gillespie." He extended his hand to her.

She hesitated for a moment and they shook hands.

"I wanted to check up on you and see if there was anything we could do."

"Can you send me home?" Either he wasn't wearing cologne or the hospital smells were overpowering.

"Not yet," he said. His skin was warm and he placed his other hand on top of hers. His touch bothered her, but maybe he could do something.

He grabbed a folding chair that leaned against the wall and opened it up as close to the bed as he could. "How are you feeling?"

"Like I shouldn't be talking to you."

"We can always get you a lawyer, but you haven't been charged with anything."

"I thought I was a victim?" Anna pushed herself up to relieve the soreness on her butt.

"Are you?"

"No." Anna tried to cross her arms but was conscious of the plastic IV catheter going into the back of her hand. "But I could still use an attorney."

"Yes, you can, though I am hoping that for now you don't."

"Give me a good reason." Anna's shoulders tensed.

"The man who held you for fifteen years, the man you consider your father, is not only wanted for kidnapping, he is also wanted by Interpol, the Department of Homeland Security, and a few other agencies whose initials I'm not allowed to repeat." He leaned back and the chair squeaked.

"For what?" Anna's hair, a ponytail held in place with a rubber band, was itchy. She scratched the back of her head but couldn't reach the spot.

"This is where things get a little mysterious. I'm not allowed to tell you in case you really are just an innocent victim."

"So my father was an international criminal, probably with terrorist ties, and numerous warrants out for his arrest? And maybe he tortured puppies while I was sleeping. We weren't hiding. We live in Brooklyn, for Pete's sake." Anna fidgeted under her blanket. She wasn't used to being in bed for so long and her muscles were feeling sore. She pulled the starched sheet back and started to get up.

"Where are you going?" Dr. Matheson said as she stood and held onto Anna's left arm.

"Nowhere, it seems." She slipped into a flimsy pair of slippers. She looked at Dr. Matheson and then at the FBI agent. She reached for her back and held her hospital gown closed. "I want to go home.

Can I go home? You guys are always looking to cut a deal. Let me go home and I'll tell you anything you want."

"That sounds tempting," he said. "But the fact of the matter is you need to do that anyway."

"Oh, please. You can send me with escorts. Maybe a few big burly types. You can post one outside my window…"

"If you don't cooperate, we can keep you from your aunt and uncle." He crossed his arms.

"That's fine! I don't want to go with whoever those people are. They are not my aunt and uncle unless they're related to my father somehow, but I'm willing to bet they're related to me in ways I'd rather not discuss." She felt a little dizzy but stood her ground.

"Anna," Dr. Matheson was speaking in a low, soothing voice. "Your aunt and uncle deserve to see you…"

"No one deserves to see me except my father. Find him and I'll pretty much agree to anything." Anna turned away from her and sat down on her bed, facing the special agent. "And don't use your Jedi mind tricks on me. You'll just make me want to throw up again. If I have a nervous breakdown, I'll sue everybody, take my house back, and go home, like I want to now." She glared at the agent. "Can't we just skips those steps?"

"We know he was abusing you." Gavin leaned forward and looked her in the eyes.

"Are you saying that you want to check if I'm still a virgin? Even my dad would have to get a court order for that." She turned to Dr. Matheson. "And I thought you were on my side. He's asking inappropriate questions and probably thinks I have Stockholm syndrome."

"You do have Stockholm," she said.

"Oh, this is a nightmare." She looked at the doorway. So close yet so far. "I just want to go home. Why can't I go home? I have homework to hand in. Classes to go to. People to hate." Her eyes were tearing. Why did she always cry at the slightest provocation? "I think it's my turn to feed the rabbit in lab."

"They still have live animals in school?" he asked.

Anna stood up. "Yes, but we don't have any rabbits. I'm allergic and I have asthma. I love pets and I can't have any."

Dr. Matheson grabbed Anna's chart at the foot of the bed.

"Allergies? Asthma? They haven't run any specific tests on you, but you don't really show any symptoms of either. Are you sure?"

"You want to give me an apple and see me swell up? Will you send me home then?" What was wrong with these people?

"You're in the top of your class. Teachers are impressed by you. Students are threatened by you. You tear through classes like an adult attending first grade," Agent Gillespie said.

Was he impressed? Maybe she could leverage that.

"Maybe you're smart enough to have figured out what your father," he made air quotes, "was doing and maybe you joined in."

"Why don't you arrest me? I'm tired. I want to get some sleep and go home so I can go to school tomorrow." She sat down. "This bed is so uncomfortable."

"That can be made better or worse. Have you ever been to jail?" The agent leaned back.

"I was hoping to avoid doing that given my new lifelong ambition is to become head of the FBI so I could fire you."

"I will wait for that day with bated breath." He stood. He was only a little taller than Anna. "Anna, or Carpenter, or whatever name you feel like using right now, we're here to help you. You were kidnapped fifteen years ago and we finally found you..."

"As we expertly hid from the world in the wilds of New York City..."

"...and all we want is to know what happened in those intervening years. Where did you live? Who did you know? How were you able to go to school, get a social security card, go to the doctor, to the hospital, without half the world knowing that you were alive and well?"

"I guess Andrew..."

"Arnold," he said.

"...whatever, is smarter than you give him credit for. Fifteen years is a long time. Are you guys that incompetent?" Anna's defensive posture: poke him with words. Her fist might be next.

"Not usually." Gavin brought his face closer to Anna. He looked into her eyes.

"You're creeping me out." She walked over to the door. "Why is there a cop at my door?"

"We want to keep you safe."

She walked back and stood in front of him again. "Right, from the man who kidnapped me for fifteen years and punished me for not eating my vegetables by making me watch Oprah. On second thought, keep him there. I don't really want to watch any more Oprah."

"I think we're done here. Get some rest." Gavin turned toward the door. "I'll be back tomorrow."

"Maybe I won't be." Anna walked over to him. "Arrest me or let me go home."

"Get some rest. I'll be back in the morning with some food. I've stayed here before and you don't want their breakfast."

Anna swung at him with her fist and he caught her arm at the wrist. He held it an extra second and let go.

"I know you find this hard to believe, but I'm here to help you."

Dr. Matheson walked out of the room, promising to be back in the morning. Gavin stood there. "I think you know something.

"You're a straight A student, yet you lived with a man who was obviously not your father for years. You seriously expect me, you expect everyone, to believe that you didn't spot inconsistencies?"

"You obviously know my family history so you won't have to ask me much."

"That's the problem, Carpenter."

"Don't call me that."

"Why? Don't like your first name? Reminds me of Karen Carpenter. I'm a big fan. Jesus was a carpenter. Carpentry is a noble profession." He crossed his arms and leaned against the doorway. "Your history starts seven years ago when you moved to Brooklyn. What were you and Arnold doing the previous eight years and how did you stay under the radar for so long?"

"How did you find us?"

"I guess it won't hurt to tell you. An anonymous tip. Someone who obviously cared for you and figured out who you really were," Gillespie said.

"Are. When I find them, I'll be sure to thank them personally." Anna walked back around to the far side of the bed and lay down.

"Good night, Anna. I'll see you in the morning."

Anna didn't reply. *Maybe I'll die tonight. Maybe I'll die and this will all be over.*

6

THE MOST IMPORTANT MEAL OF
THE DAY

Anna stood past the threshold of Special Agent Gavin Gillespie's conference room wearing handcuffs. The tall, muscular police officer who stood behind her spun her around. Gavin walked over holding a brown paper bag. "Did you get a good night's sleep?" The officer unlocked the cuffs.

There was a scent of men's cologne. Her father hardly ever wore cologne, but when he did, she always knew. She could detect it from the furthest corner of their secure home.

Date? she would ask.

When I want to talk about my love life, I'll send you a text. And, no, not a date. I don't have time to shower, the man who was no longer her father would reply.

The ratcheting sound of the handcuffs kept her lips in a straight line. She was exhausted from all of the questions running through her mind. Her attempt at an extracurricular jaunt had failed and the robo-cop who was her personal prison guard decided she needed to be humiliated. *Good job, Mr. Officer.*

The FBI guy wore cologne. To impress her, or did he always wear it? Maybe he was trying to impress Dr. Matheson. He had less hair than she remembered from yesterday, but his navy blue suit fit better.

The dark color hid his paunch. She wanted to roll her eyes. *Yeah, that's impressive.*

She rubbed her wrists and looked away from Gavin. She wore the same orange t-shirt and jeans as yesterday, refusing to have someone return to her home to get her a fresh set. Imagining someone going through her things made her stomach queasy. After a few seconds, she tugged at a chair and sat down.

Gavin pushed the bag toward her. "I got you another breakfast burrito. I assume you're still hungry."

Anna put her hands on her lap and stared as though examining the fake wood grain table top.

"I had to throw the first one away. When they told me you'd tried running away, I thought, that's not the Carpenter I know. I bet you she must have gotten a look at the hospital food."

"I want an attorney." She sat back and looked at her lap.

"You understand that you are not being charged with anything?"

"I understand you can go f...frak yourself. I want a lawyer." Anna stood up and walked over to the table at the far end of the room toward the flat screen monitor. Two clone potted plants sat like lumps on either side of it.

He sighed. "Okay." He stared at her. "You know we're the good guys, right? You don't have to talk to me, but we've spent a great deal of time and effort looking for you and all we want are some answers."

"Sorry I'm not grateful for being detained." She pushed a large vase with fake flowers off the table. It shattered into a few dozen large shards, spilling dirt and plastic on the rug. "Oops."

"I didn't like those anyway." Gavin strode over to her. "We can hold you as long as we like. I could send you to Juvenile Detention just for being a smart-ass. Do you know what obstruction of justice is?"

She knocked over another vase.

A voice behind him at the doorway responded. "Yes, it's when someone purposely interferes with the work of an officer of the court." A tall man wearing jeans and a clean and pressed button-down stood holding the door open. "Or something like that."

"And you would be?" Gavin asked.

"My name is Ray Stoddard and if you ask my niece another question without her legal guardian present, that would be me or my wife, I'll not only sue your ass, I'll kick it." The room was silent, as everyone stood frozen by his words.

"Well," Anna said, "gotta go."

———

The elevator door closed behind Anna, and Ray and Marcie Stoddard. Anna unhooked her arm from Ray and retreated to the furthest corner of the compartment as soon as the doors shut. Ray was a head taller than her and Marcie was the picture of a dutiful wife. Marcie had followed them both and started gently crying before the elevator arrived. Anna felt Ray's gaze.

Anna couldn't maintain eye contact. "Why is she crying?" She scrutinized Marcie. She was about Anna's height and wore a floral print dress that was tight around her waist. "Why are you crying?"

Marcie pulled a tissue out of her tan purse. It had multiple exterior pockets and wasn't very big. She pulled the tissue from an inside compartment. "I'm sorry." She sniffled a little. "You look just like your mother."

Anna took a step back and hit the wall. "I don't like either of you. I mean, I'm grateful you came in there and saved me. They were threatening to arrest me, but I just want to go home."

Marcie sobbed and put her hand to her mouth.

"Where's home?" Ray asked. It was morning, but he already had stubble on his face. His salt and pepper hair was thin but covered the top of his sunburned head.

"Brooklyn."

"You should come with us."

"I don't want to seem ungrateful..."

"But you will."

Anna blinked back a tear. "I just want to see my dad."

"Where is he?"

"If I knew that, would I be threatened with imprisonment?"

"They can't arrest you. At worst, they could put you in a foster home. Even New York isn't that stupid."

"Oh, just try them." The doors opened and they stepped out. They walked out of the building in silence. Once outside Anna walked away from them.

"And where are you going, young lady?" Ray seemed to be doing all the talking.

"I told you. Home."

"You can at least give your aunt a hug. We've come a long way for you."

"And as I've said, I'm very grateful..."

Marcie eyes filled with sadness. The same eyes Anna saw in the mirror some mornings. The mornings when she looked at her dad and didn't see her eyes, or her smile, or any similarities, in his face.

Their behaviors matched: they were both workaholics. Was that genetic or environmental?

Agent Gavin was right. There were a lot of little things that just didn't add up.

Dad? Am I adopted?

Don't be silly, Squirrel. You look just like your mother.

She walked over to Marcie, gave her an awkward embrace, and then turned to Ray and did the same.

Marcie held the tissue to her mouth and looked away.

"Okay, well, thanks for getting me out," Anna said. "I guess I'll be in touch." Anna wasn't sure what else to say.

"Why don't you let us give you a ride?"

"The subway is faster, and," Anna glanced away and then back at Ray, "you don't know the way."

"My cell has GPS. Just because we're from Pennsylvania..."

"No, no, I get it."

"If you really want to stay in that house all by yourself, that's fine. We respect your decision." He put his arm around his wife. "But you don't seem in a position to be by yourself as of yet and we can either stay here with you for the next few days or take you back to our home and try to help you pull your life back together. You've had a rough few days."

"My life is fine, thank you." Anna bristled at the thought of them in her home.

"And I can respect that, too. You're family. But you might need some help."

Anna felt pain in her chest. Help? Who did he think he was? She didn't need his help. She would figure this out.

But looking at them made her sad.

Her boring life had just gotten worse.

No. She was not giving up without a fight. Her dad was coming back. He had never left her alone for more than a day or so for work. He always came back.

Always.

"We can bring you back as often as you like. I'm sure the school would understand. Your friends certainly would. I'm sure that an attractive girl like you probably doesn't think about homework much, but we can help, and, well, we'd love to have you stay with us." He hugged Marcie a little tighter. "You're free to move out whenever you like. We don't have much, but we can probably help you find a place in a few months."

———

Anna sat in the back seat of her new uncle and aunt's green car, staring out the rear passenger window at the passing lampposts. They seemed like bars that were too far apart. While there was no new car smell, it felt comfortable. She didn't like it. Her life wasn't over.

Her father would come back. He never left her before and he wouldn't start now. Even the few times when he wasn't there she just knew he was around.

He always came back. He would always come back.

He will. I know he will.

2006

2007

2008

2009

2010

2011

2012

7

―――――

GRADUATION DAY

May 14, 2012

The sky was a deep summer blue and there were almost no clouds. The air was clear, the humidity low, the grass a lush green, and the trees full.

It was a perfect day for graduation. Franklin Field at the University of Pennsylvania overflowed with the yearly mass of humanity there for their commencement ceremony, graduates spread out from the goalpost to the forty-yard line. Dark gowns proliferated with a swath of yellow and blue and red depending on what sash a graduate or faculty member was wearing. The Astroturf was crispy and hot.

The only shadows came from the overhanging bleachers of the U-shaped stadium where thousands of parents sat and still only took up a small percentage of the seats around and behind the graduates. The soon-to-be-ex-college students sat on beige metal chairs with textured plastic backs on which they leaned back and felt the give of experience. The ground staff had covered the football field with the grandstand and the chairs in record time and would put it all away in record time as soon as they received the okay to erase their work until the next ephemeral event.

Anna Wodehouse, soon to be twenty-four years old, was in among the graduates, under duress, and gave up paying attention to the ceremony speeches as soon as they started.

This is why smart phones were invented.

With earbuds in place, the ceremony was just so much white noise. She was thirsty, anxious, and bored. Those went unnoticed. What mattered was the knot in her stomach.

She was graduating. Her birthday was in another month. Her reason for getting up in the morning was about to change.

And it was seven years.

The woman to her right, Holly Myers, elbowed her to get her attention.

"You're bored."

"What?" Anna pulled out her right earbud after tapping her cell phone screen.

"What are you listening to?"

"The Steve Jobs commencement. Stanford. 2005," Anna said.

"It should have been you giving the valedictorian."

"I'm too shy." She stuck the earbud back and tapped her phone. Steve Jobs continued.

When I was seventeen, I read a quote that went something like: "If you live each day as if it was your last, someday you'll most certainly be right."

Holly nudged her again.

"What?"

"You should have given the valedictorian."

"Oh, Holly, I would never have done it. You know I just want to be ignored."

"You'll never be ignored."

Anna's eyes opened. That was something her father, no, Arnold whoever-the-hell, that jerk she didn't care about, that idiot she hated, told her once. She felt a knot in her throat. Questions, conjectures, recriminations, pain, loss, hope all swirled in her brain and she pushed them down where they belonged. Especially hope. Years and years of hope.

"That's not true," Anna said, "and I am going to prove it. I am going to get the most non-descript job I can and lead the most boring life possible..."

"With a major in Math and Poly-Sci, and a minor in accounting and who-the-hell-knows-what-else, I'm not really sure you can cut it at MacDonald's," Holly said.

"I have an offer in cable. And my second major is Computer Science. I just happen to have enough Poly-Sci credits."

"Snore." Holly motioned with her head off to the left. "I think I see that reporter again. The one you almost tossed off the roof."

"I did not almost toss him off the roof."

"Between Tae Kwon Do and all that gun training I'm surprised anyone talks to you. But I think I see him."

Please let her be wrong! Anna turned. She gave a low groan.

"Why is he here?" Anna asked.

"One guess." Anna might actually have to toss him off the roof this time. He had been sending her email incessantly during her exams and she made it very clear that she was not interested.

She stuck the earbud back in.

No one wants to die. Even people who want to go to heaven don't want to die to get there. And yet death is the destination we all share. No one has ever escaped it. And that is as it should be...

She pulled the earbud out. She had listened to Jobs' speech numerous times, but this time felt different.

"You okay?" Holly asked.

"Yeah." She scanned the stands. "I'm fine."

———

The dark blue caps flew in the air. Anna held hers and almost let it join the others, but she hugged it instead. When all the other caps had fallen, she counted a beat and then threw her cap up as high as she could muster. A lone blue square twirling in the air.

———

Anna gave Holly a hug and promised to stay in touch. She was pretty sure that would never happen, but why stop lying now? While Holly had been a good friend, she and Anna traveled in different circles. Or more accurately, Anna didn't have a circle.

She did her best not to touch the crowd of students that were fighting their way to the stands while she scanned the faces of the fathers and brothers and uncles and grandfathers. *This would have been easier if I had set up the facial recognition software like I wanted to.* She had been working at a feverish pace to finish the project, but there were times when she didn't have the energy. Did she really think she'd get a hit?

A familiar outline went behind a group of people. Anna made her way through the crowd. Where did he go? He was a little older, but...

She looked back and forth, her hair twirling around her face. She ran and caught up. A whisper left her lips. "Dad?" She touched his shoulder.

"Anna!" Her aunt's voice was clear and happy.

The man turned.

Not him.

Anna apologized and spun toward the familiar voice. Her aunt and uncle stopped just short of slamming into her and lifted her off the ground with smiles that were the widest of all the people she knew. They were the only people she knew.

"Hi," Anna said. She did her best not to look away, and remembered to smile.

Her aunt's eyes shone in the bright sunshine and a tear trailed across her cheek, leaving a mark in the light dusting of makeup. She hugged her again.

Uncle Ray squeezed her left arm. "Well, young lady. The only thing left is a doctorate and I would be afraid to ask in what."

Stop looking around. "Thanks," Anna said. *He's not here.*

"Your parents would have been so proud," Aunt Marcie said. She pursed her lips. "And your father, too."

Anna glared at her and then felt guilty. "Don't. I don't care."

"Carpenter!" The reporter she had been trying to avoid appeared out of nowhere.

"Let's go," Anna said to her uncle.

"Wait," the reporter said. "I just wanted to congratulate you. You're almost legendary in these parts. Your grades are unbelievable." He put up his hands. "I haven't seen your transcript. I just hear things."

"Please, just leave me alone."

Another voice came from behind her. "Carpenter, there you are, can we just ask you a couple of questions?" It was a female reporter, dragging along a camera crew and microphone.

"No, please..." She turned and there was another camera. And another. What was going on? Voices were shouting at her. Blades sliced the air above her. Helicopters.

"How have you been doing since you were rescued seven years ago?"

"Have you thrown yourself into your studies because of your psychic trauma?"

"Do you give thanks to Almighty God for having saved you from that monster?"

"Do you have anything to say to the kidnapper?"

She turned to the face that exhaled that last question. She grabbed the microphone from his hand and looked at him, not into the camera, and said, "I hate him. He brought me nothing but misery and pain. I hope he rots in hell and that he never knows happiness ever again." She threw the microphone to the floor and walked away from the surging group of journalists who continued to follow and hurl questions at her.

———

As they approached the car, Uncle Ray unlocked the doors with his key fob and held her door open. Just before she entered the car, she collided with him and held him tight. The warmth of her breath doubly-heated her cheeks. "I am so lucky to have you and Aunt Marcie."

Where's Dad? Why won't he come back? She let him go and entered the car.

Uncle Ray closed the door with a firm push. They all sat in silence. Uncle Ray glanced at Aunt Marcie who didn't look back. He started the car.

"It's okay. I don't care that he wasn't there. I don't." She started to sob. "I don't." She covered her face as the car sped away.

8

A WIDOW, A CHILD, AND A DEAD FRIEND

June 1, 2012

Terrell Garrison felt awkward sitting in the love seat next to Darlene Kirby.

He'd driven up north on the Taconic State Parkway that Friday morning, dressed in jeans, a green polo shirt, and black sneakers, grateful to be going against traffic. His trip would be long enough without the added aggravation of a traffic jam. The road, which had been resurfaced, was smooth with the occasional bump as the earth made sure the drivers wouldn't forget who was really in charge. The foliage and dynamite-blasted rocky hills did their best to transform the city feel of the Bronx and Southern Westchester into the long-forgotten rural feel that was New York at the turn of the century when construction started on the Taconic back in 1925.

The turn of the century. History fascinated Terrell, but not for the last few years. Time took on a different dimension a few years ago. He looked at the passing trees and couldn't remember anything about them. While his knowledge of botany was rudimentary, he prided himself on learning what he could as he discovered the history of an area and simple facts about trees was something that he enjoyed.

Walking through a state park or through a local historic area was as appealing as a good brandy or a good cigar (something he indulged on occasion). He had to know more. There was always more.

Now they were just trees. Blown-through rock formations. Trash on the side of the road.

When he reached for his water bottle in the holder to his right he found that it was empty. He cursed the lack of rest stops.

The blue sky had the morning fuzziness of blue felt and the lack of clouds to match. He knew it was going to be a scorcher even before he got to Del's house.

Darlene's house. Today was the day that belonged to the life insurance company.

When he woke up this morning, he thought for sure that he wouldn't feel the way he always did at this time of year.

When Del Kirby disappeared.

Muscle memory delivered him to his destination. Did he remember the packages? Of course he did. He had wanted to put them in the trunk of his car the night before, but he also knew he lived in the Bronx. He placed them against his front door instead so he wouldn't forget.

Terrell wanted to visit more often, and promised himself he would, but somehow the year always got away from him.

Another year had got away from him since Del went missing.

Now sitting close to Darlene, he could smell her Obsession. She wore a plain dress that looked like it was form-fitted for her. She was elegant. "How have you been doing? Really?" he asked.

"I'm good. Del Jr. turned eight a few weeks ago." She examined the glass-topped coffee table. "We missed you."

He heard running upstairs and smiled. Del Jr. was overflowing with energy even for an eight year old. Eight!

"How are things at the Bureau?"

The living room was exactly as he remembered it from last year. Just enough furniture to feel lived in. A lot of photographs. Pictures of Darlene with Del Jr.. Del Jr. with Terrell. Del Jr., when he was just born, with his father, Del Sr. Photos of Del Sr. and Terrell, graduating from college together. Graduating for Quantico. The person who was always there for Terrell during the years when things weren't so good. The friend who made sure Terrell never forgot there was more to life than just catching bad guys.

The house smelled fresh. Alive. Not the home of someone who had passed. He hated euphemisms. Dead.

"How many years has it been now?" he asked.

"You're one to ask. You know."

"Seven," he said. "Seven years."

"Now," Darlene leaned forward, "he's legally dead. Will you accept that?"

"No." It was Terrell's turn to look away. "I know in my head that Del is gone, but there's just something..." His eyes unfocused. All he saw were colors and shapes.

"Have you found anything?" She crossed her legs and held onto her knee with her right hand. "I know you're still looking."

"Nothing." Terrell's cheeks grew warm from the embarrassment. He reached over the side of the love seat, to the bag he'd brought with him. "I thought maybe Del Jr. could use some more building blocks..."

Darlene took the bag from him. She still wore her wedding ring. "Thank you."

Bounding down the stairs came a small bolt of lightning in the form of a boy. He jumped up and hugged Terrell.

"Hi, Uncle Terrell!" He let Terrell go and started to run around the couch with his arms extended out. An airplane. A less-than-three-foot airplane.

"Stop running." Darlene held her hand out to him. "Stop running. Your Uncle Terrell brought you a birthday present." The plane changed direction and landed on his mother's lap. He wore miniature gym pants that were baggy the way well-worn clothes get baggy. His t-shirt was green and had a comic book superhero on it. She pulled the boxes out of the bag. One box of pirate figures. Another box of aliens. Another larger box with an aircraft carrier. The little boy's eyes lit up with each successive reveal.

Terrell's chest get tight. *This is my best friend's son. Del, if you could just see your son.*

In a flash, the boy once again became an airplane and took off for parts unknown, the boxes left behind for a later time. Terrell remembered those days.

"I don't want you to do that again." Darlene stood up. Even at five foot four she was an imposing presence.

"Do what?"

"Spend that kind of money on Del. I know you're single, but you don't make that much at the Bureau. You have to start saving for your turn."

"Oh, you can't deny little Del the opportunity to get presents from his absentee uncle." Terrell smiled. His cheeks felt sore. He got up and towered over her, so he stepped back slightly.

"Yes I can." She took a step toward him. "You're a good man, Terrell, but you have got to let go of this. Del is dead."

"And I'm going to find out what happened to him and who did it."

"Are you any closer?" she asked.

He pursed his lips.

"Are you?" she asked again.

"No, not yet."

"You need to stop coming here. Del Jr. loves when you come over. I love when you come over, but this is not good for you."

"I am capable of figuring out what is good and not good for me..."

"No, you're not!" She stopped for a moment and lowered her voice. "I know what you're going to do after this. I know where you're going."

"I want to know. I have to know." Terrell walked around the love seat, touching the curve of the couch. The flower pattern felt rough.

"And you think I don't. You've shut down your life over him."

"I know what I'm doing."

"Get out."

"What?" Terrell looked at her determined face.

"Get out. Being here is part of the problem. If you can't let go of Del's memory then you can at least let go of us."

"But what if that day never comes?" What if that day never *ever* comes?

"I stopped waiting years ago. Del was not a runaway. He was not some irresponsible father who decided to use his job as a way of disappearing and absolving himself from the people he loved." Darlene's eyes watered, but not a tear ran down her cheek. "He was not a suicide. He was murdered." She walked over to the door. "Get out."

Terrell walked behind her. "What are you doing?"

"Tough love, baby." She swung the door open. "Don't let it hit you on the way out."

He grabbed the door and slammed it shut. "I decide when I'll let go of my friend's memory. I decide! You had him for two years. I had him for nine. Nine years! From high school, Darlene! From high school. He convinced me to join the FBI."

"I've heard this before."

"And I was your best man."

"I was there. Get out. Go visit other dead people." She started to open the door and he pushed it closed. She opened it again and he closed it. Again.

She slapped him.

Terrell blinked. He felt the tears in his eyes, but they weren't from her wake-up call. *He was my family and some bastard took him away.* He swallowed. He hugged her and she resisted at first and then hugged him back. After a few seconds, she pulled away but stayed in his arms. When was it going to feel better?

"Marry me."

"How many times are you going to ask me that?" She looked amused.

"Until you say yes."

"I don't want to be a pity wife." She pulled his arms away but held onto his hands. "You don't love me. I'm just your last connection to him." She kissed him on the cheek with the softest of lips.

The woman Del had chosen and who had chosen Del. Was he waiting? Waiting for what? For Del to return and be the brother

Terrell never had? Del was his brother. Even when events conspired to keep them apart they always found time. He remembered...

Darlene turned away from him and headed into the house. "Don't come back. I stopped waiting. Find who killed him and do what you need to do to them if that will make you feel better."

He wondered what he would do the day, oh, if that day ever came! Would he have the courage, the anger, to take another human being's life if he knew for sure that person had killed Del?

He knew the answer. That was what he was waiting for.

Darlene walked away from him. "Show yourself out."

9

———

WOODLAWN

Terrell sat on his canvas and plastic folding chair with Del's case file opened on his lap surrounded by the dead. In the midst of the beautifully manicured lawn, the *chick-chick-chick* of sprinklers watered the lush, green grass. He flipped through the worn pages and knew that he would have to print the file's contents again. Soon. The last time was six months ago and the condition of the files were a testament to his inattention to paper abuse.

This was the third neighborhood he'd known growing up. The first, in a torn-up ghetto where a building fire forced them to move, was the furthest from his memory. The second, in the Bronxdale projects across the street from the local parochial school, was where he learned to hate petty thievery (*Dad, they took my bike!*), violence brought on by fragile emotions, and the inability of local cops to do anything. Having been with the Bureau for so many years, he had a better understanding of the pressures brought to bear on people, especially the police, but he never developed the patience to deal with them.

The third neighborhood was here: a few blocks from the Woodlawn Cemetery where he commuted to and from college, and he did his best to ignore how much his parents loved where they lived. The area seemed to cycle between getting better and getting worse and Terrell, who couldn't understand his parents' fascination, grew tired of it. The neighborhood felt like sunburned skin, or an ill-fitting sweaty suit. He vowed to move away the first chance he got (the smells alone drove him crazy), but he moved back in with them during the last years of their lives as his father was diagnosed with prostate cancer and his mother died soon after.

He looked up, but the bright sunlight was too much for his eyes. He put on his aviator-frame sunglasses, and from his perch on the south end of Woodlawn Cemetery on 211 Street and Hull Avenue in the Bronx, he could see his car. He never liked this spot and argued with his parents when they told him they had picked out a burial plot, and where it was located. This was their neighborhood, their home, and they wanted to stay. The price was also reasonable since they purchased it before they needed it (at least as reasonable as you can get buying real estate in New York). Terrell wasn't happy, but they were happy, and Terrell was never happy anyway.

A gray Corolla went by. He caught the first few letters of the license plate. He hadn't seen it before so he would store it away. His version of the license plate game he used to play when he was a kid. Five cars had gone by since he arrived and he mostly remembered them. A black Mustang. A red Camaro. A green Camry. Number six: gray Corolla. DSM-something-or-other.

Every so often he would look up at the single tombstone before him and he would direct a question to his parents. *What would we be doing right now if you hadn't died, Mom? Would you be ordering out? Cooking up a storm?* He took off his sunglasses and flipped over another page. Another photograph. Another interview. He was thirsty. The flimsy shade of the trees to his right were not enough to subdue the glare but enough for him to read.

Names. Dates. Interviews. He had combed through them over and over. Endlessly. Something would jump out at him. He was sure of it. His brain hadn't failed him yet. *Will I go out like you, Dad? In your sleep? Or like Mom, of a broken heart? On second thought, no chance of a broken heart.*

The skin on his neck was hot. A gap in the shade targeted him.

Another car. Number seven. Red Scion. Personalized. B1t3 m3. He shook his head. *Bite Me.* Personalized plates were a waste of money, but they made surveillance easier. Unbelievable how many suspects who tried to stay under the radar personalized their license plates.

Another interview. Another undercover report. Money laundering. Funds going to a construction company for work done surreptitiously. Every time he read the interview, his bullshit detector went off. Why pay for construction work no one would know about? A secret gift? Idiocy. Hidden location to do hand-offs? A meth lab? A quiet place to cut coke or eliminate competition? The report didn't state where the work was done, or who paid for it, just that it was completed and more contractors were waiting in line to do more work. The flow of money never seemed to stop.

Easy: do it in plain sight. That was how H.H. Holmes had done it in Chicago at the turn of the twentieth century when he paid different contractors to build his house of horrors. Terrell was used to telling new agents about cases like that one to show how easy it was to commit certain crimes that looked difficult to perform, but were actually quite easy:

Holmes had all kinds of chutes leading to the basement where he used to send the bodies of his victims after he murdered them. In addition, they built soundproof rooms that could only be opened from the outside that had gas pumped into them to render the victim unconscious.

All built by public contractors because they didn't know that he was constantly firing the work crews and no one saw the big picture. The house was designed to feed the incinerator.

And Holmes always fed it because he was always hungry.

Another car. Number eight: a gray Corolla. DSM-something. He blinked. No, that was number six. He took a good look at the passing vehicle. Yep, same one as before. Perfect body. Corner bent on the license plate. Must be looking for a parking space. Or lost. He would keep an eye on it.

Another transcript. He had gotten the names of a few of the

construction workers. All interviewed by the Bureau. One of them died recently. What did Del find out? What connection had he made?

He was getting tired. The visit with Darlene did not go well and her reaction this year caught him by surprise. He didn't know what to do anymore. He knew Del loved her, and she was a wonderful woman, but the whole relationship thing was beyond him. If she ever dated anyone, he would run a full background check on the guy and let him know that he was not welcome if he seemed the least bit questionable. Even with her demand that he not return, he knew that he would keep checking up on her and Del Jr. if for no other reason than to make himself feel better. *I won't leave them alone, Del. Don't worry.*

He realized that at some point he was going to have to stop talking to people who weren't there, but he was good with it. One day he would feel a sense of closure and then move on. That day was not today.

Something glinted in a window over to his right. He turned his head left to give the appearance of looking the other way. Was there someone surveilling him? Probably a window being closed. The heat was starting to get a bit much. Almost time to go.

His inconsistent monthly visits to Woodlawn Cemetery was just another part of his routine. Darlene was right; some of his best friends were dead and he made it a point to visit them all in the normal course of his life.

The window. There was no way to look through it. Too high up and too bright.

More paperwork. The heat didn't bother him that much. Much to do and he didn't want to hang out in a diner or other public venue when he could be here. With the people he knew.

He walked the long way around to his car. He could have jumped the fence, but he didn't want to give onlookers the wrong idea. With the chair properly folded and stashed in its carry bag, he headed toward the entrance of the cemetery at 233 Street and Webster Avenue where he had the car parked along the web of roads that snaked their way through the Woodlawn property.

Gray Corolla. DSM-1667. Two men sat in the vehicle. Not doing very much and today Terrell was feeling paranoid. Maybe the heat.

"Good afternoon, gentlemen." Terrell approached the vehicle and peered in. Middle-aged men. Not particularly muscular, but being armed would take care of that.

"Hello."

"I couldn't help but notice that you were circling the cemetery. Sure is hard to find a parking spot, isn't it?" He peered up and down the private road. It was almost empty.

"Yes, you're right." Russian accent. They all laughed at the joke. "We were just looking for a good spot to stop and rest for a few moments before finishing our drive."

"Well, this is certainly a good spot for that." Terrell glanced around and then back at the men. Pastel blue button-down shirt. White t-shirt. Probably Dockers pants. Driver had shaved. So did the passenger. "Where you driving to?"

"Oh, probably Manhattan. You know. To pick up girls." More laughing.

"Yeah. Well, you have a good day. Now I can tell my buddies at work how I met two guys from the Russian mafia on their way to the city to pick up girls." They all laughed. He stood up still looking at the men, and then turned and walked away.

10

THE PACKAGE

Anna walked into the imposing glass structure of the Comcast Innovation and Technology Center, at 1800 Arch Street, the newest and tallest building in Philadelphia, hoping no one would recognize her.

She decided to use a fake name just in case. When the reception security asked her for ID, she pretended to have forgotten it at home. Long drive. She couldn't reschedule. They understood and called upstairs to confirm.

They took her picture, printed out a guest pass, and pointed her toward one of the numerous banks of elevators.

The ride up was unnerving. Shiny buttons. Shiny walls. She felt the glare through her skin.

She gave the receptionist her name and sat down to wait. She crossed her legs and pulled at the dark skirt Aunt Marcie said would be perfect for a job interview. The white blouse felt comfortable, though Anna pulled at it to keep the fabric from bunching up behind her as she leaned back in the red bench seat.

"Ms. Powell?" the receptionist asked.

Anna looked up from the fashion magazine she pretended to read and stood up.

"Please come with me."

———

The interview office was small, but cold. Anna hugged herself and rubbed her arms to keep the circulation going. *So much for the short-sleeved blouse.* The desk was a U-shaped monster that took up most of the room, yet the man sitting behind it had almost nothing on its surface. A single PC with a dual-monitor set-up dominated the area to his left and a coffee cup sat to his right. The dim overhead lights made the white walls look more tan. *What I would give to have this much desk space.*

The man was overweight, but Anna thought he held it well. Not much of a double chin. Clean-shaven. Nice suit. Nice tie. Wedding ring.

No photos. Maybe he didn't have kids.

They exchanged pleasantries.

This is a waste of time.

Wait. What did he say?

"Why would you want a position as an intern?" He placed the paper copy of her resume on the desk in front of him.

His eyes were making her uncomfortable. She had seen that look before.

It was the look of incomprehension.

"I think I would be effective. There are a number of things that need to be done and I know that I can support the people who make things happen here."

"No," he said. He flipped through her paperwork. "You misunderstand me. Why would someone like you even apply here?"

She sighed to herself. "The university told me that the position wasn't filled. Is that the problem? Was there a class I should have taken? I only took five classes in broadcasting. Wasn't that enough?" she asked.

"No. I mean, yes, that's plenty. It's just that," he placed his hands on the stack of paper that represented her background, "what could you possibly learn here?"

"I can help you get organized."

"You're going to be throwing away trash." He raised his eyebrows.

"I can write. I do amazing research."

He leaned back. "You're going to make copies."

"One of my independent studies was helping children in Africa learn how to develop critical thinking skills so they could participate in their government."

"You're going to be delivering coffee."

"I really need this job. My aunt and uncle need me to start bringing home some money. They've been so good to me. I...I just want to help. There must be something I can do here."

"It's a non-paying position for the next three months and if they like you, they'll offer you a position at minimum wage." He slid her resume back to her. "You should apply as a quant at Goldman. You'd be making six figures Day One. You'll be running the place in a couple of years."

———

She sat at the lip of the fountain outside the building gritting her teeth. *Acting stupid shouldn't be this hard.* She would have to apply for something that didn't need her transcript even with her fake name. A name that was close enough to her real one so she would recognize it when someone called out to her, but not close enough that anyone would put the pieces together.

How did Superman do it? He just put on glasses.

Spiderman delivered pizza and sold his photos.

What could Anna do? She could teach programming. Math from introductory to advanced. Tae Kwon Do. Organic Chemistry. This was painful. She finally made it to the exit of academia, and the entrance to real life, and she was unemployable. Why? *Because I'm over-qualified, and my face...*

A woman holding a little girl's hand stopped and stared at her.

"Excuse me, but were you on the evening news last night? Are you that girl that was kidnapped years ago?"

"No, I'm not, and I wasn't." She felt her anger rush through her stomach and into her throat and then disappear, leaving a hollow emptiness. "That happens to me all the time." She tried to chuckle, but a burst of air escaped her lips. She pushed her black hair behind her ear. "I hate that I look like that stupid girl. My name is Carpenter."

———

Anna bolted through the door of the Stoddard's house and went straight to her bedroom.

She gave them a half-hearted greeting, climbed the stairs, and closed the door, doing her best not to slam it. The twenty-year-old home barely creaked. Uncle Ray had monitored its construction and made sure that it had enough insulation to keep their heating bill low along with the sound between rooms. The walls of her room were painted a powder blue with a lacy trim along the top that Anna had convinced them to remove, but she changed her mind at the last moment.

She paced on the clean hardwood floor, considered hiding under the sheets of her queen-size bed, and instead sat down in the cushioned wooden chair in the corner near the window. The window she climbed out of numerous times, thinking she could make good her escape.

She always came back.

Someone knocked on the door. It was so soft it had to be Aunt Marcie.

———

"So the job wasn't a good fit?"

"That building is populated by morons passing for mobile brains. They call that an innovation center? All they care about is distributing mindless programming in new and novel ways for more and more money to people who understand less and less about what they're watching while their mirror neurons give them the warm and fuzzy feeling that they could drive a truck through ice-covered roads or cook like a master chef or be someone they're not. They're so lost and alone that they don't even realize that their lives are slipping away while they feel superior because they can answer every twentieth question on *Jeopardy* from the comfort of their easy chair that was made by underpaid workers in China or the Philippines who can at least do higher-order math."

Aunt Marcie sat on the bed in front of Anna, listening to the verbal onslaught. Her lips gave a slight upward turn. "Can I get you some tea?"

"No. I don't deserve any tea. I failed today." Anna folded her hands on her lap. "How did I do that? Aunt Marcie, how did I do that?"

"Would you like me to tell you why? Or would you rather open the box that came for you?"

"Did it have any oily stains on it?"

"No."

"It could be a bomb."

"It doesn't seem big enough, but I don't know that much about explosives." Aunt Marcie took her glasses off. That was a bad sign. She was near-sighted most of the time. "You're trying too hard."

"How can I..."

"You are so wound up that everyone knows you're better than they are as soon as you walk in the room. You're tall, you're beautiful, you're intelligent. And you haven't a clue." She put her glasses back on, stood, and walked to the wooden door that had seen better days. "Come down in a few minutes. I'll have your favorite tea ready for you."

"Stop being nice to me. I'm a college graduate. I drink beer now."

Aunt Marcie smiled and walked out, closing the door behind her. Anna didn't do gratitude well, but she'd learned living with the Stoddards for the last few years. She felt that somehow she didn't deserve them. They were part of a life from another time stream and she'd crossed over into a world with aunts, uncles, cousins. To say the Stoddards had relatives was an understatement. Uncle Ray had five brothers and sisters and Marcie had a younger sister who recently widowed. All had multiple children. The wilds of Pennsylvania were different than the wilds of New York. It was warmer there.

———

The box was on her bed. Waiting. Anna looked it over. Aunt Marcie was right: no oil stains. It could still be a bomb, but she decided to chance it. She picked it up and twirled it in her hands. No forwarding address. The printed label had her old name: Anna Wodehouse. The address was correct.

No cancelled postage. "Uncle Ray!"

She heard his voice through the door. It carried from downstairs. "I hear yelling."

"How long has the box been here?"

"I found it on the steps when I went for my walk this morning."

"Thank you!"

The box was dropped off on the doorstep by someone who wasn't the mail carrier. A messenger?

Anna put the box down, sat down in her updated Aeron chair, and turned to the monitor attached to her tablet. She played back the video feed outside the door of the house. She had set up the video monitoring system years ago on a lark. It was the kind of thing she learned to do in her younger days when there was so much to do and discover.

Now, it was just something to do.

There wasn't much to rewind as her system only activated when the picture changed. No need for external motion sensors.

Uncle Ray and Aunt Marcie leaving the house in reverse.

Uncle Ray and Aunt Marcie arriving at the house in reverse.

Uncle Ray. Coming in. Going out.

Aunt Marcie. Going out. Coming in.

Some kid catching the newspaper when it jumped from their lawn and over the fence.

The morning sun went down and it got dark. Her cameras switched to green when the low-light imaging kicked in. When did this package arrive?

A car drove in reverse and stopped across the street. A man got out and walked in reverse to her doorstep. The cameras cut from one shot to another automatically based on distance to the door. She didn't see his face until he turned around to pick up the package.

Anna jumped. He was wearing a mask. She rewound to where the car left the frame.

Play. The time stamp read 3:42:20 a.m. Anna felt creeped out. Someone was at her house at 3:42 in the morning. This morning.

The car pulled up. The first camera to activate was at street level. She didn't know cars that well, but she would be able to look it up. The next camera tried to take a picture of the license plate, but there was none to be found at the front of the car. *Must be from New York.*

The driver got out, walked through the fence, and up the walk. He was carrying the box. Camera two and then camera three and four all cut in succession as he got closer and closer. The mask was either plastic, vinyl, or leather. It covered everything except for a slit for his eyes to see through. Anna couldn't make out what his eyes looked like or what color they were or the color of his skin, though she was sure he was white.

He looked around, and put the box down. He stood at attention for a moment and then turned, looking directly into the camera.

And waved.

He knew where the camera was!

She almost called out for Uncle Ray and then stopped herself.

What if?

What if the box was from her father? Hope jumped from her head to her heart and she threw herself on the bed and grabbed it. Only he would have known that she would have a security system installed to record everyone coming and going. Her nails were short and the box was sealed in wide paper tape that had threads running through it. She opened a drawer in her bureau, pulled out a pair of scissors, and carefully cut the box open. *Mustn't damage the contents.*

Maybe it was a graduation present. Or an airline ticket. Maybe it would be a note begging her forgiveness for leaving her alone all these years. *Oh, Dad, I knew you would come back.*

She opened it. The box was empty except for a photo, a thumb drive, and a note.

She unfolded the note.

Don't take this to the authorities.

She looked at the photo. High quality paper and high-end ink. High-resolution photo, probably from a cell phone. There were a number of people in the picture. Walking toward the camera, behind the people who were being photographed, was a man. She brought her hand to her mouth. *It's him.* Her shoulders tightened. Someone else found him. And that someone else found her. Why?

She read the note again. *Don't take this to the authorities.*

Right.

11

DIGITAL MEMORIES

The drive down to the FBI office in lower Manhattan from the Bronx was never a pleasant experience, but at least predictable: it was always terrible. Fighting traffic, or sitting in traffic, parking, walking to the office, getting through the lobby after displaying his PIV card, and making it upstairs was routine. Bland and aggravating, but routine.

It was afternoon. After driving to his apartment to change into a suit and one of five pairs of polished black shoes, Terrell decided to focus his day on Del's case. Normally he would spend an hour here, a few hours there, every few days to make sure his other work didn't fall behind. He had decided on the drive back from Darlene's to ignore everything else for a few hours, but the time at his parents' gravesite clinched his resolution to just drown in the seven-year-old information again. Finding himself inundated with facts, dates, locations, and names had helped him before. He needed to feel the information absorbed by his skin, embracing him, telling him things he had heard before, but in new and different ways.

This had worked for other cases. However, while he had done this every few months on Del's case it had never yielded results.

His throat was parched. He filled his plastic water bottle from the fountain down the hall and gave it another try.

Terrell slid his hand across the mass of files and papers on his desk and a clump of dust fell off the surface. *I think I've scared the cleaning people away.* Terrell's cubicle, as were all the cubicles in the cube farm on his floor at 26 Federal Plaza, was not much different than you would see at a private sector firm. Faux desks that were just flat surfaces attached to the cube walls. The square footage was a comfortable size, the areas cleaned on a regular basis by a rotating staff of cleaning companies, and Terrell's chair was an acquisition he made when a higher-up retired and Terrell switched his standard issue torture seat for the much more comfortable Steelcase. The walls were 4 and a half feet high, had flat slate gray panels embedded in a thin white frame to hold the walls up and supply them with a sense of strength, and were almost soundproof (or at least as sound-proof as an office can be with no door). The height of the walls, designed to allow a measure of privacy when an agent was working or making calls, also gave the agents a place to hide safely on the astronomically small chance someone showed up with a weapon and began firing into the unsuspecting agents. There was really only one difference between the walls of Terrell's cube and the walls of the average office: Terrell's were made of Kevlar.

There was something in Del Kirby's case files that bothered Terrell. He had the nagging feeling he always did when there was something out of place, and he obsessively needed to put it back, but he couldn't determine what it was. What was it? The mass of paper hiding his desk related to many things, but none of them from Del's file. Those files Terrell protected like the precious clues they were. Somewhere was the missing piece that would help Terrell find out his friend's fate as much as he feared that discovery.

Del's case files had been digitized almost as soon as he created them. The easiest way for Terrell, or any agent, to find what he needed was to just open a file in the Sentinel system and look at the paperwork or photos. Since he wanted to look over the information at home, Terrell had printed out every last scrap as soon as Del was officially declared missing back in 2005. He spent a lot more time on it back when he had been assigned to the case once they confirmed that Del had not simply been sick or involved in an accident. Plenty of agents through the years have found themselves unable to contact their families due to a random car accident or mugging, but that never stopped the Bureau from looking for them with the full strength and power of the U.S. government.

There had been a few suicides. Terrell knew that Del was depressed at various times in his life. He even talked about what it would be like to end it all. Terrell encouraged him to see a therapist, but they both knew formal therapy could lead to an early retirement if word got out. So, no therapists.

What about a random event that had somehow pulled him under the radar? On occasion it was a suspect who somehow found they were being made or who discovered the surveillance team and thought that taking them out would protect them from retribution. Events like that were unpredictable, but few and far between.

There was no evidence one way or another. Del had simply vanished.

Yet there was something. Was it the men in the parked car? No, Terrell wasn't leading any cases right now, just support.

He scanned the photos on his hi-res screen. There were better monitors available, but for photos it was more than enough. And typing? Who needed a hi-res screen to type?

The photos flashed by. One, two, four, six. *Wait. What?* The photos were...there was something wrong. Wrong? No, must be his eyes. He blinked to clear his vision.

The photos seemed blurred.

Terrell went through the photos in his file and pulled a random one out for examination. Sharp, color, faces were distinguishable. Back to the digital case file. *Flip, flip, flip.* There was the digitized version of the same photo. The faces were definitely blurred. Why hadn't he noticed that before? He held the picture up to the screen. It was different, but was it different enough?

He pulled out his cell phone and took a picture of the hard copy photograph. He could still make out the faces. He grabbed the photo and went to the copy machine against the wall just outside his office. No special settings so it would come out in black-and-white.

Soft, but he could still see the suspect's eyes in the photo.

"Sentinel support."

"Hey, good afternoon. This is Special Agent Garrison. I was just taking a look at some photos..."

"Case file number?"

Terrell read it off the screen.

"What seems to be the problem?"

"I've got some photos that don't match the hard copies. I made hard copies from the system about five years ago and the hard copies look better than the originals."

"Hold on, please."

Support. A love/hate relationship.

"Sorry, Agent Garrison, but the photos are the photos. They were entered over seven years ago and haven't been touched at all. Are you sure?"

Terrell bid him a good day and went back to the files.

The files dates. Nothing had changed. He opened a random file and compared it to his hard copy. Another file. Another file.

What the hell? The information was changed. The vast majority of a given report was the same, but additional information had been redacted. While that was standard procedure when information unrelated to a case was discovered, his hard copy had the information in full view. He checked the date. Unchanged.

What the hell was going on? He decided to take another step back. He pulled out a full listing of the files as they were when he printed everything out.

He held the print out against the screen.

There were files missing. Terrell cursed at himself.

"Support...what's your name?"

"Dave Harcourt."

"I'm sorry, Dave, but we have a problem. Get your supervisor on the line."

"Hold on, sir."

The phone went silent. Terrell continued looking at his printout and the screen. They couldn't be more different. If someone had made it into Sentinel, they had bigger problems than just Del's disappearance. Sentinel was the successor to the Virtual Case File system that had been started in 2000 and abandoned in 2005 after $170 million dollars had been spent and the Bureau had nothing to show for it. Embarrassing, but it appeared to be business as usual in the software industry.

"Special Agent Garrison?"

"Yes. I think there has been unauthorized access to Sentinel and the destruction of case file information. And to who am I speaking?" Terrell could feel his brain compartmentalizing the situation; this could be about Del. It could be about the Bureau. It could be both or neither.

"This is Joe Vanderman. I'm the manager for Sentinel support. We're locking down all the files and started a system audit. We'll need whatever you've got so we can prove before and after."

"No problem. I'll get you copies of everything I have including folder listings that show which files have been deleted."

"Thanks. Get that sent over as soon as you can. I think you just started a fire storm."

"Understood." He hung up. There had to be red lights going off all over Bureau IT right now. Was this just his files? How many other agents were affected?

He turned to his keyboard and continued searching. One file, another file. What was in the missing files? He would have to compare his hard copy to the system listing.

As Terrell opened a file related to another interview, the Sentinel window closed. He pulled his hands away from the keyboard. *What the...?*

He opened another window and searched for the case. Gone. He picked up the phone again.

"Dave? What the hell is going on?"

"Hold on, let me check..."

Two agents walked over to his desk.

"Hi, guys." He looked at their serious demeanor and leaned back in his chair. *Great.* "What's going on?"

"Special Agent Garrison?"

He nodded. *Oh, this is not going to go well.*

"Sir, please step away from your keyboard and come with us."

Terrell pushed himself away from this desk while holding onto the phone. "Dave, I have two very serious looking men at my desk. Is there something you want to tell me?"

"Ah, sir, I don't know any more than you do," Dave said.

"Did my access just get pulled? Or was I somehow magically transported to the folder where the case files live?"

"I would follow those two men if I were you."

12

ROOM WITHOUT A VIEW

Terrell watched Agent-in-Charge Han Gilson enter the room that looked less like an interrogation room, or even an office, and more like a library. The difference, in this case, was that the walls, floor, and ceiling had a specially designed wire mesh running through them, turning it into an area disconnected from the rest of the world. Cell phones with five bars just minutes earlier had none. Inbound and outbound signals of any kind were neutered. The room, the practical application of a Faraday cage, was the equivalent of a black hole. The Sensitive Compartmented Information Facility, or SCIF, was the last place Terrell wanted to be.

He was leaning against one of the metal bookcases, tapping it with the back of his fist when Gilson approached him. Terrell didn't move. *Too bad, let him come to me.*

"I guess you're wondering why I called you here today," Gilson said and smiled.

Oh, I am not in the mood for this. Terrell had dealt with Gilson before. A nice guy, but in it for the pension. By *it* Terrell meant civil service. Gilson would have been at home at the Department of Motor Vehicles as much as the FBI.

"What's going on, Han?" Terrell asked. "I've got people to question. Crimes to solve. Coffee to drink." He pushed away from the bookcase but stood his ground. The bookcases extended well behind him with at least ten others to either side of him. In addition to being a surveillance-free room, this particular SCIF was a research facility. Scattered throughout the expanse of paper were desks with PCs that had secure access to the outside world.

Terrell had left his jacket on his chair, but his white tailored shirt, which normally fit him quite comfortably, was sticking to his back. He twitched his shoulder every few seconds in the hope that the movement would pull the shirt straight.

Three agents sat at a long, light blond, wood table for eight. One of them looked up at Terrell and Gilson and collected his things. The others followed suit and walked toward the shadow of the back room to continue their work.

Gilson motioned to the chair and Terrell sat.

"This had better be good," Terrell said.

"You've been reassigned." Gilson crossed his legs.

"I don't do cyber-crime."

"How do you know what I'm assigning you to?"

"I found a leak. I don't know if it's related to a current case, a cold case, or just wants to piss me off."

"It's not a leak, or a break-in," Gilson said. "But this assignment might be related to your case."

Terrell leaned forward and clasped his hands together. "And?"

"Once you get back, I'll make sure you have access restored and you continue working on Del's case the way you always have."

"This isn't the X-files. Del is an active agent who probably disappeared in the commission of his duties."

"I like how you say 'is an active duty agent,' not 'was an active duty agent.'"

Terrell felt his cheeks grow warm.

"I know. That's why I'm sending you out to interview a WitSec before he gets moved to a new location." The armpits of Gilson's white button-down were starting to show sweat soaking through.

Terrell felt a chill. "WitSec? Are you kidding?" He folded his arms.

"We're not protecting Del's murderer, are we? In WitSec?" *No way in hell. If I find out that Del's murderer has been in Witness Protection I'm going to go ballistic.*

Gilson looked up at the ceiling for a moment. "No. Jesus H. Christ, Terrell. If we knew that, we could close Del's case and that information would just be sealed. We'd give Darlene some closure and make sure all of her benefits were in place." Gilson loosened the tie around his thick neck and then crossed his arms. "The file on this guy is available to you. Read up on it and get ready to pay him a visit."

"Where is he? Outside of the metro area?"

"Yeah. He's in the UK. Or on his way."

"The UK?" Terrell fell back. "What about my current cases? I've got people out in the field."

"Your cases have been handed over to Quinones. He's been working them with you so they'll be fine."

Quinones? Yes, it was true that Quinones was involved in all the cases, but...Terrell could think of no objections. He turned out to be an excellent addition to Terrell's group, but handing over the primary role?

"I guess they would, but why do this at all? If the guy is still in the States, can't they just hold him a little longer? An extra day?"

"No," Gilson said. "This came in at the last minute and his travel can't be changed without potentially risking his life."

"You know what I have to say about that, right?"

"Lucky for you we're in an SCIF."

Terrell knew his choices were limited. What could this man know that had been overlooked all these years? "How do we know this guy is legit?"

"We just know."

"What do you mean 'We just know'?" *What the hell?* "International WitSec. Are you telling me the Agency has something to do with this?"

"I'm not telling you anything except that you have to talk to this guy and find out what he knows. No one knows Del's cases like you do. And no one has as much invested." Gilson leaned in. "State asked for you specifically."

"State?" Terrell's stomach clenched.

"I assumed you would know who. You have a lot of friends over there." Gilson smiled as Terrell slowly blinked.

"This can't be happening."

"Oh, yes, it can. I didn't say what kinds of friends you have over there. You certainly impressed them with your uncanny ability to get the job done."

Even if it meant that I arrested a few of them. "No good deed…"

God, he hoped he wasn't being set up. If anything went wrong while he was overseas there was no predicting what could happen, and he was having enough fun with his current case, which involved the daughter of a Senator and the CEO of a major software company. Organized crime just wasn't what it used to be.

"What about Sentinel?" Terrell asked. "I want to be available to the investigation team. I know those files inside and out and can tell them what's been changed and what's been deleted. This is a bad one, Han."

"Yeah, yeah, it would be if we didn't already know who did it," Gilson said.

"What are you talking about? We know who…?" Terrell watched in disbelief as Gilson nodded his head. "No."

"NSA under the auspices of the State Department authorized the redaction of certain documents related to work being done by various federal agencies." Gilson eyes reflected a measure of resignation. "And, from the looks of it, you tipped them off."

"No way in hell!"

"You mentioned some term that got flagged and the right people, or the wrong people, found out."

Terrell couldn't think of what he'd done. What had he been looking for? He didn't remember putting in any requests for information. There was nothing to ask for.

"I can't imagine what it was. Are you kidding me?" The new world of 24/7 surveillance was getting stickier and stickier.

"Be grateful. We wouldn't have gotten this lead otherwise. Del stepped out onto the metaphorical freeway and was overtaken by events we still haven't pieced together. They're giving us this opportunity to get some information from the horse's mouth because they've been following you following this and they're prepared to let us question him to get our own intel."

"All right. I'll question him. What do I do then?" Gilson stood and Terrell joined him.

"Come back. File a report that will probably be sealed and classified. If you can confirm that Del was killed in the line of duty, we start to petition State for more information so we can find the bastards who did it. I don't care if it causes an international incident. I knew Del before I became Agent-in-Charge." He looked Terrell in the eyes. "He was a good man. Is. A good man. I know what it's like to have a family destroyed because of a case. We'll straighten this out."

"Okay, boss. I know I don't have much of a choice, but this is what I would have done no matter how this conversation ended." Terrell thought again about how State had requested him specifically. "Who asked for me?"

"We're not allowed to know that either. All I know is that WitSec guy was moved recently due to some police action. Go figure. Somebody in WitSec getting in trouble with the law."

13

———

WITNESS SECURITY

"You have to sign an updated memorandum to make it possible for you to continue in the program." U.S. Marshal Edison Myrick, the latest lead case officer for what was already an interminable case, was getting tired. He had dealt with this man before and it was always exhausting. Most days he could work his way around things, but for some reason today he was on a short fuse. *Breathe in*. Let the patience return before Myrick pulled out his weapon and pistol-whipped him.

The plain, gray, metal chair Myrick sat in always made his back hurt. Or maybe it was the man in front of him who was the pain in the ass. Myrick enjoyed the job of protecting the innocent, people brave enough to step forward and destroy their old lives for the general good. Selflessness was something he didn't see too often, and as he occupied the otherwise simple conference room, he knew he didn't see it before him.

The room smelled musty, the vent on the wall was more of a prop than a conduit for air-conditioning, and he was hungry. The mystery man, in his pressed Dockers, white button-down and insufferable attitude, was pushing Myrick to the point where Myrick considered walking out and letting some other fool fight this battle. He blinked and opened his eyes wide. He knew he wouldn't leave. The lack of cool air in the room had an effect on them both and the process of hiding what they were doing didn't make the task any easier. The room had a glass wall, but the blinds had been drawn and closed. If the mystery man decided to try and kill Myrick, the only indication would be a muffled cry in the soundproof room and maybe one of them being thrown against the glass.

He slid his rubber-soled black shoes on the thin pile carpeting. If either of their faces was dragged on it, he was sure it would leave a mark.

"I told you: I'm not signing until you bring my daughter to me." The man paced the room like a caged animal. His square-ish body moved in smooth thumps highlighting the man's solid frame.

His clothes looked tailored, but Myrick knew they weren't. During one of his encounters with him Myrick compared him to a bear with the grace of a leopard. Maybe he *was* a caged animal.

"Okay. This is how it is: you know how the program works. You sign; we protect. There is nothing new here. You know the rules. You've been living under them for years. Your daughter is safe. We have a detail on her and no one has ever gone near her." This man needed to understand that he was posing a greater threat to his daughter by not cooperating than by signing.

"I don't care anymore. I haven't seen her in years. I want to see her. Can't you at least give me that?"

Edison felt for him. He had two children of his own and he didn't know what he would do if he couldn't see them. However, he also knew he wouldn't willingly place them in danger just for a peek. The forty-to-fifty-something-year-old man was not easily placated. How could someone so meticulous about his appearance be so damn irritating?

"The guys who want to kill you might have someone keeping an eye out for her. If you suddenly appeared, that could easily spur them into action and kidnap her. Is that what you want?" Tactic number one in persuasion: remind the other guy what he really wants. This guy didn't just want to see his daughter; he also wanted her to be safe.

"Look, I've done crazier things and survived. What I need now is a chance. That's all." The windowless office in the safe house was furnished for a minimalist setting. The pacing man seemed an overpowering presence. "Just a chance. Take me to her area and then turn away. I'll take care of the rest. I'm telling you I've done this before."

Had he? Did it matter? Myrick picked up the phone and dialed one of his colleagues who was waiting for the paperwork so he could begin the process of overseas cooperation. Witness Protection International.

"Harvey? Please send a cab for our guest. He has decided not to continue with the program. What? Yes, he understands what this means to his safety and well-being. Yes, he accepts all responsibility for what can occur to him and his daughter." Myrick hung up and looked at him. The stunned look on his face was unexpected.

"You know you're going to be fired for this," he said.

"I'm a civil servant. We don't get fired; we get promoted."

"When does the cab arrive?" He tugged at his shirt as if he were wearing a tie.

He didn't seem like the tie-wearing type. Myrick was not often wrong about those kinds of behaviors.

"They'll call up. You realize you're going to be dead within a few hours of leaving here. Right? The cabbie might be one of them."

"I'll take that chance. I have to see her first. I don't care if they kill me after that."

"Are you an idiot?" The man shot a look of anger at him. "I'm sorry. That was uncalled for. Look, they're not going to ask you for a schedule of events. They are just going to kill you. Maybe quickly, maybe slowly, but you will be dead before you get anywhere near her."

"Yeah, well, maybe I can get help from someone else," he said.

"Others?" Edison felt a lump form in his stomach. Was he going to tell Myrick something he shouldn't?

"There are others who can protect me. Really protect me," the man said.

People? What people?

"No one can protect you like we can." *Here it comes.*

"I was involved in a lot of things. There are numerous governments I can turn to that would help me out." He stood a little straighter.

"You've been in contact with other governments?" Myrick considered jumping at him.

"Not yet, but they're Plan B."

"Doesn't work out? Do you think this is a negotiation for a pay raise or a settlement on sexual harassment?" Myrick stood up and pulled out his handcuffs. "I can arrest you, right now, on suspicion of espionage, conspiracy to communicate national defense information to persons not entitled to receive it, the retention and willful disclosure of classified information, and the unauthorized disclosure of national defense information." The man's eyes opened wide for a moment and then resumed a calmer appearance. Edison slid open the cuffs. "Feel like turning around?"

"You can arrest me, but you won't." He held his hands out. Large hands. Large wrists.

"I would Mirandize you, but I'll leave that up to the locals to do that."

"I have people on the outside who have recordings I've made. Disclosing what I know. The things I still haven't told Justice, but will...on the condition you bring me my daughter!" He slammed his hand on the table, causing the phone to jump.

Myrick stood for a moment and decided it was time to lower the temperature. "You care about your daughter, correct?" The man sat down and nodded. "You realize that one of the conditions of your protection was her detail."

"What's your point? Those are different memoranda."

"As soon as you walk out that door her detail becomes a memory."

The man's face relaxed and he became slack-jawed.

Myrick said, "And you go to jail anyway where you will not be allowed to see her. Do you realize that?"

"Why would you endanger the life of an innocent victim?" the man asked.

"If anything happened to her, we would handle it like any other murder case, but that would be after the fact."

"And if I sign?" His shoulders sagged. His look said *I have run out of viable choices.*

Myrick tried to believe it.

"Life goes on like it has for the last few years. You will be safe, and more important, so will your daughter." Myrick hoped the man would buy that assurance. Myrick didn't.

———

"Your new name is Fletcher Burkholder. You will be briefed on your new identity when you arrive in your new location and full support will be given to assisting you in assimilating into your new environment." Myrick could see the pain in his eyes. He held out his hand.

"Welcome back to the program, Fletch."

———

Fletch looked at the Marshal, whose name he had already forgotten even before they shook hands. *I missed her growing up. I was always there for her and now I haven't been there for years and she doesn't know why.*

She probably hates me and I deserve that. I have to see her. Even for just a little while. Long enough to get her out of here. He didn't know the date they were turning on the program, but when they did, everyone would know.

Everyone would know. He would make sure of it.

14

OTHER INTERESTED PARTIES

Fletch looked down at US Marshal Edison Myrick's unconscious body in the men's room. *His disciplinary hearing is not going to go well. Maybe I shouldn't have hit him so hard.*

The locations for WitSec varied, but part of the process would occur at the offices of the U.S. Marshals. He had been in this building before. This was shared space: Secret Service, Marshals, and FBI could all be found here, as well as State law enforcement personnel. Offices above, cars in a garage below. The building, located near the White Plains Metro North train station, had little foot traffic and just enough moving cars to give the impression that the sleepy area was not asleep.

It was warm out. Fletch knew because, like the dog that did nothing in the nighttime, the air-conditioning did nothing on the floor he was on. The heat was like a subconscious scraping against the back of his neck and the inside of his parched throat.

The building was only nine stories and had an underground garage with the usual assortment of commuter vehicles for the law enforcement personnel, and visitor vehicles that were either there on business or would be towed. The office building was marginally maintained, but clean so the marble tiles on most floors sometimes squeaked regardless of what someone had on their feet.

Fletch thought the building designed in early Brown. Beige walls trimmed with dark wood. Brownish tiles. Fluorescent lights that reflected a cross between glaring white and some shade of tan. Doors of dark wood, desks that looked like they came off the same assembly line as the doors.

Clean, but brown.

Fletch knew the routine. A four-person team (usually men, but sometimes a woman); one would prep the vehicle and the other two would secure the area. The remaining member would stay with the witness and escort them down to the waiting car. Fletch would have to wear a mask if he was going outside, or if there was a chance that he might run into a member of the public during the escort process. Not likely in this case, but the Marshals seemed skittish today.

He decided to leverage skittish.

The other three went to do their job. The remaining marshal, Myrick, who had walked him through his paperwork, stayed with him. Fletch decided to go to the men's room. After a few minutes, he called out to the marshal who entered with his gun drawn. Fletch hit Myrick's jaw with the force of a bat or a pipe. Not wanting to leave him on the floor, Fletch moved him into a stall and sat him up as best he could.

Where was the black cloth mask? He had to get to the garage with very little wasted effort. He considered wearing the mask for the cameras, but they had already photographed him entering the men's room. Surprise was all he could hope for. In a few minutes, the lead would radio Myrick and when he didn't respond, they would go into lockdown.

He found the mask in Myrick's jacket. He would put it on only if he needed the anonymity. He was a large man with a large head and the mask was uncomfortable. But waste not, want not.

After cleaning his hands, Fletch entered the otherwise sparsely populated hall, got in the nearest elevator, and took it down to the garage. As it opened, he peered around the doorway and saw no one. The garage had three levels and he knew the transport vehicle was on the floor closest to the exit. The agents didn't want to drive the car that far.

That meant he would go to the lowest floor. He needed a car and his time was measured.

Fletch learned a long time ago that human beings were human beings even when they were law enforcement. Someone always forgot to lock their door; someone always left their spare keys in the glove compartment. He needed to find a car with both and he could hear the clock ticking. He hated hot-wiring ignitions.

God Bless the United States! There were two separate memoranda: one for him and one for his daughter. He had fought for them both and made sure that if he violated his, it would have no impact on the second. The feds would have to continue to protect his daughter even if it set off a manhunt for him. What a bunch of idiots. He would turn himself in. In due time. First, a quick trip to the only member of his family he loved and used to love him in return. The one he fell in love with the moment he held her in his hands the day of her birth.

The car population was sparse. This was either going to work or fail in record time. He ran to the nearest car and tried the door. Locked. He ran to the next nearest. Also locked.

This went on for the next few cars until he tried the door to a navy Honda and its door swung open, inviting him in.

He didn't bother to look around.

Jumping into the driver's seat, he leaned over and opened the glove compartment. This was a button ignition so he needed the dongle or he was going to have to check another car. The glove compartment was empty. He felt below the steering wheel to see if there was a holder. He stopped. *I'm an idiot.*

He pressed the button and the car started up. If the dongle was in the car, he didn't need to have it in his hands; it just had to be within proximity. Somewhere in the car the dongle was safely stored for the convenience of its owner. And Fletch. He closed the door.

The door promptly opened and the car turned itself off.

"Hey!" The man who opened Fletch's door was not happy. "Who are you?"

"Oh, sorry," Fletch said as he got out of the car and swung at the man who was a head shorter than he was. He missed.

The man hit him in the lower sternum, knocking the air out of him. He hadn't had that happen in years. He swung at the man again and the man blocked one arm. Then the other. Fletch jumped to take the man down to the ground, but he somehow managed to push himself out from under him.

Fletch was on the ground when he heard a magazine being slapped in a gun grip.

The man was smiling at him. He wore a dark blue suit, white shirt, and dark tie. "You fell for that car trick way too fast."

Fletch tabulated his options. The elevator was nearby. The ramp to the next level to his right. The car behind him. He was larger than his opponent. His shoulders tensed and he relaxed them.

The man had a gun. *Fuck.*

"Who are you?" Fletch asked.

"You have nothing to say. I know who you are. You think that we don't know what you've been doing or what you've been saying, or not saying." He motioned with his gun. "Sit down."

Fletch turned himself until he was sitting on the ground facing his assailant.

The man reached under his jacket. He pulled out a pair of handcuffs. He tossed them on the ground in from of Fletch. "Put them on."

"No."

"Put them on. We've got a long trip ahead of us."

"Why don't you just kill me?"

"Someone else wants to do it. You know who."

Fletch swallowed. He could never get up and jump the man before he would shoot and kill him.

"Handcuffs, please," the man said.

Fletch reached over and took the cuffs. He closed one bracelet on his left hand.

"Behind you," the man said. "Breathe wrong and you're dead." The man gripped the gun with both hands in a relaxed position and took a step back.

The handcuffs clicked into place.

"Turn around slowly and show me your hands."

Fletch did as he was told.

"Okay, turn around."

The man stayed a good distance from him. There wasn't much Fletch could do.

"Alright. So what's the plan?" Fletch asked.

The man smiled and raised the gun to adjust his aim. "I shoot you right here."

The muscles in Fletch's face relaxed and his eyes widened. He felt a hot ball of anger forming in his chest. "I thought we were going to see..."

"No. I just wanted to make sure you couldn't do anything." He aimed his gun at Fletch's face. "Kneel. I have to absolve you."

Fletch raised himself enough to change positions. What would it take to overpower this man? Nothing came to mind. He couldn't outrun a bullet.

"I guess Witness Protection didn't work out for you," the man said.

"I...I was going to see someone."

"I guess you're going to miss your appointment."

Fletch's knees were on the hard concrete. He breathed deeply. He looked up at the man.

"All I ever wanted was to do was what was best for my country. My family..." He sighed and stared at the ground with unfocused eyes. "I made the wrong decision. Great." He glared at the man. "It ends in an empty garage with a bastard and a gun."

The man walked up to Fletch and put the gun against his head. "Yeah, I guess that's what happens when you lie to your case officer for the benefit of yourself. You are so full of it I think I'm going to be sick soon." He put his left wrist up to his mouth. "Security. Notify the marshals that I have Fletcher Burkholder in custody."

They both heard the elevator door open and two marshals ran from around the corner. "Put your hands where we can see them!"

The man stepped away from Fletch and slowly lifted his hands in the air. U.S. Marshal Torres kept his gun trained on him while the other marshal trained his gun on Fletch.

"Gentlemen, my name is Norris Mullen. I was in your security booth when your witness decided to take a stroll on his own." Torres reached into Mullen's jacket and extracted a wallet. "I fully expected him to run so I left my car unlocked and ready to go just in case. When I saw him taking the elevator to this level, I ran down the stairs and caught up with him.

"Can't have our prize subject falling into the wrong hands," with his hands still up, Mullen bent down to face Fletch, "now can we?"

Torres handed Mullen his wallet. "You can put your hands down." He turned to the other marshal. "He's with the Agency."

The Central Intelligence Agency.

15

COFFEE BREAK

Anna stood in the hallway of the New York City office of the FBI flanked by two agents who were, for all intents and purposes, bored. The agent standing before her, Special Agent Gavin Gillespie, was not. And he was not amused. Anna had thrown the box into her car and drove to New York the next morning after leaving Gillespie a voicemail announcing her impending arrival.

Gillespie looked none the worse for wear. Anna didn't remember him being her height, which made him short in her book. Her seventeen-year-old self must have been traumatized by what he represented and not by who he really was.

Wearing a freshly washed pair of jeans and a white blouse, the first thing she tried to give him was the box, which he refused to touch. The second thing she tried to give him, which he accepted, was a thumb drive of her security footage.

"Carpenter," he held the thumb drive of her camera feed up for public inspection, "this is not how you should be spending your time. I thought when I last saw you..."

"When you last saw me my uncle was going to cut you a new one for talking to me without a lawyer or him being present." She leaned forward. Her hair, tied up in a ponytail, fell on her left shoulder. "I would have stayed for a few extra hours to watch that."

"So would my ex." He motioned the two agents to go.

They sauntered away, but Anna did not turn to see them go. "Look, I thought you were done with Arnold, uh, Marshall."

He turned, entered his office, and took a seat at a round, glass table in the corner opposite his desk.

"I'm done. Apparently, he is not," she said. She waited outside the office holding the box. Gillespie made a face and waved her in. She placed the box on the glass tabletop.

"Please," he said as he motioned toward the chair opposite him.

Anna sat and motioned a peek at the box. "Technically, someone who found him was simply letting me know." She stood up. "Anyway, my job here is done. I wasn't going to hold onto that, and I know you boys are just dying to find him." She bent down a little to look him in the eyes. "So get to it. And stop looking at my cleavage." She turned and took a step toward the door.

"You're an idiot."

She stopped. "I've been called worse."

"I'm not surprised. Do you think you need a lawyer?" He leaned back and hooked an arm over the back of the chair. "I would like to ask you a few questions about this." He slid the photo of her father across the table to her. "Why you? Why now?"

Anna closed her eyes and touched her forehead. "I sense a divine presence. I sense the hand of karma. I sense you are looking for reasons where none exist." She opened her eyes. "Maybe, after you examine the thumb drive in the box, you could try pulling your head out of your..."

"How do you know that's your father?"

She did a double take.

"Surprised?" he asked.

"Yes. You called him my father."

"If that is your father then he hasn't changed much in seven years."

"If you knew him, you'd know that he always looked younger

than he was." She pinched her cheek. "Good skin tone." She always thought she was going to be as lucky as he was in that department. Guess not. She lost her smile as she had a flash memory of Marshall pinching her cheeks. "I've really got to go."

"I think the photo is a fake. To see if you'll bite."

"I don't bite. Especially for photos."

"I think you're lying." He stood up and walked over to her. "You drove all the way from Nowhere, PA to deliver this package safely." They were eye to eye. "You could have sent it in the mail. You could have asked to have an agent go to your new home…"

"Not so new."

"You could have thrown it away and told us after the fact." He leaned in and whispered, "But that would have been destroying evidence and even you know that would be very naughty."

"Almost time for me to take the Bar exam. You'll be the first person to find out when I serve you."

"I'll be waiting for it." Gillespie uncrossed his arms. "He'd be proud of you."

Anna tensed. Why was one of the tenets of martial arts *not* to get into fights? "If you have any other questions, give me a call," she said as she opened the door. "Or better yet, don't."

————

In the elevator, Anna pulled out her cell phone and opened the photo gallery. There was the picture in all of its high-res glory. She expanded it until his face filled the screen. Looking at it for a few seconds, she expanded the photo even more. She examined the edges around the outline of his face, his shoulders, and his arms. Again. Either the people who added him were masters at Photoshop or the photo of Marshall was real.

Did she want them to find him?

It was a long drive from Nowhere, PA., and she sure as heck wasn't going looking for him.

———

The coffee shop was crowded and the line was long, but Anna was willing to wait for a cup of hot New York coffee even if it was from Starbucks. She sat down at one of the tables meant for someone half her size and sipped the bitter drink. *So, this is what cigarettes in water taste like.* She breathed in the aroma. She wasn't sure what it was about coffee that she liked, but this was the epitome of her guilty pleasure. In PA the nearest coffee shop was too far, if you didn't count Aunt Marcie's kitchen, and what she called coffee would insult even the British.

"Excuse me." A tall man in a suit was standing to her right. " Can I share what's left of your table space?" He smiled.

She saw the Venti paper cup in his hand and nodded.

He had a tablet under his left arm, which he pulled out and started to read as soon as he put the coffee down. "Careful. That's hot enough to be radioactive," he said. They gave each other a quick smile and he turned toward his screen.

His tablet was a two-year old Android. Did nobody understand the need to refresh their technology on a regular basis? He had nice hands. She looked away. What time was it? She had to start back soon.

Shouldn't he be talking to her if he was sitting at her table? She'd be damned if she was going to talk to him first. She looked out the window. Put her coffee next to his. Should she buy a pastry and ask him to watch her things? She cleared her throat.

Her brain screamed at her. *You don't want to meet anybody. You are an unemployed woman looking for work!*

She tapped the tabletop with her index finger and pursed her lips. What was she going to do first? She had to call Farley. CrapIsK-ing! His user name popped into her mind unbidden, but he was the one to call first. One of at least three people. He had to have some leads for freelance software work that were legal.

"Excuse me again, but do you know where 26 Federal Plaza is?"

Anna froze for a moment. Nice eyes. Voice to match. Then she adjusted. "Are you an investment banker? Broker? Businessperson? Sales guy?"

"No, why?" He gave an almost blank stare.

"Because you're an FBI agent so you already know where Federal Plaza is."

His eyes went wide for a moment and then he smiled. Perfect teeth.

"You got me. That usually works."

"It does? Do you normally flirt with the mentally disabled?" She tilted her head and looked at him with a suspicious smile. "I know: not very PC."

"So you prefer, come here often?"

"I don't."

"Oh." He blushed and turned away. "Sorry."

"No." *Oh, oh! Mistake!* "I mean, I don't come here often."

"Oh." He straightened up a little. His jacket had straight shoulder lines. "I come here all the time. The coffee is terrible at the office."

"Government coffee tastes terrible? What does that say about this?" She tilted her cup a little.

"We do our piece for the public good. Including drink dark, strong, bitter coffee," he said.

"Do you know a Special Agent Gillespie?"

"I do. A bit of a troll, but I didn't say that. How do you know him?"

Anna smiled. She could like this guy. She put out her hand. "Ann...Carpenter Poole."

"Seriously? Car Poole?" She sighed and he shook her hand.

"Garrison. Terrell Garrison."

16

THE INVITATION

Terrell Garrison. She said his name over and over again as she walked down the sidewalk and the bright sunlight turned into softer shadows as the sun found itself hidden behind a cottony mask.

Terrell Garrison.

The afternoon drew to a close, and she knew she was a going to be caught in traffic back on the way to the land of Nod. She caught herself; she didn't mean that. It wasn't that she didn't like going back to Aunt Marcie's. It was just that after seven years it still didn't feel like home. It was someone else's home. She remembered the first day she arrived. She knew she didn't belong and it took her years to realize that there would be nowhere that she would feel that sense of belonging. She would always feel like a guest. A welcome guest, but a guest nonetheless.

Terrell Garrison.

She wondered how old he was. He didn't seem that much older than her, but she was pretty certain that he was another clueless agent. She hadn't dated in so long maybe clueless was what she needed. Clueless, but with a gun.

Oh, but he was cute. *Excuse me, Agent Garrison,* she would say while fluttering her eye lashes, *but could I borrow those handcuffs for our party?*

Anna stopped in the middle of the street, realizing that while she was daydreaming she wasn't paying attention to where she was going. *Bad Carpenter.* She blinked and looked around. Where the heck was she? When she left Federal Plaza, she started walking back toward the number four subway stop. She hadn't taken the train down from PA, but the parking lot where she had her car, the one she bought with her own money from that cute idiot down the way, was in that direction. The people around her made her anxious, but she enjoyed the nervous energy.

This was on her. Where was she? She looked around and a man about half a block away suddenly stopped and turned toward a store window. Of all the people around her, why did he stand out? She wasn't sure, but she wondered if she was being followed. *Damn FBI. I bet he's a tail to see if I can lead them back to Dad.*

She would show him. She took off down one block and then another. She didn't see him anymore. If he was FBI, they probably had more than one agent working her. A standard tail would be about seven people including vehicles. She had a good memory, but seven different faces in the span of a few minutes would be too much for her. Besides, she didn't care that much.

She looked down another block. Scaffolding. Narrow roadway. Not a lot of people. Anna backtracked a bit but didn't see the original man she spotted. That was fine. One way or another if she was being followed, they would...

"Excuse me?"

She jumped at the voice behind her.

"There is a gentleman who would like to speak with you if you have a few moments."

The man motioned toward the block she had just selected as her Alamo. He was a head taller than her, full head of hair, muscular build with a black top. Serious demeanor.

"Who?" Anxiety twisted her stomach.

"Over there." He looked in the direction of the street and then turned to her again. "Please?"

"No."

"Okay. I'll let him know." He leaned in. "We have information about your father."

Anna checked around. No cameras. *Lower Manhattan is flooded with cameras!* How did she screw that one up? The man walked away.

Anna followed him. "I don't care about my father! Go take your information and shove it up your..." She had turned into the block. There was a white van and three other men standing around it. Black shirt never turned back toward her.

Get out of here. Now.

She spun. There was a man behind her. He grabbed her wrist. She slapped his ear as hard as she could, released his grip from her wrist, and then kicked him between the legs. She felt hard plastic where she made contact, but she hit him hard enough that he fell back and hit his head on the wall of the building.

Someone ran toward her. She made a fist with her right hand, swung it back, and felt her knuckles connect with the runner's nose. She swiped her leg under his, and slammed him down onto the sidewalk.

Frantic to escape, she whipped her head and saw a car and some men blocking off the entrance to the street. This would have to do; the other way was the van and more men. Now they knew what she was capable of so their tactics would change.

Time to play the helpless female. She stopped and started to scream when she felt a pinch on her arm and everything went black.

17

HUNTING DAD

Anna blinked and she was awake. The afternoon sun brightened the room through windows covered with thin, gauzy curtains that hung limp, like tired muscles. The walls, covered with a dark mustard paisley pattern, extended far for a normal room. She must have been in a suite. Her face felt the tingle of cold air shooting from a vent over to her left.

White ceiling.

Music played in the background, and then it stopped. *No, I like that song.*

She shook her head. Her mouth was dry, and there was no groggy sensation in her head, but the memory of what happened floated just close enough for her to remember, but not connect. Her short-circuited brain seemed to contain a firewall between what she knew and how she felt.

This is a hotel. This must be a hotel.

Don't remember going to a hotel. I don't remember how I got here. Is this a dream?

She was sitting in an antique-style padded chair with her wrists tied to the beige arms. She straightened her back and pulled up on the ropes that held her down. Her arms weren't going anywhere. She pulled her legs away from the chair and they swung upward. *Great! I can walk out of here attached to a large, comfortable piece of wood.*

Her years of martial arts training should have prepared her for a real event, but the real thing was always different. When someone figured out how to disable you so you were a neutralized threat.

Anna Wodehouse was terrified.

"Good afternoon, Ms. Wodehouse."

Startled, Anna jumped and tried to lean away to her left. To her right was a clean-shaven man with close-cropped salt-and-pepper hair and gray-framed glasses. Button-down shirt. Green pressed slacks. Thin for a middle-aged guy, but a bit stocky. Low center of gravity. He would be hard to knock down.

He was also far enough away that Anna couldn't kick him, or lunge at him and hit him with the chair. Who was she kidding? She could barely lift herself up, much less the chair. It was quality furniture whatever it was, and felt weighted down as well.

"Are you alright?" he asked. He leaned in rather than stepping in her direction.

She'd been taking short breaths and was getting light-headed but could recognize caution when she saw it. This was a cautious man.

"Are you going to kill me?"

He chuckled. "No." He walked over and stopped. "You have to promise not to hit me. My men weren't supposed to touch you, but they were afraid of disappointing me."

She shook her head.

"Promise?"

She shook her head again.

He pulled at the knots on her ropes and they came free.

If he'd left her alone long enough, she could have done the same.

"The two men you sent to the hospital were supposed to guide you to the van where another of my teammates would have shown you this." He handed her a tablet open to some documentation. "I hoped they would convince you to come here so we could have a civilized conversation about your desire to kill your father."

And there it was. He said it. The feeling that had been in the back of her mind for the last two years. The reason for the intense martial arts training. The reason for the gun training. The reason for throwing herself into her studies to the exclusion of everything else. All packaged up in just a few words. *Your desire to kill your father.* The years of disappointment. The emptiness that had filled her with a depth she didn't think she was capable of. She had disliked the world so much that when her father (her father!) left her for dead all she could think was, *Now he's one of them.* He had left her.

He left her.

It was true: she wanted to find Marshall Wodehouse. No question about it. She wanted to find him.

So she could kill him.

"I beg your forgiveness, but, yes, I have read your journal."

"It's not online," Anna said.

"We have a program running that sends us your files on a regular basis. We've been doing everything we could to protect you, but the people he works for are rather motivated."

"What do you mean?"

"I'm not sure, but the people your father works for seem to have decided that you're a distraction. That he's liable to make a decision they will not be happy with, and so they've decided to kill you."

Anna blinked. They wanted to do to her what she wanted to do to him? Really?

"He wouldn't want me killed."

"He doesn't. They've decided that without him. He's important to them and they can't afford to have you around any longer.'

"How do I know it's not you?" Anna asked.

"You're still alive."

She put the tablet down on a nearby table and made a beeline to the door. She opened it. Two men were seated outside. She walked past them and they did nothing to stop her.

She pressed the elevator button.

The man who had been questioning her stuck his head outside the door. "We've never been formally introduced."

"You're the man who kidnapped me. I seem to encourage that in people."

"Come back. I have a few things to show you." He leaned against the doorway. "You see," he motioned toward the door, "you're not a prisoner."

The elevator dinged. The door slid open. Empty. She turned. "Can you talk to me out here?"

"I could, but I wouldn't want everyone to know our business." He tilted his head toward one of the security cameras. "I won't be more than a few minutes." He stood straight and removed his wire-frame glasses. "It shouldn't take longer than that."

"I have friends at the FBI."

"Less friends than interested parties. If anything were to happen to you, I'm sure they would be all broken up."

———

Once in the room he handed her the tablet again. He had one in his own hand. "We're screen sharing so you can look, but not touch."

"Why me?"

"Why did some man kidnap you so many years ago and raise you as his own?"

"No, why do they want to kill me?"

"You're a distraction to Marshall. He doesn't think well when he's distracted." The man sat in a chair opposite her as he motioned to a chair for her to repose. "But you already know that."

Squirrel, I'll help you later. You know I can't do more than five things at once.

But, Dad!

Anna examined the tablet. It was not like one she had ever seen. She watched as scanned documents and filled-in web forms flipped past. The man dangled his arm over the chair rest.

"I read you liked technology." He lifted the tablet's twin. "Something out of Corning." He shook the unit in his hand and it bent and straightened out. "We get nice toys." He smiled at her but not with his eyes. "Read this."

Anna scanned the thin sheet of glass she held. "I don't understand."

"My apologies. I forget that even someone with a better-than-4.0 GPA would have a problem cutting through the disinfected words of internal bureaucratic reports." He pointed to his tablet. "Do you see where it says, Asset X? That's your father."

"And how would I know that?"

"Hold on." He flipped pages on his unit and Anna saw what he saw. "Here's the file that lists your father as an official/unofficial asset of an internal think tank that did more than just think."

"I don't see his name anywhere."

"Do you see the entry for Sam Pharaoh?" She nodded. He flipped back to the original page she was reading. "What do you see?"

She silently read the entry. "It says that Sam Pharaoh is being designated Asset X because of the outcome of some operation that didn't meet the operational objectives."

"That's spook-speak for people died and he was responsible, but they didn't want to lose access to him. So he became Asset X and continued doing the things he was hired to do even though he shouldn't have been."

"Like what?" Anna got angry. Why would he show this to her? Why would he encourage her to hate him even more? Her reasons for hating him were very personal. She could care less about patriotic ideals.

"Like work out technical and social technologies to infect the computer systems of countries both friendly and unfriendly to the United States."

"Social technologies?"

"Yes, his bots were so smart that they never had a problem getting through firewalls or any other form of security that would normally keep him out of a network, but the air gap was another story."

Anna knew an air gap was the physical distance between unconnected computers. To infect a system, the payload had to bridge the air gap.

"Marshall is as socially inept as they come," she said.

"He's brilliant. He didn't need social skills to work out how to hack them. Especially on a certain date over twenty years ago, in India, when one of his payloads jumped the air gap and was delivered to its target by the child of a chemical engineer who installed her infected game on Daddy's terminal. She was dead a few hours later when the payload shutdown the safety systems of the chemical munitions plant where he worked and she and her family lived...and died.

"The death toll was over two hundred thousand men, women, and children who did nothing more than go to work, school, and home every day."

"Accidents happen."

"Yes, they do. Except for one little detail." He walked over and sat down next to her. "The plant was being run by the United States in a clandestine operation together with a friendly government."

"But you said he worked for the government."

"He did." He put his tablet down on the coffee table before them. "Apparently, Sam Pharaoh decided that the plant, which I will admit was being run in violation of a handful of international treaties, had to go. And to teach the parties involved a lesson. He made sure that the chemical release would make the area uninhabitable. The U.S. and Indians gave up trying to clean it up ten years ago. That was just one of the many operations that Sam was in charge of that caused permanent damage to the internal infrastructure of countries doing joint work with the U.S.

"There is a group within the U.S. intelligence community that is working in direct opposition to the wishes of the U.S. government and wreaking havoc on all its operations. It's well-funded by outside governments and has been using your father to discover operations, operatives, facilities, and anything else that they can leverage to gain an upper hand against our government and our economy."

He picked up the tablet again. *Flip, flip, flip.* He turned his screen to her. There was a picture of Marshall along with identifying information. "This group that is working within the structure of the intelligence community changed Sam Pharaoh, loving husband and at the time not-yet father, into Marshall Wodehouse."

Anna very carefully placed the glass tablet on the table. She did her best not to slam the unit in the man's face. *I think it's time to go. Dad is an international criminal. Maybe he* was *torturing puppies while I slept.*

"Your father is in witness protection being protected by the very people he has harmed time and time again."

"Find him and do what you want. Don't ever, ever contact me again or you'll wish you had killed me when your minion took unfair advantage and shot me with a sleeping dart."

With that, Anna walked out.

18

911

The drive back to Littleton, PA was quiet. Anna felt her chest thump for the first fifteen minutes or so until fear gave way to anger which then gave way to frustration. The void between knowing and doing was getting larger. They had dropped her off near the garage in an unmarked car, and drove off without another word. She wanted to say, *No hard feelings! Sorry about putting your friends in the hospital!*. But she decided to get into her car instead.

With an hour left to her trip, she called the Stoddard's using a Bluetooth set-up she had installed in the car herself.

No one answered.

I-78W cleared up, but the humidity wrapped around her head like a hot blanket. On more than one occasion, she had to pull into a rest stop just to stand and breathe. The other cars sat oblivious to her, a sea of colored metal sending thermal columns to the sky as cheap lift to the turkey vultures overhead.

It was dark when she arrived. The homes were far enough apart that she knew all the neighbors, the children, the pets. She especially knew the cars.

There were two she didn't recognize even in the dark. Two black vehicles. Almost muscle cars. The cars were not near her driveway.

She pulled into her driveway and pretended the cars weren't there. She would mention it to Uncle Ray first; Aunt Marcie didn't need to be told yet. She had a short anxiety fuse. It was about 10:30 p.m. and the house was dark. Was that right? Uncle Ray was an early riser so he was usually in bed by 9 p.m., but Aunt Marcie still waited up for her. The porch light was out and the house was otherwise pitch black. Not even the kitchen lights illuminated Aunt Marcie's domain.

Anna walked up the front steps. If someone attacked her, the cameras would give the authorities something to work from. *Stop thinking such negative thoughts.* She wouldn't be attacked. She wouldn't be shot with another sleeping dart. No one would try to kill her. At least not tonight. She gave everyone the night off.

She stood before the door. The light preceded her standing there by a second or so. She never understood how Aunt Marcie always seemed to know when she made it up the stairs even when Anna practiced her soft walk. She did her best not to make a sound.

No light. No movement. Her pulse raced. She felt above the dusty doorjamb and found the spare key. She so seldom used it that she had asked Uncle Ray to put it away. He told her he would take care of it, but somehow it was always there when she needed it.

The screen door opened with its assortment of creaks and crackles. Uncle Ray needed to fix the lower section. Bugs were always finding their way in. Anna had offered to fix it, and even did once, but it never lasted more than one season.

Locking the door behind her, she stood in silence in the foyer and opened the inner door slowly. She always did that. She hated disturbing them, but this time was different. Was there someone in the house with her who was not her aunt and uncle? She walked in the dark toward the living room. There was a selection of pokers by the fireplace and she felt a need to hold onto something, something long and thin with a hook at the end.

Her father's employer wanted her dead. The house was empty. They had better not have touched her aunt and uncle. She would take down a few of them first. As she reached to turn on one of the table lamps a shadow went by a window and she cursed under her breath.

Poker in hand, she went toward the back of the house. Another shadow. And another. She had to call for reinforcements. She grabbed the nearest wireless phone.

"This is 9-1-1."

"Mrs. Hawthorne?" she whispered. Anna tutored Mrs. Hawthorne's son. A sweet boy, but definite problems with acting out hostilities toward his absentee father.

"Carpenter, is that you?"

"Yes." She faked a half-sob. "I think someone's broken into the house. I'm inside and I'm afraid to move."

"Try to get out of the house before you hurt someone. I'll have a car there in a few minutes."

"Thanks." She hung up. *Time to hurt someone. Death to the barbarians!*

She started to turn the knob of the back door when the front of the house was bathed in light.

There was a knock at the back door.

"Carpenter?" *Knock, knock, knock.* "Open up. This is the FBI." Silence. "It's Special Agent Terrell Garrison."

She pulled the door open and held the poker up. They both looked at each other until Garrison spoke.

"And I thought we hit it off at the café," he said.

———

"Your aunt and uncle are in protective custody."

"What happened?" They stood outside on the porch with the

light of the two vehicles pointing toward her aunt's house. The light bothered her a little, but the emptiness was worse.

"We got word…"

"From who?"

"Does that matter? You, your aunt, and uncle are in danger."

"If there's a sniper out there, I would be dead already." She leaned against the porch railing.

"We almost arrested someone about three hours ago. A local field office got someone here as soon as we found out and we moved them. Whoever he was he was a professional. We found his stash nearby. Enough firepower to take the three of you out."

"He'd have to try." *Was the man in the hotel telling the truth? Was someone out to kill her?*

"He'd succeed. I need you to come with me."

"No, I'm staying right here." She thought a moment. "Keep Aunt Marcie and Uncle Ray safe. I don't think they'd believe I could take care of them."

"I don't believe it myself." He opened his jacket back and put his hand on his hip. "You did hear me say that we almost arrested someone? This isn't just a credible threat. This *is* a threat."

Anna looked at the lights and vehicles and other agents standing by the cars. "I know. But now you're looking for someone, and I want to stay here." Maybe plans were about to change.

"What's wrong?" Terrell asked.

"Nothing's wrong. I'm tired of being taken out of my house. Tired. Of. It." She stared at him.

"There is a credible threat of death here."

"I can take care of myself."

"Speaking of which, where were you?"

"What do you mean?" The back of Anna's neck felt hot.

"We were done at the café with plenty of time for you to get here before we moved your aunt and uncle. Stop for a movie or something?"

Anna wasn't sure how to lie about her unwilling car ride and hotel meeting. Or should she tell him the truth? "I had some personal business."

"Oh, some guy?"

"Yeah, some guy." She crossed her arms. "None of your business."

"Yeah, except that one of our guys followed you until you made him and we had to send someone else, but before he had a chance to see where you went, you disappeared."

"Like you said, I made him."

"And you lost him."

"Yep."

"And you went straight to your car or to Don Juan?"

"To my car. I had to drive to him."

"Really? Well, that's rich because we started tracking your car as soon as it went by, oh, the hundreds of security cameras that bathe Wall Street, and one of my other guys trailed you all the way to..." He pulled out a notebook from his pocket. "Oh, yeah. To here." He put the notebook away. "Lying is not a good way to start a relationship. Where were you for ninety minutes after you lost my guy?"

She would not be intimidated. She stared him down but remained silent.

"Carpenter, there's someone out to kill you, and I don't know who or why. I can only assume it has to do with the man who held you captive all those years."

She closed her eyes. *This is getting tiring.* "He did not..." She sighed. "Whatever. You have to go. I have job interviews tomorrow and work to do." She turned to the door. "You must have a job you do, don't you?"

He waved his hand and the headlights went out, leaving just the yellow glow of the porch light and the sounds of the occasional cricket. Anna had stood on that porch innumerable times, but couldn't picture any of its detail at that moment. She wanted to get inside and lie down.

"Call me," Terrell said.

He held out one of his cards and Anna took it.

"Sorry, I'm already in an exclusive relationship."

"Your dad's not coming back."

"Now you're getting creepy."

"I'm serious. He knows there are people looking for him and they don't mean him any good."

"Yeah, and then there's you."

"We can protect him."

"Yeah, until you throw him in jail."

"Maybe we won't. You wouldn't press charges."

"I think there are other charges that might matter more. Your buddy Agent Gillespie made it pretty clear that the government wants him for more than just kidnapping."

"We can help him with that, too."

"Thanks, but no thanks. I'm done with that part of my life. That loser can figure it out himself." Anna entered the house, locked the door, and turned off the porch light.

———

Terrell walked back to the waiting cars and the three agents who had accompanied him west. The gravel on the otherwise paved road crunched under his shoes. *Why did she have to lie to me already?* The air was cool. Terrell pulled at his tie and thought about how long it would take to get back to the Bronx.

"Keep an eye on her," he said to the one he was leaving behind. "Don't be seen until we think she needs to see you and check in with either Gillespie or me in the morning. I don't want anyone else to know what's going on."

19

BREAKING AND ENTERING

The house was empty and Anna felt every square inch of it. The first floor. The second floor. The hallway past the living room and toward the kitchen. She was sure that if she tried hard enough, she could imagine someone up in the attic waiting for her to get into her fluffy-quilty bed so they could climb down and kill her.

Oh, stop.

The silence hummed in the background. No light snoring from Uncle Ray. No aroma of tea brewing in the kitchen as Aunt Marcie waited for her to come home.

Yet she didn't feel the difference from any other day. Being alone was just another day in not-paradise. And yet...why did she remember the snoring? The tea? Aunt Marcie waiting up for her?

She kept the lights off except when she entered a room. She didn't want to waste the electricity. She had explained to Uncle Ray last year how much money he would save if he went solar, but he wasn't impressed. Uncle Ray didn't impress easily.

Her head hurt. She wandered the house, turning lights on, turning lights off, until she made it to her bathroom, washed up, and then followed the light switches to her second-floor room as she left a scented trail of toothpaste and mouthwash. She'd had days like this at

UPenn and would crash as soon as she lay down. *Rest might have to be earned tonight.*

It was after midnight when Anna, wearing an oversized t-shirt with no writing on it, gave up trying to sleep, and decided it was time to take a closer look at the thumb drive she found in the box.

The thumb drive she had told Special Agent Gillespie she had not touched, but in fact had copied, and given him the copy. It was not a large drive (only 32G), but it had a bevy of interesting programs some of which she had even heard of: TALON, RADON, CONVERT, DEWSWEEPER. NSA and CIA programs designed to hack into foreign systems (and weren't all systems foreign?) or piggyback onto network packets to get the information they needed. Were these for her use, or just to get her arrested?

One was called WITSEC.

She flushed thinking about clicking on the program. What would happen? How did the thumb drive even work on her box? When it started up, it commented that it found a key that somehow she had on her notebook. Had someone hacked into her box? She was going to be embarrassed about the photos of scantily clad (or worse) actors, but at this point if someone had hacked into her box, it was a little late anyway.

Hacking into a system that she was not allowed to enter was an automatic felony. She didn't know who these people were, but they seemed to be with the government. Who or which group in the government? No one seemed to be forthcoming with that information.

Her notebook beeped. There was unauthorized network activity. An open-source network alarm noticed the activity and was doing everything but yelling. The thumb drive was calling home. She yanked it out. Her shoulders tensed and her heart thumped in her chest. This was bad. Programs that she should not have, much less use, were telling someone that she was about to use them.

Or maybe it was calling the authorities and she should expect a knock on the door sometime soon. She paced the room. This was outside her expertise. What should she do? Burn the drive and bury it in the backyard? No, throw it off a bridge and into the river. It probably had a GPS tracker. *Oh, jeez, they probably know where she is already.*

What should she do? What would her father do? What would someone with half a brain do?

Keep going. The felony was committed and she could plead ignorance as to what the drive had and hope for the mercy of the court. She sighed. *Right.*

Anna slid the thumb drive back into the USB slot. The Dolphin file manager opened and there was the program listing again.

WITSEC.

She had her programs set to run on a single click. This was it. Now or never. She clicked. A window opened. A message about unauthorized access flashed by so quickly Anna couldn't read it. WITSEC had logged into the Witness Protection Program database.

Anna started a search. A window had opened requesting parameters for her query. WITSEC took care of parsing her criteria and turned it into the Witness Security Request Query format that the system was expecting. *How interesting.* She found the user interface for the penetration system was far superior to the actual system being hacked. What kind of a focus group did the developers have during the development of penetration tools? *Analysts*, Anna thought. People whose jobs depended on them getting more information than they needed in ways that would accomplish that with little fuss and bother.

She also realized that no one would ever know what she had done unless this was part of an elaborate set up.

———

After an hour of paging through search results WITSEC beeped. *Intrusion detected. Last message: Erasing audit trail. Protocol mimicking: Israeli.*

Paging through the list of names was like playing Sudoku. She lay in bed and flipped thought the names on the touch screen of her notebook. What added up and what didn't? There was no Marshall Wodehouse listed. She supposed she shouldn't be surprised. Her father was smarter than that. Why would he go into Witness Protection? Was that why he never returned? But why wouldn't they let him communicate with her? Even witness protection let the witnesses take their families with them.

Unless their families weren't wanted.

———

The next morning, after staying up most of the night, Anna had a name and a place. She looked at Google Maps satellite photos. She went to overseas tourism sites. She looked at flight times out of Philadelphia.

She fell asleep for about an hour.

She went through her drawers and found her passport.

She was going to London. No one threatened her aunt and uncle and, if it was the man who said he was her father, or the people who were protecting him, then she had a few things to say about that.

She also put Terrell Garrison's number in her cell. Just in case.

20

DEAL OF HIS LIFE

Fletch wore his mask as the team drove him to a secluded airstrip in New Jersey where the government kept a few private jets for just this occasion. The road was just-paved smooth. The large street lamps towards the front of the terminal was almost all the airstrip used for lighting. From behind there was just enough light for visitors to know where they were, with the runway illumination enough for the pilots to take off and head to wherever it was they needed to be. Colorado, California, Texas.

The United Kingdom.

Fletch would bypass customs and immigration, but the Brits would know that he entered the country, and that he was now their concern if he was stupid enough to get into trouble. Fletch had no intention of ever getting on their radar. He had money to pay his bills, and he was otherwise a man of few needs.

Sitting in the sweaty smelling vehicle, Fletch felt his hatred of the marshals increasing the more he thought about what he was about to do. He clenched his hands and his stomach twisted. He considered running, but where would be the gain? This was all his own doing, but how the hell had he let himself get into this? Bringing his little girl into the program was going to be hard enough, but now that she was older would she even want to be part of it? He knew nothing about her life these past years. Did she still believe in him enough to want to join him?

No, she couldn't join him. He was leaving and that meant leaving everything, and everyone, behind. Not dragging his family into it meant that the only person whose life would be affected would be his. He could live with that. This was a hell of his own making. And she would be safe.

He couldn't bring himself to ask. He knew the marshals were right.

She would be better off without him.

The fleet of black SUVs pulled into the airstrip that appeared to be privately-owned but was really operated by the Department of Justice. The high-pitched wail of the engines signaled that the jet was ready to go, waiting for its passenger and his entourage.

———

"Do you think you'll ever talk about the things you don't want to talk about?"

Fletch didn't remember the marshal sitting in front of him. *He must be new. Wet behind the ears.*

He sat in his comfortable seat and watched the man start to dig a hole. How deep would it be? Would Fletch push him in or would he push himself?

"Rumor has it that Justice has information that links you to at least one other program." The marshal leaned forward. "I hear things. I have friends up in the hierarchy and they would be very grateful for your assistance."

Fletch's stomach started to roil. He looked at the man for a few seconds until the man turned away. *What a pussy.* Fletch straightened himself and peered out the window of the jet. He normally enjoyed flying, but today was a day of final choices. When he arrived in the UK, there was no telling when he would return. Maybe never. He would have to make peace with that.

"You know any messages from Justice will come through me." The marshal sat forward again. "And from you to them."

Fletch continued his examination of the plane window.

"What I'm saying is," the marshal snuck a peek at his colleagues and made sure they weren't paying attention, "I can help you. If you help us." The man looked up at Fletch. "If you help me."

What next? Veiled threats?

"All I'm saying is that Justice has cut loose the occasional witness who was, shall we say, uncooperative."

Fletch unbuckled his seatbelt with a flick of his thumb and brought his face up to the marshal. "Are you saying that Justice thinks I'm holding out on them?"

The marshal pushed himself back. "No, no. Not at all." Fletch felt his face flush along with an itch on his knuckles. "Just that they know you have at least one more project under your belt," the man lowered his voice, "and that they could use the intel."

Fletch sat back and looked out the window again. This was idiotic. He told them that he would never talk about the final project. Never.

"I have friends. In Justice. For the right information," the marshal crossed his arms, "we could see about getting you together with a certain someone on a regular basis."

Fletch did his best to keep his voice down. "And if I leave the program and go underground? Then you and your people would be screwed. I love my country. I don't want the wrong people doing things, but it's getting harder and harder to tell the good guys from the bad ones."

"And yet it's the only leverage you have to stay in the program."

"I've hit marshals before. Keep it up and I might have a new name for my list," Fletch said.

"If you surface in the UK, you'll be dead in no time. We'll make sure that never happens, but going underground on your own is not the answer." The marshal gave Fletch a strong, confident stare. "Look, you're going to be living overseas for a few years, but if you play your cards right, we can work out some sort of arrangement where you can see your daughter on a regular basis."

A regular basis? "I think you need to stop talking. I've made my peace. Her life means everything to me and if leaving her will keep her safe then that's what I have to do. So do me a favor and shut up."

"I understand. I can respect that." The marshal pretended to see something outside the window. "I just wanted to make sure you knew that Justice is sending out feelers and that things can change. You can make them change."

Fletch had been feeling tired for a few months now and this was not making him any more energized. One more program. There was always one more damn thing they wanted to know. In this case, it was the one thing that Fletch knew he could never do. If he even mentioned the program there was a chance he would be shot out of the sky. Hell, that could happen anyway. They didn't know what he said or didn't say. He promised, in exchange for immunity, that he would tell them what he knew without getting him into the ultimate trouble. The kind where there was no protection from. Ever.

Was he willing to do it for one last visit? One last conversation? Was he willing to talk about the program that would get him killed just for naming it?

Maybe this guy was different. Maybe he was the one who could pull this off. *And if not, I can always get him to get me what I want. I've done that before.* Was even the possibility of time with his daughter worth it?

"What's your name, soldier?" Fletch asked.

"Tompkins. Alonso Tompkins. Deputy Marshal."

"Maybe there's something we can do, Deputy Marshall," Fletch said.

HUNTING MARSHALL

21

HEATHROW

Anna walked through John F. Kennedy International Airport on her way to the ticket line. She was tense and concerned. Even though her documents were up-to-date, the FBI could make life difficult for her by cutting her off at the pass. If the WitSec information was any indication, London was where she needed to be though she had to admit she wasn't sure how well immigration would take her sudden trip to the UK.

Maybe they would care; maybe they wouldn't. Some things you couldn't look up and research was her primary information source for the present. While she was pretty adept at finding answers, there were some things you had to experience firsthand.

Like being arrested at the airport for losing her protection detail.

At her moment of greatest distraction, she collided with another moving object. Somehow she had been looking the wrong way or not paying attention, but she slammed right into an Indian woman who fell on the floor along with her and apologized to Anna more than she had thought possible for a single person to do. On her hands and knees, Anna picked up her purse, which had just about exploded all over the concourse floor, while the woman ran for her flight. Anna collected all her things. Her flight wasn't for another two hours so Anna took her time.

Until she picked up her passport. It felt wrong. It felt new and heavier. She opened it and her eyes went wide.

Annette Powell. Oh, jeez. She looked up and tried to find the Indian woman when something about the passport caught her eye. The passport had her picture in it. *OMG. I'm Annette Powell.*

Anna did her best not to look around. She picked up the remaining items from the floor, put them in her purse, and went to the ladies' room. *That bastard from the hotel got me a fake passport.* It was perfect. But — and this was where Anna was certain she would be caught — none of her other IDs matched. She pulled out her wallet to see if there were any photos of her to compare against.

She almost dropped the purse. Her library card, driver license, and insurance card, even some new membership cards: they were all made out to Annette Powell. How did they know what wallet she would use? She realized she only had one so that one was easy. But the work was done so fast! How did they know she would decide to go to London? Time to worry about that later. She had to pick up her ticket. Her ticket! She made a fist and struck her forehead. It was made out to Carpenter Poole.

She did her best to walk with a confident stride to the check-in kiosk and run the credit card for Annette Powell. A ticket came up. Virgin Atlantic to Heathrow. The name on the ticket: Annette Powell.

She was a little ticked off. She could have done this on her own. In fact, she did. They changed what she had already done to make sure she could actually leave the country. How would they get her back? Maybe they had no intention of bringing her back. Maybe they had other plans. Again, things to worry about later.

———

At Heathrow, she approached the self-service kiosk at the immigration barrier and scanned the passport booklet. She didn't want to look up but couldn't help herself. With the British e-passport paperwork she found in her purse she could bypass the normal line to immigration and just scan her passport. Obviously, not a coincidence. The system scanned the chip in her passport and let her in.

Anna walked out of Customs, through the airport, and into the United Kingdom, ready to find her father, not ungrateful for the help, but wary as to what it would cost her.

22

HOSPITALITY SUITE

A few hours later, Terrell Garrison, dressed in a gray suit sans tie, stepped off the plane in London, and made his way to the immigration line. He was in the back of the plane and exited as slowly as the plane full of passengers would allow.

He scanned the room. Large, airy, and filled with the odor of sweat. Cameras. Armed personnel. Lines longer than you find at Disney. Not that many immigration agents. No suspicious-looking passengers so this should be just as tedious an experience as it looked. He picked up his bags, moved them a few feet, and put them down. Again. And again.

Then he was next.

The officer greeted him and held out his hand for Terrell's passport.

"Good afternoon, sir. Did you have a good flight?" The official looked at him and scanned the passport. As Terrell answered, the man interrupted him. "I'm sorry, sir. Would you come with me?"

Terrell picked up his bags and followed the man down a long corridor. "Something wrong?"

"Not at all, sir. Please follow me."

Please let this be a welcoming committee. I could really use some dinner.

The official opened the door to an empty room. As Terrell entered he turned to the man. "How long will this be?"

"Someone will be here to see you soon, sir. Quite alright." He nodded and closed the door behind him.

A few minutes later, an older man came through the door and said, "Good evening, Agent Garrison. You're under arrest."

The older man extended his hand to Terrell. The grip was firm and Terrell felt the man's chapped skin scratch his palm. The mixture of stale air, flat lighting, and low blood sugar was starting to get to him.

"At least maybe now I can get something to eat." They both smiled. "Did you really have to get me off the line and stick me in here?"

His stomach dominated his thoughts and, while he wasn't shy about voicing his current need, he didn't want to offend his host who had gone out of his way to meet him.

Conrad Chapin wore a clean, pressed gray suit that had seen better days. It looked fine, but it was shiny at the elbows and knees. "I'd say I wanted to catch your attention, but you were already examining the entry area as if you were searching for gaps in our security."

"If we had as much money to spend on cameras and security as you do..." Terrell continued to smile. It was good to see his MI-6 contact again. "I'd say you owe me breakfast, but since it's dinner time I would gladly pay to eat anything at this point."

They sat across from each other. The room had multiple chairs but no tables. It looked more like a waiting room than an interrogation area.

"I'm afraid you will be eating without me. I have a few things going on, not the least of which is you. This man you want to interview, he did finally arrive yesterday. For such a big man, he seemed unusually skittish. Deservedly so."

"What's that? He's unusually British?"

They smiled again, but Conrad's face relaxed and the smile was gone in a few seconds.

Terrell continued, "Listen, I'm here to interview him and then head back home. I don't think

he's going to have much for me, but the powers-that-be insisted I talk with him. Have you met him yet?"

"No, can't say that I have, but I've already been perusing the reports. Your marshals are with him for another day or so and then he becomes our problem. And a problem he has already become." Conrad dragged his chair next to Terrell. "I would truly appreciate a briefing on this man as I've been told that someone wants to kill him."

"Conrad, that's why he's in WitSec. If no one wanted to kill him, he could have just stayed home sipping margaritas by his pool."

"I don't mean kill him in some abstract future sense. I'm telling you that we have serious intelligence that someone has been sent here from the States to kill him and, quite honestly, we don't know who it is.

"Are you really here just to interview this man?"

Terrell blinked. When it rained, it poured. First the Stoddards and Carpenter, and now this. "Conrad, I swear to you, I am here to interview this man in reference to a cold case. I think he had some information about a murder and I need to know what he knows. Have the marshals been told?"

"Of course. There is always some measure of time that goes by between our discovery of information and the passing of it to the people who need to know, but it does get there eventually."

"What do you know?" Terrell was starting to worry. The marshals would take care of their man, but what happened that turned this on?

"Not very much. We are taking care of it."

Terrell stood up and extended his hand. "I know you are. I need to get out there and see this man."

"I'm afraid that's not possible," Conrad said. "Yet." He shook Terrell's hand.

"I need to see him."

"I know you do."

"Why is he here, Conrad?" Terrell wasn't sure that he would be able to ask someone about this, but Conrad was connected. He had spent the last few years making his way up the British organization.

"He's here because you sent him here."

"Ah, the royal you. I didn't send him. Most people in witness protection don't make their way overseas. Certainly not to some place as cosmopolitan as London, though I assume he'll be kept somewhere slightly less populated until you find him employment."

"From what I understand he won't be working in public any time soon."

Terrell nodded. "So he's being kept underground."

"Not literally," Conrad said.

Unless the bad guys find him. "Why is he here?"

"That was my question to you."

"The British don't want him here? His papers went through faster than I've ever seen," Terrell said.

"He requested the transfer." Conrad sat back.

"I didn't realize our cousins were so accommodating to our WitSec members."

"And given that his location is under our control I will make sure you get escorted there as quickly as possible." Conrad glanced at the door and then back at Terrell. "Just not yet."

"I have only so many hours to do my job, my friend."

"I promise you, you will see him." Conrad looked back at the door.

"What's on your mind? You seem distracted," Terrell said. "And you never seem distracted."

Conrad pursed his lips and looked like he wanted to sit, but thought better of it. "Your brethren at the Agency have been acting rather interesting lately. You wouldn't happen to know…"

"I do my best to stay away unless I really have to work with them. Let's just say they can be over-enthusiastic."

"For all we know this entire operation might be compromised simply by your being here."

"You think the Agency might be involved. And you think that maybe, just maybe, I might be here for more than just a friendly chat.

If the Agency wanted him dead, he'd already be dead. Getting that kind of information is easy for them."

Conrad sat and crossed his legs but didn't look at Terrell.

"You're not telling me something," Terrell said.

"I'm always not telling you something."

23

THE HEART OF THE MATTER

"We've lost her."

In a nondescript office park, just outside of Arlington, VA, were the adjunct offices to the U.S. Marshal Service. The Marshals, under the auspices of the Justice Department, took care of judicial security, fugitive operations, and asset forfeiture.

And Witness Protection.

In all the years that the program had been in effect there had never been a death to anyone under their protection who followed the rules and let the marshals do their job.

The words, *We've lost her,* were not words that made federal prosecutors happy.

The participants in the conference room had been discussing another case when the call came in. They asked that any news about Fletch and anyone associated with him be directed to them immediately. While Fletch did not know many people, many people knew about Fletch.

The Director spoke first into the Logitech speakerphone. "What happened? I thought we had around-the-clock details on her."

"Yes, Madam Director, but it seems that she evaded them. Again."

"Again?" She looked around at the leadership sitting around the conference table.

"Yes, ma'am. We stay out of her way as part of the agreement. We just make sure she's safe."

"Alright. Find her. If she turns up dead, this won't just be a PR problem. Thank you, Stephan." She hung up the speakerphone. "We finally get the latest shit storm around him under control and the one thing that keeps him calm is gone."

"How soon do we tell him?" An older balding man toward the back of the table spoke up.

"I vote for never," she said, "but I'm going to give our guys an hour to find out what they can."

———

Almost two hours later, Fletch walked into the living room of the safe house. Deputy Marshal Alonso Tompkins was already sitting off to the side and watched as he entered. The room, tastefully furnished in early-Ikea, had yellow walls with framed photos of people Fletch didn't recognize. First floor room. Two windows. Boring window treatments. The light streaming through the glass was gray and darker than it was a few minutes ago. He could almost smell the ionized air.

A storm was brewing.

Fletch reminded himself that the average person was a dullard. No focus. No sense of urgency. That was one of the reasons people were so easy to kill. On an assignment, he would dress as casually as he could to soften the perception of his size. Just part of the job. On his own, he never wore jeans if he could help it, much less pullover shirts. It felt sloppy and Fletch hated sloppy.

He was certain the photos had pinhole cameras in them.

"I'm not saying anything else until..."

"That's why I brought you here," Tompkins said. "I'm afraid we have some bad news." Fletch thought he saw contempt in the man's eyes. What did he know?

"It's about your daughter."

Fletch's thoughts of sitting vanished as his legs became taut, and he prepared to run. No, he would get all the information he needed and then kill every last one of these men before leaving. He knew he could do it. They had never seen him do it, but he had cleared a room of armed men before.

The two additional marshals straightened. Fletch knew it was hard to miss him positioning himself. You didn't have to be fast to clear a room. Just accurate.

Fletch stood and waited. He looked Tompkins in the eyes.

Tompkins stood and took a step behind the richly upholstered sofa. "You daughter seems to have vanished."

With that Fletch grabbed the coffee table and held it before him like a shield and ran toward the nearest marshal. He could feel the man's body under the tabletop and Fletch pressed down like the table was a giant trash compactor. He felt someone grab his left arm. He let the table go and swung a crushing fist into the face of the man who held him.

Two down.

He turned and started to charge Tompkins.

Tompkins held up an X26 police-issue Taser and shot it straight into Fletch's chest. The term in the Taser manual is neuromuscular incapacitation, which translates into shutting down the muscles of the recipient using a shaped pulse of electricity. Fletch had been Tasered before and continued plowing through to his goal, but this time he went down. The Taser was a much higher voltage then he had ever felt before. He crashed into the floor and felt a sharp stick hit him hard on the shoulder and the back of his head.

———

Fletch woke up with his hands bound behind his back and his legs tied together at the ankle with not one, but two plastic zip tie hand-cuff cables. He wasn't sure what they were trying to accomplish, but now that he was frustrated the one thing he was sure of was that they had now made him dangerous.

"Mr. Burkholder." Tompkins stood to his right.

Fletch was prone on the sofa and managed to pull himself up. One of the agents helped straighten him out.

"That was really stupid," Tompkins said.

"Yes, it was."

"I mean me," Tompkins said.

"So did I."

"I shouldn't have been so cavalier about the news. I thought you would take it better so we could explain what we were doing to remedy the situation, but you seemed to have taken the news rather badly."

Fletch thought of lunging at him but knew that would not get him the tactical advantage he was looking for. He would wait.

"Again, I apologize. The two marshals you sent to the hospital are probably wishing you had taken the news better as well, but," he nodded at the two new faces in the room, "that's part of their job." He took a few steps away from Fletch. "I hope health care here really is better than the U.S."

Fletch sat back and decided it was time. "Let me go."

"Mr. Burkholder, please..."

"Let me..." Fletch closed his mouth and sighed.

"We can't let you go. As soon as you walk out that door you will be hunted down and killed."

"If you don't let me go, I will wait until you're all asleep and kill you one by one."

"That's certainly encouraging." Tompkins leaned on the windowsill, pulling on the curtain just so. The curtain rod bent downward. "My job is to keep you alive. I intend to do that for as long as I am directed to."

Fletch could feel his anger pull back. He had to leave and he had to find her. He wasn't sure how he was going to do it, but it was now the only thing he had to do. Nothing else mattered. They had taken her. Somehow, they knew that he was ready to talk.

"I've been very accommodating all these years. You and your buddies have done a good job, but it's obvious that the people who want me know what's going on and are willing to do anything to stop me from saying anything more.

"Keep me bound, put me asleep, Taser me a few more times. I don't really care. I'm not saying another word until you find her. You have one day to do that. If that is beyond your power then I am done here. If she's dead, you had better kill me instead of telling me because I will kill you all."

24

WALLS

"I need to talk to the man under your protection."

Terrell didn't enjoy wearing sunglasses, but the brightness of the afternoon sun left him the choice of expensive eyewear or blindness. The unpredictability of the weather was frustrating; first the sky was clear, then it was filled with clouds, and now it was clear again. With almost no humidity, the heat didn't feel anywhere near as harsh as it might have been, but Terrell's skin still absorbed more heat than he liked. He felt bad for the young men before him, dressed in full uniform, having to do a professional job in conditions best suited to college students on spring break.

The moors extended in every direction around him. When he first drove up, he thought, *Stay off the moors*. Then he smiled and continued. The memory of the movie *An American Werewolf in London* was fresh in his head even though he hadn't seen it in years.

"I'm afraid I don't know what you mean, sir." The soldier at the checkpoint just outside of the town of Chattingham looked friendly in the way all Brits looked friendly: a look of seriousness and maturity, and a sense that they were talking to a child. "However, access to the neighborhood is currently restricted, and I am afraid you do not have the requisite permissions needed to proceed."

Terrell knew he was going to hate this part. "Listen, soldier, I am here at the request of MI6 to talk to an American who is..." He could feel his frustration growing. "Could you please check my name against your roster again? I hate to have to call my contacts, but this is important." He smiled at the soldier who was younger than he was but had a much larger gun. He handed over his FBI ID card. "Please."

The soldier took the card and walked back over to the olive-drab-covered truck which reminded Terrell of World War II movies.

Terrell had been to the UK several times before and always enjoyed the experience.

The soldier returned.

"I'm sorry, sir. We called in direct and the word is still that no one is allowed access. In fact, we've been instructed to tell you that you need to call in to your office for a change in plans." The soldier gave him an apologetic look. "Cell phone coverage is quite poor in these parts. Would you like to use one of the phones in the truck?"

———

"What the hell is going on?" Terrell was on the phone with the case officer for the U.S. Marshals here in the UK, Deputy Marshal Alonso Tompkins. Tompkins sounded relaxed and unfazed.

"Nothing worth discussing. The subject has simply had a change of heart. He has decided not to cooperate any further."

The audio quality was less than that of a cell phone, but Terrell had no problem reading between the lines: This was their man and they were deciding who would talk with him.

"Any chance for an answer? The man was good with talking a few days ago and then really wanted to talk to us just the other day." Terrell took in the surrounding moors. A stark beauty of flat land broken up by stone boundaries for as far as the eye could see. The occasional cloud hung overhead, sending a shadow over a sharply defined piece of ground.

"I understand, Special Agent Garrison. All I can say is that in his current state of mind we may have to reconsider keeping him in the program. I am not at liberty to say more than that."

"Given his propensity to change his mind," Terrell said, "how about if I stay in the area for a bit and wait him out? I don't have a lot of time, but maybe you can convince him to give me a few minutes. I've come a long way, but that doesn't matter as much as the fact that I could really use some information about a cold case that I think he can help with. Are we good with that?"

Silence.

"Yeah, I think we're good with that." Terrell heard some papers rustling in the background. "I have your contact info. If I lose it, I'll contact the embassy."

Why did Terrell feel like Tompkins was going to lose his contact info anyway?

———

Another call.

This time Terrell decided to go behind the curtain.

"Tell me what's going on, Conrad."

The soldiers must have felt bad for Terrell to let him use their communications truck for so long. The heat was hard to escape. At this rate, he was going to need a local place just to cool off. Maybe grab a pint.

"I knew you'd call eventually. The message came through my office and I thought of you immediately. Your people lost something your man wanted. He is quite upset from what I understand."

"What did we lose?"

"Do you know anything at all about this man?"

"I don't even know his new name," Terrell said.

"Well, just because I like you, and I know I can trust you, I can tell you that his new name is Fletcher Burkholder. Not a particularly British name, but I suppose it will have to do for now."

Terrell made a mental note: don't tell Conrad things he shouldn't know. And buy him a bottle of whatever it was he drank. He wasn't sure, but for some reason Laphroaig came to mind.

"C'mon, Conrad. What did we lose? What does he care about?"

"A family member, my friend," Conrad said. "His daughter. Apparently, she didn't join him in your program years ago and he had just cut a deal that would include her. The problem is...she disappeared just as she was about to be picked up."

"Please don't tell me these things. How the hell did we do that?"

"I'm sure I don't know, but she had been under protective surveillance for years."

"Conrad, I need to speak to this guy." Terrell hated asking this kind of favor, but he wasn't sure if things weren't unraveling faster than he could handle them. "If he goes underground, I'll never get to talk to him and this case goes cold again."

"Or still, in your case."

In the silence, Terrell could hear Conrad thinking. "I know what you want. What do you need?"

"I need to get in there. I need you to coordinate permission with your people and my people to let me get to him."

"That's actually easier than you think. Let me make a few calls and see if we can't get you in there. Your questions have nothing to do with why he's in witness protection."

Terrell turned and saw the soldier walking toward him. Did they all have to be so serious?

"Then I have a favor to ask of you," Conrad said.

———

"Tompkins? Special Agent Garrison."

"A pleasure to hear from you again."

"I'm sure." Terrell looked at the soldier and wondered who he would have to call to get past him. He wasn't rushing a checkpoint. "Just checking in. I've made a few calls to assure the powers-that-be that my interview is only about my current investigation in a cold case."

"Well, that is mighty neighborly of you."

"Everyone says that about me." He saw cars going through one at a time with Terrell's on the shoulder. There were times he wished he could stay for a few weeks and just enjoy some of the places he worked, but this would not be one of them. "One last thing. If the reason that your man doesn't want to talk to anyone is because he thinks I'll be questioning him about his latest offer to discuss things he is not supposed to discuss, then please assure him that I promise to avoid any mention of plots to invade the United States."

25

ROOM SERVICE

Anna couldn't afford much. She entered her room at the low-key Shellington Hotel in the outskirts of London and gave it the once over. All it contained were the expected bed, bureau, large screen TV, and bathroom.

The tub/shower combination was smaller than she had in her dorm. *Showering might be dangerous.* At least the white porcelain toilet and sink were clean.

Her sigh accompanied her sagging shoulders and slow blink. A shower. That was what she needed. Everything would be better after she washed up.

A few minutes later, the shifting water temperature and unreliable pressure caused her to leave the new and unwelcome experience and just get dressed. The fresh clothes didn't quite feel comfortable, but the coolness against her skin was enough.

This was not where she planned to be right after leaving UPenn. Her dad must have been there. Maybe in the shadows, but he would have been there. She gritted her teeth.

Stop being such a sap.

Someone knocked. She didn't call for room service. She leaned against the door, placing one hand on the doorknob and the other against the door, which felt cool against her palm.

"Ms. Powell?"

"Yes?" The room was devoid of anything she could use to defend herself.

"I have some additional toiletries from housekeeping." She opened the door a crack. A lone man in plain street clothes with a cart holding some toiletries. She opened the door and reached out for the items.

"Thank you."

As she reached for the bottles he dropped them and grabbed her wrists. He pushed her in hard and she fell to the floor. Then he pulled the cart in and closed the door. Anna stood up and lunged at him, but his left hand went up and deflected her attack. This one wasn't going to be as easy as the two back in Manhattan.

She ran to the other side of the room, grabbed a portable coffee pot that was on the table next to her, and threw it at his head. The man caught the glass container, put it down, and ran at her. Before she could move he had the bed sheet in his hands and over her head.

She landed on the floor with his hand on the back of her head, softening the blow.

"Truce?"

"Truce," her muffled voice said. She felt the weight of his knee lift off her hip and she pulled the sheet off.

The man stood by the door with his hands up in front of his chest. "I don't know who you are, Ms. Powell, but they told me you might want to blow off some steam. I guess you did."

"You started it."

"My mistake." He had a fresh cut on his hand. "I just came to drop a few things off."

"Toiletries?"

"I think these might help you a little more."

———

The equipment was laid out on her bed as if they were the clothes she would wear for the day. A tablet. Three burner phones. An ear piece.

And a gun. Something that would very difficult to find in the UK, but useful if you're looking to kill someone.

She knew what the other equipment felt like, and she was rated sharpshooter in the gun club she had joined during her last year at UPenn. Part of her scholarship was a stipend to be used any way she liked with the tacit understanding that she would end up buying beer or pot or shoes. Anna bought bullets.

She picked up the gun. Standard black. A nice grip. Balanced. She popped the magazine out. Standard six-round clip. She slid it back in. What would it be like to fire it at her father? She felt a tickle in her stomach. She would find out soon enough. The dry air of the room was making her thirsty. The collection of equipment angered her.

She picked up one of the burner phones and checked the contact list. One entry that read *Call Me.*

Asshole.

She threw the phone back on the bed and knew what she would do with the equipment. A gun in the UK. A part of her felt guilty. She had never broken the law before. And though she knew guns, she had never owned one. Somehow the thought of the gun didn't bother her as much as the computer. She couldn't trust it. It might be useful; it might not. Using it might lead someone to her and she would rather trust herself. The one thing she knew was that the authorities, and the not-so-authorities, had access to the web and would find her in no time if she wasn't careful. Hacking into the Witness Protection database was a felony by any definition of the word, but she was willing to take the chance to find any clue that would lead her to her father.

Anna tried to remember when the anger had overtaken her. She wasn't sure. One day, Aunt Marcie found her out on the porch reading. No, she was studying. The one thing that gave her a sense of control. She sat down across from Anna, pulled at her dress, and smoothed out the fabric on her lap. Somehow, her movement was always smooth. Effortless. Anna copied her aunt by trying to smooth out the fabric on her dress. The book fell off her lap.

"Are you going to help me with dinner?" Aunt Marcie asked.

"Can I do it after I finish?"

"When will you finish?"

"In another two months."

Aunt Marcie chuckled. Her eyes were bright and proud. "Your uncle's worried about you."

"No, he's not. I fixed my room, helped with the groceries, and showed him how good a shot I am."

"He did mention that we should hide all the guns."

"You have guns?"

"No, but if we had any, we should hide them."

They smiled at each other. Anna wondered if this is what it felt like to have a mother.

"Aunt Marcie," Anna glanced away for a second before looking at the well-defined brown eyes of the person she had met just a few years ago, "what was my mother like?"

"She didn't take shit from anybody."

Now Anna stared at the gun back in her hand. She was so done waiting to be saved. Time to save herself. *Bastard*. Where was he when she needed him?

Not here. Not there. Not where she needed him. And she needed him so much these last seven years.

No matter. Time to rid herself of her demons.

Starting with the crap on her bed.

She picked up the notebook and two of the burner phones and tossed them in the trash. She got the remaining phone and selected the one item in the contact list. She was sure that the number was going to a secure line that no one could trace, much less tap.

"Good afternoon, Ms. Bishop."

"Fuck you." Her hand was shaking. She had never spoken like that to someone before. And a stranger! She hung up and tossed the phone into the trash with the rest of the equipment. Her focus was undeniable, but who was she becoming? She wasn't sure, but Carpenter Poole was someone no one knew and Anna Wodehouse was someone being pushed into the background.

It was time to learn new habits.

26

POLITE CONVERSATION

Tompkins sat in one of the safe house bedrooms and wondered how he was going to get Burkholder to talk. Talk about what? He didn't know yet. Burkholder had been close, and then the idiot protection detail had lost the girl. Well, woman. Hard to call someone in their twenties a girl.

Tompkins had shot Burkholder with enough voltage to kill a horse and yet he survived. He had read the man's file from cover to cover and it was certainly impressive. This was not the first time he had sent agents to the hospital.

The room smelled hot. Tompkins felt boiled in the only comfortable antique-style chair in the room; blue upholstery and pale wood finish. If there were any birds on this side of the world he couldn't hear them. The only sounds were the men chattering amongst themselves. He suspected that, unless it was a cool evening, he would have a hard time sleeping. He would let the other agents worry about keeping an eye on Burkholder. The heat sapped his energy. He was going to have to go back inside and talk to his charge to calm him down. Sending him back to the States was out of the question. They would find the girl. This wasn't the first time had disappeared, but they'd never been able to get him to agree to anything before with her as a bargaining chip.

Maybe he was just getting old. Burkholder had been in the program for years. He was always getting special treatment and wasn't allowed to get a job that would put him at risk. The challenge was that every job put him at risk.

Who was he? The marshals always knew the background of whom they were protecting, but Burkholder was different. He was a spook for sure. There were a few people like that in the program, but they were typically the easiest to deal with. A lot of education. A lot of ties to government or at least foreign governments. They received the royal treatment and were retired. No extravagance, but things were good for them. Had they served the U.S. well or ill? It was not up to Tompkins to make that decision; that was above his pay scale.

Something that Tompkins knew was that Burkholder was his ticket. Here was a man who had information that everybody wanted, but no one could get him to reveal it. He must have come up with some incredible intel to get into the program. Information so hot that it wasn't even allowed into his file. Burkholder, who had already changed identities ten times during his tenure in the program, was not a lightweight in any sense of the word.

Time to bait him some more. Promotions wait for no man.

———

Tompkins was blacking out when Fletch let go of his throat and Tompkins fell on his knees to the floor.

That went well.

The two new agents were holding Burkholder when he pulled his arms out of their grip.

"You need to learn some manners," Fletch said. He turned and strode to the far corner of the room and sat down in a smooth motion.

"You're right." Tompkins massaged his neck. He had authorized the removal of Fletch's plastic cuffs. His voice sounded scratchy. "My mistake."

———

Fletch was grateful to be uncuffed because now he could think. Being bound constrained his mind. The safe house constrained his being. The small rooms had low ceilings, short doors, and small windows that were a constant reminder that he was not free. Not home. Not in control. Breathing felt hard.

"Thanks for removing the cuffs."

"You need to stop worrying so much about what happens next," Tompkins stood with the care of someone who didn't want to seem threatening. "We'll take care of everything. You need to start thinking about yourself."

So that's it. He wants me to think he's my friend.

"I always do. Can't you tell?"

Tompkins pulled himself into a chair. A Queen Anne.

"Feeling a little out of breath?"

"Just fine, thanks," Tompkins said.

What does this twerp want? Fletch gripped the armrests, felt his muscle tense up, and relaxed them. His shoulders sagged. He relaxed his face.

"I want to help you get what you want," Tompkins said.

"I don't need you to do that. I don't need anyone to do that."

"And yet..." Tompkins let the statement hang in the air.

My daughter is gone.

"Guys? Would you leave us alone for a few minutes?" The two marshals looked at him and then over at Fletch. Fletch never dropped his gaze from Tompkins. "It's okay. Fletch is over his tantrum."

Oh, I would enjoy breaking this guy's neck, but he wouldn't be worth the effort. Better to destroy his credit history.

The men left them.

Tompkins stared him down. Fletch decided to play the game. He kept a steady gaze and then looked away. Tompkins gave a little smile.

"I can help you."

"Are you special? What makes you think you can succeed where the full force of the FBI and U.S. Marshals have failed?"

"Maybe I am."

"What do you know?" Was Tompkins a plant?

"Everything." Tompkins let the word leave his mouth slowly.

"Then you don't need me. And you're really here to kill me."

"No! No." Tompkins put his hands up in mock surrender. "Why would I do that when we can help each other?"

"How?"

"Finish telling me what you had agreed to talk about before."

"Why? The one thing you were supposed to get right you screwed up."

"Let's get one thing straight. I didn't screw up. The protection detail screwed up. And they'll have her soon enough." Tompkins sat back. "I read your file. You're a patriot."

Fletch felt a knot turn in his chest. "Really?"

"Really."

Fletch knew he was lying. His file contained the barest of information. All part of the WitSec deal.

"Look, why can't we start again? The Bureau has an agent who wants to interview you about a seven-year-old cold case. I can send him away..."

"Seven-year-old case?" Fletch thought for a moment. What happened seven years ago? It was all a blur sometimes. Sometimes not.

Seven years ago. Was he about to be OBE? Overcome by Events? Maybe he could leverage this cooperation with the true powers-that-be and get the attention he needed to get out of this mess. This mess of his own making. Tompkins was easy to distract and he didn't need to keep him distracted for very long. All Fletch had to do was give the word and he would be out of here. He didn't want to play that card too soon as there was the chance that he would be found and his life ended sooner than he was ready for.

"Maybe we can help each other. Who is this guy?" Fletch asked.

"Someone you agreed to see a few months ago. I think he's finally calling in his dance card."

What a mess of metaphors. What an idiot. Fletch leaned forward and bent his head down in a position of defeat. He counted to two and looked up.

"I'll talk to him. Maybe you'll see that I am cooperating. When my daughter is found then we can talk about the other thing."

Tompkins eyes lit up.

Let the games begin.

27

DESPERATELY SEEKING ANNA

Anna stared at her screen and hesitated before committing her next felony.

Her claustrophobia under control (the mind was nothing if not resilient), Anna sat at the foot of her bed and decided to check on the status of her prey. The bedspread was cool, but the mattress was too soft for her. Sleep was going to hurt tonight. She had checked the pillows earlier and they were just the right level of firmness. She would have preferred her own pillow with its smells and texture, but sacrifices to a higher cause, and all that.

It was midafternoon. She had heard so much about the rain in Britain, but so far, the weather had help up. It was actually a nice day.

The question in her mind was whether to use the supplied notebook to break into WitSec again, or her own. Her biggest concern was that she was being set up. With her notebook, she knew that the MAC address was masked (it changed every few seconds), and she automatically routed her packets to various places around the world so her traffic was just part of the noise. She wanted to believe that she had gotten the idea on her own, but her dad, Marshall, whoever, had told her about it. He said it was like a distributed denial of service attack only without the attack part. That just meant that her packets would be routed randomly to various machines around the world that had bots installed on them to accept the traffic, encrypt it, send it off to another machine, and then another and maybe even another, unencrypt the packets, and deliver the final message to the source. She thought it was more like Tor, only Tor was a volunteer network.

Marshall had told her on numerous occasions the network she used was run by the NSA. She never asked her dad how he knew that. She thought he was kidding. Once she was on her own she did her own checking. Slowly and carefully, but she checked. It wasn't Tor. Was it NSA? She didn't bother asking and waited for the police or someone to show up and arrest her. Nothing happened.

Whatever it was, she didn't want to find out so she stayed off it. Now she had the USB thumb drive and it was doing something similar. She knew she was going to regret it, but it was time to go back in.

She inserted the thumb drive into her unsuspecting PC that was already invisible to the network. The WITSEC window opened again. Why did that one open? If they knew Marshall was in WitSec, why didn't they just go get him themselves? Anna was just an extra complication. A wrinkle.

Unless they didn't want the exposure. She didn't know who they were and telling the police or the FBI certainly wouldn't help her. This was getting ugly with every step, but she was going to see this through.

After a few minutes, Anna noticed that her hard drive was busy writing. Was the program downloading the WitSec files? She hoped not. There could be no more incriminating evidence on her machine. This was going to be the last time she did this. Her new top priority was wiping her notebook of all her personalizations. She knew that one of the things that would identify her PC on the web was all the little changes she made, along with everyone else, to make their computer set-up their own. Fonts, colors, programs. All of it was as good as a fingerprint in terms of identifying a computer.

Once they identified the computer, they had the owner even if the owner was not the person who used the machine during the intrusion. She knew that due process broke down at that point. In Anna's case, they would have her.

The program went through its cleanup and shutdown.

Wait! Where was the information?

An Excel window opened. Well, in this case Open Office Calc. Maybe not as easy to use as Excel but also not as bulky. She used to give thanks for things like file type associations, but that was a long time ago. Now things just needed to work.

The database was laid out in a standard row and column set up. Names, locations, comments. Links to more information. The window title stated: *Last Updated 30 Seconds Ago*. Her heart raced. This was so illegal she was tempted to delete everything and go hide under her bed or get back on a plane and forget any of this ever happened. Would she even make it out of the UK?

She looked for the name she had found last time: Burkholder. The comments area was in a different color than the other columns. New information. Something about...not being able to find his daughter.

Not being able to find his daughter?

They were looking for her! He wanted to see her! She closed the notebook and felt a knot in her throat. He was looking for her. He was in Witness Protection and he had decided it was time to bring her into the fold.

She couldn't help herself. She started to cry.

Stop. This wasn't helping. She had to get to him and she had to do it soon. They were spending all of their time on protecting him and looking for her when she was spending all of her time looking for him.

She had to find the database files and remove them. Where would this program have stored them? Since she was on Kubuntu, her favorite Linux distro, she knew how to navigate the landscape and find what she wanted. Only it was nowhere to be found.

That was suspicious. She did a quick umount and found another drive partition that had not been there before. There it was. In an encrypted partition. The last time she saw something like that was when she used the now-defunct TrueCrypt to encrypt her file system. *Had they had ported and updated TrueCrypt? Whoa. These guys are kinda cool. Bad asses.* Bastards, but bad asses nonetheless.

She had deniability and so did they. Unless the authorities were given the information necessary to find the encrypted drive partition, in which case she was going to jail.

That would not be a satisfactory lifestyle choice.

There was very little for her to do next. In fact, the one thing that she had considered doing from the beginning now seemed to be the one thing that she should have done as soon as she had arrived in the UK.

Go to the U.S. Embassy and tell them who she was.

28

MOVING DAY

The email received later that day belied its importance:

From: U.S. Department of Justice
United States Marshals Service
Office of the Attorney General

To: All Local Field Offices

Subject: Project Clockwork

Project Clockwork effective immediately. Confirm receipt.

Office of the Attorney General

At any given moment, there are 17,000 witnesses and family members in the Witness Security Program across the United States using various aliases, jobs, and locations where no one would find them.

That would be true for another hour.

———

"This is very civilized," Tompkins said.

The living room where Tompkins had taken Fletch down was rearranged enough it hid the earlier struggle. The blood on the carpet, from the agent whose nose Fletch had broken when he shoved the table into his face, would wait until the professionals came in. He knew he should have felt guilty, but that was for novices. He had his goal just as surely as Tompkins had his. The coffee table surface had the barest smear of red.

Fletch put his glass of water on top of it. When the beading water met the remaining blood, it would look fresh again. Something to remind Tompkins of cause and effect.

He looked over at the Deputy Marshal and thought of the item he had secreted into the furniture. He needed just a few minutes alone and he would make a call on the cell phone he had stolen on the way from the airport. Untraceable and effective. Could he have waited until tonight? Perhaps, but every moment he waited was putting his daughter in more potential danger. He couldn't allow that.

"As long as you're talking we can keep it that way," Fletch said. "When are you going to bring me the new terms?"

"When are you going to tell me about the one thing you didn't want to talk about?"

"I've told you people everything I know."

"On the plane. You said you had more. I know you have more."

"I do," Fletch said.

"Then let's take this forward. The sooner we get going the better." Tompkins' leg was shaking and he clutched his hands together like they were cold. He was probably sweating more than usual.

"I only deal with the Bureau." Fletch slid forward in his seat. "Why do you care?"

"I care as much as you do."

"I care about keeping my mouth shut. You have no idea what you're up against."

"You could tell me."

"You would lose your job." Fletch smiled. "Maybe I should." *Who is this idiot?* Fletch couldn't believe Tompkins was willing to break protocol. This was enough for him to lose his job if it ever came out. Fletch would make sure it got out. "I tell you what, why don't we talk about why you don't want me talking?" He cocked his head toward the window. "Especially by a window with an open curtain."

"We have soldiers up the road. The moors make everything visible for over a mile. No snipers here."

Soldiers? The British were being rather complete. Fletch realized that MI6 would be involved. They would know Fletch was hot. The Brits would never allow him in without a full understanding of what they were getting themselves into.

"Perfect. When the missile strikes, it'll leave a clean crater." Tompkins frowned.

Fletch could see him getting a touch anxious. "Oh, don't worry so much, Deputy Tompkins." Fletch tilted his head. "You wouldn't want to worry."

"I'm not worried." Tompkins moved on the couch. Away from the window.

"I'm safe as long as I don't talk. You're safe as long as I don't talk. And you want me to talk. Your superiors must not like you very much."

"They like me fine."

Fletch flexed his biceps. The joker had easy buttons to push. "They must. They sent you to England. They sent you to protect me. Well, they sent you to manage the case, which means you have to manage the agents. The ones who are in the hospital right now." Fletch looked back and forth and then lowered his voice. "Who are those other guys? I don't remember them."

"Those are marshals sent from the U.S. embassy."

"Are you sure? I've been in this program a long time." He rubbed his hands together. "I don't remember them."

"What happens if you talk?"

"I don't know, but I've spent most of my life trying not to find out."

"Tell me," Tompkins said.

"I'd have to kill you. They would have to kill you."

Tompkins paled.

Novice. Bush league player.

"If you don't tell me you'll have to tell someone." Tompkins' tongue touched the top of his upper lip.

Fletch saw his hands shake just so.

"I'm not talking until my daughter is found."

"I agree. You shouldn't talk to anyone because she might not be missing for the same reason she's been missing before."

"You mean she snuck past some of the most well-trained agents on the planet?" Fletch smirked and crossed his leg.

"No one was killed. If someone wanted to kidnap her, they would have left a trail of bodies."

"Maybe they knew that she'd evaded your guys once before."

"The protection detail is not made up of marshals."

"Right. They have real professionals."

"Professional enough. Talk to me."

"I'm in no rush."

"Neither am I, but this would make things easier later."

"Easier?" Fletch had him on the hook. "What I have to say will never get easier. For anyone."

"It will get easier for you."

"I'll be dead."

"Not right away."

"As long as you're willing to admit that my time will be limited." Fletch could feel the man before him becoming more and more confident. Cat playing with a piece of string.

"Everyone knows that." The phone was under one of the cushions. Fletch knew who he would call first. Someone with the connections he needed without the complications of his previous employer, who'd made it necessary for him to enter WitSec. The U.S. Government.

————

The door burst open and the two agents who had left him alone ran in with guns drawn.

"Let's go!" one of the officers said.

Fletch was about to take a swing at one of the men when they both grabbed him by the arms and led him out through the house, in which he had not even gone to the bathroom.

"Deputy? Time to go!" the officer repeated. Fletch wasn't sure what was going on, but something had changed.

"The Embassy called." The agent was talking to Tompkins as Tompkins was making sounds of objection. "We received a Clockwork alert."

Tompkins started barking orders. Fletch was almost out.

"What about my daughter? What does this have to do with...?" They were outside. An SUV convoy flanked by two military trucks was waiting. "What's going on?"

The men remained silent as they pushed his head down as if he were entering a police cruiser and was on his way to central booking.

The opposite passenger door opened and Tompkins jumped in. "What are you waiting for? Get in and close the door."

Fletch could feel the distance of the phone still in the living room and considered running back in to retrieve it. No, the moment was gone. He would have to find another way.

Tomkins stared at him. "Word came down that you had to be moved so we're moving you."

"What?"

"The only thing you need to know for now is that you just became hot again and we have to move you somewhere safe." Tompkins clicked his seatbelt on. "Don't worry. You'll have plenty of company."

"Company?"

Tompkins patted the back of the driver's seat. "Let's go!"

The SUVs revved up and took off. Frustrated, Fletch thought about the phone. The only lifeline he had at the moment. He felt his heart drop. They had never moved him without warning the way they just did. News of his daughter had not come in so whatever it was had nothing to do with her.

Or maybe it did. Every moment was a new moment.

29

HIGH CEILINGS AND AIR-CONDITIONING

The U.S. Embassy, located at 24 Grosvenor Square in London since 1960, was the official diplomatic mission of the United States to the United Kingdom. As the largest American embassy in Western Europe it served many functions. One function was as the symbol of the US/UK alliance that had seen minimal interruption since the Revolutionary War when the U.S. told its British parent it was all grown up and moving out. Anna knew this because she looked it up before leaving the Shellington Hotel that morning.

Being outside, finally doing something instead of obsessing about felonies committed and yet to be committed, had raised her reality front and center. The streets with no shadows, the occasional bit of trash on the street (which seemed to increase as she got closer to the embassy) stood out during her nondescript walk to Grosvenor Square. She could see the edge of the massive park to the rear of the building and wondered if, once this was all over, she would have time to play tourist and see the sites. She frowned. *Stop fantasizing. Nothing is going to go well today no matter how it turns out.*

An otherwise clear blue sky had a few clouds that dogged Anna, and kept the area she inhabited colored in a flat, dull, gray pallor.

There was a crowd of people ahead of her, but they couldn't be heading to the embassy as well, could they?

Anna arrived earlier than she expected and knew it was the right thing to do. That was, arrive early. She hated going places late and hated business hours that made her wait. The embassy's hours of operations were 24/7, but their hours to the public were from 10 a.m. until 3 p.m. which made for a short day for someone. What she didn't expect was to find so many people in line before her. She made her way forward and when she got to the guard at the front gate, she wasn't sure what to tell her. Not that Anna hadn't been practicing for the last hour while she made her way to the guard. It was that she was so excited about seeing Marshall that she wasn't thinking past any given moment.

"Good morning."

The female officer greeted her in silence but looked her up and down.

"My name is Anna Wodehouse." She stood and waited for a response. "You guys are looking for me." She leaned toward her and whispered, "You have Marshall Wodehouse."

"Passport, please."

Anna straightened up, reached into her small purse, and extracted the document. As the guard took it from Anna she stood and turned.

"Come with me, please."

Wow. Could it be this easy?

"I really appreciate this. The ride here was kind of boring, but hey, this is England, you know?"

They walked down a corridor where the only sound she heard was their footsteps against the polished marble floor. The air was a touch stale. The building looked like it had been around for a while. "Where are we going?"

The guard continued without answering. Anna continued to follow.

They arrived at another room. She handed Anna her passport and motioned for her to sit down. The room was filled with people.

She walked over to a red container, pulled a ticket, handed it to Anna, and walked out.

Fifty-seven.

She was waiting on line with fifty-six other people. For what? Didn't they understand why she was there? This had to be a mistake. They were holding Marshall and he was being uncooperative because of her!

She was thankful she hadn't brought the gun with her. The metal detector at the main door would have been a problem. She clasped the paper ticket and looked around the room. None of these people had as important a mission as she had.

There were people there in suits, in shorts, with their kids, their bags, their problems. The man at the front, whose number had to be fourteen given the display, was waving his hands to a woman behind the teller's window. She didn't look impressed and let him go on until the man stopped and when she answered him, he started again. Anna heard her saying, "Please have a seat. Please. Have a seat. Someone will be with you shortly."

Here was her chance. As the man walked away Anna got up, cut off the next person who stood in her way, and started the long walk to the teller window.

Excusing herself to the elderly woman whose turn it was, Anna strode to the window. "Hi."

"Number fifteen?" The woman was rather attractive. Shoulder length dark hair, thin wireframe glasses. Definitely plucked her eyebrows.

"Ah, well, no. Good morning," Anna said.

"I'm sorry. You're going to have to sit down until your number is called." Using a pencil she clutched in her hand, she pointed at Anna and then at the display.

"No, you don't understand. When the guard," she pointed over her shoulder, "brought me here, I thought he understood what I was talking about."

"You're going to have to sit down." The woman put the pencil down and looked at a monitor to her right.

"My father...Marshall Wodehouse is looking for me."

"So you're a lost minor?"

"No, I'm twenty-four. Haven't been a minor for a long time."

"Please sit down. When it's your turn, I'll be able to help you the same way I have helped everyone else this morning."

Anna checked behind her before she turned back. "If you ask me, the people here beg to differ, but I get your point."

"Please, ma'am..."

Anna placed both her hands on the edge of the window. "You're looking for me."

The woman shook her head. "I don't understand."

Anna spoke through her teeth. "My father is in Witness Protection."

The woman's eyes opened just enough that Anna knew she understood.

She picked up her phone and punched in a three-digit extension. She kept her eyes trained on Anna and spoke too low for Anna to hear, but she was sure she heard words related to WitSec.

"What did you say your name was?"

"Anna Wodehouse."

"May I have your passport, please?"

Anna pulled it out of her purse again and handed it over.

"When you hear your number called again, it will be someone from the legal attaché's office. Please have a seat and thank you for your patience."

"No, thank you." Anna returned to her seat.

This was awesome! Legal attaché. Now she was getting somewhere. This was much easier than she had expected. Even cutting the line was a cinch. She had never done that before either. Ordering something on-line meant you never waited.

She clenched and unclenched her hands. Anna knew that her expectations were going through the roof as she rubbed the palms of her hands along her legs. She sat back and breathed. *Breathe in. 5-4-3-2-1. Breathe out.* She repeated the pattern twice. Her shoulders relaxed and her eyebrows flattened.

With her eyes closed she smelled the mixture of cleaning fluid and sweat. The room echoed just enough for her to know that it had a very high ceiling that was probably the bane of their existence before they installed air-conditioners. Heat would float up, and just sit there. Opening the windows would just make it worse. She wondered what it must have been like to work here during the bombings in the 1940s.

"Fifty-seven!"

Her eyes flew open. "Here!" She stood and held up her piece of paper.

The guard looked at her and motioned for her to follow him. *Rude. Very rude.* He had a rather large gun on the right side of his belt. She wanted to make small talk but noticed he was not in a talking mood. "Is there a bathroom I could...?"

"After your meeting. There's one down the hall."

How could he stand to wear a hat? She looked over at another guard. Also wearing a hat. They went down a flight of stairs and she felt blood rush to her head. She wasn't paying attention. Where was she going? If she needed to get out...

The guard stopped before a door with a man's name on it and *Legal Attaché* printed below it. This was her moment of truth. He opened the door and Anna stepped through.

30

THE ATTACHÉ CASE

Anna sat alone. While it didn't look like an interrogation room, she remembered her past experiences, and decided she would listen to her gut. Her gut said she was hungry. And that she was being watched. The room, a drawing room really, was just another office. Who worked here? Were there rooms where they delivered good news and others where they delivered bad?

Her brain was on high alert. Her electrified senses made her surroundings light up in ways she hadn't experienced in years. The lights were bright, the colors were vivid, the smells outstanding. She heard and felt her breathing in the silence, though she thought she heard a hum permeating the air. Probably the resonant frequency of the building.

Where were the cameras? Probably in one of the paintings. It would be easier to hide the pinhole lens in a textured surface like an oil painting than in wood, but she knew that would work as well. *Ah, paranoia, your teacher is Marshall.*

So, what were her paranoid fears? They could deport her. They could arrest her. Worse, they could ignore her. This could turn out badly because there was no way for her to change their mind. She could feel the anxiety in the pit of her stomach. She wanted to stand and pace, but she closed her eyes and cleared her mind.

And waited.

Then the door opened. The man who strode toward her was tall and thin. His dark blue suit fit perfectly with the requisite amount of white sleeve showing. Perfectly knotted thin paisley tie. She couldn't tell his age though he had quite the receding hairline, but no wrinkles around his eyes or forehead.

"Good morning, Ms. Wodehouse. Quintin Hardwick." *How disappointing. No British accent.*

Anna stood and shook his hand. Firm. Dry. She felt no confidence in his confident grip. She nodded to his greeting.

"So what can I do for you?"

No wasted words for him.

"I want you to take me to my father." No wasted words for her.

"Who is?"

"Marshall Wodehouse. I have reason to believe that he is in Witness Protection and that he's looking for me."

"That's quite a mouthful. And who is Marshall Wodehouse?" He blinked, tilted his head to his left, and furrowed his forehead.

Anna blinked. "He," she looked away for a second, "he is the man who allegedly kidnapped me, but who also disappeared..."

"So you are looking for the man who kidnapped you and hasn't been brought to justice?" He dragged a chair over and sat down in front of her.

Anna sat, too. His thin tie reminded her of the Sword of Damocles. It even swung a little back and forth like a pendulum. She knew that everything she said was going to tell him something, and Anna wasn't sure what she wanted him to know. What if he jumped to a conclusion that she hadn't considered?

"No. Well, yes." She stared into his blue eyes. "I understood that he was looking for me. I want to, I want to..."

"Kill him?" The statement came out of his smiling mouth.

Anna's eyes opened in shock for about a second.

His expression changed even as he responded to his own question. "I know I would."

She relaxed her eyebrows. Her face was always such a giveaway. "That's, that's just stupid." Again, she glanced away and then returned his gaze. "He wants to see me."

"Has it occurred to you that if he is, in fact, in Witness Protection, he won't be seeing you?" He studied her face. "Why would you want to see him? Why aren't you warm in your bed?" He smirked.

Anna was worried.

"Why are you even here?"

"I told you, I heard that he was looking for me and he was in Witness Protection..." *I don't believe this.* Anna gripped her knees and brought them together.

"First of all, what good would Witness Protection do if anyone could look up someone's name and find them? Not very good protection, one would think?

"Secondly, how do you know he's in WitSec?" He blinked. Twice.

"What was your name again?" Anna asked.

"Quintin. Quintin Hardwick. Assistant to the Legal Attaché."

"Quintin. Well, Quintin, Mr. Hardwick, I don't know anybody. Yet I know that he's looking for me and I also know that I'm looking for him. It seems like a fair bit that wherever he is, we should see each other." She folded her hands on the table. "I would really appreciate it if..."

Quintin placed Anna's passport on the table. "Forged passports are not a way to get on my good side."

A rock fell in her stomach and down both legs. *Oh my God. My passport.* She had been waving it around like it was her ticket into the inner sanctum and all it did was implicate her in a fraud. She almost jumped out of her chair.

"So tell me, Ms. Wodehouse, or should I say Ms. Powell, how did you get into this country?"

Anna looked to the door. Her hands started to sweat and she involuntarily swallowed. She wasn't sure how she was supposed to answer him. *Damn it! The passport.*

He looked at her as if he was examining a specimen. "Cat got your tongue?"

"That's old."

"What is?" Hardwick asked.

"That saying. It's from the 1800's. I can't believe people still use it."

"I've been at this for a while."

"Where is my father?"

"Is that why you're looking for him? You think he's your father?"

"OMG, you're telling me that you haven't read my file?"

"Not everything is at the speed of the Internet."

"Yeah, especially since everything we do on it is Hoovered," she said. The words came out on auto-pilot. This meeting was now a bad idea.

I have to get out of here.

"I don't know your story. At least not your entire story." He crossed his legs. "Care to tell me about it?"

He's acting too cavalier. What did he know? He must know everything. No, he hasn't had that much time.

"Find me Marshall. Find me my father. I know you're looking for me and here I am."

"Having a fake passport is a serious offense."

She considered telling him that breaking his neck would be considered a serious offense as well. She had a sudden and singular thought: *Run.*

She stood up and retched. "I think," she grabbed her stomach, "I think I'm going to be sick."

Quintin stood and leaned in toward her. "Are you...?"

She swung her fist as hard as she could, almost lifting him off his feet as she connected with his lower jaw. The knuckles of her right hand burst into pain, but she felt his face buckle as he reeled back in shock. She hit him again for good measure and he fell to the ground.

Her stomach twisted. *Oh, no.* She threw up on him before she could look away.

Time to go.

31

PISSING CONTEST

As a rule, Terrell didn't hate tourists. He wasn't in the position to be a tourist all that often, but he had an appreciation for their raison d'etre: to inject money into the economy and for people on both sides of the transaction to realize that, while they might not have all that much in common, their complimentary agendas served them well. A view into another culture could be done with relative safety and desire, and money would exchange hands, which always made everybody happy.

Being jostled in the middle of the street by an ocean of people moving to and fro through the streets of London made Terrell realize that today wasn't one of his love days. In fact, if one more person knocked into him, his call-to-action might alert the authorities. Perhaps the horrible smell coming from the nearby alley put him in a sour mood to start with. Could it be dealing with that squirrel Tompkins? Or the mayonnaise wall of sound coming from all around him.

He felt like he was in Times Square on New Year's Eve, only without the overwhelming signs and lights, just the ocean of humanity that washed over him leaving the feeling of aggravation and anxiety. In New York, he welcomed wading through the ocean of energy. London felt different.

The job he had to do seemed to be under someone else's control.

He was out of his element and his choices had gotten him nowhere. Had gotten him to a crowded street with only one place to turn.

Terrell made the call and Conrad answered.

"I think you might be out of luck soon," Conrad said.

Neither man was happy about it.

"Get me in to see him," Terrell said.

"I don't know why you call me when things like this happen. This is your government taking it on the backside. Her Majesty's government is simply extending the courtesy of making sure he doesn't die on our watch."

"I just want to know that if I need you, I can call you."

"My dear boy, of course you can always call me. Especially given your present circumstances."

"My what?" Terrell asked.

"Your circumstances. Oh, don't play coy with me. We received the emergency alert along with all the other people who care."

"Conrad, please stop playing games. What are you talking about?"

"I don't know what you call it in the States, but we just received an alert that your entire witness database has been compromised. Everyone in your lovely witness security program needs to be picked up and given new identities. We confirmed the message and are now in the middle of moving an undisclosed number of very unhappy people to safe houses we don't have, to locations that don't exist, to prepare new identities that we don't yet have."

Terrell stopped. The occasional person bumped into him. He didn't know the marshal code for total bloody screw-up, but he could imagine what was going on back in the States. No wonder he couldn't get face time with that man. Who the hell messed up this time?

Terrell checked in with the Bureau and was told that no one was closer to understanding who was responsible for the break-in or why. Was it the Chinese? The Russians? Anonymous? God, he hated the Internet.

The car he had rented to get around was becoming an annoyance.

It was too small and sounded like a go-kart. A man his size needed something that sounded like a machine for a man his size. No matter. He was on his way once again. A new location, a new day. Just outside of London was the man who might have the answers about Del he needed for the last few years. Who this man was didn't matter to Terrell. If he was in international WitSec that meant that whatever he dropped the dime on was pretty damn serious. Terrell appreciated the danger the man was in by even talking to him. Once he received his new identity, Terrell might never see him again. Time meant something, and he didn't have a lot of it.

Of course, now that the database was compromised, he was either going to be shuffled around for a lot longer, or disappear even quicker.

How the heck did they even break in? These were systems that even the NSA couldn't get into. Well, maybe the NSA because if they or the Agency needed to get a hold of those data repositories, they just had to ask. They had the run of the hen house as far as Terrell was concerned. Nothing was beyond their reach. The Bureau sure could have used that kind of power.

———

"You can't see him." The young, short Deputy Marshal who stood before Terrell was trying to stare him down but had to look up to do it. *WTF?*

"Deputy Tompkins, I understand the situation you've found yourself in..."

"No, Special Agent," the words sounded like he used them for the first time, "you don't understand our current situation. The fact that you're even here has compromised this man."

Terrell smiled as he thought about how to persuade this kid that he was authorized and not going anywhere until he got to speak with Fletch Burkholder. "I don't know everything that's going on, that's true, but I've been in this kind of situation before."

"No one has been in this situation before," Tompkins said.

"Unless you want to tell me about some Bureau database that suddenly went missing, shutting down a major program, and costing the government of the United States a few million dollars to correct."

"No, thankfully that has never happened. However, if I don't talk to this man, I won't get a second chance once you give him his new life. This might be the only chance I get." Terrell's tie hung loose around his neck. He loosened it more with the passing thought of wrapping it around Tompkins' neck. *No. That would ruin the tie.* "Deputy Marshal. I was told that I could expect your cooperation in this."

"Yes, and that was before all hell broke loose."

"This doesn't change anything. No one knows who broke into the database or why. Until we do, all we can do is keep protecting these people." Terrell pointed toward a door. "Protecting that man." Terrell let out a breath. "I just need a few minutes."

"I think you need to leave, Special Agent."

Terrell couldn't believe it. A twerp of a U.S. Marshal was going to show him the door. Their standards must be slipping.

"There has to be something we can do," Terrell said. He opened his jacket and put his hands on his hips. "Talk to me. Is there someone I need to get on the phone? Is the problem that your man wants reassurances that this won't come back to haunt him?" Terrell heard people moving in the other room. Pushing his way in wouldn't get him what he wanted. "You know how far his immunity goes. I don't. All I want are some answers. If he lies to me, I'll never know." Yes, he would, but he didn't need to tell Tompkins that. "Just a few minutes."

Tompkins looked up at Terrell, then at the British soldiers who stood at the door, and waved them over. "Gentlemen, Special Agent Garrison is leaving. Please show him out." Tompkins turned and walked away.

"Whoa! Whoa!" Had Tompkins just waved him off? "What's going on here? I'm not here to have high tea with him."

"Gentlemen, please show him out."

As one of the soldiers touched Terrell's arm, Terrell pulled his arm back and pulled out his cell. The follow-up to the call he hadn't wanted to make to begin with.

"Hello? This is Special Agent Terrell Garrison for Conrad Chapin." He glanced at the soldiers for a moment and smiled at Tompkins. "Yes, I'll hold." When Conrad came on, he spoke to him for a few seconds and then handed the phone over to one of the soldiers.

When the soldier handed the phone back to Terrell, he and his twin returned to their position at the door. Terrell put the phone back in his jacket, sat, and crossed his legs.

"I need to talk to Fletcher Burkholder. I need to talk to him now and if you have any objections, you can file that paperwork into whatever office you work out of back home."

Tompkins stood frozen in place. He pursed his lips.

"I'll sit in on the interview," Tompkins said.

"You'll sit in on anything you like, but this interview will not be one of them. When I'm done, I will leave Mr. Burkholder, or whatever his name is, to your care to keep him safe and sound for whatever it is he's done for the fine people of the United States." Terrell struggled not to smirk.

"Now, either bring him to me, or take me to him."

32

POINTS OF PERSUASION

When Anna was bumped as she escaped from the embassy, she didn't think twice about it. Her mind was nowhere close to where she was at the moment. *OMG! What the heck was I thinking?*

They knew her name.

They knew her fake name.

They had her passport.

They knew she was looking for Marshall.

She had to get back to the hotel. Could one or more of the authorities be following her to her room?

She held her purse close to her. A phone rang, but not noticing it at first, she kept walking with her head down. She had turned right on Blackburne's Mews as soon as she left the embassy and did her best not to look up at the technology that most Londoners ignored every day: the overhead security cameras.

Her heart pounded. *Stupid, stupid, stupid.* The number of people on the street had thinned and the smell of exhaust fumes washed over her as a double decker bus lumbered by with a sound that scraped the inside of her eardrum like a metal table dragged across a concrete floor. She was an amateur. How the hell was she supposed to make this work?

When she got to Upper Brook Street, she hung a left and an immediate right onto the alley that was Shepherd's Place.

Now that she'd managed to make an absolute screw up of her trip, she had to somehow get out. Get out to where? Back to the U.S.? Maybe she should go pay Edward Snowden a visit.

Her purse vibrated and rang. She looked down, walked over to the side of a building, and opened her bag.

BEEEEP. BEEEEP.

Where did that come from? The phone said *Unlisted.*

"How does it feel to know that you're so close?" It was the Voice.

She hung up and when she passed a trash can, Anna tossed the phone in as she worked out the most surreptitious route back to the hotel. Did it matter? Now the cameras saw her ditching a phone. They would put two and two together and figure out it was a burner. Aside from not having breakfast, and throwing up what little she had, her stomach was doing somersaults. *Okay. Okay. Next thing to do is head into a café and get something to...*

Two men slammed into her and lifted her off the ground. They pulled her into an alleyway. She tried to scream, but one of them had his hand over her mouth.

"Don't make a sound. Don't."

She stifled a cry and then shook her head. Her arms were pinned and her back was up against a wall. The man to her left held a cell phone up to her ear.

"Why do you do these things? Don't you know..." It was the Voice. The man from the hotel back in New York.

"I'm going to be picked up by the police!"

"We're here to help you. Why do you fight us so much?"

"Tell your goons to let go of me."

"I will. Eventually. For now, I want you to hear me out. This seems to be the only way to accomplish that."

"What do you want?" Anna took in a breath. "Seriously, I can hardly breathe."

"I'm sure even you realize how stupid a move that was. What

made you think that going to the Embassy and asking about your father was going to help?"

"I found him. He's looking for me." Silence on the other end. "Air. Could really use some." She looked over at the two men and they loosened their grip. She relaxed her shoulders. "Why can't you send me coded messages like everybody else?"

"This is the twenty-first century. Phone calls are so much more civilized. What do you mean he's looking for you?"

"I mean he's cutting a deal to tell them more about something, but he'll only talk if they bring me to him."

"Really? That is good news." The sound of his voice and his words didn't match. Down beat on the last few words. He wasn't happy.

"Get me out of here. Get me back home." The bricks she was lodged against bit into her sore back.

"What you did was very stupid. I would emphasize it more, but I've already told you twice. If you don't let us help you, the police will arrest you and you will go to jail for a very long time."

"I'll take you with me." Anna tried to shake her arms loose and managed to strike her shoulder on the wall. The pain screamed up her neck.

"We will never be found and you'll have a phantom to blame for your problems."

"So, you're a real help then."

"I can help you get out. Just do your life's calling."

"I think you set me up. I think you wanted me to go to the Embassy and have them see me."

"If your job, your task, is to kill someone, the last thing you want is to have the people protecting him to know your face. The only good thing is that they don't know why you're here. You are an enigma and they are going to chase their tail trying to figure out what you are doing here."

"Lucky for you."

"Why?"

"If you had been arrested, there's no saying what could have happened to you," the Voice said.

"What do you want?"

"What do you want?"

"I want to go home," Anna said.

"Interesting that you've never used the term 'home' before. Always, 'my aunt and uncle's,' 'my hotel room. Never 'home.' Feeling homesick?"

Anna pursed her lips. What was it that her father was involved in?

"If they capture you, you'll be tried in the UK and maybe extradited to the United States. That will take time. Time you don't have. If your father really is in Witness Protection then he will vanish without a trace and you will never find him."

Maybe that wasn't such a bad thing. Maybe she should run. Maybe she didn't deserve to see him again much less kill him.

"I don't want that to happen. He deserves what you're bringing him," the Voice said.

"How do I know that you won't just hand me over to the authorities once this is all done?"

"I have a plane waiting for you. As soon as you're done, my people will bring you to a hidden airfield, and we'll get you out."

"Your boys seem perfectly capable of this." She gave her two companions an incredulous look. "Why not just use them?"

"Let's just say that I knew your father and I believe in poetic justice. He deserves his fate."

"You're starting to worry me."

"Don't worry about me. Worry about the people who are now looking for you. Tell one of the men to take the phone."

Anna pushed the phone away from her ear. "He wants to talk to you."

The man listened for a moment and then he and his companion stepped away from her. He put the phone back up against her ear. Anna took it from him.

"Now what?"

"Your friend there is going to give you another burner phone. Keep it with you. As soon as you're done, you call and tell them you're ready. We'll know if you've kept your end of the deal."

"So now we're dealing?" Anna restrained herself from throwing the phone as far as she could.

"Who are you looking for? Tell me his name," the Voice said.

"Fletcher Burkholder."

"And what are you going to do when you find him?"

"I'm going to kill him."

33

THE INTERVIEW

The drive back after his conversation with Conrad left him feeling queasy. He hated calling in favors and hoped not to call one in now. It left a taste in his mouth that he was sure wouldn't get any better. His suspicions as to the outcome of his upcoming conversation were not positive and the appearance of the British officers and the U.S. Marshal's upon his arrival to the safe house did nothing to allay his fears.

They showed him into the room and left him alone with his subject.

"Good afternoon, Mr. Burkholder." Terrell looked him over. Tall, white, large hands. Intelligent eyes. Terrell saw him doing the same.

Fletch nodded. "Agent Garrison, I believe." Neither man extended his hand.

"Thank you for agreeing to see me. This case is rather important."

"The pleasure is mine." Fletch motioned to the chairs.

Terrell thanked him as they both sat. "I don't want to take up any more of your time than necessary. I realize time is life. I just have a few questions..."

"Did Deputy Dog out there try to keep you out?"

"Excuse me?"

"Deputy Marshal Tompkins. The clown who's my case officer for the immediate future." Why was he badmouthing the marshal?

"He's been trying to get me to talk for the last few days."

Terrell held up his hands. "I don't want to get in the middle of anything."

"Don't worry. You won't. I won't allow it," Fletch said. He sat in the chair with his arms draped over the back of the chair and his legs splayed open.

His body screamed alpha male. He was in control. Terrell would play to that.

"As I was saying, I just had a few questions I was hoping you could answer." Terrell reached into his jacket and pulled out his mini-notebook.

"Aren't you a throwback? Using paper and a pen."

"I'm not a very good typist."

"You're not a very good interviewer."

Terrell smiled. "I've been called worse." He leaned forward. Let Burkholder think he was being submissive. "Seven years ago..."

"What do I get for talking to you?"

Was Burkholder sneering?

"For talking with me? You get the full thanks of the people of the United States. And our continued protection." He leaned back. "I've never seen someone as scared as you."

Burkholder didn't move. "If you knew what I knew, you'd be scared too. Do you know why I'm in this program?"

"I suppose you want to tell me."

"I don't. And I'm not telling."

Terrell put down his notebook on his lap. "What do you want, Mr. Burkholder?"

"Deputy Dog knows. And he won't get it for me."

"I can't promise anything, but maybe I can help," Terrell said.

"Can you find a missing person?"

"Missing?"

"This is going to be a waste of time." Burkholder pulled his arms in. "I'm not in the mood to converse until I get what I want."

"And that is?"

"A person. Someone I care about." He leaned in. "Who is missing."

"The marshals are looking for this person?"

"That's what they say," Burkholder said.

"What do you say?"

"I say they're full of it." Burkholder looked away. "Do you know who they're looking for?"

"I haven't read your file."

"Then it doesn't matter. You didn't care enough to even read my file."

"I'm not allowed. Your name was redacted in a case file and I was able to track you down because of your witness number." Terrell wondered what was going on. He wasn't going to mention knowing about Burkholder's missing daughter.

"Give me what I want and we'll talk."

"Really?" Terrell wondered what his next move would be: another call? The time in New York was off by four hours. Someone would be in the office. "Who is it?"

"Ask Deputy Dog."

"Mr. Burkholder, I assure you that if the U.S. Marshals are looking for a relative or other loved one..."

"They lost my daughter."

Great! The long slide downhill.

"They'll find her. Is this the first time?"

"No. She loses them on a regular basis." The voice of a frustrated father.

Terrell could hear his dad: *You walk around like you're lost.* A parental lament.

"Then she'll show up."

"Maybe not this time."

"If you're not going to address my questions..."

"Don't threaten me! My immunity extends to everything. If I killed you right now, I wouldn't be prosecuted."

"I'll try to bear that in mind." Terrell put his notebook back in his jacket and stood. *This is a waste of time. Time to call the office.* Out came his cell phone.

"That's it? You're not going to argue with me about this?"

"I don't even argue with my girlfriend."

"You're an idiot. Maybe I will kill you."

Terrell put the phone back in his pocket.

"I really want to talk with you. You know something about a murder. An FBI agent named Del Kirby."

"I don't know the name." His eyes took on a faraway look.

"Mr. Burkholder, now I know you're lying to me." Terrell lay his arms on the armrests. He jacket was open.

"Get me what I want."

"What do you know about the murder of Del Kirby?"

"Nothing." He looked at Terrell's jacket and then at his face. "Probably nothing."

"Probably?"

"I can't talk about it. If I even tell you that it sounds familiar, they might kill my daughter."

"Who?" Terrell was about to sit down when Burkholder suddenly came at him.

"You should have read my file." Burkholder grabbed Terrell's lapels and took a swing at him that connected with an immense amount of pain.

Terrell grabbed a nearby lamp and tried to throw it, but the electrical cord caused it to bounce back toward the table with a loud crash. The door opened and the two marshals ran in and subdued Burkholder as he was lunging at Terrell again.

"Tell me about Del Kirby." Terrell was standing a few inches from Burkholder. He refused to raise his voice. "Was he murdered?"

"Get out!" Burkholder shook the two agents off and strode to the other side of the room. "This interview is over."

———

Alone now, Fletch was too busy to feel more than anxiety. He reached into his pocket and pulled out Terrell's cell phone. All Fletch had to do was catch a glimpse of it to know he had better things to do than incriminate himself over something he had no control over, even if he had recommended it.

He dialed a number that he knew he would never forget. The number led to an encrypted line that the cell tower registered as non-existent.

"Yes?"

"Did you take her?"

"Have you told them anything?"

"Of course not."

"Then we haven't taken her." The voice on the other end let out a breath. "Should we?"

"No. I've never asked them to bring her in and I won't."

"Now you know that is a lie." Fletch's neck tensed up. "You asked for her to be brought to you. You've been talking to the FBI about helping to find her."

———

Terrell put the towel down and thought it was time to call the main office. There had to be another way to get Burkholder to talk.

His phone was gone. In that split second, he knew he'd been taken. He threw open the door and ran toward Burkholder, who was talking to someone on it. Tompkins was right behind him. As Terrell reached for the phone, Burkholder held it aloft and hung up. He threw the phone across the room.

"Who were you calling?" Terrell asked.

"What do you care?"

"I just want to make sure you didn't burn my minutes on a call to a hooker."

Burkholder brought his face close to Terrell. "No hookers. They're waiting for you to get back to the hotel." He turned away with a disgusted look. "But it turns out your phone makes a great microphone."

Someone listened in on their conversation through his cell phone? *Who the hell is this guy?*

34

———

THREATENING FLETCHER

"You realize you've just lost this phone." Tompkins held onto Terrell's phone and felt good about what he was about to do. "We've examined it and there isn't a trace as to where he called. We'll have to wait for the final determination about the call itself and what the cell towers can tell us, but your phone is now evidence."

"Yep," Terrell said.

It was hard to tell what the FBI agent was thinking, but that was as close to a resigned affirmative as Tompkins had ever heard. He knew he screwed up. This was not good and his interview was never going to happen.

———

Terrell couldn't believe he had made such a stupid mistake. This was one way to burn the Bureau's money – come all the way out to the UK and let the interview subject take control.

He knew this wasn't going to end well.

Tompkins was talking with one of the other marshals. "When do we move him again? Any word?"

The response did not sound hopeful.

Terrell headed for the door to the room that held his subject as Tompkins called out to him. "Whoa! Where are you going?"

"I have an interview to conduct." Terrell turned the doorknob and re-entered the room.

Fletch stared out a window, crinkling the curtain with his hand. He didn't seem to notice that Terrell had entered.

Terrell closed the door. He didn't slam it and Tompkins didn't call out or say anything that would cause anyone to think there was anything wrong. Everyone already knew that.

"Tell me about your daughter," Terrell said.

"You cell phone just became evidence," Fletch said.

"Evidence for what? We can't prosecute you for anything." Terrell stood by him but in front of the wall before the window. Burkholder let go of the curtain and leaned against the wall. "So you're looking to be shot by a sniper?" Terrell asked.

"They know I'm looking for her. It might not matter anymore."

"Look, I don't know what you know, or don't know, or why you're even in the program, but I could really use some information from you. You owe me for my phone."

Burkholder turned his head and then continued staring out the window.

"Hey, I don't have it anymore so they can't listen to us." Terrell peered out on the moors and then at the large man next to him. "C'mon. You owe me for my minutes."

———

"The man you remember as FBI, you don't remember his name?" Terrell asked.

"No."

They sat on the same couch this time. Burkholder seemed to be thinking so hard he slumped with the effort.

"I only remember because we didn't kill a lot of people back then. There was no need to."

"And you're not going to tell me what the need was that suddenly made this possible?"

"No," Burkholder said.

Terrell knew he should feel anger. Hurt. Instead his heart simply felt spent. "If I show you a picture, do you think you might remember him?"

"Maybe."

Terrell pulled two photos out of a file folder. One was Del Kirby's Bureau photo and the other was a casual shot. Walking with someone Terrell didn't remember. Burkholder looked at the two photos.

"Did you kill him?" Terrell asked.

"No comment."

"You're a man with anger management issues, but I don't think you did it."

"No comment."

"You know who did."

"I'm sorry, Senator. I don't recall."

Terrell smiled, but not with his eyes. "Good. Wisecracks. I'll take that as a yes." He retrieved the photos and returned them to their place. "Why?"

"No comment."

"Oh, stop."

"No comment."

"You have full immunity. We can't do anything to you." Terrell's frustrated voice took over as he neck became tense.

"No comment."

"Why? Why? What did he know?"

"Maybe." Fletch shrugged. "Maybe he didn't know anything."

"So why kill...?"

Fletch's voice rose and he motioned to stand, but remained seated. "I don't know. I don't know anything, like I said. But, maybe by the time his assailants figured out he didn't know anything," Burkholder looked Terrell in the eyes, "he knew too much. Sometimes that happens."

Terrell could feel the frustration building in his chest. Del had died because he knew nothing, and then found himself unable to escape a bad situation. "So this agent was just a victim of bad timing?"

"How would I know? How long have you been at this? You know how often that happens." Burkholder kicked the coffee table a few inches. "Wrong place, wrong time."

The door opened and Tompkins stuck his head in. "A word?" Terrell pointed to Burkholder and then himself. Tompkins pointed at him.

———

"Fletcher Burkholder. I'm going to kill him." The scratchy voice on Tompkins phone was a recording.

Terrell couldn't believe his ears. "You've got to be kidding me."

"This was intercepted about an hour ago. They don't know the voice, but the intent is rather clear," Tompkins said.

This trip really has been a waste of time. Terrell thought about next moves. He knew his was to leave. "Sounds strange, though."

"In what way?"

"You said that the guys who intercepted this noted that everything before and after the call was too noisy to get a good read on the rest of the message." Terrell reached into his pocket for his phone. Not there.

"What's your point?" Tompkins asked.

"Isn't the message rather obvious? I mean, the odds of us getting to hear it are rather astronomical, but," he rubbed his forehead, "we did. And the only part worth listening to is the part we can hear."

"I'm not in the coincidence business. We need to get him out of here."

"I want to ask him a few more things. Just five more minutes."

"Special Agent? Don't you think you've already done enough damage?" Tompkins held up Terrell's phone and ice bag.

35

GETTING IN POSITION

It didn't take Anna very long to pack what few things she'd brought with her. She knew the people at the embassy had followed her as far as they could, using the street cameras. She was still too new at this thing to be any good at avoiding them. At one point, she sat in a chair in the corner and waited for the police to show up like they had that day seven years ago. Her eyes glazed just a touch. The memories were starting to have less and less of an impact on her, but for now the one thing she remembered was the shock. The loneliness. The abandonment.

She focused on her breathing and thought about holding her legs close to her, but didn't. The chair wasn't that comfortable or large enough to start the process of self-incrimination and second-guessing.

Her father was never coming back. More than anything she wanted to know why. Was that what motivated adopted kids to seek out their birth parents? To discover what they may, or may not, have done to make them less than worthy?

She was startled by a bump against the brownish wall. More bumping. What were they doing that needed them to hit the wall so often?

She looked along the bottom of her door. Shadows moved back and forth like ghosts at a train station. People leading normal lives. That could have been her. She was smart enough, but not motivated enough. She envied people who knew their direction. Their strengths and weaknesses. Anna could only think of her weaknesses.

Maybe she was the ghost?

Sometimes she thought of hurting herself again. Those were times she was not proud of, but they would always exist in her mind as proof that she still felt something. She wondered what it would be like not to hurt any more.

She was sinking. *I have to stop. If I go, he goes first.*

The phone chirped. She jumped toward the bed, but before grabbing the phone, she stood up, straightened her hair, and then reached for it as if she was making a date wait. Random parts of conversations filled her mind.

They're moving him.

What? Why?

Because they know something, that's why. What could they know?

The phone chirped again and she dropped it. She picked it up and answered.

"You seemed to have caused an international incident."

"Listen, I'm not in the mood," she said.

"I'm not kidding. Apparently, the work you did to find your father accidentally got discovered and things are rather disturbed in the Justice Department."

"That was your software. What do you mean it got discovered?" Anna started to pace. She waved her hands as if the Voice was in the room with her.

"The software obviously had a problem."

"You mean a bug. You gave me buggy software to break into a government system. Every time I think I'm starting to work with you, you do something stupid. I thought the software shouldn't have been writing the database to my box. I saw it and I knew that was bad news."

"Don't worry. It's only caused everyone in the program to be moved."

Anna let her head tilt back and closed her eyes. "Everyone?"

"It is getting rather expensive helping you find your father."

"How expensive?"

"When you consider there are about seventeen thousand people in the program at a cost of about $10 thousand each..."

"$170 million," she said.

"I hope he's worth it."

"He's obviously worth it to you. Your software did this."

"A moot point. It's not where the arrow was aimed, but what it hit. And you were the archer."

"I've told you once before you need to send me back."

"And we will. As soon as you're done. You're closer than you've ever been."

"Where is he?"

"Don't want to keep hunting?"

"Not if you can give me that answer."

"We have a connection. After you found him the first time, we've been keeping track of him. We know exactly where he is.

"You have to draw him out. You can't let them see you or his protection detail will kill you," the Voice said.

"If I just go to the police, they can take me to him," Anna said.

"They'll arrest you on illegally entering the country. You won't ever see him. Certainly not long enough to finish what you came here to do."

Anna walked over to a bureau, pulled out a ball of clothing, and dropped it on the bed.

"How do I draw him out?"

"I'm afraid you'll have to work that out. Perhaps you can let him catch a glimpse of you. He seems fond of standing in front of windows."

"Why don't you kill him? You know someone tried to kill me before I left."

"Who do you think notified the authorities that someone was trying to kill you?"

Anna stopped. He had saved her life? "How are my aunt and uncle?" she asked.

"They're fine. They wonder why you don't join them."

"Once this is over."

"Yes, once this is over."

She unrolled the ball. The gun fell out. "I don't like this burner phone."

"Better than the average smart phone."

"It weighs a ton. And you're on it."

"Time to go to work," he said.

———

Time to go to work. Right.

Anna sat with her notebook open on her lap as she browsed for a new destination. She decided she didn't want to come back to the Shellington, but wherever she went next had to be for a better reason than just a place to sleep. Coming back to any hotel didn't make sense to her, but she needed something to give her the feeling she was thinking a few moves ahead. The mildewy smell, the tired bed, chair, windows, and curtains were about all she could take. Even the AC sounded like it had been working well past retirement age.

Maybe it was time for an upgrade.

The Pestana Chelsea Bridge Hotel. That looks like a nice place to stay.

She booked a suite.

———

Anna stepped out of the hotel with her handbag slung on her shoulder and the gun hidden toward the bottom of the bag. She hated the bag. Not enough pockets. She wore a pair of sunglasses and loose hair. She wasn't used to it, but she hoped it made her look different enough from how she looked when she went to the embassy that they wouldn't notice her.

She flicked a glance at one of the cameras without turning her head. Were they watching her right now? Were they just waiting for her to come out? She quickly walked up the street, checking for cars that might be there for reasons other than belonging in the neighborhood.

Nothing.

Were the British authorities just as bad as the Americans? She entered and left the embassy, not doing much to hide who she was. If they were looking for her, they were doing a piss poor job. She had to be wanted for assault, at least. She hoped she hadn't hurt the attaché too much. It wasn't his fault that Anna panicked and ran. In any other circumstance, she would have asked him out for a coffee, or a tea in this case. Would he have accepted? He was probably married. Or going out seriously. An exclusive relationship. Or he didn't have time for a girlfriend. All the latest excuses.

Doesn't matter. Time to go find Dad and show him how much I miss him for leaving me alone for seven years.

———

The directions to the safe house came in a text a few minutes later. She mapped it on her phone. She would have to take a cab most of the way and then walk so she could get a lay of the land. If she needed to hide or run, she had to make sure she could.

Her dad was in the middle of nowhere a few days ago. Now he was in the middle one of the neighboring areas just outside of London. Yeah, she was going to have to figure out how to get him to come out alone. And avoid the police. And the U.S. Marshals. And anyone else who thought they had a problem with her.

She waved down a cab and gave him an intersection about half a mile from the address.

36

SHOOT TO KILL

A feeling rose in Terrell's chest, spread to his shoulders, and tickled the back of his head like a piece of steel wool. The U.S. Embassy hallways were enormous, the front lobby even more so, and yet human beings gravitated into his space unbidden. The late afternoon light streamed through the large, plate glass windows of the embassy lobby and the echoes of dozens of footsteps bounced around him. Light-colored marble tile. A man with a long stick and a rubber ball attached at one end rubbed scuffmarks off the floor.

He looked back down at the picture Conrad had just downloaded to his phone via secure link. The picture was not as clear as he would have expected out of the cameras circling the U.S. Embassy, but the cameras had been there for a few years. A young woman on the street. The face was not as clear as her clothing, but clear enough. Hard to place her age. Light complexion. Dark hair.

He put the phone back to his ear. Was he feeling protective?

"So that's her?"

Conrad called him on the new Bureau phone Terrell had acquired from the local FBI office at the U.S. Embassy. "That's her. The bloody fool decided to talk to her without security and she knocked him out cold."

Terrell wasn't sure what crime had been committed that he had to give up his cell, but he was more than willing to relinquish it. The phone was the last link to whoever he was hiding from and Burkholder wasn't talking about who that was. If this was the kind of person WitSec was protecting, Terrell was glad not to be involved. The few answers he had received were enough to tell him that Burkholder was involved in something big. Really big. So big that the reason he was in WitSec was because it was the perfect permanent security detail. After talking to Tompkins' boss, Terrell got confirmation that Burkholder had to be kept alive until the day he decided to talk, but no one knew when that day was. He had never asked to see his daughter before, but he was becoming almost obsessive about it.

Something was about to happen — Burkholder knew it — and he was running out of time. Seeing his daughter was an emotional plea that someone like Burkholder never made unless the stakes were so high that he was afraid for someone's life. Not his. Hers.

And now this woman. Asking for someone in witness protection. Could she be looking for Burkholder? That was not the name she gave. It could just as easily be one of his previous aliases. Terrell didn't bother getting any details so he didn't know who she was asking for or what her name was. She had a fake passport and that was enough.

"You know we need to verify that photo with the pictures taken of her in the embassy. She doesn't look familiar to me so she's not on any of the immediate watch lists. But then the picture isn't exactly one of your best." He walked through the streets again, away from the U.S. Embassy and toward his hotel.

"How did your interview go?" Conrad asked.

"Oh, about as well as can be expected."

"So you didn't get what you wanted?"

"No, but I think I got what I came for. You and I need to compare notes a bit before I head back. Do you have time for dinner?" He knew that Conrad would be available even if it was late into the night. He and Conrad got along and had a great working relationship. At least, that was what Terrell hoped. Conrad could just have been milking him for information. Sometimes it was hard to tell when help was sincere or with a price. He corrected himself: *Information always came at a price.*

"I think I can make an exception for you." Conrad chuckled on the other end of the line and then got serious. "You realize that we have our own people looking for her?"

"That's what I would expect. Is that not protocol anymore?"

"Terrell, as I mentioned earlier, your timing is rather interesting. Yes, that is protocol, but there are some things that just seem, well, odd."

This was the conversation he had hoped to have a few days ago. Well, he had the time now.

"Anything you need to tell me right now?" Terrell asked.

"Her passport. It was fake," Conrad said.

"Old news."

"It was registered with e-passport."

"Are you kidding?" That was near impossible. In fact, the only thing immigration worried about these days was academics poking holes into the system. No one got through the new immigration system. Overall, the only people who tried were the amateurs. Even the intelligence community was having a hard time deciding what to do about the improved immigration system. Without the ability to create fake passports, new identities were always going to be problematic during travel.

"Not only am I not kidding, you must understand that the only way she could have gotten into the system was with help from someone on the inside, or some group that has access to the system to begin with. As usual, the Chinese are a favorite, but it could just as easily have been Anonymous. Or an American agency."

"Your systems are better than that and my people aren't that stupid."

"I know, but the possibility that she's with a foreign power means that we have to take her entry into the UK with utter seriousness. We have to find her."

"So what's the problem? Find her."

"We're trying. But I must admit I fear for your life."

Terrell stopped. "What are you telling me, Conrad?"

"I'm telling you that we have not sent this picture to your comrades at the Bureau or the embassy yet. And that's on my order. Even how we found the picture is unusual."

Maybe Terrell wasn't going home after all.

"We have people, very few people, coming through with fake passports anymore. How did she do it?" Conrad asked.

He didn't need to hear anymore. A foreign power with a strong cyber-muscle did it, and there weren't that many of them around. After the US there was China, Russia, maybe North Korea.

"You have to send that picture in," Terrell said.

"I will, but something's not right."

Terrell briefly thought about Anna and her father and just as quickly jumped back to his present predicament. What could not be right?

Conrad continued, "We need to talk. I'm hearing things that don't add up and haven't been adding up for," Terrell was sure he could heard the gears in Conrad's head turning, "shall we say, a considerable amount of time."

"Okay, okay. Under any other circumstance we wouldn't link her to Burkholder, but she mentioned WitSec so we make the leap and connect her even though I'm hoping they're not connected."

"It almost doesn't matter anymore. We received orders from your government about her even before we had the street photo. I haven't seen the orders, but they seem rather serious."

"How serious?"

"I didn't know myself until we had to notify Scotland Yard about her," Conrad said.

"Alright. This is what I'm going to do. As long as I have some kind of connection with Burkholder, I get to pretend I care and make sure nothing happens to him. I'll head back to the safe house and try to keep everyone calm. I don't need a dead witness on my hands."

"Or perhaps a dead American female."

Terrell was about to push his way through the door to the outside when he stopped. "Why would I worry about that, Conrad?"

"The orders that were given to your people, and to Scotland Yard, which made its way down to the Bobbies, are shoot to kill."

And there it was again. The heavy feeling in his chest. Why would he feel protective about Burkholder? Or was he feeling protective of someone else?

37

———

LOST IN THE CROWD

The cab dropped Anna off a little further away than she had hoped, but distance was good as it gave her time to think. The street was the kind of place that Anna would expect to see on a postcard, or billboard. Clean, a lot of small shops. If she had been blindfolded and dropped into this area, she would have known she was in the UK, but not have a clue as to how she knew that. Most of the shops had freshly painted professional signs with either white or yellow serif lettering on a black background. In the distance, she heard a police siren and it reminded her of a police series she watched on PBS one time years ago. The sound of the Doppler-shifted police siren recalled her room in Brooklyn, but not for very long. She turned a corner and the smell of rotting meat struck her.

Right. Stay on point.

The one odd thing was the lack of time to think things through. She felt like a puppet and she wasn't happy with that. She hated that she didn't know the guy's name she was working with — he certainly wasn't working with her — and that always made the conversations awkward.

A passing police car flew by with full lights and sirens and just missed her before she crossed the street. She stopped long enough to read the instructions on the asphalt to Look Right as the car came and went before she even had time to register that she was almost hit.

These guys are as bad as New York cops. Note to self: Always look right. The squad car had been going in her direction. She thought, in a twisted sort of way, that the car was good luck. She could follow them and then veer off and head to wherever it was that they had Marshall. She was within a mile. She noticed the crowds and thought that was good luck, too. A lot of people so a lot of ways to get lost in a crowd if she needed it. Her hands felt sweaty.

Her bag vibrated. Would they ever leave her alone?

"You're not making me less nervous," Anna said.

"If that will keep you focused, stay nervous," the Voice said.

"Say what you have to say and then leave me alone." Anna turned to face the stop windows as much to look inside as to avoid the street cameras.

"Your stunt at the embassy has made your life more difficult."

"How much more?" She walked faster.

"Very much more."

That was it. It was over.

"Can you get me out?" she asked. Anna slowed herself down.

"We are not deserting you. You will be picked up and taken to a plane that is waiting for you just outside of your area. You're heading home. There is no need to do this now."

"I'm not leaving yet. I'm within a mile of where he's being kept." Anna did her best to keep her voice down and still walk toward her goal. "I can do this." *I can do this. I can make him pay attention.* Her pace picked up.

"I know you can. You don't have to. There will be other opportunities."

Great! He was being protective.

"This is one of them. I can do this. Get me out after."

"I would like to agree, but things don't look good for you. Your picture is being circulated."

"I look different than when I went to the embassy." She stopped and examined her reflection. She looked different.

"Good. But that doesn't change that things have gone from bad to worse."

Anna almost slipped as he spoke. *You're not helping!* She slowed her pace to a walk. Her father wasn't going anywhere.

"Remember that man who was sent to kill you back in Pennsylvania? There's another one. And he's part of the protection detail around Marshall. He knows what you look like and he's dressed up like one of the locals."

"I'm going to be shot by a Bobbie?"

"I'm glad you find some amusement in this."

"We are not amused." Damn it! She was walking too fast again. Anna could feel a level of hyperactivity starting to kick in. She knew this was a normal part of how her body reacted to stress. The higher the stress, the higher the hyperactivity. "Look, you got me in, I screwed up the follow-through because I thought I knew better, and now I know better." She walked with confidence though the crowd. She knew that she would be at the cross street soon enough. So many people. So many ways to get lost.

"If you're serious about this..."

"As serious as a heart attack," she said.

"Then you're going to have to find your way to the back of the building where he's being kept. He is on the first floor because that is the easiest to secure and he seems to like looking out the rear window."

"He does?"

Must be a new habit. Marshall hated windows. Almost every window in their house had windows treatments that were closed the vast majority of the time. The materials were beautiful. He had an eye for fabrics. She used to hide behind them when they would play hide and seek. She never liked hiding in the closet. One time she was so frantic to find a place to hide that she ran into one of the closets and was so scared she couldn't get out. It was dark and she was five, and she was shivering. When he hadn't found her after a few minutes, he opened every door, moving every bed, couch, table, wardrobe that he could find until he opened the closet and found her. She jumped out screaming and held him until she fell asleep in his arms.

The afternoon air was a little chilly. She drew her jacket closer while still holding onto the phone.

"After this call throw the phone away," the Voice said.

"Got it, boss."

"Not boss. Benson. And don't forget to dispose of the phone."

"Right," she hesitated, "Benson. Why are you telling me your name now?"

"We'll be on the lookout for you. On your way to the safe house there's a hardware store, Romany's, an ironmongery, so remember where it is. On Brewer Street and Great Pulteney."

"Ironmongery. Is that a brand?"

"Pay attention. That's just what they call hardware stores. Get back there as soon as you can and we'll pick you up. The confusion should be enough to give you time to get there safely."

"If something goes wrong, I won't have a way to contact you," she said.

"I have people all over the area."

Anna turned and looked behind her.

"Don't look around. Every camera in the neighborhood is trained on you and they'll use that as a marker to follow you later when they figure out which one of the dozens of people walking around are the one who did in your father."

If you live each day as if it was your last, someday you'll most certainly be right. Anna walked faster.

"Take a breath. Blend in. Don't do anything that will make you a target. Remember, he has a security detail and someone is out to kill you. The one thing you don't want is be an obvious target."

"You're right. I should be an unobvious target."

"Your father knows you're coming."

She stopped. "He does?"

"It will be the only way for you to draw him out. He will want to meet with you. That's why he's willing to stand by the window. He'll find a way to get to you."

He was waiting for her. She slowed her walk as she pondered that knowledge.

He was going to come out and meet her. Would he even recognize her? She was different. It was seven years after all. She grew a little. She was wearing stylish sunglasses. She had on a jacket he'd never seen before. He was so particular about her dressing habits. He knew every item in her closet. He used to say, as he tapped his head, that his pattern matching software was not that good so he had to make sure he knew what she looked like and what she might wear on any given day.

What would he say about her gun?

38

OBSCENE CALL

Terrell's cell displayed *Private*. It was a new phone, but that didn't seem right. Was that the default setting? No, it should have shown the incoming number.

Terrell's hotel, the Union Jack Club on Sandell Street, was not a location he was used to staying at, given how seldom he came to London, but at Conrad's recommendation, he had decided to try. Being across the street from the Waterloo Station Tube stop should have meant something to him, but he was already frustrated by the fact that he had to drive out into the middle of the English countryside to ask mere questions of a man who had perhaps earned his protection, but maybe didn't deserve it. The hotel turned out to be an oasis of calm for Terrell. Now if he could only return to the States in one piece.

Burkholder was in the middle of something and that something was starting to make itself known. His security detail was good, but there were just too many things. Del, Burkholder, the young woman. How were they related? Why had Del died when he didn't know anything, but then knew too much?

His BS detector was starting to go off and he wasn't happy about it at all.

He answered the cell. He hoped it was a telemarketer or an obscene phone call. He needed the downtime.

"Special Agent Terrell Garrison?"

Terrell stopped short on the blue and gold rug in the lobby on his way to the elevator. The voice was muffled and deep. Whoever was calling was using an audio filter to change the sound of their voice. He looked at the phone again. No other information except the elapsed call time information.

"No. He's not here right now. Would you like me to get him?"

"Tell him someone is on their way to kill Fletcher Burkholder. The woman from the embassy incident. If he goes to the corner of Waterloo Place and Pall Mall by the Royal Opera Arcade, he might be able to stop her before she gets there."

"Who's calling, please?" *Click.* "Hello?" The caller was gone. Someone was on their way to kill Burkholder? He cursed to himself. What wasn't Conrad telling him this time?

He dialed the first number he could think of. Conrad's voicemail kicked in. Terrell hung up and ran out of the hotel. Who else did he know? Another call to make. No point getting into his car. A cab would be faster.

"United States Marshals. Deputy Marshal Owen speaking."

"Connect me to Deputy Marshal Tompkins here in London. I just received an anonymous tip that there's going to be an attempt on the life of his witness."

———

"I think you need to stay away," Tompkins said.

This was going to be one of those calls, Terrell thought.

"Deputy, I swear to you that I am only here to help. I wouldn't be calling you otherwise. Your witness knows what's going on and isn't saying. He is putting all of you at risk."

"This has happened before and we weathered it rather well."

It had? Terrell made a mental note to check that out. A witness with multiple attempts on his life was obviously being followed by determined people. Was that why he was brought to the UK?

"I know you can." Persuasion 101: Let the other person think you agree with them before disagreeing. "I'm just calling to let you know that whatever was done before had better be instituted again. I don't have confirmation, but better safe than sorry." Terrell chin still ached from his encounter with Burkholder. "In his case, I might make an exception."

"Understood. Get yourself to the embassy and coordinate this from over there. I know you'll be a better help there than here. All we need is Fletch having another episode."

Tompkins was calling him Fletch? Terrell was never happy with anyone calling a witness by their familiar name to other law enforcement personnel. Not professional. There was a level of comfort that a witness needed, but outside of that zone they were another resource and had to be treated as such. What was Tompkins playing at?

"Right. The embassy. Listen, lock him down. Hide the security. Make the target look appealing. Take her down. Got it?" Terrell asked.

"I'm pretty sure we've got it."

Terrell managed to flag down a local police car a few blocks from the hotel. The single officer was not used to accommodating requests from random American law enforcement officials, but he made an exception for Terrell.

At least, that's what the officer told him. The main dispatch connected him with Scotland Yard. Terrell stood outside the squad car with the officer a measured distance away.

"Right, so use my cell number to track where the call came from. I've already notified the people on my end and they're doing what they can, but I know your people will do better faster."

"Thank you, Agent Garrison. This is probably the confirmation we were looking for."

"No problem." He was about to disconnect when a thought occurred to him. "What are your men going to do when they find her?"

"She will be given minimal opportunity for surrender. I expect one of the security detail will shoot her."

"No, you can't do that."

"I assure you we can. We will, in fact, be doing that if there is the slightest possibility that someone matching her description is found in the area. Their orders are to detain anyone matching her description. If she resists, she will be forcibly detained. If she actively resists," meaning with a weapon, "they will take the appropriate measures."

Jesus Christ. "Okay, I understand. I would prefer that you simply follow her and get the subject out of the area. She is more valuable alive."

"They all are, but we can't afford to lose any lives. Are you telling me this tip is not necessarily reliable?"

"No, I'm not telling you that..." Was he really having this conversation? *Don't kill the target.* They are always more valuable alive and you didn't have to explain anything to their closest living relative when you accidentally killed the wrong person.

"If this is a credible threat, and you seem to think it is, then we need to act with all due haste on this. Were you given any additional information?"

"If I tell you, you'll just kill her," Terrell said.

"As I have already told you, we will attempt to apprehend her first. What happens after that will be completely up to her."

"No, there is nothing else. Get to the safe house and lock it down. Don't move him yet because the target will be scared away. You want her as much as I do. Prep the area, but hide your men. If she sees too much activity, she's liable to call it off," Terrell said.

"We don't want that to happen. Are you sure you don't have any other information? It sounds like it was a quick call."

"It was," Terrell said.

"You realize that if anyone is withholding information, we can arrest them as well."

Are you kidding me? Now we're doing veiled threats?

"I understand. I will be sure to get back to you with anything else that I might remember." *Right.* First he would let the Bureau know what was going on. He didn't want to find himself being detained just so the Brits could send a message that even U.S. law enforcement couldn't mess with them.

"Don't worry, Special Agent. Our Special Forces team will do you proud."

Terrell ended the call. *Special Forces? Great. Guys with bigger guns.* He pulled his phone out and looked at the picture of the young woman again. What was it that was so familiar?

He would work it out as he went along. Time to move. "Officer, may I ask a favor?"

"Of course, sir."

"I need you to take me to Royal Opera Arcade on Waterloo."

"Yes, sir."

The officer jumped in on the right side and Terrell jumped into the left passenger side to sit next to him. The officer grabbed Terrell's wrist as Terrell started to put on his seat belt.

39

RANDOM NEXUS

Kevin and Paul looked out their second story window and knew there was a plainclothes cop walking in their alleyway. There was just something about the way they walked or looked around that gave them away. The two friends had known each other for years growing up together in this otherwise quiet section of London and the one thing they knew, a shared knowledge, was who was a cop and who was not. The other thing they knew was that the police were there to be pissed on. *Simply returning the favor.* They saw police or plainclothes cops coming and going through the years and ignored them as much as possible or ran away from them otherwise.

Kevin had decided that the weather meant more video games while Paul wanted to go out and look for that girl he liked from school. This afternoon, what Paul wanted didn't matter. Kevin was hiding out from his mates and Paul's place was as good a place as any to hide out. Paul room was comfortable and had a great view of the alley. It was usually empty, except for things like disgustingly old dumpsters, but on occasion, they would see one of their mates, or a teacher, making a buy. The homes were brown and shades of brown. Roof brown, brick brown, dark door brown, and, Paul's favorite, poop brown.

In the police report that would be written up after the incident there was mention of a possible connection between the alleged assassin and the two boys and much attention was drawn to them and their plight as lower-income children in troubled households; right now, they were just 2 boys out to play a prank.

Paul suggested setting up the speakers at their window.

———

In the middle of the mobilization of London's law enforcement personnel Fletch Burkholder stood by the window facing the alleyway and waited. He knew that making himself visible was a bad idea, but no one knew what he and Special Agent Garrison had discussed, except for Garrison and the assholes on the other end of Garrison's phone. He had learned to hate cell phones over the years, given how often he was involved in leveraging them to surveil more people than he cared to acknowledge. It all looked so romantic and dashing on television.

"Where can I get some water around here?" Fletch walked into the living room where another marshal sat reading a local magazine. Fletch refrained from shaking his head at his surroundings. Now that they were in London proper things could be even more British: the ceilings felt even lower, the water temperature varied when he tried washing his hands, and the sink looked like it had seen better days twenty years ago. And the walls? When did that shade of yellow become a color?

The marshal motioned toward the kitchen. Fletch walked over to the sink, found a glass that didn't look like a reject from a horror movie, poured himself some water, and leaned against the counter.

Whatever was going on couldn't be related to him. If they wanted him dead, he'd be dead, even if it meant launching a missile strike. But they were subtler than that. In the middle of London, it would be much easier to simply break in and poison his breakfast. They knew his habits. They knew everything they needed to know.

How did he screw up his life so bad that the people he worked with for so many years were now out to kill him if he said the wrong thing?

He returned to the window. A lone man wearing a short jacket and his hands in his pockets walked down the alley. Just another Brit out of central casting.

Fletch turned and yelled out, "Can someone get Tompkins on the phone?"

———

"I'll talk to him later." Tompkins motioned the officer away and stood with a small group of plainclothes officers at the corner of the row homes. He hoped this would be over soon, but knew that there was no predicting what would happen next. Special Agent Garrison was a good source of intel after all.

———

Fletch blinked his tired eyes. Waiting was never high on his list of useful tasks, but he also knew it had kept him alive so far. He walked back into the living room with the bored officer. He saw the folder on the coffee table and almost reached for it, but stopped until the officer gave him a glance. He nodded ascent, and Fletch opened it on his lap. The first thing he saw was the photo.

"Look familiar?" The officer looked over the edge of the publication.

Fletch didn't hesitate. "Not at all." He held up the photo of the woman. The camera was fairly new and the level of detail was quite good. He always knew when they were using the UK cameras, they were getting the best that could be offered in surveillance video. Yet, the face looked blurred out.

"That was taken outside the US Embassy. Are you sure?" the officer asked.

Fletch said nothing.

The Brits would not have been happy to know that the U.S. had tapped into their system almost as soon as the first batch of cameras were operational a few years ago. While the U.S. and Britain were partners, the U.S. was light-years ahead in terms of system penetration and was not afraid to use it, even against its friends.

Hesitation to do the things that needed to be done had killed more people than Fletch cared to remember. Hesitation would have tipped off the officer that Fletch knew something he wasn't telling. He returned the photo to the folder, stood up still holding onto it, and returned to his room.

Kevin and Paul wore headphones as they played another video game that they had picked up at the local game trader, and were quite caught up in shooting down the enemy army that had invaded their otherwise destroyed city.

40

LOUD SOUNDS

The cameras had been on as usual, but this time the officers were watching the neighborhood with the care reserved only for their children or a recalcitrant politician. Giving a quick look to the cameras a little further out was when one of the duty officers thought he saw something.

Crowds were crowds and they were out in full force this afternoon. Trying to place a face or a kind of walk or something out of the ordinary was plain difficult given the number of people that populate any major city and London was one major city. He looked. He examined.

He yawned. This kind of work was more taxing than being on a beat and even the most experienced officers admitted it. The more experienced the more stir crazy they became. Sitting and staring. Sitting and staring. Sitting and...

In a succession of blinks, the cameras in the neighborhood around the safe house began to shut down.

The officers around the safe house began receiving text messages: *Subject may be in the area. Cameras are out.* There was a universal, but unspoken, recognition: the messages told them nothing they didn't know a few minutes earlier except for the cameras.

Cameras are out.

———

In a well-known, but very secure, area of London all hell was breaking loose in the central dispatch area where all the various street cameras were monitored for both their streaming video and their status. Their status was what was at fault. They had all entered into hard refresh mode: first they took themselves off line, checked in with the central administration looked for updates, took care of downloading the updates, installed the updates, confirmed the installs were correct and not compromised, and then restarted themselves.

The first cycle was going to take about 5 minutes per camera, but at least they were all happening at the same time.

After the first cycle the administrators realized they were in trouble: the cameras were restoring their firmware to a previous state and going through the cycle again. They would have to go to every camera and manually update the firmware to stop the cycle from repeating.

All 300 cameras.

At the time, no one thought to check where the hard update command had come from.

———

Anna rounded the corner of the otherwise empty neighborhood and walked to where an alleyway split the block in half, giving her access to the rear of every three-story flat. She knew she was alone. She had thrown the phone away and had changed her appearance again when she entered a café she found on her way. Before, she had loose hair and wore thin reflective sunglasses. Her hair would have gotten in the way, more so if it started to rain. She wrapped her hair tight and put on a pair of sunglasses that took up most of her face.

She felt silly in the glasses. She never wore sunglasses unless she had to and she almost never did. They were heavy and did not improve her looks. She would live with the fashion nightmare for the moment but would ditch them the first chance she got...if she got away.

When, she corrected herself. *When*.

As she walked down the alley, she noticed that there was a torn open section of fence. The text was right; this was the spot. There was a dumpster opposite the yard the fence was meant to protect. She approached it with a slow step, but one of familiarity. She wanted to be mistaken for just another resident. Was there a special term for neighbors? Apartments were flats. Elevators were lifts. Neighbors must have a special term.

She was certain they called homicides "homicides".

She walked along the wall opposite the fence with the gap. One step. Two steps. She peered over the sunglasses and saw the beginning of the picture window surrounded by worn brick and badly placed mortar.

"Excuse me, miss!"

She stopped and then took another few steps. She could see more of the window.

"Miss!"

She turned and saw that the man pointed a gun at her. Chocolate brown pants, light brown windbreaker, bulky chest that didn't match his height. He was wearing a vest.

She took her hands out of her pockets and raised them.

"What have I done? What have I done?" *Would helpless female work?*

"Put your hands on your head and don't move!"

Oh, no. She placed her hands on her head. *It was a trap.* The officer approached her but never took his eyes or his gun away from her.

"I thought British police didn't have guns?"

"Be quiet! Put the gun on the ground."

She sized him up. Disarming him was never going to happen if he didn't come closer. She hadn't taken out her gun and yet he was sure she had one. *C'mon. Come to me.*

He didn't move any closer.

Then the shooting began.

―――――

Paul looked out the window and saw a man and a woman in the alley before the man took his gun out. He thought it was time.

Kevin was so immersed in the game that he didn't notice Paul walking over to his stereo watching exactly what Kevin was doing. Paul knew it was almost time for Kevin to reload and that he usually just threw away his current weapon and would upgrade to something bigger.

Kevin was out. Down came the menu. Up came the selection of armaments. *Awesome!* Heavy-gauge repeater with armor piercing bullets.

Paul changed the audio output to the speakers with the flick of a switch.

―――――

The air filled with the sound of gunfire. The officer looked toward the window to his right and Anna lunged at him. She knocked the gun out of his hand, and he swung but missed as he tried to get her back in position. She had to get out of there. She should have listened to Benson the first time. The operation was compromised and she had to go.

Her bag fell from her shoulder. The officer grabbed his gun and began shooting toward the sound of the gunfire. She didn't see anyone firing, but the explosions were overwhelming.

The follow-up sounds came. Background music. It was a video game. The officer looked at her and then at the ground. Her gun had fallen out of her bag. She gave herself one last turn and smashed him across the face. He fell unconscious.

She looked at the picture window. There was a man in front of it with no one else around him. He had somehow, miraculously, not seen her.

She fired three times toward the window. The first shot caused the plate glass to shatter. While the man turned away from the falling glass, Anna aimed and fired again. And again.

What now?

She ran.

PART III

THE CHASE

41

CRIME SCENE

The decoy safe house started losing personnel as soon as the call came in from the real safe house: the woman had appeared where she wasn't supposed to be and the few officers protecting Fletch had been caught with their knickers down.

The worn brick facade of the homes on Frith Street made it difficult to tell one house from the other. The police cars, in white and green, blended with the gray shadows of the clouds that covered everything. The quiet neighborhood became a riot of sirens, and colours, and people who had not seen this level of activity on their block in years if at all.

Tompkins was seething. Someone told. Or someone was listening. He ran around the building to the alley (*doesn't smell any better here than in New York*) and found the injured officer being placed on a gurney for an ambulance ride to the Royal London Hospital, which, with no traffic, would be about 9 minutes, but today would be about 30.

"What happened?" Tompkins grabbed at the injured man's clothes and stopped the EMTs from pulling him into the vehicle. The gurney felt cold. "Where did she go?" An officer to his left put his hand on Tompkins' shoulder. Tompkins released his grip and the officer slid into the ambulance. Tompkins turned to the man to his left. "What the hell happened?"

"I can tell you what didn't happen: the man on the roof was patrolling the front of the building when the woman fought this officer to the ground here in the back. And some kids."

"Kids?"

"Playing video games. They put their speakers to their window and started playing their game. Lots of explosions and firing."

"Arrest them. They were probably working with her," Tompkins said.

"We have some officers going over to the flat right now."

———

Fletch looked out the shattered window at the chaos. Shards littered the floor with the occasional piece cracking under his heavy step. The locals had tried to shove him into a squad car, but, in so many words, he told them he would rather stay for the parade. Some of the persuasion involved disarming two of the officers and tossing their guns in the squad car. Tompkins wouldn't let anything happen (*good ol' Deputy Dog!*) and these people seemed to be used to this level of stupidity.

Whoever that woman was she knew what she was doing. Her aim didn't suck; she had no intention of killing him. If she did, he would have been dead.

That was a very screwed up warning. A little heavy-handed, but he knew a warning shot when he saw one.

When the first bullet hit, everything went into slow motion. Glass shattered. The momentary explosion of sound that gave everyone bad hearing for at least a few minutes. After a certain number of incidences involving gunfire, the slow-motion effect was something he was used to. He also got a look at the shooter. Not a good one, but the photograph he had viewed earlier, which had not interested him in the slightest, was now quite interesting.

The safe house was going to need a paintjob and some new furniture.

He walked into the parlor. There was one British officer standing by the front door. They nodded, alpha to alpha, and Fletch decided to go to the kitchen. There had to be a back door somewhere.

The kitchen. Were all rooms in the UK designed for midgets? Low ceilings. Small rooms. How did anyone move around? The Brits were not short people. At least not the ones Fletch had seen so far. Old stove. Old table. Old chairs. Even Ikea had better furniture than this.

Another officer. Guard. Prison guard. Holding a rather large weapon. An MP5. The Brits have been upgrading.

"Let's take a walk," Fletch said.

"I'm sorry, sir. You're not allowed out for now."

"Oh, screw that."

The officer, wearing a navy protective vest, took a step before the door.

Fletch was just taller than he was and didn't have a weapon. "Come with me."

"We've been told you have to stay indoors. At least for the moment," the officer said.

"Call it in."

"Step away, sir."

Fletch looked into his eyes and stepped back. The man spoke into the radio attached to his left shoulder.

Fletch poured himself a glass of water and a cup of coffee from a nearby carafe. He drank the coffee as he watched the man. It didn't look good. He held the glass of water in one hand and the coffee in another and walked back over to him.

"I'm sorry, sir. You have to wait."

"You're right. You look thirsty." Fletch slammed the glass full of water into the man's head, dropping him to the floor. He opened the door with his now free hand and stepped out as the ambulance pulled away just past the gap in the broken fence. The grass was brown and crackled with every step he took toward the collection of people standing around, wondering what happened. Tompkins was the first to notice him.

"What the hell are you doing out here?" Tompkins stomped over to him. "Is the blown-out window not enough of a sign? How about the squad cars and ambulance?"

Fletch sipped his coffee. "Didn't notice. Whatever was going to happen has happened."

The officer who Fletch had hit with the glass came running out with his weapon pointed at Fletch. Tompkins waved him off. The man stood there and aimed his weapon, blood dripping down the side of his face where the glass had exploded.

"Stand down, soldier," Tompkins said.

Fletch took another sip of his coffee, and didn't turn around. The officer aimed his weapon one last time and then walked away.

"You hit him, didn't you?"

Fletch shrugged.

"What did you see?" Tompkins asked.

"Not a helluva lot. I heard gunfire, saw glass flying in every direction, and then I saw a running person. No one I know." Fletch continued his walk to the alley.

Tompkins walked with him.

"So this was an attempt on my life?"

"You don't look very concerned," Tompkins said.

"Am I supposed to be?"

"Whoever these people are they knew about the decoy safehouse. And they almost got you."

"They're not that smart." He stopped and gave the area a cursory glance. "They're just smarter than you."

They both heard a commotion behind them. Six fully armed officers came through the back door and stood behind Fletch. He put his hands in his pockets and sighed.

"If that photo was any indication..." Fletch said.

"You saw the photo? I think we have a positive ID."

"It was in a file on the coffee table." Fletch shook his head. "If that photo was any indication, you guys got done in by a girl." He looked over his shoulder. "You should be embarrassed." He took another sip.

———

In the house behind the real safe house officers were everywhere. It was a 2-story flat, as were all of the buildings on the block, and there were officers standing at the door, at the foot of the stairs, at the top of the stairs, at the doorway to the boys room, and 2 DCIs, Deputy Chief Inspectors, in the room.

"What were you boys doing?" The Deputy Chief Investigator was talking to Kevin who was sitting in the chair where he had been playing his game. Kevin kept looking at the floor. "You need to talk to me." Kevin looked up at him. "What happened?" The DCI touched his arm. "Why did you do this? Did you know the woman?"

The room was a typical boy's room. There were posters, magazines and video games everywhere and a sense of uncontrolled chaos that pervaded the area.

"Kevin?"

The DCI heard the ambulance getting closer. The siren was piercing. He stood and looked around the room. The speaker on the floor. The 42-inch LCD TV that Kevin probably got for getting mediocre grades. Kevin didn't look that smart. They were probably not going to get very far in asking him questions, but he knew that this might be one of their only chances to speak with him directly. This was one of those cases. The kind that the evening news cared about.

"Let's get what we can from here." The DCIs nodded at each other knowing that rather than a boring night at the station house filling in paperwork this was going to be a bad one. Whoever the officer was who fired at a virtual attack was going to lose everything.

The emergency personnel arrived with an orange plastic pallet that looked more like a surfboard with holes toward the top. The EMT looked at the blood soaked floor and knelt down next to Paul's lifeless body.

42

EMERGENCY EXIT

Where is everybody?

Anna turned the corner and walked a beeline to the ironmonger's. She saw an otherwise empty street with the rare bit of litter blowing by with the occasional pedestrian taking a calm stroll up the block. She was happy for the lack of shadows from the cloud cover. Her heart raced. Her foot hurt where her heel hit the man's face. She had practiced the move so many times that the spin was all muscle memory. In the heat of the moment, she thought only long enough to know that things had not gone as planned. She remembered the fight was short. She panted and tried to swallow, but her mouth was too dry.

She closed her eyes and breathed in. *They'll be here.*

Where are they?

A large black cab turned the corner, pulled up, and its door swung open. "You called for a cab?"

She looked up and down the block again. "Yes, I did."

She tried to get in with a sense of calm, but it was all she could do to keep from running again. Even the musty smell of too many passengers and not enough disinfectant did not stop her from entering. Fight or flight? She had done both. She slid in the black seat as the cab started its journey.

The driver hadn't asked her where she was going.

"Excuse me, but...?" she asked as the cabbie tossed a cell phone over his shoulder. It fell at her feet.

"You should put on your safety belt," he said.

She grabbed the phone from the grimy floor, sat back, and put on her seat belt. "Just in case." She felt the buckle snap into place. She could rationalize running from the embassy. Even from the officer she knocked unconscious. She wasn't sure how she was going to feel about a car chase through the streets of London. The situation was not improving and neither was her state of mind. She had lost her gun, they now knew what she looked like, and the street cameras were going to draw the entire planet to her location.

She thought for a moment. If she had her notebook, she might have been able to reset the traffic lights so her ride could flee uninterrupted. Maybe even turn off the cameras.

No. She never could have turned off the cameras. They must have firewall upon firewall and passwords upon passwords. The best she could have done would be to re-configure the traffic lights. She was sure she could do it, but it probably wouldn't be enough.

Anna jumped as the cell rang.

"Are you alright?" Benson said.

"Of course, I'm alright." It was all she could do to keep from yelling. "I thought you said he wasn't being protected."

"He's always under protection."

"I almost got shot!" She lowered her voice. "I almost got shot and someone let loose the sound of gunfire that was obviously recorded."

"I had nothing to do with that."

"It saved my life. It distracted the cop long enough for me to disarm him and..."

"You disarmed him?"

Anna blinked and looked out the window. "I have a history," she said.

"I forget that you didn't have much of a social life. Black belt, right?"

"Third degree. I just didn't like to compete."

"Thankfully. Fewer people in the hospital."

"I'm sorry, but you and your people are morons. I could have been killed."

"Did you think that murdering someone was the same as taking an exam?"

The word felt different coming from him. *Murder*.

"I told you I could handle it on my own and all you did was make sure I failed. Was that the plan? Because it sure looks like it."

"No, Anna. It wasn't. But finding him was. And you found him. It's safe for you to stand down."

"Stand," she gripped the phone tighter, "down? Are you crazy? After all that I've been through so far? There is no way in hell."

"This is not a test."

Wasn't it? "Call it anything you want, but I am finishing this. Are you telling me that you're going to bring him to justice or something?"

Benson sighed. "Something like that. Your father will be dealt with. You have my word."

A police car approached from the opposite direction. Anna turned inward. It whizzed by, followed by another and then another. Maybe Benson was right? How was she going to do this on her own?

"Fine. I need instructions on how I'm leaving so that when I'm done, there won't be any lag time. My flight has got to leave on time."

"When you're done?"

"Benson, do you understand that if I had followed my own advice, he would be dead? Dead. Not wounded. Not mildly surprised. Not ordering take-out. Dead.

"He's not because of you." The palms of her hands popped with sweat. Something felt wrong in the pit of her stomach. The words didn't ring true. She shook her head. Too many cobwebs. The scent of mildew in the interior of the black cab caused her throat to itch. "I don't believe it."

"We did the best we could."

"No, I think I'm having an allergic reaction to the moldy aroma in this cab." She looked at the cabbie who turned his head toward her. "No offense."

"None taken," the cabbie said.

What was she going to do? What she always did.

"Benson, figure out how to get me the information I need to get out of here. You're obviously following me somehow and I know it's not my phone because I don't have one with me."

"We're trying to protect you."

"OMG. Why don't you just kill him yourself?"

"I already told you: we just want to find him. I know you have a score to settle, but we need him alive."

"Then why send me?"

"Because we knew you would find him."

"Figure out how to get me the gosh darn exit information and I'll be in touch." She hung up, rolled down her window, and flung the phone out. She said to the cabbie, "Do you have another one of those?"

He lobbed another phone over his shoulder. She thanked him and sank back.

God, it's hard to find good help these days.

She closed her eyes. No more distractions. The wind touched her face and cooled her hot cheeks. *This is bad. Oh, this is so bad.* Was killing him really the answer? Anger churned in her stomach and shot up her chest. The nights she made excuses for his being gone. He didn't know where she lived. He was dead. He had amnesia. He was being held captive by terrorists (he was a government agent, after all).

One night, a few weeks after she moved in with the Stoddards, she packed her bag sure he was going to come get her. She fell asleep waiting.

So many nights. Going to class, and doing the one thing she knew how to do better than anybody. Better than him!

Yes, killing him was the answer.

43

REMOTE VIEWING

The temperature in greater London was going up. The clouds parted and let enough sunshine through that everyone knew the afternoon was going to be a scorcher with the added enjoyment of rising humidity. Everything was bright and in focus. The passing cars, the walking tourists, the too-tiny dogs wearing too-tight leashes going for their walk. Anna threw away her light jacket since she didn't have any place to put it, and decided it was almost time for Plan B: Send everyone away while she recuperated and worked out what to do next. Then she could move on to Plan C.

Her skin felt clammy, the goosebumps pushing out on her skin. She rubbed her arms and crinkled her nose. The aroma of trash did nothing for her hunger; her mouth watered and she wished she had had enough forethought to pick up some snacks on the way to her new hotel. Time for that later. She was still too wound up to think of snacks, lunch, or even dinner.

At the Pestana Chelsea Bridge hotel, located on Queenstown Road, the first squad car arrived. Anna knew it was a police car because she had seen plenty of PBS cop shows and the cars looked just like that one: lime green and white with a light bridge on the roof. Her stomach twisted. Maybe it was just the rotting food.

One time, she had to be less than ten, she had asked her dad (*Marshall!*) about a half-eaten bird she had found on the sidewalk outside their apartment shortly after they arrived in New York. She had seen plenty of photos of animals decomposing on various image sites on the web. The bird in front of her house looked like it had been cut in half. He stopped and stared at it. He pointed out the various parts that were still left and she was just fascinated that he knew so much about pigeons. She thought she was going to throw up and then didn't.

That was how she felt now, only she was the one who was going to be cut in half and she had too much work to do. *Time to delay becoming a dead pigeon.* Anna sat down at her PC. During her time at UPenn she had navigated through the dark web many times. She was always amazed at what she found and what others were finding and disclosing. Was this where her father lived? Were these the places he really hung out at? She drew comfort in the knowledge that they didn't share any genes. Anna was not a part of him nor he her.

It was time to play with traffic.

———

"Are you ready to go?" Tompkins asked.

Fletch was fed up with this man. Tompkins had worn out his welcome. Who could Fletch talk to about transferring him somewhere? Anywhere.

The safe house was like any other two-story location: a kitchen to one side, a living room to the other, a staircase, and bedrooms on the floor above. Not comfortable, but not a bad place to have a beer. That reminded him: Where could he get a beer?

"Okay, so you're not listening." Tompkins stepped around to face him. "Now that the decoy safehouse didn't work out, it's time to move you. And that would be now."

"You don't seem as concerned as you were earlier," Fletch said.

"Earlier, someone stole the entire WitSec database. Now, we just have to move you so whoever wants to kill you doesn't."

"What about the 'assassin'?" Fletch made air quotes. Whoever she was she could not have anything to do with his former colleagues. That was the sloppiest execution he had ever seen. And she left the one person who could identify her alive. She was obviously not a professional.

Never leave clues to your failed work.

"I think the locals have that well in hand," Tompkins said.

"Then I would rather stay here until they get back to you." He leaned against the wall of the kitchen where he and Tompkins had strolled into. "It could be a trap." He crossed his arms.

"You could only hope." Tompkins poured some water into a kettle. "Want some?"

"I prefer coffee to tea," Fletch said.

"I prefer hamburgers to fish and chips, but we all adjust." He turned on a burner and set the kettle down on the flame. He adjusted the flame higher.

"You can adjust. I want to get back into a routine. I have lots of things not to do." Fletch had to admit that the last few days have been more exciting than the last few years. Sitting around in the middle of nowhere exercising and watching the telly were not high on his list of to-dos. At one point, he had almost forgotten how much he hated WitSec, but he also knew that being under constant protection was his choice. It was the only one he had been given. He would never have gone to prison and he always held out hope that one day he would be reunited with his family. What little family he still had left.

———

The first indication that something was wrong was the sudden appearance of green traffic lights.

The first volley of police cars to the Pestana Chelsea Bridge hotel did not arrive all together though they had tried. Traffic was such a snarl that they had to send officers in full gear to direct traffic, clear intersections and get the various emergency vehicles to their desired location.

The dead-end street that was Queenstown Road was blocked off with cars that couldn't get in as other cars could no longer get out. As the hotel was on the Thames the cool smell of the water permeated the air even as the clouds kept the sunlight indirect.

The slight turn-off to the hotel was impenetrable which led the Special Operations Force Firearms Unit, the British version of the American SWAT team, to simply get out of their vehicles and run to the hotel as quickly as they could. The Armed Response Vehicles, or ARVs, would arrive when they arrived. If necessary, they would work with the vehicles and the men inside from a distance. Traffic notwithstanding, time was of the essence and they knew it.

The first of the operations officers arrived and began to clear the lobby. The officer-in-charge approached the reception desk, pulled out a photograph and placed it on the counter. "Has this woman checked in? She may or may not have used the names Annette Powell, or Anna Wodehouse."

———

A couple of miles away, Benson walked around his desk at the NSA offices in the UK to get another drink of water and then sat down for the play-by-play of what was transpiring down by the Thames.

Anna said she had not turned off the street cameras and yet here she was making them do pirouettes like they had all gone to Julliard. The rootkit on her notebook was telling them everything they needed to know about what she was doing and what she was doing was quite effective. In fact, she didn't need to turn the cameras into psychotic ballerinas given that now traffic around her hotel, and the latest safe house, was in such a pretzel that the Force Firearms Unit had to get there on foot.

She was rather good, this non-daughter of Marshall. He would see to it that she was taken care of one way or another.

A shame she wasn't just another civil servant running intel for Uncle Sam. With her combination of looks and brains she would have gone far.

If only her face wasn't known to the entire world now. She would be on the BBC tonight for sure and that was going to be bad for business. Benson flipped between street cameras showing the two hotels, and Scotland Yard audio feeds.

"...We have confirmation: subject is in the Pestana Chelsea. Lobby cameras confirm her arrival..."

"Team Lead at the Pestana: lock it down."

"Officers still arriving. Traffic is being cleared."

"Roger, that. Continue lock down. Do not approach the target. Repeat: do not approach the target."

Amateurs.

44

WALKING AWAY

Anna sat on the rough ground, looking at her notebook screen. She had four windows open on her hi-res desktop; one was a map of the area from British Traffic, another was a traffic cam (*How easy was that to hack? I gave them too much credit*), another was the hotel infrastructure dashboard, and the last was an elevator camera that cycled through various elevator banks. What an interesting view.

The camera showed the Force Firearms Unit sending officers into the elevators.

———

The Pestana has 5 banks of elevators. They were brought down to the first floor and passengers were escorted into the bar area where they were questioned and released. The cars was then further examined for any remaining passengers or items. The SO Force Firearms Unit, or CO19, officers went into each of the elevators and unscrewed the ceiling panels leading into the elevator shaft. One officer pushed his colleague up the narrow panel and onto the roof of the compartment.

The officers signaled to each other across the shafts, looked down and signaled to the officer in the car who then sounded off into their radios: "Clear!"

When all 5 cars were on the first floor, the elevators were disabled with one heavily armed officer standing on the roof of each.

———

Another group of officers sealed off the stairwells. One officer per lobby door and another officer at the exits of Anna's floor. Given that there were about 10 exits between the main building and the adjacent buildings, and that all of the roof exits were also closed off there was a total of 30 officers in play just at the doors.

As law enforcement personnel ran, and then walked, to the hotel it took some time to get enough officers into position.

They started with the lobby. The front doors were locked and guests were escorted out one at a time.

It would be impossible for her to walk out.

———

I wonder if it's too late to give myself up. She looked at the hotel dashboard. *Whatever. In for a penny, in for a pound. I guess that must be a British saying. I'll have to look it up later.*

———

The sprinklers started to go off on every floor, but just in the hallways. Inside the rooms not a drop was spilled. In the stairwells there was a light monsoon.

"CQ. CQ. Sprinklers on in stairwell 5."

"And stairwell 9." Every stairwell called in except for one: stairwell 7. They were sure there was something special about that location so another officer was dispatched in due haste.

Anna just couldn't figure out how to active it. *It must be under repair.*

―――――

In Scotland Yard, the cyberterrorism unit began their hunt for the culprit who was snarling traffic and hiding the population by aiming cameras at the sky.

They expected to find the network packets coming in from either China or a random Middle Eastern country. Not knowing why the attack occurred meant that all large scale options were in play. They were sure something definitive would happen which would give them a better sense of where they should be looking, but nothing much happened once the traffic lights went green and the cameras pointed up.

Within a few minutes, they found where the attack had come originated. The Pestana Chelsea Bridge hotel.

―――――

Anna marveled at what she had wrought. Or more accurately, what her notebook had wrought. She donned her white ear buds so that she could monitor the police bands. The accent was always so easy to understand.

Something caught her attention. They found the source of the infrastructure attack? And how did they do that? For a second she panicked. *Hold on. How could they do that?* Was she not routing her packets anymore? She looked at her Linux processes. Everything appeared normal...Oh, no! Her packet router had crashed! She slammed the notebook shut.

Stop. Think.

Think.

Okay, the program crashed. That could be the only explanation. Programs she had written along with some of the smartest people on the planet had crashed. Was there too much load? A memory leak? A rootkit screwing with system resources or network communication?

She cursed to herself. That bastard Benson. His software must have installed a rootkit. No wonder her machine rebooted on its own shortly after she inserted his USB key. How could she have been so stupid?

Wait. She had some of the best malware and virus protection anywhere. His key had installed and rebooted the machine without the anti-virus software going insane?

Wow. His stuff was good. That was bad.

So...too late. They knew where she was. Well, whatever. They were already storming Asgard. No point crying over unencrypted packets.

She opened her PC, restarted the packet router, and reset her MAC and IP address. She kept swearing at herself while she restarted the four windows she had up before. The traffic cams came up first. They were still twirling except for the one she kept trained on a subsection of them to let her see what was going on.

She turned that lone camera around. Where was this? *Great. The U.S. Embassy.* Another place she didn't want to see again. She hoped Benson was true to his word. This was not going to be the kind of thing for which she would get a slap on the wrist. This would be hard time. Federal time, but hard time nonetheless. Unless Interpol got involved. How did that change things? International court? She didn't find international law that interesting. Studying mold was more interesting than law, in her opinion.

She stood up. She was not going to hang around long enough to find out which jurisdiction was going to care. It was time to go.

In the distance, she heard the blaring of sirens. Fire trucks. They were never going to get to the hotel. She hoped that there were no fires in this London neighborhood for the next few hours. It would take them that long to clear out enough streets to get everything back to normal.

The alleyway she used as her command center was narrow and had blackened brick on either side for as high as she could see. The sunlight cut across the building, putting the entire alley in shadow which let Anna look at her screen without any annoying glare. She took a deep breath and coughed as the acrid fumes of the dumpster filled her lungs. The alleyway of the restaurant where she had decided to stop was gross even by New York standards. They would get a Health Department Grade-Pending-Stay-Away certificate. Leaving the hotel at the first sign of the police was the luckiest things she had done so far. They were serious. Now they needed to see how serious she was.

She slung her duffel bag over her shoulder and did her best to walk in absolute defiance of her amygdala and hypothalamus. *Fight or flight is overrated. Time to check on Dad.*

45

CALL TO HIGH PLACES

Fletch was in over his head. Tompkins had had enough and now was the time to show him who was boss. The safe house was no longer safe and he had the Brits breathing down his neck to move. Move where? Only MI5 knew for sure.

"I need you to get in the car, Fletch. We'll move your unpacked things, but you have got to be taken to another location," Tompkins said.

Fletch sat down on a flimsy aluminum folding chair reserved for a member of the protection detail. The chair buckled enough that Tompkins hoped it would collapse on itself and teach Fletch a lesson. Even a folding chair shouldn't have to go through so much. *Oh my God, he could act like a petulant child.* Tompkins watched Fletch cross his large arms. The back of Tompkins' shirt was pasted to his skin like very wide adhesive tape. Between the attempt on Fletch's life and the weather, Tompkins couldn't keep up with his laundry. On the other hand, Fletch's pressed striped shirt fit him to a T. As big a man as he was, his clothes fit him like they were tailor-made. Maybe they were.

"Listen, Tompkins, I know you mean well, but we're staying right here. Whoever that woman is, they're going to arrest her in just a few minutes. Are you telling me that we can't spare a few minutes?"

"We're guests in this country. They tell us to move, that means we move. Are you new to this?" Tompkins could not believe what he was hearing. The one thing he had to do, the only thing he had to do, was protect this man. And yet that seemed to be the one thing that Fletch didn't want.

"Then treat me like a goddamned guest. Leave me alone. Or bring me some tea." He motioned to the LCD TV. "You could turn on the TV until the news announces they found her and then we can go find out who she is."

"Why do you care so much?" Tompkins looked over at the blank TV screen and then back at Fletch. "Did you recognize her?"

"No, I'm just interested in knowing..."

"Oh my God, you recognized her." Tompkins turned to the officer standing by the door for a moment. He might need him soon. "Who is she? She's not your daughter."

"How would you know? Seen any pictures?" Fletch crossed his legs. "It's not her in any case."

Tompkins had not heard a bigger lie in his life. "Okay, I'm going to let you in on a secret: we already know her name."

Fletch sat up. "And?"

"I'm not telling you until they catch her."

"Good. I'm willing to wait for that moment."

Tompkins motioned to the guard who walked over with his MP5 at the ready and stood before the men.

"Is there a problem, gentlemen?" the guard asked.

"No," Tompkins said, "not yet. Please escort Mr. Burkholder to the vehicle behind the lead outside."

"Yes, sir." The officer looked down at Fletch. Even sitting, Fletch sat high in the folding chair. "Mr. Burkholder?"

Fletch jumped up and the officer jumped back, aiming his submachine gun at him.

"Sir, while you are under my protection, I will not hesitate to..."

"What?" Fletch asked. "Shoot me? Go ahead. If you want to lose your pitiful pension."

The officer stood frozen in place with his finger on the trigger.

Fletch slowly raised his hand and turned to Tompkins. "May I use your phone?"

"Of course not." What was he up to?

"Your phone, please. I need to call the State Department," Fletch said.

"Are you kidding?"

"Dial the number or I will shove the phone up your ass before this kid can fire off the first round."

Tompkins felt his face flush. It wasn't because he thought about what would happen if he could get Fletch to talk...

Tompkins dialed the main switchboard to State.

A recording kicked in. "Thank you for calling the Department of State of..." Tompkins handed the phone to Fletch.

Fletch listened and started responding to the prompts of the IVR, the Interactive Voice Recognition system, which always drove Tompkins crazy. He wished he could get the person who invented that alone in a room for an hour.

Fletch held the phone to his ear. Someone must have answered. "Yes, can I speak with the Secretary of State? Who's calling?" He looked at Tompkins and winked. "I'm sorry, dear, but if I told you then I'd have to kill you." He gave a loud guffaw. "Just kidding. Just kidding." He lost the smile in an instant and stared at Tompkins, who rubbed the sides of his legs. "Please tell him that Deputy U.S. Marshal Tompkins is on the line." Fletch rocked on the balls of his feet just once. "Yes, U.S. Marshals. It's of national importance." He winked at Tompkins and then at the guard. "Thank you."

Tompkins was ready to take the MP5 from the officer and use it on Fletch himself.

"You know who this is." Fletch's voice lowered an octave. Tompkins had not heard that tone before. "Yes, it's me. I can't tell you where I am, but apparently your boys had a break-in and lost the entire database." Fletch stood up straight. "I have a member of the U.S. Marshals here with me and he doesn't want me to stay put for a few minutes. Seems to be in a hurry to get me out and about." Fletch's hand tightened around the phone. "Yes, of course you can speak with him." Fletch handed the phone back.

Tompkins felt his cheeks grow hot. "Good evening, sir."

"Good evening, Deputy Marshal. This is Secretary of State Monahan. Do you recognize my voice?"

"Yes, I do, sir. I apologize for the late evening intrusion."

"Not a problem," Secretary of State Monahan said. "Always ready to help our people out in the field. I should say my people."

"I appreciate that, sir," Tompkins said.

"Good. I am only going to say this once and then I am going to hang up."

Tompkins gritted his teeth. He loosened his jaw muscle, but he gritted again.

"As long as that man is not causing an international incident, do as he says. Do your job, but do as he says. If he wants to stay in once place for a few extra moments, pretend he's going to the bathroom."

Tompkins looked toward a window. Fletch returned to his sagging chair and looked into the distance with a smile.

"No, pretend you're going to the bathroom. Like you're doing now."

Tompkins refused to look over at Fletch. "I understand, sir. I appreciate your time and, again, I apologize for the interruption." The line was dead before Tompkins finished his sentence. Tompkins ran his tongue over his teeth as he turned off the screen to his phone. "I didn't realize you had such interesting friends," Tompkins said. "A shame he's all the way over there and we're all the way over here." He turned to the officer again. "Please escort Mr. Burkholder to the car." He motioned another officer over. "And please put Mr. Burkholder in cuffs for the trip to the new location. It appears he's not in a cooperative mood today."

Fletch's face visibly relaxed. "I'm feeling very cooperative. If you want to put the ties on me, feel free." He put his wrists together in surrender.

"That won't be necessary," Tompkins said. "I promise to let you know when they catch the woman who was sent to kill you." Fletch walked past him and he could feel the tension in Fletch's walk. "It's not your daughter."

"Just remember you promised. The Secretary of State will be happy to hear how well you kept it." Fletch winked at him again.

46

ROOTKIT REMOVAL

It was late afternoon when Anna spotted a coffee shop from about a block away and made a beeline toward it. Not a lot of people in the area, but enough that she fit in as just another young person going home from work. The noise from traffic and people chatting with each other gave the scene the appearance of normality she didn't feel, but needed so she could do the work she had to do. A quick stop at a few local clothing shops gave her resources she knew she would need for the duration of her trip. Her gray duffel bag now was stuffed with clothes that were all easy-to-fold and could be worn at a moment's notice. She had changed into a pair of jeans, a white short-sleeved shirt, and another light jacket. Not being much of a traveler, she had to look up advice from other travelers before she got on her flight.

Research was, after all, one of her strong suits.

The Cafe Nile on Clapham High Street was perfect. The neighborhood was blue collar and the Clapham High Street Tube Station was nearby. She hoped not to have to run to the Underground, but she would if she had to. Nothing like desperation to silence all fears of capture.

She bought a coffee and sat down at a table in the corner, away from the otherwise-inviting windows. The hot, black, unsweetened liquid scalded her mouth, but reminded her that she had escaped arrest, somehow still in the outside world. She was going to need at least an hour to get her machine back in working order. That meant a quiet place and focus.

Job One: Find and remove the rootkit. Sony BMG had gotten into trouble a few years back by installing digital rights management software that phoned home, interfered with CD copying, and opened the user's PC to exploits by malware unrelated to Sony's attempt at controlling the user's listening habits. Even rejecting the licensing agreement didn't stop the software from installing, and it infected millions of PCs and affected about half a million networks, before class action suits and government investigations led Sony BMG to remove all copy protection from their CDs.

Idiots.

She opened her PC. The Kubuntu login screen appeared and she entered her user name and password. Everything looked normal.

This was the part she hated. It was the part that everyone thought was so easy but was never simple. The assumption in the Linux user community was that Linux boxes were just not a large enough part of the PC population to warrant things like viruses and other malware. While that was true, the average person hadn't even heard of Linux. It just meant that when a Linux box was attacked, it was devastating.

What was the best thing she could do? Reformat her drive and reinstall everything. She wandered around her drive, peeking at running processes and executing diagnostic tools. If she were home, she would do exactly that. She had available snapshots of her work so she could afford to start from scratch. Not this time.

She thought of home. Aunt Marcie and Uncle Ray. She hadn't thought of them in days. She hoped that they were okay and that whoever or whatever it was that they were subjected to was minimal. Aunt Marcie cried at the least provocation and Uncle Ray had a parochial view of the world that didn't include round-the-clock protection from people who might be after his niece.

Her chest felt empty. Not as bad as seven years ago, but the sensation was familiar. Anna had never been in a position in which she felt she needed anyone except her father, yet those two people whom she had never met before took her into their lives like a long-lost relative. *Which I'm not.* She sighed as she poured through the various places where Benson might have hidden intrusion software. If the USB key installed a kernel-mode rootkit then she was really in trouble. She would never find it without reinstalling the kernel and that would not guarantee she'd found everything.

She wrote a few scripts to kill any packet sniffers and set up a daemon to auto-start her own programs if the script found that they had gone down for some reason. Any of the other rootkit programs that might have been on her system like key loggers or log wiping utilities would stay until she was either back home or in jail.

She hated being a sysadmin. Doing this for herself was one thing, but at least she didn't have to do this for anyone else.

The coffee was cold and disgusting. She left a few hours later, after ordering less coffee and more tea, and some snacks to keep herself going. The sun was down, and the traffic on Clapham High Street was cleared as far as she could tell. Anna felt like she was back in Brooklyn when she was growing up as a teenager. The store a few blocks from where they lived was one of the few places her dad would let her go on her own. He had always been so paranoid about leaving her alone.

A few hours, and about 30 minutes of wandering, later she sat with her back to the door of her latest location and knew it was a bad idea. She couldn't see who was coming in or out, and someone out shoulder surfing might see what she was doing. The longer she typed the more vulnerable she felt. Either she was going to hide her face or hide what she was doing, but she couldn't do both. She decided to hide what she was doing.

The PC was first. She turned it around and then changed seats so that now she was facing the door, her screen facing her, and her back was to a wall. *So many damn details when you're on the trail of a wild animal.* She thought of Marshall and rolled her eyes at herself. *Yeah. Dad, a wild animal.* She tried to remember if he ever killed any animals when they lived in the Midwest or even when they moved to Brooklyn when she was ten. Maybe a cockroach. He didn't have any problems smashing a water bug. Those were just gross. She remembered him saying, "I have previous bug killing experience." She thought it was cute then. Now it just angered her. *Why do I hate him so much?* The more she thought about it, the more she realized that she wasn't sure.

MI5. If anyone was going to have information about where her father was, it was the UK equivalent to the FBI. There was no official witness protection program in Britain so any kind of deal like this would have to be coordinated by MI6 and then handled locally by MI5.

She hoped.

After making inquiries through a few discreet IRC channels, she discovered where to go to get the information she was looking for. She was used to using IRC the way it was intended: as the precursor to Instant Messaging and every other form of chat in the world. The difference was that the hard-core geeks found commercial IM to be pointless. She couldn't blame them. So much time wasted learning the latest dance craze instead of working toward a cure for cancer. She would never understand the rest of the world no matter how hard she tried.

She was done. The MI5 system could send out notification when records changed so she registered herself for any alerts given certain parameters. If she was lucky, they wouldn't notice the new alert settings until after her father's location records were updated and the system sent Anna an automated alert letting her know his new location.

47

CHANGE OF PLANS

Fletch sat in the back of the SUV with Tompkins again. Fletch was a model member of the program. He kept to himself. He never dated. He didn't object to the idiocies they would subject him to on a regular basis. He was a homebody. How many more times were they going to have to move him? This killer thing was a ruse. It was an exercise in stupidity and no one seemed to notice it but him. At this rate, he was just going to ask to be released and allowed to stay in the English countryside somewhere. He could spend the remainder of his days watching sheep out his window and staring at the local women.

After all, there might not be many remainders left.

The convoy had stopped outside of Heathrow. Just another blind alley in case they were being followed. It was evening and he was hungry. Years ago, when it mattered, he was built, ripped, whatever they called it today. He didn't think about women because the work he was doing kept him in situations in which the last thing he wanted to do was worry about a family back home or have them worrying about him. That was the least he could do. It meant that his life felt incomplete now, but back then there was no time to contemplate the future. A future without a future.

The line of SUVs pulled up at the hotel, and the usual cadre of men poured out to secure the area before he and Tompkins entered the building. He hoped they had a restaurant.

———

The hotel restaurant was empty. At this time of night, the kitchen was closed and there might be a guest sitting at one of the tables while their bored child scrawled an original drawing or on a page from a coloring book. In this case, the Marshals called ahead and made sure that the manager on duty would open the kitchen and clear out the restaurant before Fletch and Tompkins entered the area. The two men sat as far away as possible from the large plate glass windows on the other side of the room. With darkness on one side of the wall and a bright, well-lit dining area on the other they were visible targets. Fletch gulped in stale air-conditioned air and cleared his lungs with a hard push from his sternum.

He wanted a beer and, when it arrived, he swallowed every drop with a desperation that surprised him. He wasn't that thirsty.

"You're heading back to the U.S.," Tompkins said.

Fletch had been taking a juicy bite out of his Salisbury steak. He chewed, swallowed, and placed his knife and fork down. "I think you must be talking to someone else. I am not leaving the lovely island of Great Britain unless I'm in a body bag." He was just enjoying his dinner and now Tompkins made it a meal to forget. "Seriously, this is getting tedious," Fletch said. "I realize that they haven't caught that vicious killer yet, but I thought we were finally getting in sync."

"This wasn't my decision. Something happened in a political channel and it was decided that you would be safer in the U.S." Tompkins had a slight smile.

The bastard was enjoying this. Was this revenge?

"You had better be serious about this. I don't have much of a sense of humor left," Fletch said.

"Oh, I'm serious. The day after tomorrow you're winging your way back to lovely New York City." Tompkins took a sip of his Merlot.

Fletch considered throwing his Harviestoun's Schiehallion lager at him. "Oh my God. I left the United States specifically because it wasn't safe...for me."

"So you say." Tompkins stared at him.

"Yeah, so I say, and since it's my mouth that needs protecting, my say means a lot."

"Not as much as you think," Tompkins said. He had not released his wine glass since the conversation started.

"More than you think." Fletch thought about chain of command. "Okay, I'll bite. What idiot decided this?"

"I don't know. Above my pay grade."

"That would be practically everyone," Fletch said.

"The rumor has it that State decided to move you." Fletch lurched forward and Tompkins put his other hand up. "I had nothing to do with it. I should have gotten in trouble for moving you and I probably will, but for now this is all on you."

"That's why we're near the airport." Fletch cursed under his breath. He was going to need his own weapon again soon.

"The only reason you're not leaving tonight is because of scheduling; otherwise, I would have put you on the next flight and you would be on your way."

"To New York." This was not a development he foresaw. Why would he be sent back? "Listen, I know we haven't gotten along, but I need you to delay this somehow."

"Can't you just call your friend, the Secretary of State? I'm sure he has all kinds of things to tell you."

Ah, payback.

"I will, but if they follow protocol then I'm being sent back because the Brits don't think they can protect me and the U.S. is just bringing me back to hide me away somewhere."

"New York apparently."

Fletch slammed the palm of his hand onto the table. The otherwise empty restaurant echoed with the noise. Fletch took short breaths. *Damn it. Damn it. Why don't they just kill me?* "I can't leave the UK. Please don't make me leave the UK."

"Fletch, don't sweat it. Look at it this way, once we find your daughter, it will be easier to convince her to come with you if you're in the country."

"Are you doing this just to piss me off?" Fletch grabbed his beer glass and was grateful it was strong enough not to shatter in his grip. "What is wrong with you?"

Tompkins' eyes opened wider. "Sorry. I've been told before that I have problems delivering good news, but I would have thought you would be happier. You're going home. You said being here was like being in exile."

"It is being in exile, you moron." He lifted the beer glass about an inch and slammed it on the table. "It's self-imposed. I want to be away from the U.S."

"But your family..."

"My family is non-existent. My daughter is it."

"I'm sorry."

"Read the damn file. Know your mark. It's easier to lie to them that way."

"I'm not lying to you."

"I need to make a call."

———

Fletch stood at attention in his room as he spoke into the secure cell phone.

"You can't be serious. How is any of this my fault?

"I understand. I get it. But...

"How can I help but take this as an affront? Everyone else is dead, except...

"No, sir. The information is safe with me. I take my responsibilities to the U.S. seriously. Even now.

"I know that you will authorize everything in your power to keep me safe. I understand.

"Thank you, sir."

Fletch sat down on the edge of the bed in the hotel room that would be home until his flight was cleared. Home. The hotel was an echo of so many of the places he had visited on the job, especially New York. Cream-colored walls. Dark wood furniture. LCD televisions. He liked New York, but now it was the last place he wanted to be.

His call had been in vain. The decision, made in the back channels of bureaucracy in total ignorance as to the kind of information he knew, was done and there was nothing he could do to change or stop it. His former commanding officer, now Secretary of State, had succumbed to politics. He did everything he could to make it sound appealing to Fletch, but the bottom line was this: Fletch was returning to the land of milk and honey to die.

48

Q AND A

The world was dark for Special Agent Terrell Garrison. He wasn't sure what was going on, but he woke up faster than he ever imagined possible.

OMIGOD.

He registered dozens of things at once. Cushionless chair. Incomplete darkness. He couldn't move his arms or legs. Canvas sack over his head that smelled awful. The sound quality in the room was near dead. Since he couldn't move his legs, he couldn't tap the ground with his shoes.

He wiggled his toes. No shoes.

He tilted his head to look down. His shirt and tie were gone. His chest was bare. He shook his head to reposition the hood, but it was too large and loose. It shook, but it neither revealed any visible gaps nor came off. Terrell flung back his head over and over again, but the hood stayed on.

He took stock in what he knew and what he could do.

It all added up to zero, except that he was in trouble.

"I hope you're done."

Terrell jumped at the sound of the voice. Someone was there with him and knew he was awake. *Damn it.* The voice sounded mechanical.

"Who are you?"

"Not to inflate your sense of self-worth, but what matters is who you are. If you are not who I hope you are, I will kill you as the mistake that you are."

"My name is Terrell Garrison." No point mentioning the Bureau. It might set him off.

"Special Agent Terrell Garrison?"

Terrell bowed his head just a little. *They got me. Fuck.* "Yes, yes, Special Agent Terrell Garrison." He turned his head toward the sound of the voice. "And who might you be?"

"I understand you spoke with Fletch Burkholder the other day."

"What did you use on me?" What was the last thing he remembered? "That cop. He used something on me?"

"Fletcher Burkholder, please."

"That must have been some powerful stuff. A propofol derivative?" *Keep him talking. Delay the inevitable.*

"Fletcher Burkholder."

"No please this time?" Terrell wiggled his toes. "It's a little cold in here. Did you have to take my shoes? And my underwear? I mean, I'm proud of my baby-maker, but..."

Terrell felt pain run up his leg and through his hip and into his chest as a board made of some very hard material smashed into his leg. He couldn't tell if anything was broken. A yell escaped his lips.

"Buy me a drink and I'll tell you everything you want to know," Terrell said. He knew how to speak with confidence. Other ways of talking got him out of trouble and others got him information he needed.

"There's not going to be a lot of talking going on," Smooth Voice said. "I am going to ask you questions and you will answer them."

Terrell heard breathing next to his face.

"This is a joke-free zone," Smooth Voice said.

Was that something in his mouth? Terrell tried to head butt him, but Smooth Voice pulled back. No retort. A professional. Terrell hated professional interrogators. Even the ones from the US had given in and started using violence as a way of getting the answers they wanted. That only created information that could be true or false, but no way to confirm unless you had additional intel. Or you knew for sure you had the guilty party.

He knows who I am.

He heard crinkling. Aluminized paper? *Tap, tap, tap.*

"Last chance. Fletcher Burkholder." Terrell heard him come closer.

Terrell tried to move his other leg to kick him. No good. "Let me go and we can talk." He felt the pinprick of a syringe on his bare leg. He waited. Nothing. Pointless truth serum?

One-Mississippi. Two-Mississippi. Three-Mississippi.

"What are we waiting for?" Terrell asked.

His body itched. Smooth Voice said nothing. He didn't have to. All he had to do was wait. Terrell's arms and legs hurt as they slowly began to swell up and push against the restraints that were holding him in place.

He was having an allergic reaction. His throat closed up. He tried to breathe and could barely gasp. *Breathe. Gasp. Breathe. Gasp.*

Breathe!

Breathe!

He wanted to reach for his throat, for his face, but he couldn't move. His hands were stuck fast and his vision sparkled. His wrists were in pain from the swelling. How long had he been sitting there? He gulped some air, but it was getting more and more difficult. He felt every second. They were longer than he had ever experienced. His fingers, his skin, everything that was stretching hurt more than he thought possible.

Short quick breaths. Another. Another.

Oh, let me black out. This bastard's not going to let me die.

Another pinprick.

His throat opened and he began gulping in air. Epinephrine.

Breathe!

"What the hell was that?" The swollen parts of his body would stay that way for hours.

"Fletcher Burkholder."

Terrell heard Smooth Voice unlatching something to the right side of the chair. His skin tingled from frustration. How could he get out of this chair?

The chair tilted, disorienting him. He was effectively on his back, but floating. His legs pushed down on his hips.

The chair was on a pivot.

"Fletcher Burkholder."

"You already know I saw him. What the hell do you want to know?"

"Tell me what he told you."

"What do you care? He didn't tell me anything worth repeating."

"Humor me," Smooth Voice said.

"Let me go and I'll tell you everything you want to know."

Silence. Terrell heard metal scraped on the ground. Was that a bucket?

"I expect we will be here for a long time discussing this. If you tell me what you know, I'll let you go."

Terrell heard sloshing.

"If you don't, I'll let you go anyway, but you will not be the man you are now."

"Let me go and..." Terrell did not get to finish his sentence when he began to drown. Water poured on his face in waves and he felt his throat spasm to keep the water from entering. More water, more water, no air, more water, more water. He shook in the chair and felt very little movement.

More water, more water, more water, more water, more water.

The chair tipped forward on its pivot until Terrell spilled the contents of his world all over the floor and he could breathe again. His entire body was soaked and the canvas hood stuck to his face like a layer of paper maché.

The chair straightened up.

"Fletcher Burkholder."

Smooth Voice never got upset. As if this was his job. Was this his job?

"I'll tell you what you want to know, but..." A shot of pain flew through his head from the left as something struck.

Again.

And again.

49

BRITISH HOSPITALITY

Another café. More free wifi. Anna could not believe her luck. At this rate, she'd be able to stay out all night until the alert came in and then she would start the next phase of her hunt. The gun the cabbie had given her would come in handy since there weren't a lot of gun vendors in London.

She didn't want to stay out all night. What if the alert never came?

What if it didn't? What if they moved her father and she never found him? What if she did find him?

What happens the moment she confronts him and has to decide...

Anna shook her head. She was getting tired. *Stay focused. This is the wrong time to night to overthink this.*

The latest coffee shop was snug between two other shops: a grocer at the corner and some place called *whitehorse* (one word, all lowercase) which didn't tell her at all what it was. A bed and breakfast? A bar? A toy store? *Whatever.* She had other things to worry about.

The café had a milk chocolate brown sign that advertised internet (*shouldn't that be upper case?*) with tables and chairs in a little fenced off area outside. At this time of the afternoon, Anna expected a lot of young people to be out. They would give her cover while she did what she had to, even if she would have preferred to have thrown away all her equipment and start again. The best way to have a clean starting point was to have a clean starting point and none was better than having fresh hardware.

She was dragging. Brixton Hill was flat, but she didn't want to stop just anywhere. She looked around. This wasn't just anywhere. This was nowhere.

Perfect.

Anna grabbed a table, but not the perfect table. That one was just out of reach. She drummed the tabletop. Sipped her soda. Nibbled on the mini-sandwich she would be able to devour in a second.

Yes! The couple at the inner corner table started to collect their things. Anna stood, grabbed her drink and snack in one hand, threw her two bags over her shoulder, and navigated in the most awkward way possible to the target table. The couple laughed and nodded at her, and she nodded and laughed. *Move! I have work to do!*

She was set up in a few minutes. She could see the door. No one could see her monitor. *Perfect.*

Over to her right were two kids. No, she looked over again and decided they must be in their early twenties. Both scrawny, spiky haircut, tattoos down their necks, and MacBooks at their fingertips. She knew there was a reason she didn't like Macs.

After a few minutes, she realized that the two guys kept sneaking a peek over at her. She was certain that even though she had bathed yesterday that her overall appearance was not interesting enough to warrant their attention. The one with the strangest eyes kept peeking over the top of his screen. Ugh, he was wearing mascara. What was he doing?

She opened her wifi packet sniffer. There were three boxes using the free wifi, one of them being hers. The other two belonged to Beavis and Butthead. Beavis pushed his chair back.

Oh, God, please, no. Don't let him come over here.

He stood up and walked over to her.

"Hey."

Anna looked at her screen. "Hey."

"My friend and I are having a fight, well, we're talking about my sister."

"You have a sister?"

"Well, yeah. I was hoping maybe you could give us some female advice. What with you're being a girl and all."

"Please go away. I'm a lesbian."

"Aren't lesbians girls?" He glanced at his companion in confusion. "Oh! Way cool! I'm gay." He was rail thin and looked like he missed one meal too many.

"No, really, I'm kind of busy and really, you should go back to your friend." His hair was flying in every direction like it had exploded on his head. Anna was starting to itch.

"Cool." He kind of bounced as if he was made of a stretched-out piece of metal. "So, what are you working on?"

"Oh, nothing. Just some school work."

"You're still in school? Cool. You must be really smart." His mascara-outlined eyes widened in mock appreciation.

Her PC dinged. Yes! The alert! "I'm sorry. But I really do need to get back to my work." She waved him off and stared at her screen.

"What are you working on?" He reached for her screen and started to turn the unit around. She stood up and before he could turn the PC, she grabbed his hand, twirled him around, and had his face on the adjoining table.

The twenty-something at the register turned and picked up the phone. Anna panicked, let Beavis go, and raised her hands up.

"No, no. I'm sorry! Look. I let him go." She helped Beavis off the table and then pulled her hands back. "See," she said, "Everything is alright. He's fine. I'm fine. We're all fine." She smiled as Beavis took a step toward her.

"I'm not fine," Beavis said.

He tried to grab her hand and she pulled it away. He tried again and again with no positive result.

"Seriously, that's not going to work."

He grabbed her shirt.

"Oh, that is seriously not going to work." She held tight to his wrists, turned them outward, straightening out her own wrists, released one arm, and twisted the other arm behind him. "If you move too much, you're going to break your arm and I'm not going to feel the least bit guilty."

"Excuse me, miss?"

Anna looked toward the door. Two police officers had walked in. She closed her eyes for just a second.

"Oh, good evening, officers."

"You having any problems with this punk?"

"No, no. You see, he was trying to pick me up..."

"No I wasn't. I was sniffing her packets."

"You were sniffing her what?" one of the officers asked.

"Her packets off the wifi. Her packets are all encrypted and I thought-" His eyes shifted back and forth. "I wonder if she's up to something. And when I tried to look at her notebook, she slammed me head down on the table."

The situation was getting out of control. Anna started to pack up. "I'm sorry, but I have to get going. This guy is a lunatic and you should arrest him." She looked at the screen and read the address in the alert. She closed the unit. "In fact, I would like to press charges against him. Could I do that?"

The officers looked at each other. Were they afraid this would pan out into work instead of a doughnut run?

"Officers, I demand that you let me press charges against this molester." She took a step over to them. "I think he's been stalking me."

"You're a tourist, are you?"

"What gave it away? My clear American accent or my laidback attitude about crime in your lovely city?" She turned back to the table and continued shoving things in her bag. "I want to press charges."

Beavis's eyes never left their hazy state. "I don't know what this lady is talking about. I went over to check her stream."

"Officers! I'm feeling very threatened right now." Anna put her hands up and took a step back. "Really, you have to do something about this."

The officer on the right made a face and reached for his handcuffs.

50

____

OUTBOUND ALERT

A few minutes earlier one of MI5's systems began to complain. When the notifications arrived, the systems analyst was unsure what to do.

This had not happened in a very long time. At least not in the three years that Gerry Flaherty had been in IT for the Security Service.

While he was embarrassed at the use of the term Whiz Kid, he knew enough of cyber security and networks to earn his salary every pay period. He had tried numerous times to gain a promotion but was passed over three times already due to political moves rather than experience. There were times when he felt slighted, but that didn't bother him in the least. He knew that his time would come and every single day he went to work, he thought perhaps this was his day.

The Protected Persons Systems (PPS) was the official listing of the unofficial version of the Witness Security Program in Britain. Gerry had been involved on the periphery and had supplied many suggestions as to how they could both set up the enterprise database and secure it to keep everyone who didn't need to get to it from getting to it. Gerry thought maybe he was too paranoid sometimes, but one thing he was sure of was that his superiors were not paranoid enough.

He remembered sending email to some of the upper management within MI5 about some of the holes he had found (definitely not features) and how he could insure that the problems would be taken care of. He remembered not receiving a reply to his missives, but his colleagues began visiting less and less. Then he was passed over for the last promotion he had put in for.

The PPS was just another database. It had a basic proxy, but once someone was in the main network, protected twelve ways to Sunday he was proud to think, an intruder could find almost anything they wanted.

The PPS was Gerry's baby. It was small, self-contained, and open to prying eyes if you knew what to look for. It was, after all, just a small MySQL database with a few choice extensions added. Gerry had set up a flag to notify him when anyone, and he meant anyone, had touched the database. While he had not been told to add it, he took the initiative and requested permission, in writing, well, at least in an email, to put in the extra check. No one expected the database to amount to much except as a scheduling point between MI5, MI6, and the U.S. authorities on those few occasions when they had someone who could not safely be kept on U.S. soil.

A few minutes ago, PPS sent him an email: Someone had entered a Movement alert on some Yank near Heathrow. Gerry could only assume they were sending him home, but they could be sending him anywhere.

Gerry looked at the notification alert on one of the three monitors in his cube. The alert had been sent a few hours earlier, but his cell hadn't registered it. He knew he should have demanded a better phone. How could he do his job if he couldn't even receive penetration notifications?

He called over to Network Infrastructure. "John? Gerry here."

"What do you want now, Gerry?"

"Well, hold on, this is important. I think there's been an intrusion." *That should get his attention.*

"And none of the other systems caught it?"

"Not that I see so far. That's why I rang," Gerry said.

"Alright then. Give me the network segment."

Who knew the network segment of any of these systems? "Look for the Protected Persons database. It should be in the organized crime segment." Gerry could hear his counterpart typing. Gerry was a little worried. The penetration happened on his watch. Not something of which he was proud.

"What am I looking for?"

"Check out any access made about five hours ago."

"Five hours? Hold on." More typing. "That's strange."

"Yes?"

"An outside connection came in about five hours ago. It was routing from the outside through a local ISP through the VPN, but that one says it routed from China."

"Bloody Chinese. Will they ever let up?"

"Hold on, hold on. I can see the ISP logs and the packet looks like it came off a Tor node."

"Bloody Tor. In China?"

"Gerry, relax. You said it added an alert off your database?"

"Yes." Gerry drummed his fingers on his desk. He stopped and placed his free hand on his lap. No use getting anxious. He always made impulsive decisions when he was anxious.

"Check your database. Did any alerts go out?"

Gerry turned to the right screen of his three-screen set-up. "Not yet." He checked his cell again. Bloody hell. "Yes, an alert did go out about five minutes ago."

"To where?"

"How the hell would I know? That's why I called you." Gerry was getting nervous. His system had been penetrated. Information had made its way out of the fortress that was MI5. No one was going to be happy.

"Wait. You say it looks like it came off a Tor node?" Gerry looked over the alerting list for the database. "The alert. Whoever they are may have come in through a secure stream, but they entered a Gmail address for the alert." That was rather simplistic. "Hold on, let me see who that account is registered to." The Brits, along with the Americans and every other country on the planet, had tapped into Google about a year ago. They were still sorting through the ocean of information, but they were making good use of what they had.

There was the Gmail account. "John, I found the account where the alert would have been sent. Can you check the status of the account?"

"You mean if they've been there lately?"

"Check, please."

"Okay, I found the ISP where the request was routed. That is quite strange. When they hacked into the system, the packet coming into the ISP was from a Tor endpoint so the packets would have been decrypted before being sent to the ISP which then sent it to us. The machine accessing the email is wide open. I have an IP address, browser type. Everything. It's like they forgot to turn on please-hide-me-from-the-police mode."

"Location, if you can spare the admiration," Gerry said. He rolled his eyes.

"Hold on. Found the ISP who routed the message."

This was taking longer than Gerry expected. He would have to send some more suggestions for improvements to the user interface. The user experience was broken.

"How much trouble do you think there'll be when I call who I have to call?" Gerry asked.

"Found it. The ISP sent the email back to the IP address I already found and, bingo! Got it."

"Give me the address so I can make a few calls. This is going to be an interesting evening." Gerry knew the protocol and started to enumerate the list of people to call to make this happen. First he would call the City of London Police. *Let's pick up that bloke before they have a chance to leave.*

He was worried, but then thought that maybe his day had come. Time to send the police to Cafe Tana.

51

PRIDE AND PREJUDICE

Anna had been fighting with Beavis and the police for much longer than she should have been, but stepping into fresh air helped clear her head. The tables in the outside eating area were empty and the lights from the police car lit up the neighborhood in its narrow radius.

Beavis stood by the police car wearing cuffs as Anna got in his face. This was fun! Why had her father always make her act so politely?

"What is wrong with you?" she asked. The officer tried to hold her back, but she shook off his hands. "You think because I'm a woman you can do anything you want? I am a citizen of this great country. Who the heck are you?"

"You're a citizen?" the officer asked.

"Excuse me," Beavis said, looking at the two officers, "but is this necessary? I have my rights too and she is being offensive."

"I'll show you offensive."

The officers were doing everything not to look at her. It was amazing how the police outside of New York didn't know how to deal with an out-of-control woman.

"Excuse me, miss, but you'll have to step away from him."

"I will do no such thing! Who do you think you are?" She had never had a moment like this. Was this her exhaustion speaking? No way. This was exactly what she should have been doing days ago.

She blinked a few times. Her arms did feel a little heavy. And her legs weren't doing so well either. How long had she been waiting for that alert?

"Miss, please," the officer said. He was the taller of the two, wearing that silly white and yellow hat.

"What time is it?" Anna asked.

"About two a.m., Miss...?"

She stopped. She needed a name. "Bennett. Elizabeth Bennett."

"Miss Bennett, please. You have to calm down."

"Hold on," Beavis said, "Elizabeth Bennett? From *Sense and Sensibility*?"

"No, you moron, from *Pride and Prejudice*. You act like you know computers, but you have no basic understanding of clean data. I'll bet your inverted index was dropping terms."

"You were using Tor. I liked that," he said.

"You shouldn't have been sniffing my packets," she said. "None of your business. A girl has to protect herself."

"I thought you were cool. Now I know you're just an American psycho." He stepped forward. He looked more and more like a praying mantis.

She took a step toward him. "I'll show you an American psycho..."

The officer stepped between them again. "Please, miss. Miss Bennett." The other officer was already in the car filling out paperwork. He poked his head out the window.

"Excuse me. What did you say your name was?"

"Boris Thatcher," he said. "Like Maggie."

"And you, Miss?"

"Elizabeth Browning...Barrett," Anna said. Was she getting lightheaded? She had not stayed up this late since UPenn. That felt like a million years ago. She rocked a little and then stumbled.

The officer who was standing next to her leaned in. "Have you been drinking?"

Anna blinked. This was not a good idea. What was she thinking? It occurred to her that she didn't know how she was going to get out of here. The fun drained out of the moment. "Is this the way you treat guests in your country? Have I been drinking? Of course not. No one's asked me out for a drink."

Beavis turned away. "Not surprising."

In the distance, Anna heard police sirens. Those were not related to her she was sure.

"We'll need you to come to the station with us, miss."

"You do?" *Damn! Forgot about that.* "Ah." She looked around. The radio crackled and she glanced up at the sign for the café. Cute name, Café Tana. "Would it be alright if I went to the ladies' room first? You know, the loo?"

The officer nodded.

They are so polite here!

"Thank you." She pretended to lean in toward Boris and held her head up high. It was time to go. Even her oxygen-deprived brain was telling her that she was about to overstay her welcome. Besides, her dry mouth was telling her it was time to rehydrate.

She went inside and asked the clerk where the ladies' loo was.

———

A few minutes passed. Boris leaned against the car. "Can I go too? I haven't gone all day." He was so thin the officer wondered where he had the room for pee.

"Let's wait 'til she comes back," the officer said. God Almighty, he hated dealing with tourists. The Americans were almost as bad as the French. Especially the ones from New York. What a bunch of entitled little twits. "How's the paperwork going, Carter?"

The officer in the car leaned against the headrest. If Carter closed his eyes he was going to buy a coffee just to pour it on him. "All done. She just needs to sign. We'll have to take her in just to finish up, but she could probably head back to her hotel or to her mate and we can just let poor Boris here go with a warning." He looked up at the young man in cuffs. "You're sorry, aren't you Boris?"

"I'm telling you, she's cute bird, but not letting me see her screen was wrong." He pointed to the front door of the cafe. "Just wrong."

The radio called out and Officer Carter responded. Boris continued stating his case to the officer standing with him, but he was not listening. All he wanted was to nip a little tea with a pastry, maybe a cookie and then head home in a few hours. The night was just liked he liked them: boring. He was grateful not to have been involved with the mess that happened earlier at the Pestana.

Carter sat up. "What's that?"

The radio was very clear. "Repeat: hold all patrons and anyone around the Cafe Tana. That's the word. Backup is on its way."

The sirens had gotten louder. The officer standing outside the car looked as three squad cars, one after another, screeched to a halt outside the cafe. He pointed at Boris. "You stay here."

He ran into the cafe. He pointed to Boris' mate still sitting at the table waiting for his friend. "You! Don't move." He turned to the young man at the register. "Where's the woman's loo?"

"We don't have one. I already told that girl. No public loo."

Oh, this is a cockup.

The officer ran through the hallway to the back of the cafe. He pushed open the beat up metal exit door that eventually led out to the sidewalk around the corner from where they were standing, and he cursed out loud at the air. He ran down the block in the only direction she could have taken.

Nothing. The streets were deserted except for the occasional man sitting in a doorway.

Elizabeth Barrett, or whatever her name was, was gone.

52

TORTURE TEST

Terrell was in pain and exhausted. He knew all about torture, but it was one thing to read about it, or even see it, and quite another to be the victim of it.

He was in total ignorance of his surroundings. What little light came through the fabric of his hood did nothing to help him see. His breathing was loud, like the sound of a child too close to his face. His eardrums had the hollow feeling he would get when he caught a cold. He yawned. He blew into his head with the little breath he could muster. His hearing filled with echoes. His butt ached from not moving. His skin was clammy and covered in goose bumps. The wooden chair was cold. And after all that water, he was very, very thirsty.

His only solace was that they hadn't broken any of his bones yet.

He knew that was coming soon enough.

Alone in the room, he let his head hang for a few moments. His neck hurt so he leaned his head back, but not too far. He was still swollen from the allergic reaction he had to whatever it was they gave him. He had childhood allergies, but none had hit him quite as hard as that shot did. He would have to find out what that was once he got back to the office.

He would get back to the office. He could not let himself think about what Smooth Voice had said earlier. They would let him go, but he wouldn't be the same man. They were going to beat him until he was almost unrecognizable or they were going to drug him and fry his brain or something in-between.

Was this what Del had gone through? He wanted to feel angry, wanted to rip his arms out of the restraints through sure will, but he was scared. This was something out of the movies. This was the interrogation from hell.

A door opened. It had been a few minutes (A few seconds? A few hours?) since Smooth Voice had departed.

"So, when do we get to talk over a drink?" Terrell asked. The words were raspy and muffled. His throat was swollen and his head bruised.

"Special Agent Terrell Garrison."

From his right, he heard a voice similar to Smooth Voice's, but it wasn't him. Through the worn canvas he thought he saw something in the man's mouth. A voice box? Terrell willed himself to head butt him but could not get his neck to move.

"I don't know why you won't let me help you."

"Help me? You could help me by undoing these." Terrell pulled at the restraints with little energy. His voice rasped. He hadn't had any food or water for who knows how long. He stopped trying to keep track of time. Nothing he could keep track with.

"Tell me about Fletcher Burkholder."

"Nice man. A little bit of an anger management problem." Terrell waited for the blow to his face, or his legs, or chest. Nothing.

"True, he does. But he was always a man to get the job done."

"Oh, so you two are buddies. I'll be sure to let him know you said hi," Terrell said. *Now I understand why Burkholder is under lock and key. Still don't know why, but, right now, who cares?*

Smooth Voice 2 patted him on the head. Terrell was too tired to care. *Could you massage my shoulders too?*

"What did he tell you?"

"You didn't have a microphone there? You didn't think to bug his room?" Terrell asked.

"We didn't know where he was. We don't always have the back channels we need. Some systems are just that hard to break into," Smooth Voice 2 said.

"I know a bunch of people you can hire to do that. Most of them are Russian, but there are a few Americans who would do it."

"What did he tell you?"

"Let me go and I'll tell you," Terrell said.

"If I let you go, you're liable to think you can overwhelm me."

"Oh, yeah. No chance of that happening. Is this what you did to Del?"

"Who?" Smooth Voice 2's hesitation told him it was a lie.

"Oh, don't play dumb." Terrell pulled his head back. "Hey, don't hit me for that. You didn't ask me any questions."

"Del?" The sound of material. Shoes brushing on concrete. "Del Kirby?"

Terrell took in a painful breath.

"I don't know any Del Kirby."

"Well, except for the fact that I didn't give you his last name, I might have believed you." Terrell slowly shook his head. "I'm going to kill you when I get out of here."

"Lucky for me," Smooth Voice 2 said.

"Your luck is running out. If I found you..."

"Except that I found you. I always find who I'm looking for."

"But not Fletcher. Not Fletch. And you sent someone to kill him."

"No, just someone to find him." He put his hand on Terrell's bare shoulder. He was standing behind him. "What did he tell you?"

Terrell thought about the file. He thought about some of the random things in the paperwork. Construction contracts. Suicides. Money laundering. "He didn't tell me anything."

Something slammed into the front of Terrell's face, making his head snap back and strike the wooden chair. He didn't feel any of that until after the initial explosion of pain from his nose breaking.

"Fletcher Burkholder. He used to be a friend. Now he's just

annoying."

Terrell fought through the pain. *I am going to kill this bastard.* He regained control. "No, bees are annoying."

"I kill bees every season."

Terrell couldn't answer. This was like a bar brawl with the asshole's friend holding you down. He tried to breathe, but his nose refused to cooperate. He wasn't sure how long it was before he spoke. "I'm sure you do." Blood ran down his nose and into Terrell's mouth. He spit onto the hood. "Can you clean some of this blood off my face? It's affecting my memory."

The sound of material again. Away from him. Tearing. Must be a table. Walking toward him. The hood came up, bright lights, concrete floor, a white hand holding a paper towel. He wiped some of the blood off and then lightly touched his nose. Terrell winced.

"Sorry," Smooth Voice 2 said. "Just trying to help."

"Yeah," Terrell spit onto the white hand, "just trying to help." The pain made it difficult to think. The hood covered his vision again. He heard steps coming toward him. Something pushed against his head. Metal. The smell of gun oil. "If I go to the bathroom here, will you wipe my ass?"

"I have no qualms about killing for my country. I also have no qualms about killing for myself. And I have no qualms about killing to keep my country's secrets." Smooth Voice 2 was tense.

He was the good cop while the other guy was the bad cop, but it all came to the same thing. Talk or more pain until you do. Secrets. Code words. Del's file. The word came to him. He saw the word in the file in a flash of memory. Maybe there was something he could learn from Smooth Voice 2's reaction.

"You mean like Halon?"

The gun went off and Terrell's hearing on the right side of his head rang from the shock wave of the explosion of the gunpowder. He yelled and moved his skull to the left of his shoulder to release the pressure. It didn't stop .

There was another voice. They exchanged words.

Footsteps receded. The door closed.

53

SLEEPING IN THE LIFT

Anna approached the off-white parallelogram that was the Hilton London Heathrow Hotel from the east parking area. She zipped her jacket up in deference to the cooling breeze and let her hair cover her face just in case any photos were being taken. Who was she kidding? This was England; all they did was photograph everyone. In the not-so-distance, planes pushed themselves away from the ground with a muffled roar that gave the night a loud looping soundtrack. Her arms were frigid and she couldn't stop shaking. *It's just the cold. It will be warmer inside.* She could smell and taste the diesel fuel along with car exhaust and her stomach had the hollow feeling it always did when she was hungry or undecided. Waiting in the shadows of the parking lot on the north side, she saw a pair of young Hispanic-looking women walking away from a beaten-up, old, beige car toward an employee entrance. She ran up to them and introduced herself.

"Perdona, pero es mi primer dia de trabajo. Me pueden ajudar entrar? No me dieron una llave," she said. *Excuse me, this is my first day at work. Can you let me in? They didn't give me a key.* She gave them part of her life story of coming to England to help pay for food for her newborn baby, and how she found the job at the Hilton through a friend.

In she went, leaving the trees and the dark behind her.

She followed the young women some distance down a tired corridor, and excused herself by saying she forgot her things in her car. She promised to meet up with them later for some coffee. They nodded and continued in.

She found a well-lit closet filled with uniforms of all different types in various sizes and dark colors. Her mind exploded with a myriad distracting questions. Were they stylish? Were they the latest in hotel fashion? Who supplied them? Who actually made them? Questions piled up in her head. She had never been to the staff section of a hotel before. The distractions were all around her. So many things she'd like to ask.

Answers she would never get. *No answers today. Well, maybe one.*

She grabbed a uniform and went into the nearest bathroom, which was not as close as she had hoped. Another member of the staff saw her. There were cameras all up and down the hallway and she awkwardly held up the uniform in front of her face, as proof of being in the right place. Of belonging.

Her hands shook.

Into the bathroom. Into the uniform. Her fingers fumbled with the buttons of the blouse. She had her purse with her sans PC and almost everything else except some basic covering to hide the gun. She would carry her purse with her for as long as she could and then she would hide the weapon in some towels. She looked at herself in the mirror. The uniform was a little tight. Black with a white top. The top button refused to stay closed so she left it open. *That'll be a distraction for someone.*

Tonight was the night.

She had to find his floor.

Daddy! I'm here!

———

She ran into a few more women who were on their way to various parts of the hotel. She hoped that no one mentioned the new girl as that might cause some problems. Where were the security guards?

Her hair was in a bun and she took off her glasses. Anything to make ID'ing her more difficult was the order of the day. Thinking back, she realized that she should have purchased either lighter or darker makeup to put on, as well. Oh, well. For her next murder. She walked down the hallway through which she had come and started her walk toward the front of the building. Her stomach twisted. She stopped for a moment and stood behind a rack of freshly laundered clothing. She closed her eyes and cleared her mind. *Think only of the moment.* The next step. And the next. How would she find him? What would she say?

I'm sorry, Squirrel, he would say.

Fuck you.

There were a number of people walking around and no one paid attention to her. A terminal being used by another member of the staff entered her field of view and she made a beeline to it. Just as she approached, she turned to the side and started grabbing linens and towels.

The person moved off the keyboard. She glanced around and the others continued to ignore her. She must have looked like somebody else because this was too strange. Nobody noticed a stranger in the staff area? She put down the linens and examined the menu on the screen.

"Excuse me?" The voice came from behind her.

"Yes?"

"Shouldn't you be on four helping to clean up after that band of idiots who ransacked the room an hour ago? They need all the help they can get," the man in the black suit with the white top said.

"Yes, sir." She grabbed the stack of linens.

"And leave your purse in your locker. It's going to get lost and then you'll be sorry."

"I'm sorry, sir," Anna said. "You're right." She turned away from him and then turned back. "I'm sorry, sir, but may I ask you a question?"

"Of course, but hurry, please."

"A call came in from the room where the police are."

"Yes, yes."

"I am sorry, but do you remember what floor they're on?"

"Of course not. It could be 8 or 9. Drop those off and go to 4, please. They need you much more there."

Eight or nine.

Anna stood in the otherwise empty elevator and watched the numbers increase on the board.

3

4

5

Anna held the stack of linens and towels in her hands. The gun was nestled in the middle where she could slip her hand in and pull the trigger.

6

7

8

A soft ding emanated from the walls. She closed her eyes for a moment and reopened them. She put a smile on her face.

She was ready for her close-up.

The door slid open.

Two men dressed in dark clothes stood in front of her. She smiled, nodded her head, and stepped out of the elevator. The two men entered behind her as she debated left or right. She took a few more steps and peeked around the corner. The corridor was empty. There should have been security somewhere. At least a guard by the door.

He must be on nine.

She turned around and found the men holding the elevator open for her. She smiled and nodded at them again. They smiled back, entered the elevator, and gazed at the floor while she waited for the jolt of heaviness she always got when an elevator was moving upward. She felt herself get lighter. She looked up. No! The elevator was heading down. She hadn't pressed the button for 9 and the men were on their way down.

Damn it! She pressed 9 over and over again. *Calm down. Act normal.* "I really meant to go up."

The men chuckled and nodded.

She cursed under her breath. *Just go to 9. Everything is fine. One step at a time.*

Each man grabbed one of her arms and pulled her back against the wall of the elevator as she dropped the linens and towels.

And the gun.

"Hello, Anna," the man to her left said.

Police?

The man squeezed her arm and she felt a pinprick.

She was asleep before she fell to the ground.

54

———

WATER UNDER THE BRIDGE

This was much more trouble than Anna had anticipated a few hours earlier.

She blinked and woke up in the back of a dark van with gaffer's tape over her mouth, wrists bound behind her back, ankles twined together, and a jacket tied around her chest. A large man sat before her in the dark. He wore an oversized jacket, but even at rest his arms strained the fabric. The emptiness in his eyes scared her like never before. The police in the alley were nothing compared to the lack of feeling she saw in his black pupils.

The van was bare except for the chairs she and her guardian sat in. Every time the van hit a bump or a pothole, the noise it made was unbelievable. She calculated that the echo increased the noise by at least 50% or more.

When she left Café Tana, it was 2 a.m. It was around 3 a.m. now and all she could think, was: *This is it.*

This is it.

This is it.

Where were they taking her? She would ask except for her mouth being sealed shut.

Her father would never have allowed this to happen. He would have stopped her long before she had decided to try to kill someone.

Why did you leave me, Dad?

The streetlights made mesmerizing streaks on the walls. The van was white. The floor was black. Rubberized. She tried moving her arms. She could move them up and down just a little, but these men were professionals. They had her locked tight. In the man's right hand was a sub-machine gun that leaned on the floor. Her heart raced audibly. They didn't even have the radio on.

She tried to talk. All that came out was mumbling. The man looked at her and then looked away. He wore a ski mask. Black gloves. Black boots. Paramilitary?

Her eyes teared. *Oh, please, oh, please, let me go.* What were her choices? She could try jumping toward the door and hope that it would pop open so she could fall out. And be run over by the car behind them. She could try running to the front and cause the driver to crash the van. And kill her anyway.

She had done some magic when she was younger. Was there some escape artist trick she could use? That took preparation. Wires. Fake something or others depending on the trick.

There was nothing she could do but wait. She hated waiting. Low boredom threshold was one of the reasons she took so many credits every semester.

Mr. Black Ski-Mask stood up and spoke to the driver. She didn't understand what they were saying. Was he speaking too quietly or another language? Or was she still recovering from whatever drug they had given her? Where had that happened? Right, the elevator. Where was her gun? It must have fallen when she let everything go and these monkeys wouldn't have left it behind.

Her gun. Getting her gun would be a good thing.

She stood, or tried to. The plastic ties on her wrists were attached to another loop of something that was attached to the chair. They thought of everything. There was no way anyone could get out of this. Even Houdini would be a goner. *Lucky he's already dead.*

The view out the windshield had changed. They were heading

out of the city. *No, no, please don't leave the city.* There were fewer lights, fewer cars. If it weren't for the banging of the van, she was sure she would be able to hear the wildlife of the London countryside. Owls, maybe. Crickets?

She almost fell out of her chair, but the loop attached to her wrist ties gave her leverage to pull herself back. Could she kick that bastard in the face? No point. His buddy would just shoot her or, worse, beat her. Even her saliva decided to desert her.

The van rocked for a quick second and then stopped. It was dark outside and she had no bearing as to where she was.

The doors opened onto a field. Or maybe it was the shoulder of a disused road. Mr. Ski-Mask, who had returned to his seat earlier, pulled out a knife. He got up, reached behind her, and sawed at the loop holding her on the chair.

Maybe he'll let me go. Maybe I can run and he'll just shoot me. She felt the restraints on her ankles. She started to cry. Her words were muffled as she tried to speak in her defense.

Please don't do this. Please!

Mr. Ski-Mask dragged her out of the van as she tried to take in her surroundings. It was so dark. In the distance, she could see the lights of London. They looked so pretty. She screamed, and the sound echoed in her head. *Please don't kill me. Please don't kill me.*

The driver took one of her arms and Mr. Ski-Mask took the other and they dragged her into the forest. The tips of her shoes left a line in the dirt as they went into the dark with a single flashlight to show them the way.

"You know we could just do her right here?"

"Shut up. We have to take her to the bridge."

The bridge? Was she being exchanged for someone? Was this out of a Cold War book?

They came out into a clearing with a bridge that extended out forever over a river that looked like it was hundreds of feet below them.

They were going to toss her over the railing.

Her brain went into overdrive and she started to scream and

wiggle and do everything she could to get them to let her go. The driver lost his grip, but Mr. Ski-Mask made sure she didn't fall on her face. The driver clutched her arm again and continued the short walk over the long bridge.

Her heart beat so hard she felt sure it was going to explode through her chest. Shaking her shoulders, her head, even pulling her legs did nothing. Her arms were held fast so she couldn't break loose and at least waste some time as they would have to pick her up again.

They lifted her up and placed her on the railing in a seated position. She heard the water down below rushing through the ravine but could only see it as a shadow scraping across the darkness. One push and she would fall back to her death. Seconds and then it would be over.

The driver twitched. "Wait a second." British accent. He reached into his pocket and pulled out a vibrating cell phone. He took off his glove. "Yeah?" He listened for a few seconds. "Roger that."

He pulled her off the railing. "He says to bring her in."

"Roger that," Mr. Ski-Mask said.

55

LEAVING ON A JET PLANE

A group of five men walked across the Heathrow tarmac in a secluded section where private and government planes were kept. A Cessna Citation XLS+ pulled up, making the unending engine wail of a plane taxiing, prepping for a long flight. The air was thick with the smell of diesel fuel and just enough light to let the pilot avoid running over his current passengers. The wind was agitated.

Three of the men wore dark suits and surrounded a fourth man wearing a mask. Tompkins walked behind him, holding onto a clipboard. He gave the paper a quick glance and put his arm down.

Fletch, wearing the dark mask and a long black overcoat, turned to him. "So this is where I tell you how much I'm gonna miss you."

"No point lying."

The plane door opened downward, revealing the steps to the passenger compartment. The doorway flooded with bright yellow light and the promise of comfort. The sound of the engines pierced Fletch's ears, but he had heard worse. Much worse.

Fletch had been in private jets before. He always thought they were overrated. However, the alcohol usually made the trip worth it. He was going to need a lot of alcohol on this trip.

"Why aren't you coming?"

"As hard to believe as it sounds, I have family here," Tompkins said.

Fletch nodded at his unwelcome companion. There was nothing else to say. It was time to return and discover his destiny. He would fight it. He always did. But he couldn't help but feel betrayed.

The pilot climbed out and approached Tompkins. A woman in her late thirties or early forties dressed as you would expect a pilot to be dressed, only with a feminine flare to her walk. Stylish. He might see her again during the trip. Then again, probably not. His right arm itched. Fletch let it be.

"Once you're on board, you can take your mask off. It obviously won't stop a bullet, but at least any photos won't mean anything," Tompkins said.

"Yeah, because the rest of me doesn't give away who I am to someone who's looking for me." The human shield surrounding him notwithstanding, Fletch knew what a sniper could do from any of a number of positions around him. He could take Fletch out and be gone before anyone realized the direction of the bullet.

The pilot put out her hand to Tompkins. "Deputy Marshall?"

He reached out and shook her hand. "You have some paperwork for me?"

Fletch watched a plane disappear into the darkness. His human shield followed along as he took a step away from the plane and surveilled the darkness and noise that was Heathrow. At one point, he had spent almost seven years in Great Britain. That was in another life that wasn't this one. England had felt like the home he should have remembered or at least should have known better. The people he had managed to meet, and there weren't many, were smudges in his memory. There was no point remembering people who meant nothing. He stayed out of their way and interacted with them only when he had to. Life was so much simpler that way. When you saved lives, or took them, there was no time for thought. Only action. Was he still a man of action? He wasn't sure.

He knew he really was a model member of the program. Stayed out of trouble and never got involved enough to let anyone in. *That won't count for much when my time comes.* How good or bad you were meant nothing in the hands of God.

"Fletch?" He turned back at the sound of Tompkins' voice. "Your ride is here."

The pilot motioned with her right hand toward the staircase.

Fletch walked over to Tompkins. "Any word on my daughter?"

"No. They have some leads, but..."

"I would never have told you what you wanted to know," Fletch said. "I know how much it means to you, but it means more to me."

"I know it does. I know it does." Tompkins held out his hand and Fletch shook it for a quick second. Weak grip. "You'll be fine."

Fletch started his walk to the plane. "Of course I will. You guys are never wrong and no one has ever died on your watch."

"You can take that to the bank."

"Yeah." He walked up the stairs knowing, hoping against hope that he would get to return.

But he knew better. They were flying him back to bury him.

56

FRIENDLY CONVERSATION

Anna blinked.

The light was too bright for the first few seconds. She covered her face and took in a deep breath. Stuffy smell. Sweaty man. She put her hands down and squinted. The room was made of concrete. She assumed she was underground, no windows after all, but she also knew she could be in a room off some garage. Was she still in Britain? She sat up on the mattress of a bare, metal frame bed that had seen better days. She sat up and got dizzy so she leaned back against the wall for support. She blinked a few more times.

Benson sat on the edge of a gray, standard issue, boring-as-all-hell desk. He looked the same as the day they met at the hotel in New York except he wasn't wearing his gray-framed glasses. New York. What a bastard. Where was her jacket? She stood to go at him and instead fell back as her head did its best to readjust to its surroundings and failed. She took in a breath.

His arms were crossed and he looked at her like she was barely there. This was the man she thought of for the last few days as a friend. A sloppy, professional friend, but a friend nonetheless.

"They were going to toss me off a bridge," Anna said. She leaned on the mattress using the palms of her hands. It felt as thin as a piece of paper.

"Yes, they were."

"I guess you told them to?"

"I did." His arms stayed crossed. He didn't move.

Anna wanted to jump up and slam him against the wall. Maybe jam a pencil in his eye. Break his arm in twelve places. She stood up and shook her head.

"You can come at me if you want. I decided you had to go because you were careless. You did everything wrong."

She took steps toward him, each surer and faster.

He stood but didn't flinch. "You could have led them back to me and everything that you were trying to do and everything that I was trying to do would be for nothing."

"I was there! I was one floor away from his room! I had the gun you gave me," Anna said.

"Yes, the gun I gave you." He picked it up off the desk. "Unregistered. Light. Doesn't show up in airport x-ray machines. Doesn't set off metal detectors. Do you know what this gun says?"

Anna wanted to grab him by the throat.

"This gun screams well-funded operation outside the mainstream. This gun screams professional organization.

"I was not going to let you do that. You did your job," he said. "That was all I wanted. All I needed."

"Which was?"

"Find your father."

"I found him a couple of days ago!" Was that a paperweight on his desk? His temple looked like a good spot.

"And you broke off all communication with us. All communication. How insane was that? We were keeping you safe. Keeping you from harm."

Was this man kidding? "Tossing me off a bridge was keeping me safe?"

"You brought that on yourself. You should have called in. I would have told you to pull back." He walked around his desk, opened a drawer, and pulled out a pair of plastic bags. "Look. Your travel kit. A new passport. Some money. You would have gone home, and we would have taken care of your father and all would be right with the world."

"But you said..."

"You weren't supposed to kill him. You were never supposed to kill him."

Anna stood in shock. What was the point of having her there?

"But you knew...?"

"You are a brilliant young woman. If you decided to go into intelligence, you would have a great career ahead of you. If you decided to go into anything, you would have had a great career ahead of you. Instead, you set yourself up where your face is so well-known that all I can do is get rid of you."

Anna's eyes went wide for a second until her anger flared. "Why am I still alive?"

"Because my latest intel tells me he left. He's gone. You found him, and now he's gone. He's on his way to the U.S. and when he gets there, we'll lose him again."

"I can find him again." *First I'll teach you a lesson.* She took another step toward him. Her head cleared a little more. Things were coming into focus.

How good a fighter was Benson? His stance was solid.

"Thank you, no. I would much rather you just go away." He got closer. "And you will stay away. I have rarely spared anyone's life I didn't have to, and I didn't have to spare yours."

"You're kidding."

"Marshall betrayed his country. He betrayed his family. He betrayed me." He stood as close as he could to Anna. She could smell his breath. A smoker. "He betrayed you."

"Oh, my dad did something to you? What? Slept with your wife? Took pictures of you with that sheep?" Anna was in his face. "What did he do? I know what you told me about him already, but you are taking this a lot more personally than I would have ever taken it."

"My job is to protect the United States."

"Who are you?" she asked.

"Marshall betrayed his country to more foreign countries than I can count."

"There are just over two hundred of them. I'm sure you can count that high."

Benson took a step back and circled her. "Snowden was nothing. Those were programs that should have been leaked. He shouldn't have done it, but that's part of the intelligence gathering game. Nothing he revealed was unknown to the rest of the ICs of the world." Intelligence communities. "You father told them about systems and projects that no one but the upper echelon of the government know about. Things that would give these countries reasons to go to war with us. To start attacking and killing every man, woman, and..."

"Oh my God. Could you be any more dramatic?" Anna took a quick glance at the desktop. Nothing of any value or substance.

But there was the paperweight.

"They do the same thing to us. All the time. And we do it to them. I know my father's a jerk and a traitor and whatever. Puppy torturer," Anna said.

"The people who tried to kill you are still out there."

"Out there?" She looked him up and down. "He's in here."

"You're alive because I want you to go back and see that I'm telling you the truth. When we arrest him..."

"Who are you?"

"He will get capital punishment," Benson said.

"I don't care. Who are you?"

He grabbed her wrist. "You have to keep this entire operation to yourself. Not your aunt, not your uncle, nobody. You must never ever talk about this to anyone. One thing I'm good at is chasing down traitors."

He squeezed her wrist. She tried to break free.

"The burners, the cab, the money, the passport still in the possession of the Embassy. Everything. Do you understand?"

Anna thought, *Next stop: Federal prison. This man is as nuts as they come. I am not going to jail for him. For killing my dad, yes. For helping out this nut job, not so much.*

"I understand. I'll be quiet." The words slipped through her teeth. "Let. Me. Go." She was alert. It was 5 a.m. if it was anything, and she was wide awake. She was getting out of here.

Anna grabbed the paperweight and slammed Benson on the side of the head as hard as she could. He saw her arm coming at him and he tried to move out of the way, but failed.

As he fell past her waist, she brought her knee up to his face. The concrete floor was next.

"That was for trying to kill me." She bent over his prone form. "I hope you can forgive me." *Idiot.*

CONCRETE, BLOOD, AND SECRETS

On the off-chance that she managed to get out of wherever-the-hell-she-was Anna took the gun and the plastic bags that contained her new ticket back to the United States. The ticket was just a ruse anyway. That would give them all the information they needed to pick her up. She was going to have to figure something else out.

She went through Benson's pockets. She thought of slamming him between his legs but found something better. Car keys.

The only door in or out of the room was closed. It looked rather flimsy. Was it locked? She dragged Benson under the bed before trying it. For a skinny man, he was rather dense. Maybe it was his head. After pushing and prodding, she got him totally under the bed. Except for his feet. Big, black, uniform, rubber-soled shoes.

That would never work. Oh, well.

She tried the doorknob. It turned. She pushed the door open, expecting a guard to be standing right outside it.

No one.

She stuck her head outside the door and decided she was either underground or in the strangest warehouse she had ever seen. Concrete everywhere. This was probably the basement to some building. Where was everyone? The acrid smell of dust was everywhere. She saw a number of doors heading down the hallway and wondered what was behind them. Could Benson have other people helping him out, looking for others? *He's one fry short of a Happy Meal, that's for sure.* And he tried to have her killed. She imagined that hitting him with the paper weight wouldn't do anything to endear her to him. *Tough. I hope he has a permanent impression of China on his skull.*

A door opened. A short man wearing glasses with some of the thickest lenses she had ever seen exited a room.

"Guards!" he yelled. She ran at him and he tried to run away. The door was left ajar.

She turned the corner and found him standing with a scalpel in his right hand. *Oh, very dangerous.* She threw one of the plastic bags at him and while he was distracted she knocked the scalpel out of his hand. She did a roundhouse kick that connected with his chin and then palmed his face as hard as she could with her right hand.

Another one on the concrete. *Really, they should have carpeting. That's just polite.*

She heard running. One or two? She hid around the corner as a large man holding a rifle turned. She grabbed the barrel of the rifle and struck him in the face with it. He was stunned for a second and then he brought the barrel down and hit her in the chest. She grabbed the barrel again, pointed it away from her, and kicked him between the legs. *OW! Cup!*

She rubbed her knee just as his hand reached her throat. She seized the rifle, pulled it away from his as far as she could, and slammed it back into his chest. As she pulled it away, he got off a few shots.

Without thinking, she kicked as hard as she could toward his face and smashed into the bottom of his chin. He stumbled back and she did it again. And again.

She wheezed. *I could sure use my asthma spray.* Looking around the corner, she anticipated more people coming. Empty. The gunshots didn't seem to attract any attention. Where the hell was she? She grabbed the rifle and went for a walk.

She found another door that was pressed closed. Using the barrel, she pushed it open. No reaction. Anna entered, making as little noise as she could. The small room was filled with about ten terminals.

She stuck one key on each keyboard and each of them came up on a login screen. Great. She had nothing that would help her with that.

Yellow post-it note on screen number seven. It read: *tea-consuming-ferret*. She took the yellow slip of paper and kissed it. Returning to the door, she closed it with as much care as she could muster to minimize any noise and returned to terminal seven.

She was in. She typed Benson's name...that was not going to work. All she had was a first name. She tried it anyway. They were going to see exactly what she was looking at in the morning anyway.

The morning. It was after 5 a.m. Some shift of evil minion had to be coming soon. Her heart shifted gears and her fingers followed.

Her search for Benson found nothing. She typed in her name.

OMG. I'm in this system. She read page after page after page about herself. The ultimate vanity search. Who she was. Where she came from. She brought her hand to her mouth. The stale smell of the concrete and sweat made her dizzy. She read some more. Her life with her father. All documented. Every place they had ever stayed. She read an odd comment: *Background filled in after 2005*. After 2005? After the police picked her up? They didn't know anything about her and Marshall until the police arrived?

She started scanning the file and there it was. Her father had made a call and the voice recognition system picked him out of the all the calls being made in the United States.

Benson had notified the police to pick him up.

Benson had been responsible for her life since 2005.

But where was her father? On a flight back to the United States. Would he return to New York? Would he go into hiding again? Without the right tools, she might never find him. They might push him so far underground he might as well be dead.

She did a search for Marshall Wodehouse. Her eyes opened wide. Her father really was involved with Benson. She tried to open a special file with no title, but it wouldn't let her in. A window opened on her first attempt, telling her that she was liable for criminal penalties for selecting a file that was obviously marked Top Secret. *Well, boo hoo.*

She clicked around some more and read numerous files about her father. Where he was born, who he had married...married? She brought up a picture of Ingrid.

She touched the screen. *Oh, you're so beautiful. Hi, Mom.*

She continued reading.

And reading.

And found nothing about what Benson had told her about him. No charges brought against him. No secrets passed. No mole in the organization.

Her father had done nothing Benson had told her about. It had to be in there somewhere. She continued looking. She typed in different keywords.

Nothing.

Marshall Wodehouse had done nothing against the United States. He had various superiors during the years until 1990 when he was in a car accident and vanished off the radar. His manager was a man named Malik Palma.

———

Anna had seen enough. She ran down the corridor and then realized that she was heading the wrong way when she saw the two bodies in the corner.

What was in the room that the short guy had come out of?

She didn't have the time. She had to go. She took a step in the opposite direction. What if someone else was trapped in here? She couldn't be the only idiot involved in this insanity.

She stepped over the bodies, keeping the rifle pointed at them, and then returned down the corridor. *Stupid, stupid, stupid.* Where was that door?

She found it and cracked it open as quietly as she could. The adrenaline kept her up and she had no intention of stopping until she was as far away from here as possible...*Oh my God.*

There was a naked man strapped to a chair with a hood over his head. Blood was running down his chest. She ran to the chair and undid the restraints. The chair wobbled back and forth until she turned the pivot switch to lock the chair in place.

The man moaned. When he woke up, he tried to pull away from her. He reached for the hood but didn't have enough energy to pull it off.

"Oh my God. Oh my God..." Anna said.

"Who ah you?"

"My name is Anna Wodehouse. Who are you?"

"Ahhnna?"

She pulled the hood off his head. He closed his eyes. The light was too much.

"We have to go. I don't know how long any of those men are going to stay unconscious, but I think people are coming soon." She helped him off the chair.

He strained to stand, but she put his right arm around her shoulder and stabilized his walk.

Together, they left the room.

58

HEAD SHOT

Anna and the naked man made it back into the corridor when she realized that she hadn't a clue what to do next. Adrenaline pumped through her, but she stood still, holding him up and thought about the choice before her. Left or right? To the right were two unconscious men around the corner, and left could be deeper in than she wanted to be.

She glanced to her left. A red and white Exit sign. *Left it is!*

The man was quite heavy and wasn't moving very fast. She didn't say anything else to him as she dragged him toward a direction that seemed ambiguous at best.

"Woo ah you?" the man asked.

What had they done to him?

"I told you. My name is Anna," she said.

His face was swollen and looked like it had been struck multiple times. His skin was stretched with the aftereffects of an allergic reaction. She would know; apples were her enemy. His nose was broken and blood was caked on parts of his face and chin. Anna decided to worry about his nakedness later.

He pulled to her left and leaned his shoulder against the wall. "Wheha...is...everybody?" The words were slow but starting to clear.

"I don't know. Maybe the place is deserted." She thought about the three people she had run into so far. "Except for a few unfortunates."

"I need to sit down."

"Can we sit down later? If I ran into three people without trying, there are more somewhere."

He nodded and pushed himself away from the wall. Each step appeared an exercise in control.

As they walked she could feel his chest wheezing as he took in air.

"Did you," inhale, "kill," exhale, "any of them?"

"Of course not," she said.

"Shame."

———

The door had an actual sign on it. Anna almost hollered in mock joy but stopped herself.

Infirmary. There had to be things she could use to clean him up and maybe get him dressed. They couldn't delay for long, but he needed help.

She leaned him on the wall and held the sub-machine gun at the ready. She knocked on the door. And then knocked again.

"Open the damn door," he said.

She opened the infirmary. The room was small, but outfitted well and very white. A number of cabinets against the walls, chairs, and a table where a patient could lie down. Perfect.

She laid the sub-machine gun on the table then ran into the hallway and brought him inside. He was walking a little better, but it was obvious that he was hurting. She positioned him on the examination table, closed the door, and started opening drawers. Bandages, needles. A sink under one of the cabinets. She grabbed a wad of gauze, soaked it, and went over to her patient.

"Tell me if this hurts," she said.

He was lying down totally exposed and vulnerable to her. She felt a wave of sympathy as she wondered what they had wanted him to do. Maybe tossed off a bridge was preferable to this.

"Help me up." He leaned on his right arm and tried to sit up.

She dabbed his face, avoiding his nose. He winced at almost every touch.

"Please tell me you're not a bad guy."

"What do you mean?" he asked.

"I'm fixing you up and then you're going to take that gun and shoot me."

His eyes were open just enough to let in some light. "I'm FBI. That could mean I'm a bad guy."

"You have to walk. Can you walk?" She cleaned off his cheeks and chin. He didn't look good. Maybe escaping with him wasn't such a good idea.

"I don't know, but that doesn't matter." He swayed in a circle. "You have to get out of here. They'll kill you for helping me."

"They almost did kill me." Anna stopped. "You're American. What the hell are you doing here?"

"I can ask you the same thing," he said.

"I'm helping find a fugitive." *In a manner of speaking.*

"I have prior experience." He still slurred his words.

"I'm pretty good at what I do," Anna said.

"What is it exactly that you do?"

"Save naked men I find restrained in torture chambers."

He chuckled. "You're good at that."

It was Anna's turn to laugh. "We have to get out of here."

"You have to get out of here."

Anna felt goosebumps on her neck. They needed to leave. "I'm not leaving without you," she said.

He pushed her away.

"Oh, and that's supposed to mean something?" She poked his nose and as she put her hands on her hips, he vomited speckles of blood onto her clothes.

She shook her head, got some more wet towels, and continued to clean him up. "I think there are some hospital gowns in here."

"Great. Something for me to get twisted in. As long as you don't mind," he flicked his eyes down at himself, "I'd like to stay like this. I can be nimbler."

"Ah. The Greek gladiator ensemble," Anna said.

He jumped off the examination table and leaned against it. His hands held him up. He stood away from the table and took a step forward. Anna grabbed his arm and he pulled it away.

He looked at her through swollen eyes. She could see the level of concentration it took for him to stay upright.

Someone came through the door. Anna and the man stopped moving and watched from behind the racks that hid them from view. A middle-aged man dressed in khaki pants and a white shirt was coming straight for them. He turned the corner of the rack and saw them. His face froze in surprise. He turned to run when a bullet hit him in the back of the neck.

Anna stood transfixed. The man hit the ground with his head in a pool of his own blood. She looked over at the naked man and in his hand was the sub-machine gun. One shot and the man had gone down. She heard rattled breaths. His nose must hurt like hell.

"I think I grit my teeth too hard." He moaned, put the gun back, and leaned on the table.

"I guess you're feeling better."

He had moved so fast she didn't even see him pick up the weapon, aim it, and fire. *Vicious muscle memory.*

"I think I can walk," he said.

Anna nodded at the body at their feet. "I think you have some clothing now." Her voice shook. How could she be so callous? The man was dead.

"He's a little small," Terrell said. "I don't want the clothes to tear while I'm running."

"Beggars can't be choosers. Do you know where we are?" she asked. She got on her knees and started undressing the lifeless man.

He scrutinized the room. "A basement to some building. Way too much concrete."

She took off one of the dead man's shoes. "Nine and a half."

"I can use those."

"Good," she said.

"You okay?"

"Yeah. Yes," Anna said.

"What's the matter?"

"I hope he doesn't have any kids waiting for him to come home tonight."

59

––––––––––

GUN-RUNNING

"You have to go," the naked man said.

"You have to shut up."

Anna was getting tired of this discussion. She had managed to get this very naked man out of captivity, cleaned up, into somewhat stained clothes, and was not going to stop before the goal line.

"Look we both want to get out of here." Anna compensated for his speech problem, but it wasn't easy going. She was terrified, but at least no one had actually hit her, much less hit her over and over again. They could have. She was bound and gagged and there was nothing she could have done about it. She was much luckier than she thought. She wanted to keep it that way.

"Okay, I'm good with a gun, but my arms are kind of tired," he said. He opened and closed his hands like they were new or cold. "You held that thing like you knew what you were doing. I think if you just point and shoot..."

Oh, it was going to be like that? "That is an MP5 sub-machine gun. Not my favorite since it only has a fifteen-shot magazine instead of thirty, but not every weapon can be a Mosin-Nagant."

His eyebrows went up just a touch.

"Oh. You're a fan of the Mosin-Nagant. Into older Russians."

"I kind of like the Heckler and Koch G36 too, but the recoil always bothered me." She squinted. "I like the Germans, too."

Was he flirting? Beat up? Swollen and still flirting?

Anna reached up to his face and stopped just before touching his nose. There was a noise outside the door. She ran over and put her face against it. The man walked over with a more confident stride, but a pronounced limp.

"Getting the hang of it again?" she whispered.

"Yeah, I think I can go for a stroll now." His speech was still hard to understand.

"Not right now. I think a parade is coming through," Anna said. He had the MP5 in his hand. "That will not get us out."

"You want me to leave it behind?"

She shook her head in disbelief. She put her index finger up against her lips. "Shh." She strained to hear. "I think they're gone."

"Then let's go."

The door opened a crack and Anna stepped out into the corridor in her bloodstained clothes. Behind her the man came out grimacing with almost every step. Anna pointed at the Exit sign down the hallway, he nodded and they started walking as fast as they could down the deserted area.

"Can you run?" Anna asked. She kept her voice low.

"I'll give it a try and let you know."

They jogged in the direction of the exit, turning one corner and then another. Plain gray concrete walls and dry, dusty air. This was not the time for an asthma attack. The man was hobbling.

Voices.

They stopped, turned the first doorknob they could find, and entered the room. It was dark and smelled of old paper and trash. The floor didn't give at all under her feet.

"This is..." Anna said.

The man put his hand on her mouth.

Outside the door at least two people were talking loudly enough that the sound could be heard, but the words were muffled. They laughed. They stopped for a moment and one of the people opened the door of the room opposite them. Anna's eyes opened wide. Was the other person going to come in?

The steps receded in the distance.

Anna opened the door and they continued to the exit. If those men had come from that direction that meant there was an entrance there for sure.

"What time is it?" the man asked.

"About six in the morning. I got here around five."

"You know where we are?"

"No. I was bound and unconscious at the time."

They stopped together. An elevator bank. They high-fived. They walked up to it and Anna pressed the only button on the wall.

"What do we do if people get off?"

The man thought a moment. "We can wait around the corner until the guys come out."

"No. By the time we come around, the door might be closed."

The light on the button went dark. "It's here. Why won't the door open?"

Anna pointed to a rectangular block below the call button. "I think it needs a key card."

"Well, we can stop waiting. The exit doors probably have them as well."

Anna thought about security doors. "On the inside of the stairwell. The problem is you're not quite ready for a multistory walk up a staircase."

"Speak for yourself."

"Don't be grouchy." She pulled out Benson's hard plastic ID card and waved it in the air. "And for my next trick..." The alarm went off before she touched the card to the pad. The lights didn't change color, but red lights up and down the hall began flashing.

Anna held the car against the pad and the elevator opened. They ran inside and pressed the only button on the panel. The doors remained open. There was a keypad inside the elevator. She tapped it with Benson's card and the doors closed.

———

The orange morning sun was just starting to lighten the sky when the elevator door opened onto a parking lot with more than a few vehicles. The number of SUVs was noticeable. The black asphalt felt cool through her shoes as Anna wondered how she was going to find Benson's car. If she had the time, she would have slammed the palm of her hand on her forehead. Anna reached into her pocket again and pulled out a dongle. She held it aloft and pressed it. Benson's car chirped at them on the far end of the lot.

"You have good friends," he said.

Anna ran to the black Chevy SUV that looked like it was armored. "You wouldn't believe what I had to do to get this."

The man made a worried face. "Did you kill him?"

"I left him unconscious in his office. He's not going to be happy."

"Not as much as I am."

He ran behind her, favoring his right leg. She opened the driver's side door, ran around the car, opened the passenger door, and helped him in.

She heard shouting and closed the door without looking. Running people. Large men with weapons. She climbed into the driver's seat and took a quick view of the dashboard.

Push button ignition. Instant start. Virtual dashboard.

This was a cool car.

The first shots hit the rear window. Her eyes opened in admiration. Bulletproof.

"Who's better than us? Seatbelts!" she said.

She threw the car into drive and drove through the door in the fence.

"You know he might have a remote kill switch in here," the man said.

"Maybe. I'm betting he's too paranoid to do that. If he could do it to someone, they could do it to him."

Behind her cars pulled out of the lot. Forget about the kill switch. If they decided to use a helicopter, she was in trouble.

She had to get this man to a hospital and she had to get out of the country.

She had to save her father.

PART IV

INCOMPLETE ANSWERS

60

OUT FOR A SPIN

Anna was too busy driving to pay attention to the man. The inside of the SUV was spotless. The dashboard was clean and the virtual dashboard in focus. Everything was black. If it weren't for the vehicle spending the night in the dark, it would have been difficult to stand the heat. As it was, the passenger compartment was cool and the black upholstery comfortably contoured her backside. It didn't smell clean, but it didn't smell lived in either.

Three other black SUVs left the compound and Anna cursed herself for not taking an offensive driving course. All she knew was that if they tapped the side of her vehicle, she would spin out, lose all forward momentum, and stop dead.

She wanted to avoid the *dead* part.

That was her immediate goal as the cars sped up on the highway, trying to get her attention. *Just don't get tapped*. They were going jus over the speed limit which was 113 kilometers per hour. Anna tried to do the conversion in her head, but all she could remember was that 55 miles per hour was 88 kilometers per hour. *Whatever*.

The highway was very straight. Could she use that to her advantage? Would the other motorists help her or would the goons chasing her leave a trail of carnage in their wake to get to her?

They weren't shooting. That was an improvement. This was a public highway and there were other motorists around. There were enough UK police that they wouldn't want to draw that much attention to themselves.

She looked at her speedometer. 150 k/h. That was definitely over 113 kilometers per hour. Maybe they were going rather fast. The black SUVs were blocking all the other traffic behind them. That was probably not good. One of them broke off and started to speed up. She couldn't let him get in front of here. That would be it.

She floored the gas pedal.

Whoa! Benson's car must be on nitrous or something. It was moving.

So were the other cars. *Oh, please, oh, please, don't hit the car.* The black car was having a problem getting around a BMW on her left. She did what she could to keep it that way. The other cars were basically slowing down traffic behind her.

Driving on the left was a definite disadvantage. Of all things! Chased and having to driving on the left!

The SUV to her left tapped the vehicle on the right side, causing it to spin onto the shoulder and stop. She sped up and started going around some of the other cars. She had to make it into London proper. They couldn't get her in there, but she could just as easily have an accident or be stuck in a traffic jam and then it would all be over.

"You okay?" she asked the no-longer-naked man.

"Yeah, other than fearing for my life in this car, yeah. Why?" The muscles in his legs were tense. He pressed his feet on the floor bracing himself.

"You're blinking too fast. I don't know what that means, but if it's enough for me to notice then something is wrong." Something about dopamine activity. Great. He had a cranial injury. "Lean back and close your eyes."

"Are you crazy?"

She slammed on the brakes, letting the SUV pass her faster than he could react. Just as she passed him she hit its rear passenger fender, sending it into a spin where it stopped on the shoulder. *Ha!*

Two can play that game. She turned the wheel, got onto the shoulder, and crossed the grassy divide.

"What are you doing?"

"The other way!" The highway on the other side had a low enough volume of traffic that she could get on and take off. If that didn't get the police's attention, nothing would.

She darted her eyes everywhere. Her side-view mirrors. Her rear mirror. She even turned around.

There they were, coming off the grass. She got off at the next exit, stopped for a few seconds, spun around, and got back on the highway. Would that confuse them? Once back on the highway she drove the car onto the shoulder and got off at the next exit. She made a few turns and got back on the highway again. Where were her pursuers? Her vehicle had to have some kind of GPS so they would know where she was no matter what she did.

"Do you know how to hotwire a car?" she asked.

"Maybe," the man said. "It's been a while."

They needed to ditch the car. "What do you know about GPS systems? "

"What?"

"They must be tracking this car. If they're not, they will if they lose us. Where would the tracking device be? C'mon. You're FBI." Anna asked.

The man shook his head.

Anna could almost feel the strain on his head as he tried to focus.

"Under the dash," he said. "This is a fleet vehicle. That means," he shook his head again, "you want it accessible for repair or replacement, but safe from damage."

"Okay, I'm going to pull over," Anna said.

"No!" The man put his hand over his face, obstructing his eye and covering part of his forehead. "Have to speak softer. Keep driving. Don't hit anything." He undid his seat belt.

"What are you doing?"

The man felt under the dash on his side. His frustration was palpable. He reached along the side of his chair and the passenger seat slid back. When it locked in place, he kneeled down and reached for the dash under the steering column. "Could be in the wheel well," he said. "Or the light assemblies. Or in the upholstery."

They hit an uneven patch of road and they both shook.

The man grunted. "Flat road, please." He looked up at her. "And don't hit anything."

Anna saw the two vehicles come up onto the highway again. She sped up. The man cursed until his head was looking under the dash.

"And?" she asked.

"Don't hit anything." He reached up and shook something. "Here!"

A flat rectangular box landed on her lap. She opened her window as the man pushed himself back to his side of the car. Before he was safely seated, Anna lobbed the unit out the window to her right. She got off the highway again, made a few turns with her pursuers well behind her, pulled behind a stand of tall bushes, and slammed on the brakes.

Anna smiled at the man as he leaned on the passenger-side dash. "You really should put on your seat belt," she said.

———

"You can't leave me here," he said. The slurring was getting worse.

"Yes, I can."

"No, you can't."

They were in the rotunda of an Emergency Room. There were ambulances and medical personnel walking around. Anna wasn't sure which hospital they were at, but she didn't care. She had done what she could for this man, whatever his name was, and it was time for her to catch a flight. After all, she had her papers in order.

"Okay, okay," he said, "at least help me out."

Anna nodded. He opened the passenger door and she jumped out to help him out of the seat. He took her hand and pulled himself out of the seat with obvious discomfort, but stoicism.

"You're a real man," she said.

"You're a real pain."

She smiled and helped him to stand. She had to ask him his name. At the very least, she wanted to know whom she had pulled out of Benson's slimy jaws.

"Hey, can I see that key card?"

She pulled Benson's card out.

The man squinted at it. "Great. No name, no identifying marks. I still don't know anything."

"I don't know who did this to you, but the bastard I dealt with was named Benson."

"Benson?"

A police officer walked over in the midst of various people coming and going. An ambulance pulled in.

The man looked at the officer and then at Anna. "Excuse me, officer..."

Anna poked him in the nose. He cried out and she brought him to the nearest medic. "I'm sorry, but this poor man was just in a bar fight. I don't know his name, but I think he could use some help."

The medic smirked and the officer just rolled his eyes. "Of course, ma'am. We'll take it from here. That was very nice of you," the officer said.

"Oh," she said, "just doing my civic duty."

The man doubled over in pain trying to speak.

"He keeps saying something about being FBI, but he certainly got his bum kicked, didn't he?"

The medic gave the officer a knowing smile, nodded and led the man into the ER.

———

Anna wasn't done yet. She dropped the car off in an alley. After a few blocks she tossed the dongle in a trash bin. She needed to get to Heathrow and buy a ticket. How was she going to do that?

She went into a café and with her last remaining pounds bought a tea. *Why not? My few memories of London.*

I wonder what the FBI guy's name was. He looked familiar, but I know it wasn't that asshole Gillespie.

She pulled out the plastic sandwich bag that contained her paperwork. Along with her new passport was a credit card in her new name. If she used it, they would know where she was going and could pick her up immediately. She would have to buy five of them. Maybe fifty.

The new problem was transportation. After dropping off Benson's car in a No Parking zone, she was left with trying to figure out how she was going to get to the airport. As she walked down the block she stopped and glanced up at a camera. She didn't look anything like herself. She didn't feel anything like herself. She knew she was a mess and needed to clean up.

Wandering the streets of London unmolested made her think that either they were surveilling her or she really had lost them. Not likely.

Across the street. Now there was a hotel she could feel comfortable getting a cab. The Cavendish. She stepped inside and wandered the lobby, taking in the old-style opulence and the upper crust of London, or at least of the tourist class, as they carried their too-small dogs or their very well-mannered children.

She sat down and pretended to be waiting for someone. After a few minutes, a man with a rather large belly walked over to her with his head held high.

"Pardon me?" he asked.

"Yes?" Could he be talking to her? Was she about to be arrested?

"We just received a reminder call and apologize for not having your room ready for you. However, it will be ready in a few minutes as is your rental car."

"My rental car?" She narrowed her eyes. Who knew she was here? Even the man at the hospital, the FBI agent, didn't know she was there.

"Yes. It is ready for you when you need it. Your office just called and confirmed that we had somehow misplaced your reservation."

"My office? Hmm, okay. Could you please have someone bring the car around? I need to go for a drive."

The man turned and walked off. She called after him. "Who called in to confirm?"

The man smiled at her. "Now, now. That would be telling. He said that you would know who he was."

Something told Anna that Benson was not behind this. But if it wasn't him, then who?

61

NOSE JOB

The hospital room was both more and less than Terrell had expected, but he was happy to be lying down again. He ached everywhere. He turned his head and was comforted by the two Bobbies outside his door.

He lost her. God damn it! He could not remember who she was at first and then it hit him. Why didn't he make a bigger deal of it than he did? Oh, right, he was in pain and just conscious enough to know that he needed medical attention.

And she poked his nose.

Anna Wodehouse! He was with Anna Wodehouse! What the hell was she doing here? And why didn't she want to stay with him? Who they hell were those people?

What was the name she mentioned? Henderson? Gregson? Benton? Damn it. What was it? Benson! She mentioned someone named Benson. They tried to kill her. But why? Did she mention a bridge?

Terrell leaned back on his pillow. His head hurt from way in the back to lines of scratchy waves around the sides. His eyes were scorching. The smell of disinfectant stung a little, but it was nothing like the pain all over his body. This was not going to be an easy adjustment, but he had to get back and find her.

She saved him.

Where did she go?

His eyes were getting heavy from the morphine drip. Maybe it was time for a few days off.

Del. The bastard knew Del. His eyes focused on the wall. Fletcher Burkholder was involved somehow and so were these bastards. He couldn't think of enough curses to level at them. He was closer than ever.

"Good afternoon, Special Agent Garrison." A tall man with perfectly combed hair walked in the room. "I hope the accommodations meet your expectations." The smile was too practiced. "I'm the assistant to the Legal Attaché at the Embassy." They shook hands. "Quintin Hardwick."

"We met earlier when I arrived a few days ago," he said.

"Your nose looks like a boxer's. With any luck, they can just pull it back into place." He looked at Terrell's nose the way an entomologist would examine a freshly pinned butterfly. He stepped back and made a pulling motion with his right hand. "They're going to yank it back into place. It's going to hurt like hell."

"Thank you. That makes it all better." Terrell winced at the thought.

"What happened?"

"I wish I knew. It doesn't add up. I interviewed a member of WitSec and suddenly I was kidnapped and tortured to find out what he told me. I was pretty certain that if I had stayed any longer, they would have started breaking off body parts."

"Yes, I understand a young woman brought you in."

"Not just brought me in. We're looking for her. She's supposed to be back in Pennsylvania. Her name is Anna Wodehouse." *And I lost her.*

The Assistant Legat blinked. "You had Carpenter Poole with you? And you let her go?"

"How do you know her?" Terrell felt a pang in his chest. Jealousy?

"We have a bulletin out on her. Fraudulent passport, assault and battery...."

"Sir, I would not be here right now if not for her." *She's in over her head. What happened after we lost her back at her house? What is she involved in? I can't protect her if I don't know what's going on.*

"Well, now we know the kind of man she likes."

Terrell waited for the next statement.

"I made the mistake of playing my hand to soon. I thought, well, I thought she was a pushover. She is an accomplished self-defense practitioner," Hardwick said.

"She took you down?" Now Terrell knew she could take care of herself. The problem was: she didn't understand what she was up against.

"Let's talk about you," Hardwick said.

"No, let's talk about her. What is she doing here?"

"She said she was looking for..." At that another man entered the room and extended his hand to Terrell. He nodded and acknowledged Hardwick.

"Hello, Terrell." His FBI contact in the UK, Jarrod Orr.

"I'd shake your hand, Jarrod," Terrell said, "but you might break it."

"What the hell happened?"

"I'll have a full report on your desk in the next twenty-four hours if you would be so kind as to send over a stenographer. I'm a little under the weather as you might have noticed," Terrell said.

Orr smiled. "You're very under the weather. So under the weather that you're out of commission for the next while. Also under temporarily permanent protection. And stuck here for the near future."

Terrell was concerned. "How near?"

"At least the next three weeks. You're really injured. Don't kid yourself. You might be a young, dashing whipper snapper..."

Terrell smiled. "Give it a rest, Jarrod."

"But you just got the tar kicked out of you and we need to make sure you survive long enough to put those bastards either in prison or caskets."

"I'm good with the former, but I prefer the latter."

"Good." Orr slid a chair over to the side of the bed. "Now, tell me about Carpenter Poole."

"You're gonna be very disappointed. I was still so out of it, swollen, beaten, and bruised, that I could barely think." He leaned back. "When she came in, I remember asking her for her name. When she said 'Anna', my head registered it as important, but I couldn't pin it down." He shook his head as he remembered. "She pulled me out of the chair, led me out to an infirmary, cleaned me up, got me clothes, and drove like a maniac to this ER."

"We know. The reports on the M25 were that there were three other vehicles trying to pull her over and she managed to do some pretty phenomenal driving."

"She's insane." Terrell's eyebrows crinkled. "But she got me here. Why didn't she just leave if she was being held by them as well?"

"Who, them?"

"Damned if I know." Terrell squirmed on the bed. "God, I'm uncomfortable."

"I'm not staying much longer," Orr said. He turned to Hardwick. "I don't think you should stay any longer than you have to either. Let him rest." He cocked his head at the men at the door. "You've got them until further notice."

"Oh, yes, you do." Hardwick looked at Terrell. "I wanted to make sure that you knew that the young lady who let you out of the lion's den is our assassin."

"Excuse me?"

"Mr. Hardwick, get out." Orr said. He turned to Terrell. "You didn't hear that. In fact, you won't hear it until you get out."

"No." Terrell turned back to Hardwick. "What are you talking about? Anna Wodehouse tried to kill Fletcher Burkholder? That's nowhere near possible."

"We have an intercepted call where she says exactly that. And, no, we won't admit that we also have a voice match," Hardwick said.

"This is fucked," Terrell muttered. He glared at the FBI agent. "Jarrod, get me any footage from the ER entrance and see if we can track down where she went. That's a hard car to miss. Indents in the back from gunshots." How did he remember that? So much of the journey was still fuzzy. He heard the back of the SUV being hit and Anna made some remark. What was it? *Who's better than us?*

"About that, we have hospital security getting us the footage from when you were admitted, but we don't have good news about the car."

Terrell tilted his head back.

"Once it left the hospital grounds, the cameras went out again. It hasn't been reported stolen yet..."

"Big surprise."

"But we already found it. She left it in a tow-away zone."

"And the cameras at the tow-away zone?" Orr didn't answer. "This is gonna hurt, isn't it?"

"Do I have to tell you?" Orr crossed his arms and legs. "It can't get any worse."

A woman in a lab coat walked in. "Hello." She went to the foot of his bed and read his chart. "Mister...Garrison." She looked up with a gleam in her eye. "I'm Doctor Breaker from ENT. I understand you have a nose that needs to be straightened."

62

NEW YORK, NEW YORK

Anna Wodehouse couldn't think through the haze of the last two days. She had managed to make it through Heathrow onto her flight, refused to talk to anyone for the duration of the trip, arrived in New York, and booked a less than acceptable room in a hotel down in Brooklyn. When she arrived, she sat in a rickety wicker chair that looked forgotten, pulled her legs up, and hugged them to her chest.

Did Benson clear the way? If he did, why did he let her get away?

What if someone else helped her?

She had no luggage. They questioned her before she boarded. They questioned her before she got through U.S. Immigration. She didn't have the pleasure of talking to anyone from Customs as she not only had nothing to declare, the only thing she had was her purse which contained her fake passport.

And her gun.

Did she want to get caught? She'd actually sewn the gun into the lining of her bag after wrapping it in plastic so it wouldn't make an outline.

Benson was right. There was something about the make-up of the gun that allowed her purse to be screened, and for it not to show up on the TSA scanner or whatever the British equivalent was to TSA.

She needed money when she arrived and she sure as hell wasn't going to use the credit card that returned her to the States. Her brain was rattled, but she knew enough to get her own paperwork together.

She called her bank, supplied all the passwords and secret codes they wanted, and had them overnight a brand-new debit card to a local branch. She didn't care about that. She pulled as much money as she could out of the airport ATM and called it a day.

She saw something moving out of the corner of her eye. A baby roach was walking on the armrest. She jumped out of the chair and swiped her hands quickly over her arms and then her shoulders, neck, and hair.

This was not how she had expected things to go.

But she was alive. Great. Alive, a possible fugitive. And now she felt sorry for her father. Not her father! *HE IS NOT MY FATHER*. She hugged her arms and shivered. She wore the clothes she had purchased at the Cavendish and just charged them to her room. When she asked about the charges, she was also told that her office had taken care of it. Was Benson trying to be nice to her? If she saw him again, she was going to...she was going to...

Damn it! She didn't know what she would do. Hitting him with the paperweight was too good for him. She hoped he was pissed about what she did, and that his head had a permanent indent. She had no proof against him, and she had been in the UK illegally, trying to kill someone. How did she let herself get so wrapped up in her feelings of abandonment that she would think, for even a minute, that any of this was a good idea?

She picked up the brown corrugated box on the side of her bed. A notebook special from one of the big box retailers pretending to be wholesale. She opened the new notebook and looked it over. Backlit keyboard, 17-inch screen, 1 terabyte drive, 16 gig of memory. A nicer notebook than the one Benson now had in his possession, but nothing she could do about that.

Over the next few hours, she installed various programs that would help her protect the PC from the outside world and anonymized her own presence on the net. It took her some time to find the various programs she used on a regular basis, including the ones she had placed in the cloud at UPenn, Azure, and Amazon. The notebook was nowhere near as secure as it used to be and didn't have anywhere close to the number of programs that her dad, she corrected herself, Marshall, had given her that she had always kept. As good as the technology had gotten in the intervening years his software was just that much better. For a quick second she missed him.

Benson was trying to kill him. Did that matter?

Yes, it mattered! If anyone had a right to kill him, it was her. Benson made all that other crap up as an excuse. His file didn't show him doing anything that he wasn't told to do. And there was a long list of project names that Marshall was associated with until 1991 when he pulled himself off the network and went into hiding right after her mother's death.

He went into hiding. And he took Anna along. *That bastard took me with him in 1991. He didn't leave me. What changed in 2005?*

Anna fought herself for another few minutes and decided she had to find him. If he was back in the United States then she would find him and tell him he needed to watch his back. She wouldn't be there to do it because he wasn't there to do it for her when she needed him the most.

She sat back. Would she ever feel better about this? *God, get over it! What is wrong with you?* She brushed away the start of a tear and typed. She opened an anonymous terminal window and decided to try breaking into the U.S. Marshals Witness Security Program database.

———

The intrusion was detected almost as soon as she attempted to come in. They had rigged a honey pot, a portion of the web site to make an intruder feel at home, so they could take the time needed to find who had decided that the U.S. Marshals were a worthy target.

They would have no problem with this one. The routing signature was recognized almost immediately as one from software with a particular bug that allowed them to track the breadcrumbs back from Alexandria.

To New York.

To a network router in Brooklyn.

———

Anna slammed the notebook shut. She wasn't sure what gave it away, but they had put up an extra layer she hadn't counted on. She got in and stayed five minutes longer than she should have. *Idiot!* She was glad that she would be leaving soon, and that she had masked the MAC address on the notebook. She didn't want to lose the $800 the notebook had cost her.

She closed her eyes for a moment. She was going to have to throw the PC away. She hit her forehead with the palm of her right hand. *Stupid, stupid, stupid!*

It was over. There was nothing she could do now but head back to her aunt and uncle and hope that they didn't hate her too much. She blew out a heavy breath. She couldn't go back. The UK authorities had to have given her name to the U.S. authorities.

Her choices were narrowing down faster than she could think of them. She didn't know what it meant to be in over her head until she realized that this was it.

She was so far over her head that she needed help. Real help.

Something was buzzing. Her cell! She had replaced it as soon as she had landed and had them transfer her old number. If her aunt or uncle had called, she could hear their voice mail. She would buy a new phone with a new number as soon as she could. She would have to live off burner phones for a while.

She opened her purse and pulled out the phone. It was silent. A text message had come in. Her aunt and uncle hated cell phones and rarely texted her. It could not possibly be from an old school friend. She didn't have any.

Anna, this is Dad. I know you're looking for me. Come to the Cambridge at 85 and York.

63

———

RE-INSTALLATION

A ghost had just sent Anna a message. The address, 85th and York, was in the Upper East Side of Manhattan, an area she was not that familiar with, at least not in the last seven years, but she knew it was in the Yorkville section. Many of the buildings there had names, but...how did he know her cell number? Had he been following her all these years? Was he really still there looking out for her?

She had to stop. This was a pointless exercise. This was a coincidence. It might be him, but he wasn't looking over her like God or the Force. She was not an avenging angel and he was not a Jedi to be reckoned with. He was just a man. A boring man whom she did not miss. At all. She was sure she had wanted to kill him just the other day.

Sitting in that Brooklyn hotel, she felt like the events of the last week were ages ago.

Anna got up and closed the curtains. The dark yellow fabric felt rough and thick. *I'm exposed, it's my fault, and there's nothing I can do about it.*

She zipped up her jacket and hugged herself. She had to tell Marshall that someone was out to kill him and that they had recruited someone who loved him to do it. Her cheeks felt hot. *I don't love him. But I can't let them get him.*

The police. She should just call the police and let them handle it. She was so done with this. She had no idea what she was doing. The last few days proved that.

What would she tell them? That there was an unknown group of people who worked for the government, who were trying to kill her father, and they recruited her to do it because she wanted to? Now she didn't, and she didn't know who else to turn to?

Yeah, that didn't sound too unreasonable. They would commit her and Benson would arrange to have her killed in her padded room. She would have deserved it.

Who could she call? Aunt Marcie and Uncle Ray? They were still in hiding, she was sure. They might even have been told that she was the one responsible for their troubles. She was feeling more determined to end this, but who could she go to? Benson and friends had access to things she couldn't dream of. Connections she could use to bring them down, but she would end up in prison long before then if she wasn't careful.

Careful? She had already done enough.

She couldn't call the police. She had read too many corruption reports when she was trying to decide on a major that local law enforcement had taken itself out of the running. State police? She thought of them as Highway Patrol or Reno 911. Federal? Who did she know in Federal?

She could hear the ding going off in her head. FBI. That guy she had met weeks ago at the café. He was the one who had come to her house that night. What was his name?

She had put his card in her contact list. And her contact list was in the cloud. She started going through the few names she had. *No...no...no...no...no.*

Terrell Garrison. *Oh, baby!* She had at least one person in the entire universe who might listen to her. And he looked interested in her so he might even listen over the noise of guilt.

How did she ever get herself into this?

She dialed his number. After a prolonged journey through the FBI phone system she was routed to his phone. He didn't answer.

She left voicemail.

———

"Dispatch, this is 54. How many of us do you need to go to this hotel? If there's some pimply faced kid trying to break into a federal system I'm pretty sure we can handle him. Over."

The radio was clear in the afternoon air. "Understood, cooperate with the feds who arrive at the location. The other 4 cars are already on their way."

"Roger that. On route."

———

Anna opened her notebook and promptly killed the terminal that had given her away. She took out a thumb drive she purchased along with the notebook and copied all of the software she had down-loaded. At least she wouldn't have to go through that again.

Once copied, she began a full installation of the software. She wanted that box as pristine as possible just in case. It probably wouldn't matter, but she was meticulous about those sorts of things. She could work much easier with everything at a clean starting point. Not like the room she was in. Her room might never be clean.

Another buzz. She logged into her phone. Another text.

The police are on their way. Hurry.

You have got to be kidding. They're never that fast. They collect more forensic evidence than there are books in the Library of Congress before they do anything. How can they be on their way?

Benson. This had to be his doing. He was racking up points. Burning through his trust credits. She wasn't sure how she was going to take him down, but doing permanent damage was now on her bucket list. She wasn't going to wait that long to make it happen.

Once she got to Marshall and warned him, Benson was next. She would destroy Benson if it was the last thing she did.

Even if it killed her.

She heard a screech. She looked out her window.

Whoa! Four police cars and at least one unmarked car. Time to go.

She grabbed her purse and PC and shut the door.

She heard feet pounding up the steps, which meant the stairs were out. She didn't know if there was even an elevator.

Emergency exit.

She ran for the door, opened it, and then closed it just enough to soften any noise. She went down the stairs, grateful to be wearing flats, but not sure if she should have taken the PC with her. If the last few days had taught her anything, it was that her fondness for high heels wasn't always practical, but her attachment to her PC was unbreakable.

Down the steps.

Out the exit door which scraped against the ground and door jamb sounding like the inside of a car compartor, but left her at the rear of the building.

She took off and heard someone call out. It sounded like it came from the fire escape. If she turned around, she knew they would get a good look at her and improve the general eyewitness description that would be wildly inaccurate by the time anyone asked.

There was a subway entrance around the corner. She could get there in a flash and be on a train in no time. The transit system cameras would get plenty of pictures of her, but it would be too late. Anna was stuck with the clothes she was wearing and her bag. She would change trains every stop for a few trains, get out, walk to another station, and get on the 4, 5, or 6 train to the Upper East Side.

She had to tell Marshall someone was out to kill him.

64

MEETING THE WIZARD

Terrell Garrison was sure someone was following him. He wasn't in the mood to be snatched, so on the off chance he was right, he had his gun on the passenger seat.

All he could hear out of his right ear was a muffled cottony sound like there was water stuck inside. The doctor had told him his hearing would come back at some point, but that point might be never. Whoever that bastard was who fired that gun was on Terrell's I'm-going-to-fuck-your-face-up list. Terrell always took care of that list. He took care of it so well that it was always a short list.

He was tired. He had arrived from the UK just the other day over everyone's objections, but he had a missing person to find. On the flight over, he was hoping that the bandage across his face wouldn't seem too out of place. On top of his being conspicuous, having a wide swath of cloth covering the front of his face was annoying in ways he couldn't begin to describe. He pulled it off as soon as he arrived at Kennedy. It hurt more than he could describe, but not enough to leave it on. *Note to self: Don't break your nose again. Avoid torture while you're at it.*

He found a parking space ahead and pulled in. Terrell had to admit that he was pulling over because he still felt terrible. He hadn't checked his office line in the last hour so he was overdue. A car going by honked at him for not moving fast enough. *Welcome to New York.* A shame it wasn't his left ear that had the hearing problems.

He punched the office number on his Blackberry followed by his PIN. First call: a friend looking to meet him for a beer. He could use one of those, but not for another week at least. A local cop returning his call for information on some construction work Del had mentioned in one of his reports. Nothing seemed wrong, but the construction guy he was looking for was dead. Committed suicide. *Suicide?* That was never a good way to go. He would call him back for more details. It would probably be another dead end, but you never knew. Dead end. *Yeah, literally.*

"Special Agent Garrison? This is Anna Wodehouse."

Terrell put the message on speaker phone and put the car in drive.

"Or Carpenter Poole. I'm not sure which name you remember me with. You probably don't remember me." *Sonofabitch. She's back and no one noticed. How was that possible?*

"Um, I just wanted to say that I think I might be in some trouble and could really use a neutral party. I'm going up to 85th and York in the Upper East Side to meet with my dad, um, Marshall, the man everyone is supposedly looking for. Apparently, he's in Witness Protection and they forgot to tell anyone." Noise on the line (*did she cough?*). "Anyway, that's where I'm going. I'm going to," more noise, "him first and then disappear. I'll be in touch."

Did she just say she was going to kill him or talk to him?

He pulled out of the spot and called the office.

Someone picked up. "Special Agent..."

"Gottfried! You need to get a hold of the marshals and tell them that a wanted fugitive is on her way to one of their locations to kill a member. Got that? 85th and York," Terrell said.

"Got it. Marshals. 85th and York."

"Find out where Fletcher Burkholder is. That's an alias that only the marshals can follow, but I need to know where he is. Is he still under protection or has he been planted? I don't care. Find out and call me back." Terrell hung up and took off up Broadway. He pulled over for a quick second, reached into his glove compartment, took out a portable police light, which he slammed on the roof of his car, and turned on his siren.

Anna had simply walked backed through Immigration, got a place to rest, and found her father. Again. The entire U.S. government had spent years trying to find him, failed, been alerted to his presence by an anonymous tip, lost him again, and a twenty-four year-old-girl tracked him down again.

85th and York. Nice quiet neighborhood about to be on the news tonight.

He drove around car after car until he decided to head up the West Side Highway. That would give him more maneuverability and he could cover more ground between lights before he would have to slow down and drive around the cars that refused to get out of his way. New Yorkers didn't always hear sirens.

Traffic ahead. This was unbelievable.

A black SUV cut him off and another blocked him from behind. He unfastened his seatbelt and waited. Soldiers came out of both vehicles. He lowered his window as two of them approached. Military on the West Side Highway. The palms of his hands felt cold. *Please let this be a mistake.* His face felt flush.

"Would you come with us, please?"

"Something you want to tell me?" Terrell asked.

"No, sir." The one who was speaking was young and polite. He held a rifle across his chest. He could afford to be polite.

Terrell motioned for him to step back and he opened the door. Both men stood at attention and didn't help him out of the vehicle.

"I'm an injured man, you know."

They said nothing. Terrell closed the car door.

"I noticed you had someone tailing me earlier. Don't think you got away with that."

"I'm afraid we don't know anything about that, sir." The soldier to Terrell's left led him to the black SUV behind his car. Lincoln Navigator. 2012 model. Polished to a sheen; the tires looked like solid rubber.

Soldiers and black SUVs. *Yeah, this is going to be an interesting conversation.*

"If you guys are arresting me, you forgot to Mirandize me," he said. "And I can't hear out of my right ear so make sure you read it to my left."

The door opened into a black interior and an empty seat. A voice called out, "Please come in, Special Agent."

Terrell tried to look in, but the man's face was hidden by the glare of the sunlight against Terrell's eyes. "You're Special Agent Terrell Garrison, correct?"

"I am."

"Please step in. We've already done enough damage to traffic. We'll continue on in this car and one of my staff will follow in your car."

"Oh, please. I'd really rather not."

"We know where you're going. 85th and York, right?"

Terrell straightened up.

"Don't be so surprised. Some things we know, but there are a lot of others we don't."

There was something familiar about the way the man spoke. The hot sun baked Terrell's suit. He felt a wave of soreness wash over him. He needed to sit down.

"Please, we'll get you to where you want to go."

Terrell climbed into the SUV, hiding the pain from his legs. Once he was inside, the lighting was normal.

The uniformed man extended his hand. "Good afternoon. My name is General Malik Palma."

Terrell stopped in surprise. General Palma?

He was shaking hands with the Director of the NSA.

65

WORKING THE PLAN

Anna arrived at The Cambridge on 85th Street and York Avenue a little over an hour and a half after getting on the train in Brooklyn. She carried her purse slung over her shoulder and her PC in her hand. The weight of it tired her and she considered hiding it somewhere safe for later retrieval. If there was a later. There would have to be a later.

She walked past the three water fountains in front of the building and continued east. There was a single police car there. Maybe that was normal. She had passed another building on 84th and First Avenue on her way to York that had a mini-police cruiser in front of it.

The blue sky was almost devoid of clouds and the sun didn't feel quite as hot as it had been back in London. The shadows should have been sharp and harsh. The buildings protected Anna with a dark shadow that made the colors of the walkups look brighter than they deserved.

Anna decided that what she was going through was buyer's remorse. The more accurate term would be Killer's Remorse. Now that she had decided not to end Marshall's life she had to rationalize her decision. She hated when she had to do that. At least at a conscious level. She was fine with her brain doing things behind her back. She was used to that. It was when she realized she had made a really bad decision that she hated herself.

It was time to make up for it. If she wasn't going to kill Marshall, she would end up dying if the police shot first and asked questions later.

Strange saying. Her projects always worked out better when she shot first and asked questions later. Sometime research got in the way of discovery. She rounded the block and decided to shoot first. Up the residential street, past the local stores, and back to the building. As she approached the corner of the Cambridge a police officer walked up to her. She stopped and let him approach so he would feel in control.

"Excuse me, miss, can I help you?"

"Is something wrong, officer?" She smiled with her eyes wide open.

"I've seen you go by before. Do you live here?"

"Well! Hi!" Anna brought her shoulders up and down. "My friend lives in that building and seeing police there," she looked to the left and right with a nervous smile, "kind of freaks me out. You know what I mean?"

"I'm sorry, miss, but unless you live here, you're going to have to move on."

"Oh, but Officer..." Anna noticed a Hispanic woman coming out of the building.

"Give her a call, have her meet you down here, and she can take you up. Otherwise you're going to have to move along." He leaned in. His breath smelled of minty gum. He needed a shave. He was too old not to maintain his appearance. "You wouldn't want to make me put you in the squad car, would you?" He winked at her.

Anna wondered what it would be like to poke his nose like she did to the guy she dropped off at the hospital. Maybe poke him in the eye.

Anna broke out in a howling laugh. "Oh! No, I wouldn't want you to do that! Yeah, let me call my friend. Maybe I'll just meet her at the movie theater on 86th." She hunched her shoulders and walked up the block in the direction of the woman.

When she was far enough away, Anna trotted up to the woman who was heading downhill on York. She was middle-aged and walked with a slight stoop. Part of the invisible working poor of the city. "Perdona! Perdona!" *Excuse me! Excuse me!*

The woman stopped and didn't respond. Her face was expressionless. No wrinkles, but leathery skin. Short, with a long sleeved jacket. She looked Peruvian. Didn't she feel the heat?

Do you understand me?

She nodded.

I was wondering if you could help me with something.

No response.

My father is in that building, but before I go up, I wanted to surprise him.

The woman smiled a little.

I just want him to get a note. Do you think you could deliver it for me?

She hesitated. Anna did her best pleading look. The woman gave the barest of nods.

Very good! Very good! I'll give you $50 right now for being so nice.

Anna reached into her purse and pulled out what little cash she had. Would she need it later? If she was still free, she could go to an ATM. She handed the woman the money. The woman took it and then tried to hand it back.

I don't think I should take that.

Oh, please, you have to. I won't feel right if you don't.

It's just that I need to go home. I'm all finished with my work today.

Oh, but my father loves surprises and it would make me so happy if you would do it.

The woman withdrew her hand with the money. Anna looked around and pulled out some more money and stuck it in her hand. The woman's skin felt rough.

Come with me. I have to give you the note, but first I have to write it.

The woman smiled at her.

You haven't written it yet? What a bad daughter you are!

They both laughed.

———

Anna sent the woman on her way and looked for a side entrance to the building. She was sure there had to be one. She pulled out her cell phone and typed a message back to her father.

I'll be there soon.

66

PASSING NOTES

Fletch sat on the sofa of his new temporary home, taking in the sights. There were three U.S. Marshals attending him: two men and a woman. All wore dark pants and white shirts, but the woman wore shoes with a slight heel. She had on aviator sunglasses and sported curly hair. Very curly hair. The men were standard issue feds. Receding hairlines and almost flat stomachs. Their spouses were standard issue wives he was sure with standard issue kids who went around showing off that their father was an FBI agent. *Whoop dee do.*

Someone had sprayed disinfectant into the two-bedroom, single bath apartment. The sharp tingle of the spray tickled the back of his nose and tongue.

He picked up the mask he had worn into the elevator until he arrived in his apartment. Today's safe house, as it were. He hoped all this running around would be over soon. While he hadn't had this much excitement in a long time, he was over it. The life he might have had back in the UK was now a fading memory and nothing was going to change that. Where would he end up? They would never let him stay in New York City. He wasn't even sure why they brought him here.

"Excuse me," he directed his comment to the marshals, "is

anybody going to make a beer run? This is New York, right? Plenty of liquor stores." His military training had not escaped him. He knew given the right motivation, like feeling sorry for him, they would share in the pleasantries. Lower their decision-making capabilities.

The female marshal heard him. "No worries, Mr. Smith. Someone will make a grocery run soon." She turned back to her colleagues and eyed him over her shoulder.

I think she likes me. I can use that.

He clenched the soft black mask in his hand. The material was like silk or polyester only it breathed when he wore it. He drummed the fingers of his left hand on the sofa cushion. Other than the marshals they were alone in the apartment. He had done the tour of the apartment the other day when they first arrived and it did nothing to improve his mood. In the past he used to be as involved as a husband and father could be; civic affairs, parent-teacher night, soccer, cheerleading. The remote to the 55-inch TV was untouched on the coffee table. What could he learn on the boob tube that would be of interest to him?

The only thing making him nervous was being here. The last place he wanted to be was in New York City. How could he get them to move when even telling them that would give them something they weren't allowed to know?

There was a knock and before anyone approached the door, it swung open and a New York City police officer entered. With him was a petite Latin woman who looked incredibly embarrassed. She didn't catch when the three marshals all put their hands on their hips near their holsters.

"Perdona?" She held her hands together at her chest. She wore simple clothes and a bag slung over her shoulder.

The police officer looked at Fletch on the sofa in front of him and then at the others. "I checked the purse and wanded her. She checks out."

A fan, Fletch thought.

"Anyone here speak Spanish?" the female marshal asked.

Fletch couldn't believe it. None of them knew Spanish? Didn't they live in New York?

"Perdona," she said again and reached into her purse.

The three marshals moved in unison and positioned their hands like they were pulling out their weapons. Probably Glock 22s.

Her eyes opened wide and she started shaking her hands and repeating, "Perdoname! Perdoname!"

The female marshal let go of her weapon and walked over to the woman. She towered over her as she held her hands up, palms facing out. "Todo esta bien…"

Keystone cops. Fletch almost rolled his eyes.

"Perdona, senora. Esta gente no le haran dano," Fletch said. *Excuse me, ma'am. These people won't hurt you.* "Por que estas aqui?" *Why are you here?*

"Pues, una chica joven me dio esta nota y dijo que quería darle una sorpresa." *Well, a young girl gave me this note and said she wanted to surprise you.*

"De verdad?" *Really?*

Fletch stood up and made a confident approach to her with his hand outstretched. The woman reached into her bag again and pulled out an envelope. Her hand shook, and she hesitated for a moment before giving it to him.

"Esperas su hija?" *Are you waiting for your daughter?*

The questions caught him by surprise. "Si."

"La amas mucho?" *Do you love her very much?*

"Si."

"Ella te quiere mucho." *She loves you very much.*

Fletch stepped around the table and took the envelope. Handwritten on the outside was *Dad.* He didn't know what to say. He took a step forward and hugged the woman. He touched her hair and smelled her sweat. He didn't remember the last time he embraced someone.

Fletch let her go. "Gracias."

"De nada."

As he straightened up the female marshal took the envelope out of his hand. He took two steps, grabbed it, and pushed her against the wall.

"Touch it again and I'll show you how shatterproof that window is," he said.

The taller of the two men stood by the woman and the other took out his gun and pointed it at Fletch. "Hand that over, please," he said.

Fletch looked at the envelope again. He was holding something he never thought he would hold ever again. He opened the letter.

"What does it say?" the female marshal asked.

Fletch read it to himself. It was a short note, so he read it again. And again. And again. The words didn't matter. What mattered was who wrote them.

Someone is trying to kill you. I get that you have to hide, but can I see you one last time?

I'll be on the roof.

The police officer was on his radio. "Someone made contact. I repeat, someone has made contact."

The marshals pulled out their cell phones and started calling whoever it was that marshals called at a time like this. Five minutes ago, he would have wanted to know exactly what they were planning, how they were doing it, and who they were doing it with.

Five minutes ago. Now, Fletch didn't care.

He was in a dream. *She's here. She wrote me a note.* "She wants to see me one last time. If it's her, I'll do anything you want."

67

BLOWING IN THE WIND

"Forgive me, Special Agent." Palma squirmed in his seat. "I hope I'm not getting in the way of your investigation." He tugged at the collar of his shirt, forcing his tie to loosen just a touch. His pale skin went from red back to wan as he pulled the collar out.

The SUV pulled out into traffic. It had its own light board on the roof and wound its way around cars and through lights. Terrell looked out his window and watched the traffic from a higher vantage point than his souped up sedan. The convoy of vehicles moved as one.

"I'll hope you forgive me, General, but you are interfering in an investigation." Terrell sat back. His muscles felt tight and sore, and he turned his neck back and forth to stretch it.

"Then I also hope that you will appreciate what I have to tell you, Terrell." Palma crossed his legs in the roomy interior of the vehicle.

The only smell Terrell could detect was spray disinfectant.

"May I call you Terrell, Special Agent?"

"Please. And do tell, General. I'm all ear," he said.

Palma chuckled and then became serious. "I heard about your encounter in Great Britain. I'm glad that you survived it and were able to tell your superiors everything you could about the group that held you hostage."

"Yes, my superiors." He felt an instant dislike for the man. "They weren't holding me hostage. They wanted information and then they were going to kill me. The term hostage gives the impression that they were going to let me go." Something tickled the back of his mind. "Were they?"

Palma stared back. "The fact that you got away would imply that they weren't that concerned with losing you."

I got lucky. And I had Anna. "Only they know that, sir. All I know is that they were very interested in the man I'm heading over to see right now."

Palma turned away. "John Doe? Formerly Fletcher Burkholder. Formerly Antony Byrnes, formerly Walker Dobson, formerly, and formerly and formerly." He waved his hands toward the window. "Fletch Burkholder..."

"What's his real name?"

"That doesn't matter," Palma answered.

"I get to decide that. That can be construed as interfering with an ongoing investigation."

"The investigation into the death of Del Kirby is a cold case that you have been chasing for years now. Based on your last reports you think the group that kidnapped you was involved."

"You've been reading up on me." *So this is what it feels like to have someone looking in your shorts.*

"You are involved with Fletcher Burkholder now. I hope that after this conversation you will consider moving on."

"Moving on?"

"Closing the case. I can give you the information you want only because of how much we know about Mr. Burkholder.

"He's the one you want," Palma said.

Terrell thought General Palma sounded certain. "Is he? Are you saying that you or someone under your command had information directly related to an ongoing investigation and that you withheld that information?"

The General glanced out his window. "The weather has been beautiful these last few days."

Terrell shook his head. "Oh, I know he was involved. If you have any information, I would be very grateful to have it. If you have any files, I would be very grateful to read them."

Palma gave the smallest of smiles. "I'll have my people look into it."

"Thank you. It is a beautiful day out."

"Fletcher Burkholder killed Del Kirby," Palma said.

Terrell thought he misheard him and sat back. He put his hands on his legs. "Could you repeat that, please?"

"Fletcher Burkholder killed Del Kirby back in 2005," Palma said.

Terrell considered what to say next. *You're under arrest for obstruction of justice. Why would you tell me this? Why now?* His arms ached as he gripped his legs. "What else can you tell me?"

"Nothing. We don't know why he was killed or what Fletch, and his accomplices, did with the body."

"Del was a close friend of mine as well as my partner for many years." He unfastened his seat belt and turned toward the General.

"I'm sorry," Palma said. "I apologize. I didn't mean to sound so disconnected."

"You didn't know Burkholder was in WitSec?" Terrell was incredulous. "That's not anywhere close to possible. You're military, but you're not normal duty so I know you're Intelligence."

"Truth be told..."

Good luck with that.

"We're part of a cooperating venture between National Security and Central Intelligence. Since the walls came down after 9/11 there are a great many things we do to help our country."

Yeah, like kidnapping and torturing people. "I understand. Why did you pick me up? My phone number at the Bureau is listed," Terrell said.

"Fletcher is important to us. He has information we need and yet need to keep away from the public eyes of our enemies."

That sounded like boilerplate to Terrell. Disavow all knowledge and responsibility. Let other people deal with the collateral damage. He needed the General and his information as much as being in the same car with him was making him uncomfortable.

"Understood, General. How can I help?"

"Let us talk to him," Palma said.

"Unacceptable."

"The things he may reveal are highly classified."

"I have clearance," Terrell said.

"Trust me, not that high."

"When it comes to my cases, my clearance is always high enough." Maybe Terrell would offer to let one of his men be present at the interrogation. The General wouldn't have to ask permission for that. He just had to wave his big Intelligence gathering hand to do that.

"You interviewed him during your time in the UK," Palma said.

"I did."

"May I ask if he told you anything that could compromise this country?"

"You may ask. You can file for inter-departmental access to everything I have," Terrell said. He would be damned if he was going to give this man anything more than the minimum.

"But as one colleague to another..."

Terrell smiled. That was a good one. "As one colleague to another Fletch didn't tell me anything I didn't already suspect. He confirmed one or two things."

"Such as?"

"Put in the paperwork or give me something I can work with."

"I already did. He killed your partner."

"Information that would have been useful five years ago."

"He must have stumbled onto something he shouldn't have. And we didn't know that five years ago."

"Such as?"

"If I knew that, Special Agent Garrison, we wouldn't be having this conversation."

"But we aren't having this conversation," Terrell said. "Are we?"

Palma struck the driver's seat twice and the SUV pulled over. "Perhaps you're better off driving yourself."

"Perhaps I am."

Terrell started to open the door when a soldier opened it for him and stood at attention. They were on the west side at 50th Street. Terrell got out.

Palma called out to him. "I read in your report that they held you naked for several days without food or water. Remember, Special Agent, we're here to help. We don't want you blowing in the wind with your privates exposed. Don't let yourself get in over your head without some friends around who can help you out."

Terrell closed the door.

68

THE NEW PLAN

"Who wants to see you?" The marshal who was pointing his gun at Fletch was the first to ask. "Someone we should care about?"

Fletch couldn't believe he could be surrounded by such smart, clueless people. "I am not sure how there could be so many of you out to protect me who know so little about what's going on."

"Sir, we are not allowed to know what's going on," the female marshal said. "We only know enough to get this done. You are a highly sought target and we have to make sure nothing happens to you."

"Something is about to happen to me." He shook hands with the woman who brought him the note. He placed his right hand under her hand as he shook it, and then covered it with his left. He smiled and said, "Un placer a conocer usted." *It is a pleasure to meet you.*

"Con mucho gusto," she said. *My pleasure.* She turned and walked out of the apartment, followed by the police officer who closed the door behind them.

Fletch turned to the three marshals. "Someone is out to kill me."

"Yes, sir. That's why we're here."

"It is not the person who sent this note."

"How do you know that?" the shorter of the two men asked.

"I know because...because I know them." If it were possible to see three mouths drop all at once, this would have been the moment.

The female looked over at her colleagues. "Are you sure?" She took a step toward him. "Sir, I know what you think this is, but you're being lied to."

"Yes, I'm sure," Fletch said. "I have been lied to for months, for years now." He walked over to the door and put his hand on it. "I want to know what you're going to do about this, before I tell you what to do."

"Sir, this has to be called in. The uniform who just walked out started the process. There will be more cars and personnel than you can imagine converging on this location over the next fifteen minutes."

Fletch walked over and felt the note in his hand. He held it tight, crumpling it a little. He imagined her writing it. He taught her to read when she was five. To build obstacles from sofa cushions. They fought over dating and curfew. And not saying goodbye when he decided it was time to go into hiding. He didn't have many choices in that, but he had hope for the future. Hope that would be fulfilled today.

"Sir, we need that note."

"We're doing this my way," Fletch said.

"Your life may be in danger. You have to do it our way."

Fletch took the note, and folded it in half. "I will eat this first." He put the note between his teeth. The shorter marshal pulled out his gun again. *What a simplistic thinker.*

"Sir, give us the note," the female said.

"Only if we do this my way."

"Hold on." She pulled out her cell and dialed a number. She stepped away for a moment, but Fletch could hear her.

"Yes, yes, someone's made contact...Look, he won't give us the note. I want to run some analysis on it before he drools all over it...Yes, he has it in his mouth...He says he has a plan to get whoever it is...No, we haven't listened to the plan. The fact that he has one means it's against protocol...You get someone to authorize that and I'll do it...yeah, yeah, go do it. Bye." She turned back to Fletch. As she was about to speak she waved her hand at the gun-holding marshal who then lowered his weapon.

Fletch took the note out of his mouth. *That was really tasteless.* "So?"

"So," she crinkled her lips, "what's your plan?"

"I want her alive."

"Good, so do we," she said.

"If I give you this note, I want it back."

"Can't do that. Once you give it to me, we're sending it in as evidence in case anything happens. Once we're done with it, we'll send it back."

Fletch knew they were right. "Okay, I'll give you the note once we're clear on how this is going down."

"We already know how this is going down," Shorty said. "We're locking down this building and spending the next four hours checking every corner and crevice for whoever sent that note and holding them on attempted murder."

"Fine," Fletch said. "Everything he just said. And by that I mean none of it. I know where she is."

Female rolled her eyes.

"Okay, he or she is. You guys are going to back me up, but I am going to see her, or him, alone."

"If you die on our watch, we'll all lose our pensions," Shorty said.

"I'll be dead," Fletch said, "so I won't care."

"True enough," she said. "How about some details."

"I have to go meet her somewhere. I have to get there before this area is crawling with people who might find her and kill her."

"Her?"

"I'll get to that." Fletch was single-minded. She was going to meet him up on the roof, but he wasn't giving that up yet. "I will go alone, but you'll be nearby. Not so close to be seen, but close enough to do something if anything happens."

The female marshal shook her head. "Why are you doing this?"

"I know them. I need to bring them in. No shooting. No nothing. As soon as I have them then we make more decisions."

"Like?"

Fletch wasn't prepared to discuss that. If her paperwork was already in the system, it would be a slam dunk to get her added and taken off the radar. She obviously thought about it. He just needed to convince her. This would not be the last time they would see each other.

"So, you're saying that you'll let us accompany you to the rendezvous point, you'll meet with someone we believe wants to kill you, but you will bring them in without firing a shot," the female agent said.

"Yes," Fletch said.

"Any other requests while I go take my anti-anxiety meds?"

Fletch thought a minute. "Yes. I'll need a gun." He held the note in this hand, knowing they wouldn't do what he wanted. "If I have to kill you all to do this, I will."

"You make a very persuasive argument," she said.

"Let's just say I have prior experience."

The three marshals looked at each other.

Fletch stood holding onto the note like a winning lottery ticket. The marshals were busy rationalizing how to help him. He could tell. "Do we have a deal?"

The female had become the de-facto leader. "I think we do."

Fletch handed her the note. She held it by a corner with two fingers, reluctantly opened and read it, and gave it to the taller man next to her.

"Okay, Mr. Smith. So far you haven't really given us much of a plan, but it does sound like a good suicide move. Who do you think you're meeting?" she asked. Fletch hadn't given her the envelope.

"My daughter."

The three marshals straightened up. Shorty buttoned his jacket while the tall one put his hands on his hips.

"Really?" she asked. "We hadn't gotten around to telling you something."

69

TELLING TALES

The cars on the West Side Highway were not going to accommodate a convoy of vehicles, much less a lone man walking back to his car. Terrell's neck felt brittle. A car door opened behind him. He was done with this. There was no point continuing. He had to get to Anna.

"Agent Garrison!" It was the General. "Before we both make a mistake we may regret I think we should be a little more understanding."

Terrell limped over, favoring his right leg.

"Listen," Palma said, "we're both on the same side. That man used to work for me. He and I have a lot of history." The General rolled up his sleeves. "Let's sit down for a minute and help each other."

"General, I don't mean to be disrespectful, but I have somewhere I need to be." He pulled out his cell phone and looked at the time. He should have already been there.

"I know. Fletch is waiting for you."

Hmm, the General likes tossing confidential information around. "He knows I'm coming?"

"No, but if you're heading up to 85th Street then you fully expect to see him again and talk to him."

General Obvious. "Exactly."

"And even though he knows you, he won't cooperate."

"You sound pretty certain. Because of you? Are you going to stop him?"

"No, because he's been alone for too long."

Terrell checked out the convoy of vehicles. Three black SUVs. That was a lot of protection.

"You're not making any sense." Terrell said.

"I'm giving you what you want. I'm trading information. I'm going to give him what he wants. Until I do, he won't talk to anyone."

The SUVs were on the move again. Terrell still felt uncomfortable, but it wasn't muscle soreness. The trading of information was making him nervous. They also weren't moving very quickly.

"How much further to 85th?" Terrell asked the driver. No answer.

"The man you know as Fletcher Burkholder was a highly decorated soldier and brilliant tactician." The General reached into the seat pocket of the chair in front of him and pulled out a bulging file folder. "This is rather redacted. And you can only read that here." He handed it to Terrell. "After the war in Iraq I hand-picked him for an assignment that should have made his career. The man was incredible. Gifted in so many areas, strong as all hell."

"Great resume so far. He does have a temper problem. Do your men always drive this slow?"

"Something he developed after all this. He was a soldier first, but otherwise, I knew him personally and there was no gentler a person you could meet."

Terrell looked through the file. Pictures of Fletch. Scores of black marks everywhere. The file could be about anyone. Dates of service were covered. Addresses. Names. The file was almost useless.

"I need this," Terrell said.

"Can't have it. That man doesn't exist."

"Yes, he does. We can go visit him together," Terrell said.

"I'm only going to make sure nothing goes wrong. I'm not seeing him." he caught himself, "Fletch is not allowed to see me." He folded his hands. "I'm not allowed to see him."

Now that was going to be a story. "Tell me about what he did to deserve the full protection of the U.S. government. And who's after him, because they have been doing some nasty stuff to us after all these years."

"We don't know," Palma said.

Terrell shut the file hard enough to cause some pages to fall.

Palma said, "We don't know. We have some ideas, but until we actually talk to someone, we just don't know. Look at how easy it was to hide the death of your partner."

Terrell felt like the General had punched him in the stomach.

"What did Fletch do?" This file was coming with him. He didn't care if he was going to have to wrestle with the General's security detail.

"Listen, the easiest way to turn someone is not to turn them. You make them do something that appears to align with their beliefs, but turns out not to be. Get them caught up in something that they think is one thing, but is really something else."

"I know. Cognitive dissonance. We can't keep two different ways of thinking about ourselves in our head at the same time so we have to reconcile the conflict between the two."

"Exactly. Fletch," the General looked down at the floor for a moment and sighed. "Fletch got caught up in the wrong end of an assignment. It's simpler than you think to find yourself compromised and for you not to even realize it. It turns out Fletch was supplying a foreign country with information about a highly sensitive operation happening here in the States that would easily cause diplomatic destabilization with Russia, India, North Korea, and a number of other countries that we count as friends and partners and potentially started conflicts where none are needed."

"Forgive me, General, but most of that sounds like made-up bullshit that says all kinds of things, but says nothing. What's his name?"

"That's classified."

"What was the operation?"

"Classified."

"What connection do you have to him that you're going to see him yourself?"

"Classified."

"This is getting old. Why is he in WitSec?"

"He's not in WitSec." Palma winced. "Fletcher has an incredible number of secrets in his head that could cause irreparable harm to the interests of the U.S. But we're not savages. We could have easily locked him away or just killed him, but he did an incredible number of things for his country and his betrayal was unfortunate, but unwilling. Fletcher is in a special Federal program not because of what he's told us, but because of what we don't want him to tell."

"You're tying me into a knot. I can't know who he is, or why he's doing anything, but I'm supposed to think that this information is useful?"

"Agent Garrison," Palma said, "Fletch is a patriot. One of the real ones. He gave up his family, his friends, for the greater good of his country. He was duped into betraying his country and now we are doing what we can to take care of him while that is still possible."

"What was he doing in the UK?"

"I don't know. I haven't known his whereabouts for years. That was part of the program. I helped him get in and then he simply vanished. I had no idea where he's been for the last several years and suddenly I'm getting requests to help him because he's tired of being alone.

"Can you blame the man? Torn from his family, betrayed, an unwilling traitor, and holding more knowledge in his head about clandestine operations than most operatives know," Palma said.

"Why are you here?"

"I was called by the U.S. Marshals. They handle WitSec and FedProtect. They told me what he wanted. We had some problems doing it, but we were able to accomplish what they could not."

"Which is?"

"His wife passed away a number of years ago and his only child has been living with some relatives.

"We're bringing him his daughter."

70

CRYING FOR CAMERAS

Anna found a side-entrance to the building and waited for someone to come through. One way or another she was going to get to her father and let him know that even though she hated him she still wanted him to be safe.

She also knew that this was probably the one chance she had to do what they should have done seven years ago: say goodbye. She wasn't sure if that was all she wanted, but she would run with that for now.

The two movers who came out the side-entrance seemed appreciative of her help in holding the brown scratched-up door open while they did their work. The door gave a scream every time she slid it open just a little more to allow the movers to get by. Anna picked up a bag of stuff and followed them in.

Anna started her walk upward. The stuffiness mixed with the burnt aroma of cigarettes bothered her. Didn't they know there was no smoking allowed in stairwells? She adjusted the straps on her purse and labored on. *Someone should report them.*

At the fifth floor, she stopped and leaned against the wall. Wow, this was harder than she thought. She didn't want to be late, but she also didn't want to have a heart attack. She sat on the cold, gray concrete steps of the next staircase up, and decided to use them to cool down her legs. She opened her notebook and reached into her purse for the USB drive. The notebook had completed reinstalling the operating system and now she was going to install some of the other more interesting programs. She hadn't found any cameras in the staircase, but there was going to be one either at the entrance to the roof, on the roof, or both. She wanted to disable or redirect them before she got there so there would be no record of the meeting. You could never be too thin or too paranoid.

If Marshall was in WitSec, she didn't want to put him in a position in which they could revoke his position. It was bad enough that he had gone through the last seven years without her, and her without him, but she was willing to let him go now.

The thought came unbidden to her. *I can let him go now.* Her eyes teared the tiniest bit and she went back to the task at hand. *No crying. We'll do that later when we're in the back of a police cruiser.*

The door opened into the staircase with an echo-y scrape and a rather surprised young man looked at her. "Can I help you?"

Her eyes opened wide. "Yes. Well, no."

"What are you doing here?"

Anna burst into tears and closed the lid of her notebook. "I'm sorry! I was just looking for a quiet place to think. Is it okay if I stay here for a few minutes?"

"Of course." He stepped into the stairwell with her. He couldn't be more than twenty-five. Mustard yellow pants and jacket over a white shirt of questionable pressing. He closed the door and leaned against the bare concrete wall. "What's up?"

Gosh darn it! She sniffled. "I'm sorry. I hate people to see me like this. I'd rather not talk about it."

"Okay." He reached into his pocket and pulled out a pack of cigarettes. "Want one?"

"No! No, thank you." She pretended to wipe tears away. *Now what?* "I've seen you around. You work at the front desk."

"Yeah." He smiled. "I haven't seen you."

"I'm new. I'm moving in today. You might have seen the movers."

Especially the one with the big arms. He moved her without lifting a finger.

"Yeah, yeah, I saw them," he said. He swaggered a bit.

Jeez, showing off already.

"What's the roof like?" She prayed she wasn't going too fast.

"What do you mean?"

"I mean is there a pool up there or something?" They both laughed. "You know, for parties. This is New York, right?"

"No, no pool. I know some of the buildings in New Jersey have pools on the roof." He lit his cigarette and took a drag. He exhaled slowly. "The high-end buildings here in New York have them. We're not that high-end." He smiled. "So, you're from out of town?"

"I like going on the roof. It relaxes me at the end of the day. Are we allowed up there?" She brought her chin down and raised her eyes.

"No," he took another puff, "not really. An alarm goes off, security runs up, the police have to be called."

"You have plenty of police here today." She sniffled.

"Yeah, there's some VIP on the upper floors. I never bother with that stuff." He gave her a focused look. "You know, it means work." He chuckled, as though looking for her reaction.

"Good for you. Well, I've got to go."

"What floor are you on?"

Anna looked at the big number on the wall. "Five, silly."

"No, I mean, which floor are you moving to? You know, if you ever need anything, just call downstairs and ask for Josh."

She smiled at him. "Thanks. Josh. I'll remember that." She continued up the stairs. "Oh, and where's the security office here?"

"In the lobby. We control everything from there. Don't worry. We have cameras on all the floors. We'll make sure you're safe."

She smiled again. "Thanks. I feel safer already." They both laughed.

Josh threw his cigarette on the floor, stepped on it, picked it up, and walked back through the door.

Well, that was close.

A few floors later Anna sat down again and finished installing her tools. She was running out of time. First, she found the building wifi. Then she started a network scan. And a port scan. She found web servers on one machine and a service running on another. She opened her Tor browser and connected to the web server. Basic information for the employees. Security information for security. Where were the instructions for the alarm system and cameras?

There they were.

71

GETTING INTO POSITION

"You are all a bunch of liars! Where is my daughter?"

Female looked worried. "She was supposed to be here already. She's being escorted over." Her body language was in sync. If she was lying, she didn't know about it.

"No. I've gone through this before. I don't know what you're trying to pull, but we do this my way or I start tossing people out the window until you shoot me."

"We could do that right now," the tall marshal said. He had taken a seat by the door.

They had seemed cooperative enough a few minutes before. They had to listen. He had the note. Why hadn't they told him about this?

"They're not bringing my daughter to me and I am going to prove it." Fletch walked up to Female. "Call up the team that has her and ask to let her speak with me." Fletch was only a bit taller than her, but he wasn't trying to intimidate her. He was sure he was doing it anyway, but that was not his intention. Not this time.

She reached into her jacket pocket and pulled out her cell. She called some number and seemed to try to get the security detail contact information. "They won't give it to me."

"Why not?"

"Because," she said, "they won't tell me."

"Okay, let's look at this rationally."

Shorty was getting nervous. "Not always a good way to start a conversation."

Fletch sat down as the other two marshals found places to lean. "If they have my daughter, they would have told me so that we could have the paperwork in place to have her join. If she refused then they would have told me that, too. I'm not a baby. If she wants to join the program, she can. If not, at least I would see her again even if it's for the last time." He didn't dwell on that for too long. Everything would be fine.

"The radio silence is telling me that they don't have her and they are just using the possibility of her as a way of keeping me from seeing whoever is waiting for me on the roof. Once the police start to show up, they're going to storm it and there's a good chance she'll be dead. I don't want to have to tell you what might happen then.

"All I'm saying is that I am going up to the roof and I am going to meet with whoever is up there. You can help or you can hinder, and by hinder, I mean you won't be walking much by the time I am done.

"Help me get up there. Watch my back. Don't shoot unless I'm already dead.

"Got it?"

———

Police cars arrived at the front of the building. They were directed to close off a two block radius around the building and begin getting the general public away from the area. Police cars began parking along First Avenue from 83rd Street to 86th Street and on East End Avenue along the same streets. The sirens in the distance heralded additional vehicles.

A SWAT truck arrived ahead of the others. Three men came out in full gear and knocked on the doors of the building a block west of The Cambridge. The super had been called ahead of time to let them in.

It was not until later that the truck would be discovered to be unattributed to any law enforcement agencies involved in the operation or that the phone call to the super had come in before the call to main dispatch was made.

———

"You have his daughter?" Terrell could not believe what he was just told. "Why is he being kept from his family?"

"I know you don't have any children yet, Agent Garrison, but his daughter means everything to him."

"You don't have any children either." The General looked at Terrell with a puzzled expression. *No ring and you talk about her like a puzzle piece.* "Nothing. Just an observation." Was anything that the General was telling him true? Was Fletch guilty of anything? Or was he just guilty of doing his job?

"We didn't keep them apart. His didn't want his daughter in the program. He demanded around-the-clock surveillance on her to insure her safety, and we gave it to her. At the first sign of trouble we expected to move her away from harm." Palma clenched his teeth. Terrell could see the sides of his jaw expand. "In point of fact, I have two children."

"There are people out to kill Fletch and you just surveilled his daughter?"

"I know you think we are all powerful, but there is only so much we can do within the letter of the law."

"Yeah, I hear that a lot these days." Terrell thought that staying with the General was becoming a worse and worse idea. "I think you should let me out."

———

The convoy of SUVs came to a stop along First Avenue and 80th Street. Terrell and the General shook hands. "You know you can expect to hear from me," Terrell said.

"While I know that you realize I won't be returning your calls."

"Oh, don't say that. When I call, it'll mean something. Everyone returns my calls." Terrell climbed out of the vehicle and trotted over to his car the file still in his hand. There had to be some sort of side-effect clue he could wrest from the redacted information. At the very least he might be able to discern the system it came from, or run some kind of image search.

He knew it was a long shot.

The soldier who had been driving his car stood at attention until Terrell was seated comfortably and then closed the door for him. He even wished him a good day.

What a lot of empty and useless crap. He threw the car into drive and sped off.

———

Palma sat in the back seat of his car and watched Garrison take off down First making the right onto 82nd Street. Terrell would get there but, with any luck, not in time to make a difference.

"Privacy shield," Palma said to the driver. This was Need to Know and his driver, as much as Palma trusted him, did not have a need to know. With the soundproof shield up, Palma reached under his seat and pulled open a compartment that contained various items including radios, communication equipment and a gun. He knew he wouldn't need the gun today.

He pulled out the radio. It used a classified and encrypted communication channel.

"Sound off," he said.

"Number 1."

"Number 2."

"Number 3."

"Positions?"

"This is number 1. I have a full view."

"This is number 2. I have a partial."

"This is number 3. I have a partial."

"Sit tight, gentlemen." Palma clicked off. He would wait here. Once they were done he would arrive with the girl. He put the radio in the pocket in the seat in front of him.

Terrell had walked off with the file. He was not so inexperienced to think there was anything in the file of any value. If he did then Palma was overestimating him and he never did that.

He pulled out his cell, logged in and looked at his last received text message.

I'll be there soon.

72

FINAL TEXT

Anna stood by the brown metal door, took a breath, and pushed against the bar. The door howled and opened onto a bare roof covered in cream-colored pebbles. A hot wind blew back into the stairwell.

The alarm did not go off.

She exhaled. Silence. *Cool. It worked.*

She held on to the door and closed it, making sure it wouldn't slam. It wouldn't do to have the folks on the lower floor hear her even if the alarm didn't go off. Her heart raced. She couldn't help but blink every few seconds. How was this going to work?

The sun overhead was bright and hot. Her skin tingled. She squinted and held her arm in front of her face so she wouldn't accidentally walk to the edge. It also wouldn't do to show him that all his years of parenting had ended because the sun was in her eyes. She smelled the East River to her left. *I need a place to hide.* She jogged on the pebbles and slid every few steps. *Okay, don't like pebbles.*

There was really no place to hide except the staircase housing. What about the police? If they just showed up, would she simply put her hands up and walk over to them? She didn't know if the people coming through the door were going to be police. Anxiety overwhelmed her. She ran around the housing for the stairs and sat down.

Her breathing sped up.

Stop. Stop.

STOP.

Breathe.

Did she have time for this? He could be here any minute! *STOP!*

She took in a deep breath and held it. *5, 4, 3, 2, 1, 0, 1, 2, 3.*

She had her back to a building on 85th Street. Pretty certain it was 85th. If anyone looked out their window, she was in trouble. Anna put her purse and notebook down. What a mistake it was to bring the PC, but it was the only way she could do what she needed to. She tried to swallow, but her throat was dry.

It was almost time. Seven years. Over seven. She wasn't even sure how she was going to greet him. She wasn't going to run over and hug him. This wasn't some commercial or corny soap opera. All she wanted was to see him, make sure he was okay, and then go. If it all went according to plan, he would convince the police not to arrest her and she could go.

OMG. She was a global fugitive. There were probably federal warrants out for her arrest.

No. Time to think about that later. For now, it was about seeing him, making sure he was safe, and getting off the roof. A warm wind blew across her face. Against her better judgment, she glanced at the building behind her. If anyone was looking, they were staying indoors. She saw a glint from one window.

She put the purse on her lap. The question continued: Did she trust the police? If she did then she would talk to Marshall unarmed. If she didn't then she would talk to him with the gun.

Paranoia ran deep. She tore the lining of her bag open. She pulled out ball after ball of crumpled paper and then the gun she had taken from Benson's office. She hadn't bothered shooting it before, but now she gave it the once over.

Just another Glock. She popped out the fifteen-round magazine. She pulled off the slide and then the barrel. *Wow. This is a nice piece. A shame it will never see combat.* She put the pieces back together. Pulled and released the slide and put the gun on the ground. The routine check gave her a sense of control she was willing to hold onto as much as she would the weapon.

What if Marshall betrayed her? What if her last ditch effort to warn him was all a trick? At this point, who cared? There was nothing she could do and if they decided to kill her then she was as good as dead anyway.

She didn't want to die. *Oh, please. I just want to see him.* She thought about an adopted student she knew at UPenn. There was an entire write-up on him and his journey to discover his birth parents. What a waste of time. She just wanted the parent she grew up with. Was that really that much to ask?

What if he hated her? Marshall had such a moral compass. He would never have gone to Europe with fake papers and beat people up. She also saved someone. He would have liked that part. Would that be enough? The weight on her shoulders felt real again. She was so keyed up that every second was too long. Marshall needed to come through that door and tell her that everything was going to be alright.

Please, Dad, make everything alright.

You know what? I don't care. This might even be a mistake. Let's get this over with.

She would carry the gun. If anyone tried anything, at least she had some bargaining power. And if she didn't like his answers then she could still...yes, she could still kill him.

Her shoulders sagged. *Right.*

She heard a click. She was so startled that she slid on the pebbles and leaned up against the wall. She sat motionless and held her breath. She listened as closely as she could. There was just the sound of the breeze. She looked around the corner with the most deliberate motions she could muster. Nothing. The door was still closed and she was still alone on the roof. She picked up the gun. The safety was off. She didn't remember doing that.

She put it back in place. *Click.*

OMG! She almost forgot. She pulled out her cell phone and sent her last text message.

———

"Number 1. Subject sighted."

"What can you tell me?"

"She is hiding and holding a weapon."

"Is it ours? Have you tested the remote?"

"Yes. I flipped the safety and she looked at it."

"She's using her cell?" Palma asked.

Silence. "Yes, she is."

Palma looked at his cell and wondered how people could be so predictable and yet so passionate even as they were being asked to do things they would never do under normal circumstances.

The message read, *I'm on the roof.*

73

SECURITY RISK

Fletch reached for his mask. Was he going to need it? He was well past the point of no return. The female marshal came over.

"What can I do for you?" he asked.

She helped him with the mask. "Tell me again how this is going to work. I need to make sure that you get this right and no one dies today." She pulled at her lapels and kept her hands there.

Fletch chuckled. "No one's going to die today." He winked at her. "Least of all, me."

"And?" she asked.

He could play along. Pre-op preparation. He had done this before many times. "You and your two buddies are going to shadow me up to the roof." He pointed at her with his head. "You'll stay behind the door as if I'm alone. Got it?" He grew serious. "The three of you are going to stay behind the door."

"Got it. Until?"

"Until I bring her in." He pulled down on the mask. It was uncomfortable, but he couldn't risk the stairwell cameras taking a picture and it showing up on the Internet somewhere. He wore dark suit pants and a pastel yellow shirt with the sleeves rolled up.

"And if it turns out not to be her?"

"We don't need to go over that part." Fletch was not a nervous man, yet he was a bit shaken. What was he going to do when he saw her? Maybe the marshals were right. He should let them bring her in.

No, he had abandoned her once before. *Play a man's game, pay a man's price.* That had kept him going in a lot of situations. This was the game he played and now it was time to pay the price.

"Mr. Smith. If it turns out not to be her?" *My, she could be insistent.*

"What's your name?"

"Patty," she said.

"Okay, Patty. If it turns out to be a trick, I'll pretend to put my gun on the ground and fire it instead. You and the cavalry will come running to save me." What a crock. He'd be dead long before he got to put his gun down. "Let me ask you something. What if the gun shot is them shooting me?"

"We'll still come running." She raised her eyebrows. "Would you like to change your mind?"

———

In the building lobby security was checking cameras. Josh had gone into the command center, really just a large room with multiple monitors displaying 9 cameras each, to view the action up close.

"Hey, boss." Josh saw his boss with a cop staring intently at the setup.

Russel Harman, who had worked at the building as security for 5 years, sat at the keyboard in full control of everything that was going on. This was a far cry from protecting rental cars. "If you're going to stay just make sure you don't get in the way." He turned to the police officer to his right. "Are there any cameras you want to see more than others?"

"Yeah." The officer had missed the festivities in the lobby earlier, but he told Harmon he heard the commotion. Harmon was glad to be in the safety of an office. "Show me the roof and the stairwell leading to the roof," the officer said.

"You got it." Harman brought up a menu that allowed him to

enter the camera numbers to display. The 2 cameras filled the center monitor: the stairwell and the roof. That's strange.

The stairwell was empty; he didn't expect to find anyone there anyway. The roof camera was pointing away from the roof entrance. Harman tried moving the camera, but it stayed locked in position.

"What's going on?"

"I wish I knew," Harman said. "Let me check something." he brought up the controls. "That's very strange. The camera's position was changed and then the movement mode was disabled." He gave the joystick control and attempted to change its position.

The camera didn't move. He moved the joystick just a touch and then pushed it back and forth. No movement whatsoever.

"Hey, boss," Josh said. He was swaying back and forth looking at the 2 monitors on either side of the main screen.

"I told you to not to say anything."

"You said unless I could help or something like that." Josh pointed to the upper left hand corner of the screen to the floor number that was just visible due to its size. "That's not the stairwell camera for the roof." The floor number read 4.

The officer pulled out his radio. "Street team, the security cameras have been compromised. We have no idea what to expect up there."

———

The police officer who was part of Fletch's security detail spoke to Patty first. She pulled Fletch over to a corner.

"Things are happening. I'm not sure I like this anymore."

"C'mon. There are three of you and one of them." Fletch heard the concern in her voice and ignored it. It was time to go.

"We don't know how many of them there are." She touched his bare forearm.

"You're coming with me. I'll be fine. Let's do this. If we wait any longer, I'm going to believe you and let you do it." He nodded at the other marshals. "Is everybody ready? Time to go pay someone a visit."

———

They rode the elevator as far as they could go. When they arrived, one of the marshals stayed by the elevator, another at the foot of the stairwell, and the third, Patty, stood by Fletch at the brown metal door. Fletch reached out and put his hand on the alarm bar.

"Remember: save me only if you have to."

Show time.

74

ON THE ROOF - PART 1

The traffic snarl and the blocked streets thwarted Terrell from approaching 86th Street so he could take York south to 85th. He gave up at the police barrier on York once he had turned onto 86th. He slammed the car to a stop next to a squad car, holstered his gun, jumped out with his ID lanyard around his neck, and raced to 85th. His legs were in pain, but he had ignored them before. The traffic was so bad that he ran down the double yellow lines to the building.

What were all these people doing here? "FBI. Excuse me. FBI." Oh, screw this. He started pushing people out of the way yelling, "FBI!" A few people even pushed back. What the hell?

He found five police officers blocking the door. One of them looked at his ID and opened the door for him. Another officer approached him from the reception desk. He had his hand palm out and his other hand on his gun.

"Whoa! Steady there, Super Cop," Terrell said. "Special Agent Terrell Garrison."

"Honestly, I don't care who you are. We've been given orders by the marshals not to let anyone up. The building is on lockdown and that means you."

"Get one of the marshals on your radio." Terrell started pacing.

"And that means right now. There is someone on the roof who is a potential danger to their charge. I need to talk to someone right now!" He had one hand on his hip and the other almost touching his nose. *Not today, please. Not today.*

"Hold on." The officer put his radio to his mouth. "This is Officer Dominquez down in the lobby. I need to talk to one of the marshals."

The radio crackled for a quick second. "This is Deputy Marshal Caron."

Fletch took the radio out of Dominquez's hand. "This is the FBI. Where the hell are you?"

"Why is the FBI getting involved in this?"

Was Caron INDIGNANT?

"Are you...Okay, I'm going to say this once. Wherever you are you, get your ass down here now. And bring Fletcher Burkholder down with you."

"Who's that?"

"What is the name of the man you're protecting?"

"John Freakin' Smith. We don't know his real name."

"Again, where are you?"

"We are at the stairwell leading up to the roof."

"Are you freaking kidding me? Get him down here!" Terrell was done. He was going to tear someone a new asshole.

"Sir, he's already out there."

Terrell yelled over at the security guard at the reception desk. "Get me an elevator with access to the top floor. I need to get up there this second!"

An elevator was coming down. "Caron?" Terrell asked into the radio.

"Yes, I'm coming down."

Oh. My. God. Fletch is going to die.

"Are you kidding? I didn't want you to come down. I want you to pull him off the roof."

Terrell could feel the sweat running down his back. The roof. He had to get on the roof. Why did elevators take so long when you needed them?

Ding. The elevator opened. Terrell ran in. He yelled out to the desk. "Make this an express!"

"Just press the top floor button!"

Great. A manual process. He pressed the button. The doors closed. Terrell's chest tightened.

———

"Is that man Fletcher Burkholder?" He was alone in the elevator with Marshal Caron. It was all Terrell could do to stop himself from throttling the man.

"You asked me that already. The answer is the same. How would I know? We were assigned to him when he got off the plane at Kennedy." Caron stood a head taller than Terrell.

Terrell glared up at him with the most pissed off eyes he could muster. "Get on a cell phone, send a smoke signal, start yelling if you have to, but send a message to the other marshals to get him secured."

"Sir, by the time we get there, it will be all over and he will either have his daughter or we will have one of the people who've been chasing him."

Was Terrell really having this conversation? "You do know how much trouble you and the other marshals are in?"

"Only if it goes bad." Caron turned toward the door. "But yes, I do."

"Oh, it's going to go bad all right. Especially for you and your colleagues. I'm going to make sure of that." He hoped not for Fletch. *Please. It's not Fletch's turn to die yet.* He had to get him to talk. He would go over the file with him and fill in the missing pieces. He would get him immunity. He would get him money. He would get him whatever he wanted, but he needed Fletch Burkholder alive. Terrell did not believe for a second Fletch killed Del. He wanted to know who did.

The floor numbers didn't change fast enough. The taller the building the faster the elevators went. This one just wasn't that tall.

"Listen, sir, this is under control. Between the three of us we've been in worse scrapes than this."

Terrell almost grabbed his jacket lapels and Caron jumped back. The compartment shook.

"Oh, worse than letting your charge out of your sight? Worse than letting him into an unsecure location with someone who wants to kill him? Ever have that one?"

———

A few minutes earlier, Fletch had spoken to Deputy Marshal Patty Kirchner and pushed open the door. The roof was empty. He stepped on the pebbles and noticed grooves in the pattern on the ground. Someone was here with him. *It's her. It has to be her.*

———

"The subject has entered the target area."

"Maintain contact."

———

Anna heard the door. Her heart started to race. It was hard to think and she was never at a loss before. Gun or no gun? Gun or no gun? She picked up the Glock, stood up, and prepared to see her father again. The sun was in her eyes, but she would be facing away from it soon. She looked around the corner and there was a man looking back and forth calling out.

———

Fletcher Burkholder looked around. He was very vulnerable here. He felt it in the pit of his stomach. It was an open space and there was no place to hide for protection.

A police copter flew overhead and hovered near by, but nowhere near the roof. This was going to be an interesting reunion.

Directly in front of him was a building taller than this one. The sun gave them great contrast and the floors closest to roof level would have great shots.

Screw it. He pulled off his mask. Where was she? Where was she?

"Chloe! Chloe!"

75

THE MOMENT

Terrell bounded up the stairwell steps as fast as he could, pushing aside the marshal at the foot of the stairs and then shoving the one at top of the stairs. He leaned against the exit door as he heard a shot fired.

"No!" someone cried out.

He would remember later hearing a muffled cry of "No!" from Anna before that. As he maneuvered around the door he saw Anna running to Fletch, who was on the ground facedown. She had a hard time lifting him, but she turned him over. Terrell aimed his gun at her.

"Anna! Step away from him. The police are on..."

He saw Anna twitch as if something hit her from behind and a puff of smoke on the housing wall at the same moment she pitched forward onto Fletch.

Terrell pulled the police radio off his belt and ran behind the thick door. "Cease fire! Cease fire! That's an order!" He peeked around the door and saw the two figures. Neither moved. He looked around and came out holding up the ID he had hanging from his neck. He heard more commands coming over the radio ordering no firing.

He pulled Anna off Fletch's body and lay her on the ground. Her blood was all over Fletch's pastel-colored shirt. Fletch's own blood was starting to run out from under him onto Terrell's pants.

Whoever had fired had a clean shot through her chest almost at the shoulder. *I hope you found what you were looking for, Anna.* Her eyes were closed. Nothing he could do for her.

He turned to Fletch. Fletch's eyes were open.

"Fletch?" Terrell grabbed Fletch's face with his right hand and moved it gently back and forth. "Fletch? Talk to me."

———

"Talk to me." The voice was deep and slurred.

Fletch knew he was dying. A rooftop kill. He wondered if any of the classes he had taught kept any of his training materials. So much historical knowledge. He couldn't have executed the plan better himself. Executed was the perfect word. After the initial burst of pain and surprise his muscles relaxed and euphoria seeped in. *So this is what it feels like.* He heard a low moan.

He couldn't move. His arms and legs felt heavy. Something was blocking the light. He heard sounds. He decided to return the favor. He had kept so much to himself for so long. Palma. Marshall and his team. Scores of contractors. All great guys. *Where did we go wrong? There was something they did and they shouldn't have done it. Oh, yeah.*

"Halon." *Was that clear? I should say it again. HALON. STOP HALON. Damn it.* His mouth wasn't working. Was that...a man was next to him. What was he saying? He practiced the explanation in his mind. The Montague tubes. The program. The security system. MAD. Especially MAD. He practiced what he wanted to say. He had so much time. He hated feeling sleepy. He could sleep when he died. He explained it to himself again. Now he could tell whoever this guy was.

His vision lit up when a wave of pain shot through him.

"HALON...Halon...Halon...mad..." Wheeze. WHEEZE. "MAR-SHALL!" *My lungs. OMIGOD.* "Marshall. Marshall." He started to cry.

He thought of Chloe. *Please keep her out of New York.* "Stop it...stop it...stop..."

———

Terrell placed Fletcher's head on the pebbled roof and closed the dead man's eyes. He turned to Anna and felt her throat. He felt nothing. She was dead and he had nothing to explain what happened. He stood up and looked around the roof.

She spasmed.

She's alive! He spun on the pebbles and knelt on the ground again. As he reached for the police radio to call for help the roof door burst open and men in SWAT attire came pouring in. He raised his hands and yelled out his three-letter shield.

"FBI!"

76

MIRANDA

Terrell accompanied the EMT and the New York City Police, who had been assigned to Anna, in the elevator to the ground floor where there was a waiting ambulance to take her to Mount Sinai Hospital on Fifth Avenue and 101st Street.

A tall, square-jawed man with graying hair on his temples in SWAT gear approached him. "Are you the agent who saw the shots fired?"

Terrell stopped and watched Anna get loaded onto the ambulance. "Yes," he said.

They shook hands.

"I'm Captain Haugen. I'm glad to see you're not hurt." He put his hand on Terrell's shoulder and pulled him off to the side. "You did a good job up there."

"Captain, I don't have time." An EMT called out to him. Terrell motioned for him to wait.

"Listen to me," Haugen said. "I can't speak for anyone else, including the marshals, but I have to tell you, before we start writing up paperwork and heads start to roll, that none of my guys fired that shot."

Terrell took a good look at the man's face. He was serious. This wasn't someone covering for his men. "I don't care. Find out who did. If one of your men fired without authorization, I will hang him out to dry. Understand?"

"You're not letting me finish. None of my men were in position. We were in the middle of setting up when everything came down."

"None of them?"

"We didn't receive the call with enough time. Not a single one."

Terrell looked at the ambulance and then over at Haugen. "That ambulance needs an escort. Can you handle it?"

"Yes, sir, I can."

"Then I will leave you to your work, Captain," Terrell said as they shook hands again.

Haugen called out to some men off to the side. They were going to need the escort. Not just any escort. SWAT escort.

Terrell ran over and grabbed a seat next to Anna as they closed the doors behind him.

The area around Mount Sinai Hospital was surrounded by more police vehicles and helicopters than it had ever seen. The news vans were parked less than a respectful distance away, but they also helped keep the crowds from the main building which was all Terrell wanted.

He made his calls and sat down to work out his report in the hallway. Introducing himself to every member of the nursing staff and surgical team, he waited for news on the only survivor of the case so far.

Anna was in surgery for five hours. The bullet had entered through her right scapula and exited her chest just below her shoulder. If someone had fired at her from the distance she had fired at Fletch, she would have died.

The autopsy report on John Smith, a.k.a Fletcher Burkholder, a.k.a Garth Donnell, former military, was straightforward. He died of a single gunshot wound to the chest fired at close range. The gun, a

Glock 19 with a fifteen-cartridge magazine, was determined to have been the murder weapon. The paraffin test run on Anna Wodehouse's clothes were positive. She fired the shot that killed him.

———

Anna woke up. *How do I always end up in a hospital room?*

Special Agent Terrell Garrison sat on the chair to her right looking over paperwork. The sights and sounds of the monitors did nothing to comfort her. She smelled ether.

"Hi," she said. Her voice was hoarse and she felt sand in her eyes.

He stood and took the two steps to her side. "Hi." He touched her hand for a moment. She squeezed back as he pulled away. "How're you feeling?"

"Stupid question," she said.

"I'm good with those." She tried making eye contact, but it made her uncomfortable.

"Do you remember what happened?"

"I think so." Her throat constricted. Feelings and images flooded her mind. The roof. The man. The gun going off. *Oh, please, let this not be real.*

"Sh. Sh." He held his hand out to her, motioning for her to stop. "No matter what anyone tells you, you want a lawyer. You don't say another thing to anyone, and I mean anyone, without a lawyer present."

"Did I kill him?" Her inner voice was silent. Waiting. She forgot to breathe.

He inhaled. She knew he was thinking.

"Yes. You fired the gun."

"No, I didn't." She swallowed. *I didn't fire the gun! I didn't! I didn't! He can't be dead!*

"Didn't I just ask you not to say anything?"

"Are you a lawyer?"

"Actually my degree was in accounting. I was going to be an actuary."

"You know what they say about actuaries," she said.

I killed him. Oh my God. I killed him. She started to cry.

"I know. They're like accountants only without the charm," he said.

She smiled while she brushed away a tear and then grimaced. Her body felt heavy. How could she still be breathing? Thinking? Being?

"You need to take care of yourself," Terrell said.

She felt like part of the bed. Could she even move her legs? Her body was sore, but the pain in her right side flared. "Why are you here? Are you arresting me?"

"No, but someone else will be." He looked toward the doorway. "Soon. I'll have to testify, and I will tell the truth, but there's more going on, and I'm going to find out what it is."

"Someone needs to find Benson."

"Yes," he said. "I'm going to find Benson."

Wait. He knew about Benson? She tried to swallow. She gestured to a pitcher of water. "Did he say anything?"

"What?" Terrell asked.

"Did the man say anything, before, before...?"

She looked up at him and wasn't sure what he was seeing. A pitiful woman who shot a man in cold blood? A smart person who was trying to find an answer? An idiot who thought she knew better?

An idiot. An idiot for sure.

"No," Terrell said. "He didn't say anything."

Anna felt a wave of shame and guilt and humiliation emanating from her chest that grew and grew until it enveloped her in its rough and dark cocoon. A stream of tears she couldn't control poured out of her eyes. She put her hands up against her face, knowing it wouldn't hide her, the people she had hurt, or herself.

What have I done?

It was all for nothing.

What have I done?

———

About an hour later a man in a suit arrived, flanked by two police officers.

"Are you with the FBI?" she asked.

"Yes, I am."

"Okay," she said.

"Is your name Carpenter Poole?" He read her aunt and uncle's Pennsylvania address to her.

"Yes, I am," she said.

"Are you also known as Anna Wodehouse?"

Her nose itched. "Yes."

"Carpenter Poole, a.k.a. Anna Wodehouse, you are under arrest for the murder of Garth Donnell. You also have outstanding warrants for your arrest for fraud, assault, and battery, possession of a handgun without a license..." He went on and on. "You have the right to remain silent..."

77

SNIPER FIRE

It was the morning of the next day.

Terrell made the drive from his apartment in Queens back to the Upper East Side of Manhattan at the request of New York City Homicide. He had left the hospital late last night after checking in with the security detail and made sure they understood how important Anna was. No mistakes. No exceptions.

He needed a shower and some breakfast. As he entered the building, he could taste the eggs from his sandwich and the tender skin inside his mouth from swallowing coffee too fast. He thought about buying some breath mints but decided not to waste any time this morning. His task list was rather long.

They gave him the address of a high-rise apartment on 84th Street and First Avenue. He found a NYC police car and CSI van parked out front. Terrell had worked with the city police on numerous occasions and this was no different.

Maybe a touch different.

The well-maintained elevator deposited him on the 30th floor. The lighting in the hallway was very bright. *No muggings here.* The linoleum tiles deadened the sound of his shoes as he approached the door with the police officer in front of it. He pulled his lanyard-attached ID and hooked it around his neck. Just another day at work.

He painted a smile on his face. "Good morning, gentlemen, good morning," he said as he entered the apartment. Someone was taking photos while someone else was examining the floor and walls. The flash bounced off the light walls. Everyone wore paper booties. Two specialists entered another room. "And good morning to you, madam."

"Good morning, Special Agent," Forensic Pathologist Ema Roland said. They shook hands and she handed him his booties. She was tall, but still not at Terrell's eye level. She wore a dark skirt with matching jacket over a beige blouse.

Terrell wrapped his shoes in the paper. "Is this the guy?"

"This is the guy."

Splayed in the middle of the light brown rug with multiple gunshot wounds lay a white male wearing blue jeans and a black pullover. On the ground was a high-powered rifle on a floor mount.

"Who is he?" Terrell asked.

"Don't know. Background check hasn't come back yet."

"Great."

"But I can tell you about that." Roland pointed to the weapon on the floor by Terrell's side. "That, Special Agent, is a Remington M-24." She bent over and picked it up with her gloved hands. "Not a weapon to be trifled with. Very popular with the sniper community. Not a light rifle, by any means, but can shoot a cockroach from a distance of three hundred meters at night or up to eight hundred meters by day."

"Was that a dig at New York?" he asked.

She smirked.

"Are you telling me that this is the gun that shot my vic?"

"I have a vic. You have an alleged murderer."

Terrell wasn't sure where this banter was going, but he was grateful for it. The last few days were wearing.

"I thought ballistics already confirmed the bullet that killed your man came from the Glock your little girl fired," Roland said.

"Three hundred night and eight hundred day? So that's roughly a thousand feet at night and twenty-six-hundred during the day."

"You're a human calculator." She put the gun back on the ground. "I am, however, willing to make a bet."

He smiled at her. "I know better than to bet with you."

She returned the smile. "I bet that the rifle our vic here was found with was the one that got your girl from behind. The distance to the roof of the Cambridge is certainly less than twenty-six-hundred feet away."

"I'm betting it's about a thousand. But I have depth perception problems," he said.

"Some of us just aren't that deep." She picked up a small plastic bag from the ground. It contained a mangled bullet. "Don't worry. I'll let you know as soon as ballistics matches the striation marks." She strode to the open glass doors leading out to a small patio.

For NYC the patio was a good size, but the patio in Terrell's house in the country was nicer. He needed to go out there more often. If work didn't kill him first.

The glass doors had numerous bullet holes. There were spider web patterns, but overall the door had much of its glass blown off.

"I like what you've done with the place," Terrell said. The wind blew a gentle zephyr into the room. He smelled water.

"We found the doors open a bit, just enough to position the rifle I'm sure, but open like this." She moved the doors to match the blue paper tape on the floor on the inside of the room. The doors were open about three inches. More than enough to get a barrel through and look in the gun site to a target.

"May I?" Terrell motioned for her gloves. He put them on, grabbed the rifle and the mount, and placed it on the floor. The rug had four indents where the mount had rested. Terrell got on the floor, positioned the rifle, and peered through the scope. What was his position? What was he looking at?

And there it was: the roof of the Cambridge. He looked up. "This is my man." His side sent a bolt of pain down his leg as he tried to stand.

Roland noticed him wince. "Hey, need some help?"

He smiled. "I'd say your vic needs the help." He looked around. "Strange." He narrowed his eyes at the glass doors and where the man had been shot. "How the hell was he shot? He fired. He knew he was done and then he stood up." Terrell pretended to walk toward where the body was. "And as he's moving he's shot by...who? Another sniper?" He looked at Roland. "Does that make any sense? What was it? A Mexican stand-off?"

"Some neighbors thought they heard something, but they just saw SWAT guys coming in. And the apartment has been empty for a few weeks."

"SWAT guys?"

"Yes, and I confirmed that no SWAT teams were sent into this area." She leaned in toward him. "Why do I smell the feds here?"

Terrell ignored her. "Ammunition strong enough to go through glass, but not the floor."

"Floor is concrete. We have plenty of bullets to examine. I'm betting ballistics won't be able to match it to anything. The folks below are lucky this was somewhat normal ammo," Roland said.

"How many shots?"

"Only a handful? So far we've recovered five bullets, not counting what might be in our dead friend."

Terrell wanted to kick the dead man. After interrogating him about who sent him. "Yeah, somewhat normal. That might be the only thing normal about this."

"You're right about that. We've just completed some preliminary trajectory tests and the one thing I can tell you is that this is not going to be an easy one."

He handed the gloves back to her.

"The trajectory of the shots are about a thousand feet out there." She pointed into the sky. "Is there something you would like to tell me?"

"I was hoping you had something interesting to tell me."

"You know those shots could have only come from one place," she said.

"Technically two," Terrell said.

"Two?"

"A helicopter, which is a possibility. Or a drone."

78

LIFE

The Daniel Patrick Moynihan United States Courthouse, located in lower Manhattan at 500 Pearl Street at Foley Square, was closed to the public the day Carpenter Poole, a.k.a. Anna Wodehouse, was transported for her sentencing six months after the shooting of Garth Donnell, a.k.a. Fletcher Burkholder.

Anna was allowed to change into civilian clothes for the hour or so that it would take for the verdict to come in. Her lawyer, paid for by Aunt Marcie and Uncle Ray, fought with Anna on a regular basis.

Anna did nothing to defend herself.

She had told them everything she knew. She even described the events leading up to her saving a man from sure death at the hands of the people who'd duped her into committing all the crimes she was accused of.

The man who turned out to be Special Agent Terrell Garrison.

Her lawyer was quick to point out the numerous problems with her case, not the least of which was the disappearance of evidence. The court believed the missing evidence was immaterial. The shot to her back probably came from a rogue police officer who had still not been found.

The police were investigating.

Anna walked into the almost empty courtroom with her eyes pinned to the ground. The spectator area had a handful of people sitting in it: Aunt Marcie and Uncle Ray, and a young woman Anna had learned was Donnell's daughter, Chloe.

Anna looked up and tried to wave. Her hands were in restraints attached to her waist so the most she could do was a half-wave. The leather restraints smelled of sweat and mildew. The courtroom had no windows. She saw cameras in various positions around the court, but all exhibited dark activation lights. This was not one for the history books.

Her lawyer, Abbie Loera, married, two children, and two ex-husbands, stood as Anna joined her at the defendants' table. Abbie wore a smart business outfit that complimented her hair and made her look authoritative. Given the tone of the case, so far it hadn't helped.

"All rise..."

Anna was fixated on her case in the beginning. She knew all the players and was doing everything she could to help with information until she realized that the only thing she was doing was helping herself get sent to prison.

The problems was she was guilty on almost all counts. Given the law, at the very least she knew she was an accomplice to the murder of Donnell. And she knew that entering the United Kingdom with false papers was a crime. And re-entering the United States with false papers was a crime. And tampering with the computer systems of various governments was a crime.

And murdering someone she didn't even know was also a crime.

The judge, a doddering old man as best she could tell, entered the room and sat down.

There was no jury. The prosecution had argued against it and won. Abbie had argued for consideration given her past as a kidnapping victim.

Overruled.

Abbie also argued for immunity for help in trying to locate the people who'd set her up to commit the crimes that she willingly committed under false pretense.

Overruled.

Anna Wodehouse was going to prison. There was no avoiding it. She had read up on the federal prison system and knew what to expect. It was easier for women than men, but it was still prison. Her fear was Benson. If he had done so much and managed it all in shadows, could he inflict retribution on her in a minimum-security prison like the Alderson Federal Prison Camp in West Virginia? Should Abbie be arguing for a maximum-security facility?

No. She had already dragged her aunt and uncle through too much. She would ask to be put in a facility where they couldn't visit or at least not visit that often. She was getting what she deserved. She wasn't worthy of them. They had opened their homes and hearts to her and now she had humiliated them in front of their friends and family.

What would her real parents have thought? *If they were still around, I wouldn't be here.*

"The defendant will rise."

The proceedings were a blur now. She had put in all the time and effort that she thought she could muster and then a few days before, her brain shut down. She stopped wondering what to do, or who to call, or even to hope.

Anna and Abbie stood side by side. Abbie squeezed Anna's shoulder. Six months ago, she would have screamed from the pain. Today, it was just a dull ache.

"Carpenter Poole, you have been found guilty of the thirty-six charges held against you. Do you understand that you also have charges being held against you overseas?"

"Yes, your honor," Anna said.

"Do you also understand that you have almost no chance for parole and that you will spend most of your adult life behind bars?"

She inhaled. This was it. She looked over her shoulder as a tear ran down her cheek. What she wouldn't give to have her dad walk in through those doors and tell them this was all a mistake.

"Yes, your honor." She wiped the tear from her cheek.

"Then, Carpenter Poole, for the crimes of cyber-terrorism and murder, I sentence you to life imprisonment at the Federal Medical Center, Carswell located in Fort Worth, Texas where you will be held in the minimum-security area unless you give them reason to move you into a higher-level security area."

Abbie gave her a hug that Anna didn't feel.

She felt a hand on her right arm. It was Aunt Marcie. She leaned over the railing and gave her a hug. Anna felt her aunt's tears on her cheek. "It'll be alright. We're already selling the house. We'll be out there so you won't be alone." Uncle Ray just stood there. He put out his hand and Anna squeezed it. She would talk them out of selling their house. She has already ruined their lives.

———

At John F. Kennedy International Airport, the U.S. Marshals have a small fleet of planes used to transport prisoners around the country. After waiting in isolation for two days, Anna, in her bright orange prison jumpsuit, walked from the Bureau of Prisons' dirty white bus onto a Boeing 727 modified for the marshals and their special passengers.

An old-style staircase led up to the plane. Anna had kept to herself, but on occasion spoke with one of the marshals. They responded with single word answers.

As her escort fastened her to the worn chair, an announcement blared overhead. It was the typical flight information mixed with dark humor. She was entering hell and she knew it.

Anna felt the wheels lift off the ground.

She was done.

———

An hour later, the pilot looked down at his new flight plan and cursed. He had been flying for the Bureau of Prisons for years and, while used to last minute changes, had not considered it in his plans today. Flying down to Carswell, Texas was exactly what he wanted so he could meet up with his family and maybe even spend some time with his new granddaughter.

Why the hell didn't I let Clancy handle this flight? Now his trip to Texas was ruined, and he would be stuck in Colorado long enough to miss the family gathering.

At least there was overtime. That was always welcome, and not as common as it used to be.

Damn it. He hated last minute changes. He was flexible, but he had already told everyone. And he knew he was going to hear it from his wife. *Oh, well. Just have to make the best of it.* Carswell, Texas or Colorado Spring, Colorado, it made no difference.

He would deliver the inmate and go grab some dinner.

EPILOGUE

ON THE ROOF - PART 2

Elapsed Time: 1 minute 30 seconds

"Chloe!"

Who?

Anna held the Glock with both hands and kept it pointed to the ground. She closed her eyes, screwed up her courage, and came out from around the corner in time to see her dad walk around the staircase housing away from her. The sun was low, but the heat tickled her skin. She put her back to the wall, and walked to the opposite corner.

"Chloe!"

Anna stepped out, and look at the man who stood about twenty feet from her.

"Who're you?" the man asked.

Anna wasn't sure how to reply. This was the moment she had been thinking about for years and she couldn't remember what to say. "My name...my name is Carpenter..." She stood up straight and gritted her teeth. "My name is Anna Wodehouse. Where the hell is my father?"

His voice softened. "Anna?"

"Dad?" She pointed the gun toward the ground. "You look bigger." She shook her head as the wind blew hair over her face.

Fletch swung his arms in the air in frustration. "I knew it." His hands made a loud slap as they hit the sides of his legs. He took a step toward her.

She brought the run back up and aimed. Center of mass.

"Stop. Don't move," she said.

The man's shoulders drooped and he shook his head. He started walking back around the housing.

"No! You stay there!" she said.

"Are you going to shoot me?" He glanced at her and turned. "If you were going to, you would have done it already."

"I'm," the moment was slipping away, "I'm looking for my father."

The man had already turned away from her when he stopped and looked back. "What did you say?" he asked. "Anna Wodehouse? You're Marshall's girl?" His eyes opened wide and then went back to normal. "But you can't be. She's dead."

Dead? Anna felt a lump in her throat. This can't be. She spun away and the man before her turned as if to run. She pointed the gun back at him. This was not happening. "Where is my father?"

"How the hell should I know?" He started to walk away again. "If we're lucky, he's dead. Your father did us all in."

"What do you mean?"

"I'm done with this. Come inside. You're about to be arrested."

"Stop!" Anna raised the gun just a touch more. "I'm really good with this and I will shoot you."

The man raised his hands. "Go for it. I'm tired of hiding." He took a step toward her. "I'm tired of everyone telling me what's right," and another step, "and what's wrong," another step, "and being accused of abandoning my family," another step, "when all I was doing was my best for my country." He stood a few feet away from Anna with the gun aimed at his head. "Guys like Marshall are like guys like me: we do what we're told because we know that the orders, no matter how illegal they might sound, come from the guys who are supposed to know better." He grabbed her by the throat.

Tears streamed from her eyes, but she said nothing. She felt her body relax as his fingers tightened around her neck. His hands were large, unlike her father's.

It's okay, Daddy. It's okay. She lowered her hands as he started to shake her.

"Marshall dropped off the radar screen when we needed him the most." He brought his face close to hers. "People were dying." He let go. "People are going to die."

She noticed that something caught his eye.

He looked over her head.

———

For Fletch, everything clicked within a few seconds.

The roof was open. There were only a few buildings taller than this one in the area.

High enough to hide what was about to happen next.

Low enough for a sniper to take them out from a block away.

The girl was a decoy. *Marshall's girl? They must want to get rid of her as well.*

They were probably using M-24s. That would buy them distance.

———

"It'll be all over soon." He looked down at her. "When you die it'll be for the best."

"What do you mean?"

"This was a trap. Maybe for both of us."

"No." She felt the gun still in her hand. "You knew my father. Who was he? Why...why did he leave me?"

"C'mon. You're never going to get the answers you want." The man walked away. "Your father was a good man who screwed up."

She ran after him and almost slipped on the pebbles. He stood by the door.

"Stop!" She pointed the Glock at him again. She felt a tear run down her cheek. "I will shoot." She wiped the tear away and held the gun in both hands again. Her trigger finger rested on the barrel and not on the trigger. Safety first.

He turned. "So you're going to kill me?"

"No." The gun went off and hit the man just off center of his chest. The recoil almost knocked the gun out of her hands, but her reflexes kicked in. "No!"

The large man fell in one giant assault to the ground. Anna ran to him and fell on her knees as she reached for his shoulders. The pebbles stung her knees as she turned him over. Within a few seconds, she saw blood running down between the two of them and she knew she only had seconds to ask him what she had to.

She heard the roof door slam open as something sharp hit her in the back. She went down.

FREE DOWNLOAD!

Get a free ebook copy of Part Two of the *Kidnapping Anna Trilogy, Kidnapping Anna: ADX Florence*, and a selection of short stories, after downloading the *A. B. Alvarez Reader* by going to https://www. abalvarez.com/free-book-en/!

CONNECT WITH A. B. ALVAREZ

Follow me on Bookbub:
https://www.bookbub.com/authors/a-b-alvarez

Follow me on Goodreads: https://www.goodreads.com/abalvarez

Read my blog: https://www.abalvarez.com/bonus-content

Visit the Brushed Steel Books web site:
https://www.brushedsteelbooks.com

OTHER BOOKS BY A.B. ALVAREZ

Please visit your favorite ebook retailer to discover other books by A.B. Alvarez:

The Kidnapping Anna Trilogy

Book One: Kidnapping Anna

Book Two: Kidnapping Anna: ADX Florence

Book Three: Kidnapping Anna: The Montague Tubes

Short Stories

Hilt

Destiny

Changing Gears

Embracing Shattered Glass

Fortuna's Head

Matador

ABOUT THE AUTHOR

A.B. Alvarez lives in New York. He doesn't have any cats, dogs, ferrets, or other pets. He does, however, have a daughter whom he did not kidnap.

ACKNOWLEDGMENTS

No author is an island and I am not starting a new tradition.

Many thanks to Cee Banton, and Nadja Hicks who read this novel long before it was ready to be released and offered great suggestions (you guys rock!). A big shout out to the folks of the Saturday writers group who were nice enough to read excerpts of the manuscript and helped make the story better.

The cover selection came out of an impromptu focus group of various people including: Lindley Valcarcel, Luis Valcarcel, Silvia Velez, Cathy Velez, Victoria Velez, Elizabeth Velez, Jessica Lassiter, Cristina Valcarcel, Casey, and Marina.

While I have already dedicated this book to my daughter, I just wanted to acknowledge that she gave Anna her name, suggested London as the main location, and was always there for the odd phone call when I had questions about story structure and covers.

Where Anna has no siblings I have been blessed to have two incredible siblings who supported me in all sorts of ways. I can only hope to be there as much for them as they continue to be there for me (Hi, Lou! Hi, Silv!).

And, of course, a big shout out to Cathi Stevenson of Book Cover Express for the great cover, and to Samantha Stroh Bailey for the superb copy edit. The book would be less without the two of you. Thanks, as well, to Glen M. Edelstein from Hudson Valley Book Design for additional visual design on the excerpts.

The wonderful parts of the book are so because the folks around me stopped me from screwing it up. The mistakes are when I didn't listen.

A.B. Alvarez
New York City, 2017